THE ACTOR'S GUIDE TO
ADULTERY

Books by Rick Copp

THE ACTOR'S GUIDE TO MURDER

THE ACTOR'S GUIDE TO ADULTERY

THE ACTOR'S GUIDE TO GREED

Published by Kensington Publishing Corporation

THE ACTOR'S GUIDE TO
ADULTERY

Rick Copp

KENSINGTON BOOKS
www.kensingtonbooks.com

KENSINGTON BOOKS are published by

Kensington Publishing Corp.
850 Third Avenue
New York, NY 10022

ISBN 0-7582-0498-1

First Hardcover Printing: November 2004
First Trade Paperback Printing: September 2005
10 9 8 7 6 5 4 3 2 1

Printed in the United States of America

For Holly:
Thank you for a lifetime of love and laughter.

Acknowledgments

Once again, without the unflagging support of my editor and friend John Scognamiglio, the adventures of Jarrod Jarvis would be stuffed in a drawer somewhere.

I'd also like to thank my Writers' Group for their keen eye to detail during the writing of this book: Dana Baratta, Melissa Rosenberg, Dan Greenberger, Rob Wright, Allison Gibson, Alexandra Cunningham, and of course Greg Stancl, who is a major fan of the genre.

Thanks to Rob Simmons, Laurice and Chris Molinari, Joel Fields, Liz Friedman, Robert Waldron, Bennett Yellin, Marilyn Webber, Mark Greenhalgh, Lori Alley, Woody and Tuesdi Woodworth, Joe Dietl, Ben Zook, David A. Goodman, Patricia Hyland, Craig Thornton, Sharon Killoran, Laura Simandl, Susan Lally, Dara Boland, Liz Newman, Brian O'Keefe, Michael Byrne and Vincent Barra. I am blessed to have you all in my life.

Thank you Yvette Abatte for your wonderful friendship and for your bang up job on the website. And thank you Todd Ransom for your tireless efforts to get the word out.

My deepest gratitude to my parents Fred and Joan Clement and to Jessica, Megan, and Justin Simason for showing me how lucky I am each and every day. Also thank you to fellow mystery lover Nancy Schroeder for challenging me to come up with a better ending.

ACKNOWLEDGMENTS

Also to my crack team of William Morris agents—Jonathan Pecarsky, Ken Freimann, Lanny Noveck, Cori Wellins and Jim Engelhardt—to whom I am forever grateful.

To Milan Rakic, thank you for bringing such joy to my life.

And finally, Linda Steiner, you are a constant inspiration and I would be lost without you.

Chapter 1

"I believe this man poses a serious threat to me and society in general, and I strongly urge you to keep him locked up behind bars where he belongs." I paused for dramatic effect. There was a chill in the air. I was nailing this. Why couldn't I have been this persuasive last week when I auditioned for the role of a powerhouse prosecuting attorney on *Law & Order: Special Victims Unit*? Maybe it was because today the stakes were much higher. The guest-starring gig was fifteen grand and another year of guaranteed SAG insurance, but this performance would decide whether or not I would spend the rest of my life living in fear, looking over my shoulder, expecting to find a knife-wielding madman bearing down on me. Today I was delivering testimony at the parole hearing of Wendell Butterworth, a forty-four-year-old mentally unstable career criminal, who when he was in his early twenties, tried kidnapping me three times.

When Wendell saw me make my acting debut on an Oscar Mayer bologna commercial just shy of my fifth birthday, he became convinced that I was his long-lost soul mate from another lifetime. He kept watching TV, hoping to see me, and he did on a slew of commercials for Juicy Fruit gum, GI Joe action figures, and Kentucky Fried Chicken. When I landed my hit series a few years later and became a big star, Wendell decided it was time for a long-overdue reunion in this lifetime.

My first encounter with him was during our first season of *Go to Your Room!* He had conned his way past the security gate at the studio posing as a messenger, and found me hiding from my tutor, who was on the warpath because she found out I'd lied when I told her I had a photo shoot for *TV Guide*. It was just a ruse to get out of one of her annoying little pop math quizzes. Wendell pretended to be a production assistant sent to retrieve me for a network run-through rehearsal. We were halfway to Barstow before a quick-thinking cashier at a Mobil Station recognized me from the special "Missing Child Star" news bulletins on TV and dialed 911. I never even knew what was happening. The whole time I thought I was on my way to a promotional appearance at the network's Las Vegas affiliate station.

The second time, Wendell bought one of those "Maps to the Stars' Homes," and drove out to our Pacific Palisades house, where he locked our maid Gilda in the pantry and jumped out to grab me while I was pouring a bowl of Lucky Charms cereal. Believe me, I didn't feel so lucky that day. But fortunately, my parents arrived home just as Wendell was hustling me into his Dodge pickup. My father wrestled him to the pavement while my mother called the police from the car phone.

Finally, with his frustration growing to dangerous levels, Wendell got his hands on a Smith & Wesson and decided that if the Devil's Disciples (namely my parents) were going to keep us apart in this world, then he had no choice but to escape with me into the other world. His plan was to shoot me dead, and then take his own life. We could finally be together for eternity.

This was still a few years before the haunting and brutal murder of another sitcom child star, Rebecca Schaffer, in 1989. That's when people finally started taking celebrity stalkers seriously. Rebecca was dressing for an audition for *The Godfather 3* when a whacked-out fan rang her bell, and fired a gun at her as she stood right in her own doorway. She died at the scene. And Hollywood was finally jolted awake.

But my nightmare ended on a sweltering hot summer day in August. And as fate would have it, Wendell Butterworth would not succeed with his insidious plot. As my mother and I pulled out of the studio gate and stopped for a red light at the intersection of Melrose and Gower next to Paramount Pictures, Wendell ran up to the passenger's side window, which was open, and pressed his newly registered gun to my temple. Before either my mother or I could even react, Wendell pulled the trigger. There was a loud click. And then silence. Wendell had forgotten to load his gun. As he fumbled in his pockets for the bullets, my mother grabbed my shirt collar and dragged me out of the car, both of us screaming and running into the street, bringing traffic to a screeching halt. A quick-thinking motorist saw Wendell stuffing bullets into the chamber of his gun, and slammed on his accelerator, plowing into Wendell and knocking him to the ground unconscious.

For weeks reporters and TV journalists besieged us with requests for interviews. I almost had an exclusive sit-down with Barbara Walters until she found out I made fun of the way she talked. Hell, I was only twelve. How did I know she was so sensitive?

More disturbing details bubbled to the surface about Wendell as the press dug deeper into his past. He was initially portrayed as a wayward orphan whose parents were brutally murdered by intruders in the summer of 1971 while he slept peacefully upstairs in his room. The killers were never caught. Well, a *20/20* investigation after his attack on me revealed that there was no home invasion by unknown intruders at all. It turned out his parents had refused to allow eleven-year-old Wendell to watch the series premiere of *The Sonny and Cher Comedy Hour*, so he took matters into his own hands by butchering both of them with a meat cleaver, watching the show, then going upstairs and turning in. After all, it was past his bedtime.

After a battery of psychological tests following his arrest, Wendell was found to be deeply disturbed (let me put on my big surprise face), and once convicted (his lawyer's "innocent by reason of insanity" ploy failed), he was committed to a special psychiatric ward at Angola State Prison, where he managed to escape once and tried to find me again during our show's second season. Luckily he was quickly recaptured and transferred to an even more secure facility at Vacaville State Prison in Northern California, where he has remained ever since.

It was tough making the six-hour drive up to Vacaville to speak at Wendell's parole hearing. I hadn't seen him since that terrifying day at the traffic light outside Paramount. When I entered the sparse, stuffy room where he was seated at a table, flanked by two beefy prison guards, I almost didn't recognize him. Almost. Eighteen years had passed, and he was much older. In his twenties, he had only just started losing his fine blond hair, and he was muscled and compact. Now he was much paunchier, with only a few wisps of dull yellow hair combed over his forehead. His complexion was ruddy and pale from years of incarceration, and more than a few wrinkles creased his face. But one thing was the same as I remembered. His eyes. They were still a dull gray and they still had the wild look of a sociopath. He stared at me, and appeared to be fighting back a smile. I half expected him to jump up and grab me in a bear hug, as if he still believed we were separated soul mates. And that's why I'd made the long trip up north. Because in my heart I knew Wendell Butterworth wasn't cured. He wasn't ready to reenter society a well-adjusted, law-abiding citizen. And I wasn't ready for him to get out either.

Wendell sat quietly watching me as I delivered my speech. My hands were shaking and the paper made a loud rustling sound in my grip.

"I do not believe that Wendell Butterworth has made enough progress, and I fear that if you release him, he will continue his campaign of terror against me, as well as others."

The sound of the paper was so thunderous, I was sure the parole board couldn't hear a word I was saying. I glanced up at them to gauge some kind of reaction to my presentation. There were three of them. A corpulent man in his fifties who was bursting out of a cheap brown suit. A prim-and-proper frail gray-haired woman with a stern gaze over a pair of horn-rimmed glasses. And a handsome doctor with curly, unkempt hair and soft, caring eyes. I made eye contact with him, because, after all, he was the cutest one on the panel. He smiled at me and I immediately lost my place. I had to consult my stack of pages again. More rustling. I kept reminding myself I was in a loving, fulfilling relationship with an LAPD detective named Charlie Peters. Damn, where was I?

"I'm sorry . . . Let's see . . . campaign of terror against me . . . Oh, right. Here we go. I simply don't believe Wendell Butterworth is a changed man. And I beg you . . . for my own peace of mind, and for my family's, please do not let this man out of prison because I know it will only be a matter of time before he strikes again."

There was a moment of silence as the parole board digested my words. Then the gray-haired lady spoke first.

"Mr. Jarvis, we all appreciate you coming here today to speak with us. You make a very convincing argument."

"Thank you."

"I'm curious though. Did you read the psychiatric evaluations we sent you in the mail?"

"Yes, ma'am. I did."

"Five reputable doctors believe Mr. Butterworth has made remarkable progress, and in order for him to continue in a positive direction, he should be able to reconnect with a life on the outside."

"I don't believe that to be the case."

The cute doctor leaned forward. "Why not?"

"Look at his eyes," I said. "They haven't changed one bit. They still scare the hell out of me."

Wendell averted his eyes from me, and fixed them on the

floor. He didn't want me blowing his chances of getting out of here. Not with something as inconsequential as the look in his eye.

The gray-haired lady broke out into a smile dripping with condescension. "Mr. Jarvis, are you disputing the findings of five doctors based on the mere fact you don't like Mr. Butterworth's eyes?"

"That's right," I said.

She stifled a chuckle, and then flashed her two colleagues a look that said, "How long are we going to indulge this idiot?"

The corpulent member of the board checked his notes before addressing me. "What about Cappy Whitaker?"

"What about him?" I said.

"He was a child actor just like you. He had a rather notable career in his own right, though admittedly not nearly as successful as yours, and he, too, was a target of Mr. Butterworth's obsessions."

"I'm very familiar with Cappy's ordeal. It was very similar to mine."

"And yet, we've received a notarized letter from Mr. Whitaker supporting a decision to release Mr. Butterworth at our discretion."

This floored me. It downright knocked the wind out of me. Cappy Whitaker was an adorable moppet who hit the audition scene right about the same time I did. He had this cherubic face dotted with freckles, big twinkling brown eyes, and bright orange hair, and he made a lasting impression on the American public in a Disney adaptation of *The Prince and the Pauper*, which led to a situation comedy as Debbie Reynolds's grandson. The show lasted six episodes, but Cappy's TV Q rating was high enough to win him a memorable series of Kraft commercials, where he stood next to a ten-foot box of macaroni and cheese and wailed, "Hey, *I'm* supposed to be the big cheese!" The catch phrase caught on for a bit, and made the front of a few million T-shirts. It was bigger than that cute old lady screaming, "Where's the Beef?!" for Wendy's Hamburgers, but didn't have the lasting impact of my very own "Baby, don't even go there!" It did, however, become an instant footnote in eighties pop culture, and further endeared Cappy to the viewing public as well as Wendell Butterworth. He decided that Cappy, like me, was also his soul mate, and it was grossly unfair that they be kept apart. He staked out the apartment complex where Cappy lived with his grandmother, who was raising him after his alcoholic mother died in a drunken traffic accident. He made one botched attempt to snatch Cappy when his grandmother took him to the beach in Santa Monica one gloriously sunny Sunday afternoon, but he failed miserably when a gaggle of buff lifeguards beat him to a pulp when Cappy screamed for help. It caused quite a stir, landing the wholesome heroic hunks on the cover of *People* in their tight red swim trunks and holding life preservers. Some believe this story was the inspiration for the popular waves and babes show *Baywatch*. Days later, Wendell was quietly released for lack of evidence. He convinced authorities he was simply asking Cappy for directions to the Santa Monica Pier. That's when Wendell turned his attention back toward me.

I cleared my throat, gathered my thoughts, and addressed the three members of the parole board. "I can understand why Cappy Whitaker no longer believes this man poses a serious threat to society. He wasn't attacked in his home while eating breakfast. Mr. Butterworth didn't press a gun to his head at a traffic light and pull the trigger. I don't mean to compare emotional scars here, but I believe my experience with Wendell Butterworth was far more harrowing and has haunted me a lot longer. I respect Mr. Whitaker's opinion, but where is he? Why isn't he here? Because he didn't care enough to make the trip. I did." I pointed a finger right at Wendell's face. "Because this man is with me in my nightmares every time I go to sleep!"

Finally I had gotten to them. The parole board members sat in stunned silence. The corpulent one started making notes. The gray-haired lady stared at the floor. And the cute one, well, he looked at me with sympathetic eyes, and gave me an understanding nod. He opened his mouth to speak when suddenly a chirping sound pierced the air. Everybody sat up and looked around. Where was it coming from?

I frowned, annoyed. It was obviously someone's cell phone, and I was offended it had interrupted the impact of my speech.

The gray-haired lady looked up at me. "Mr. Jarvis?"

"Yes?"

"I think it might be yours."

She was right. The aggravating chirping sound was coming from my back pants pocket. I had planned on leaving my cell phone in the car, but I was expecting a very important call from my manager/best friend Laurette Taylor. I had been cast in one of the lead roles in an NBC comedy pilot some months ago that insiders predicted would be sandwiched in between the network's two biggest hits on Must-See Thursday. I played a lascivious massage therapist with designs on all the girls in a hip twenty-something apartment house. As a proud gay man in his early thirties, I had to congratulate myself on my ability to stretch as an actor. And the suits loved me. The networks were in the process of selecting their new series for the fall TV season. Laurette had promised to call me the minute she heard something. I checked the small screen on my cell phone. Sure enough, it was Laurette. I had to take the call. This could be one of those life-altering moments that could shift the entire trajectory of my career as an actor.

I sheepishly looked up at the bemused parole board. Even the cute doctor wasn't smiling anymore. "I'm sorry. I really have to take this." There was an audible huff from the gray-haired lady as I hastily slipped out of the room.

Outside, the drab, sterile hallway was even more depressing than the room where the parole board was conducting their hearing. It was empty except for a two-man cleaning crew mopping the floor a few feet away from me. I pressed the talk button and took a deep breath.

"Laurette?"

"Hi, doll face. Where the hell have you been? Haven't you gotten any of my e-mails?"

"I haven't been online today. I'm in Vacaville."

"Where in God's name is that?"

"Up north. Between Sacramento and San Francisco. I drove up for my stalker's parole hearing."

"I really need to get you a job. You do the strangest things to keep busy."

"They want to release him, and I'm here to make sure that doesn't happen."

"Do you know how many actors would kill to have a stalker? You can't buy that kind of publicity."

Laurette was always thinking of my career.

"Listen, I have to get back inside. They're going to make a decision soon," I said. "But I didn't want to miss your call."

"Good. Because I have exciting news."

This was it. After years of struggling to shed the baggage that came with being a former child star, I was about to land my first significant series role as an adult. I had worked so hard for this moment. I sat down on a hard wooden bench to savor the news.

"I'm getting married," Laurette said.

That didn't sound like, "The network picked up your pilot."

"I'm sorry. What?"

"I'm getting married. Can you believe it? After a lifetime of horrible dates and misfired relationships, I've finally found him. The one. Just when I came to accept the fact that he'd never show up, he's here."

"What about the pilot?"

"Oh, God, that loser? He hasn't called in months. Last I heard he quit Delta after his divorce was final and moved back to Atlanta. Truth be told, he had this mole on his back I just couldn't get past."

"Not the airline pilot. The network pilot."

"What network pilot?"

"*My* network pilot. On NBC. The one I've been waiting weeks to hear about. Did it get picked up?"

There was nothing but dead air. I figured the news wasn't good.

"Oh, honey . . ." Laurette said, her voice filled with a motherly, comforting tone usually reserved for occasions like telling a kid his pet hamster died. "It's not going to happen. They passed on it."

Now I felt just like that kid with the dead hamster.

"Why? You said all the suits loved it."

"They did. And then they tested it. I think it set a new record for low audience scores. Didn't I call you? That was something like, four days ago."

"No, you didn't call me."

"Oh, I guess I've been so caught up in this new romance, I forgot. So, back to me. Isn't this wild? I'm finally going to walk down the aisle!"

This was a double blow. First, my best friend neglected to break potentially devastating news to me as early as possible, so I could grieve properly and move on to my next career disappointment. Second, this same best friend, who always insisted on relating every last detail of her life, was getting hitched to a man I had never even heard about.

"Who is this guy? And why haven't I met him?"

"We just met two weeks ago."

I opened my mouth to speak, but felt there was no way she would not detect a hint of judgment in anything I said.

"I know it's fast," she said, reading my mind. "But it was one of those moments when you just know. We ran into each other at a screening at the TV Academy. It was some CBS Sunday night movie based on a true story about a little girl in Tennessee who was trapped in a mineshaft for eight days. The movie was crap. The kid they got sucked. But he played one of the firefighters, and believe it or not, he was quite good. He's very talented. His name is Juan Carlos Barranco."

Juan Carlos Barranco. The name sounded vaguely familiar, but I couldn't place it.

Laurette had discovered a propensity for Spanish men on our nine-day trip to the coast of Spain last summer. But an actor? I love actors. I'm one myself. But I know that most of them are one big red flag for inevitable emotional distress.

"So he's an actor, huh?" I said, hoping she'd pick up the obvious concern in my voice.

"Yes," she said, choosing to ignore it. "They had a reception after the screening, and we both went for the last finger sandwich. It was chicken salad. Not bad actually."

Laurette and I also both have to fill in complete food descriptions during any story we tell the other.

"Anyway, he graciously let me have the sandwich," she said. "And I told him how impressed I was with his performance, and then we wound up back at my place. And he's been there ever since."

"He's living with you?"

"Don't tell my mother, but yes. That's why we're getting married right away. I don't want to compromise my Catholic upbringing."

"Sweetheart, you compromised your Catholic upbringing in 1986 on our road trip to Fort Lauderdale when—"

"Don't say it. Just tell me how happy you are for me!"

I sighed. There was no way to slow Laurette down once she made a decision. She was a freight train and you just had to go along for the ride and hope you didn't derail from the high speed.

"I'm really happy for you," I said.

"Now get your ass back down to LA so we can start making plans."

"I want to meet this guy, and make sure he's good enough for you."

"Wait until you see him! He's gorgeous! And so sweet. He brought home takeout from Red Lobster because he knows how much I love their garlic cheese rolls. He hid the ring in one of my popcorn shrimp! I almost choked to death."

Laurette was laughing at the memory. I was still hung up on the fact she was planning to marry an actor. If I could just get her to talk to my boyfriend Charlie, he'd certainly tell her to run screaming for the hills, having lived with me for three years.

I was momentarily distracted when the door to the parole hearing opened and the three members of the board filed out into the hallway. They were followed by the two prison guards, who escorted Wendell Butterworth down the hall toward the processing room.

"Laurette, I have to go," I said. "Something's happening."

"All right, but call me when you get home. I want you and Charlie to be the first ones to meet my new husband. Can you believe I just said that? Husband!"

"I'll call you from the car."

I hung up the phone and approached the curly-haired cutie from the parole board.

"Excuse me, are we taking a short break?" I said.

The handsome doctor turned and flashed me his winning smile. "No. We're finished."

"Well, what happened?"

"We unanimously voted to grant Mr. Butterworth his parole."

I felt as if someone had just slammed me in the gut with a fist. I staggered back, not sure at first if I heard him right.

"You're letting him out?"

Eavesdropping, the gray-haired lady stepped up behind me and sniffed, "We asked if anyone else had anything to add, but you were out here on the phone." With a satisfied smile, she marched off toward the exit.

My head was spinning. I didn't know what to do. I thought I might pass out. That's when the curly-haired doctor put a comforting hand on my arm. I thought he might offer some encouraging words, maybe a little advice on what steps I should take to protect myself now that Wendell Butterworth was free to start following me around again.

"I was wondering," he said. "Are you seeing anyone?"

Chapter 2

After extricating myself from the curly-haired doctor's advances, I didn't stick around to witness Wendell Butterworth's official release after two decades of imprisonment. My stomach was churning enough as it was. Laurette's bombshell had shaken me up pretty good, and I had to race back to LA to judge this new fiancé for myself.

I called Charlie from the car when I was still a good four hours away from home. I knew he was working on a gang-related assault case on a homeless man and wouldn't be in his office so I left a message on his voice mail.

"Hi, it's me. You're not going to believe this one. They're releasing Wendell Butterworth so you better check the alarm system at home. Oh, and by the way, we're hosting a dinner party tonight . . . for Laurette and the actor she's going to marry. Yes, you heard me right. I said 'marry' and 'actor' in the same sentence."

When I had left LA the day before to drive up to Vacaville for the parole hearing, Charlie told me he was looking forward to the two of us ordering Indian food and watching a DVD, just the two of us, upon my return. I had a habit of disrupting his plans so I had to tread delicately.

"I know you were looking forward to coconut chicken curry and Reese Witherspoon tonight, but we don't know anything about this guy. Who he is. Where he comes from. Zilch. So I think it's best we put that off and have them over to the house. I knew you'd agree with me."

I hung up quickly, knowing perfectly well his reaction when he heard the message. But Charlie loved Laurette almost as much as I did, and I knew he, too, would want the scoop on this rather sudden shocking turn of events, even at the expense of his favorite Friday night ritual.

The next order of business on the drive home was calling every actor I knew to see if any of them had ever heard of Juan Carlos Barranco. The first six fellow thespians couldn't even manage to repeat back the name, let alone reel off a list of credits or a bio. But I struck pay dirt with Annabelle Lipton, a former scene partner from my Master Acting Class a few years back with the late Tony Randall of TV's *Odd Couple*. Annabelle and I had teamed up for a scene from Clifford Odets's *Golden Boy* that had left Mr. Randall in tears. I recently caught Annabelle in a feminine hygiene ad on Lifetime, so it was good to know the class had paid off for her in some way.

"Juan Carlos Barranco? I dated him for a while about seven months ago," Annabelle said. I could almost hear the bile rising in her throat. I hadn't seen her in over two years, but from what I remembered, she was adorably cute with a pixie cut and huge hazel eyes.

"When did you two break up?" I said.

"We never officially did. He stayed over one night because my place was close to an early-morning audition. He kissed me good-bye and said he'd be back in an hour. I never saw him again."

Some people are reluctant to talk about painful moments from their past. Luckily actors can go on for hours, all day even, as long as the topic is related to them. And Annabelle, being a consummate actress, had plenty to say. "We met at the Viper

Room. He asked me to dance, bought me a few drinks, just showered me with attention. It was right about the time I had received a small inheritance from my great aunt who had died back in Grand Rapids. Got about fifteen grand. He was working as a massage therapist at the time. That was his side business when he wasn't working as an actor. Right about the time we finished blowing my aunt's money together was when he disappeared. Interesting timing, wouldn't you say?"

"Could be a coincidence," I said, not believing a word I was saying. Neither was Annabelle.

"Yeah, right. Then I started getting all these calls from his massage clients trying to find him. It seems he offered a package of ten massages for the price of five. Pretty good deal, right? Well, after everybody paid him in advance, he took off. When people called up to schedule an appointment, they found out his cell phone was no longer in service. And the only other contact number he gave out was mine."

"Sounds like a charming guy."

"You have no idea, Jarrod."

True, Annabelle had a flair for the dramatic. She once stubbed her toe on her bathroom door jam and tooled around in an electric wheelchair for two weeks. But I believed every word she was telling me about Laurette's new love.

"Next thing I know," she said, "I see him on *90210* kissing Tori Spelling."

Of course! That was how I knew him. He played a really hot Rugby player on *Beverly Hills 90210* during its last season (I was and still am an unapologetic fan). I knew a couple of actors on that show, who confirmed rumors that he had slept with the very much married executive producer in order to get the part. He must have been good. He was signed up for a six-episode story arc.

"So why are you asking me about Juan Carlos?" Annabelle said.

"He's about to marry a friend of mine."

Dead silence. For a minute I thought the cell phone had cut out. But then Annabelle spoke in a grave, measured tone. "Tell her to get out while she still can."

I roared up Beachwood Drive, heading straight for the world-famous Hollywood sign and the English Tudor home I shared with my boyfriend, Charlie, and our loyal Pekinese, Snickers. Charlie and I both would have preferred a bigger dog, maybe a shepherd or even a Lab (a pet that wouldn't scream *gay*), but when Charlie was called to the scene of a murder-suicide involving an elderly couple driven to despair by their useless HMO, he found their cute little dog sniffing around the bodies of his former owners, confused and whining, and just a few minutes away from a one-way trip to the Humane Society. Charlie just couldn't do it. He brought her home, we fed her some left over chicken tikka (yes, it was Indian food/DVD night), and she went to sleep at the foot of our bed. She's been a fixture there ever since.

I whipped up the windy roads of the canyon, turning the last corner to see Charlie's new Volvo parked outside the house. Right behind it was Laurette's gas-guzzling Ford SUV. I knew when I hit that unexpected traffic just north of the city, I would be cutting it close. I hit the garage door opener, and pulled my Beamer inside. As I jumped out, I could hear the excited jangling of Snickers's tags behind the door leading to the kitchen. I took a deep breath, and marched inside to meet the already infamous Juan Carlos Barranco.

Charlie was at the stove stirring a pot full of mashed potatoes and boiling water for corn on the cob. I knew instantly that the steaks were probably already on the grill outside in the backyard. Laurette sat at the kitchen table, which resembled a fifties diner booth (a by-product of my gay kitsch gene), downing what I presumed from the half-empty bottle was her third glass of wine. Charlie didn't drink.

There was no sign of Juan Carlos.

As Snickers ran in circles to celebrate my arrival, Laurette jumped up and grabbed me in a big welcoming hug. "We thought you'd never get here."

I muffled a reply into her ample bosom, as the bright colors from her stylish print top blinded me.

Charlie turned around and gave me a wink. "Hi, babe." He looked as sexy as always in an open-collar J.Crew shirt and a pair of ripped jeans. Even after mucking up his Friday night plans and making him prepare a whole dinner for four because I was late, he still looked genuinely happy to see me. God, how did I get so lucky?

"So, where is he?" I said.

"He had an audition for some low-budget horror thing in Silver Lake. He'll be here soon," Laurette said confidently, obviously unaware of his history of never returning from acting auditions.

Charlie turned back to the stove and started scooping the freshly whipped potatoes into empty skins that he had lined up on a cooking sheet. I saddled up behind him and wrapped my arms around his waist.

"Twice-baked potatoes," I said. "My favorite."

"Got filet mignon, corn on the cob, tossed salad, and rolls. Am I forgetting anything?"

Laurette piped up. "Juan Carlos is bringing dessert. He said it would be a surprise. Something sweet and Spanish, I'm assuming. Like him."

I turned and smiled at Charlie. "Looks like you took care of everything. I owe you."

"Yes, you do, and I intend to collect . . . later." Another wink.

As Charlie slipped the cooking sheet in the oven, I poured myself a glass of wine and sat down with Laurette at the kitchen table.

"So . . . an actor?" I said.

Laurette laughed. "I know, I know. Trouble with a capital T. But Juan Carlos is different from any man I've ever dated."

"Or married, I hope." I added. Five years ago Laurette had married an aspiring director who was trying to mount an independent production about a family horse-breeding business set in Lexington, Kentucky. Once Laurette had secured financing through her ample contacts, and he went off to shoot his epic, the whole thing fell apart. The marriage, not the film. The film went on to win an audience award at Sundance and a successful art house career for its director. The marriage was dissolved after Laurette's husband impregnated an extra on the set who was fresh out of high school.

"Yes. Joel was a prick. He used me. My therapist says I have to stop picking men who need me professionally so I feel I have a value in the relationship. That's why Juan Carlos is perfect for me. He doesn't need me."

"Um, Laurette, honey, I don't mean to be a wet blanket or anything, but Juan Carlos is an actor and you're a talent agent. A talent agent who knows a lot of studio executives and TV producers."

"Yes, but Juan Carlos is doing just fine without me. He hasn't asked me to do him one favor. Not one. Joel and I were on our second date when he handed me his script and asked if I could get it to Jennifer Love Hewitt."

It was just about dark outside. The flashing beam of a car's headlights passed by slowly out front, signaling the arrival of the man in question. He turned around in the driveway and parked behind Laurette's SUV. Snickers's ears perked up and she scurried to the door, barking all the way. As I followed Snickers, I glanced out the window and noted that Juan Carlos drove a Lexus convertible. Very nice for someone whose last film role was "Firefighter #3" in a CBS TV movie. I opened the door, and put on the warmest, most welcoming smile I could muster. Juan Carlos wasn't the only actor in Laurette's life.

"Hi, you must be Juan Carlos. I'm Jarrod." I wanted to add, "And Laurette's best friend who will hunt you down and gut you with a knife if you hurt her in any way," but it seemed too early in the evening.

"I've heard a lot about you, Jarrod." There wasn't a trace of a Spanish accent. Maybe he was second or third generation. Or maybe he had been working with a voice coach to pound it out of him.

Despite my suspicions based on Annabelle's stories, I couldn't help but be impressed upon first glance with Juan Carlos. He was, just as Laurette promised, gorgeous. About six feet, broad shoulders, jet-black hair, and smoldering brown Spanish eyes that glistened in the light from the lamp just outside the front door. He was wearing a Hugo Boss suit, but the tie had been undone and the shirt was open, giving me more than a hint of his toned muscular smooth chest. He looked even better in person than he did on *90210*.

"Sorry I'm late," he said as he shook my hand and entered before I had a chance to invite him inside.

Laurette ran into the entryway from the kitchen and threw her arms around him. She smothered him with kisses on his face, ears, and neck. Whatever was in reach of her lips. I noticed him tense slightly as she hugged him. It was just for a split second, and then he relaxed and allowed her to maul him. Finally, he gently pulled away and smiled. His teeth were fluoride white and perfect.

"I nailed it, honey. I'm pretty sure I got the part," he said.

"Oh, honey, that's wonderful. I'm so happy for you," Laurette said, before turning to me. "See, I told you he was good."

Charlie was the next to amble out of the kitchen, and stride over to Juan Carlos with an outstretched hand. "I'm Charlie. Nice to meet you, Juan Carlos."

Juan Carlos gripped Charlie's hand, and looked him up and down. It was subtle, barely detectable in fact, but I caught it. If I didn't know better, I'd swear he was checking Charlie out.

"I better head out to the backyard and check on the steaks. How do you like yours done, Juan Carlos?" Charlie said.

Juan Carlos smiled and slipped his hand behind Laurette, lowering it until his palm was firmly clamped on her butt. "Blood red."

Charlie nodded and walked away. I thought I saw Juan Carlos peek at Charlie's ass as he strolled off, but he instantly averted his eyes when he felt me watching him. I had to be imagining this. Laurette had excellent gaydar. She of all people would likely know if the man she was planning to marry was straight or not. But it did depend on how good an actor Juan Carlos was.

"So, sweetie, what did you bring us for dessert?"

Juan Carlos frowned, and then gave us both an apologetic look. "In all the excitement about the audition, I forgot to pick something up."

"That's all right, darling," Laurette said. "I have to lose twenty pounds in six days anyway if I want to fit into my wedding dress."

They embraced again, and Laurette mouthed the words, "Isn't he fabulous?" over his shoulder to me.

That's when it hit me what she had just said. "Did you say six days?"

"Yes. You don't already have plans or anything, do you? We just didn't have time to send out formal invitations."

"No, we don't have plans. But six days? I had no idea you were going to get married so soon."

Juan Carlos flashed me a self-satisfied smile. "We both know this is it, the real deal. What's the point in waiting?"

Laurette took his hand and gazed longingly at him. I had to snap her out of it somehow. I didn't have time to get the full story on Juan Carlos in only six days. "But there's so much to plan. You have to pick out a venue, a dress . . ."

"It's done," Laurette said. "You know I've always wanted to be married at the Hearst Castle. There was a last-minute cancellation next weekend. It cost me most of my savings, but I got it. My dress is being altered as we speak. I've booked a band. Invited everybody I want to be there. There's not a whole lot left to do."

My head was spinning. I knew Laurette was a freight train when she decided to do something, but I didn't expect her speed to rival a space shuttle.

"There is one problem, though," she said with a scowl.

Finally, something I could work with to stop this madness.

"I could only afford the Hearst Castle for three hours," she said. "With setup and cleanup, that leaves approximately one hour and seven minutes for the ceremony and reception. It's going to be tight."

I was speechless. There was a momentary silence before Juan Carlos picked up the slack in the conversation. He beamed at his blushing bride. "Oh well," he purred. "More time for the honeymoon."

And then the happy couple proceeded to suck face right in front of me, devouring each other like a pair of five-year-olds chowing down on their first hot fudge sundae.

I felt sick to my stomach.

La Cuesta Encantada, or the "Enchanted Hill," is located in San Simeon, midway between Los Angeles and San Francisco, and is situated sixteen hundred feet above sea level on a sprawling two hundred and fifty thousand acres. Housing one hundred and sixty-five rooms, two spectacular swimming pools, and an astonishing collection of art and antiques, the magnificent compound was built by publishing magnate William Randolph Hearst over a twenty-eight year-period. Since Hearst and his longtime mistress, the comedy actress Marion Davies, loved hosting Hollywood royalty, including Charlie Chaplin, Jimmy Stewart, Greta Garbo, and Cary Grant, the camp value alone made it the ideal spot for Laurette's nuptials. Ever since her parents carted their wide-eyed eight-year-old daughter on a bus up to the grounds for a tour, Laurette had been fascinated with the history and beauty of "the ranch," as Hearst liked to call it, and felt it was destiny that she be married among the ghosts of the Hollywood elite. Since her first wedding was a Vegas quickie so her husband could jet off to Prague for an obscure film festival, Laurette decided to arrange a more formal affair at the Hearst Castle upon his return. But when he did arrive home six weeks later, he kept putting her off until she finally gave up on both a San Simeon wedding and her ill-fated marriage.

Juan Carlos was an entirely different animal altogether. The thought of an expensive party at a sprawling hilltop retreat looking down on the blue sea and up at the blue sky was not only a good thing, but a God-given right. Despite having no financial resources of his own from what I could see, this charmer certainly had cultivated tastes. He was more excited about getting married at this exotic location than his blushing bride was.

Charlie didn't share my suspicions about Juan Carlos's character. He felt I was being overprotective of my best friend, and should just lay off and be happy for her. So naturally my persistent suggestions that he run an ID check on Juan Carlos using his police sources fell on deaf ears.

The drive up to the tiny seaside hamlet of San Simeon took about three and a half hours, not counting the hour-and-a-half stop at the Biltmore Hotel in Santa Barbara for their remarkable all-you-can-eat Sunday morning brunch. Charlie tried reminding me that there would be food at the reception, but since Laurette could only afford to rent the Castle for such a limited amount of time, I didn't want the pressure of having to scarf down enough shrimp cocktail before we got kicked out.

Since I insisted on going back for a third serving of pineapple sponge cake at the Biltmore, we fell behind schedule, so by the time we reached the Hearst Castle, there were only a handful of guests left at the bottom to be bussed up to the property for the ceremony.

Five of us boarded a blue bus driven by a portly African-American man with a pleasant smile, and began our ascent heavenward to the estate that was so high up it often sat above the coastal fog drifts.

Charlie and I sat in the back and I watched the other three passengers, none of whom seemed to know each other. Directly in front of us was a young woman in her early twenties, with long cascading brown hair that fell down below her shoulders. She was a petite thing, very thin and gaunt. If only I had brought a doggie bag from the Biltmore, then maybe I could feed the starving little bird. Her face was striking, with gorgeous green eyes and full Angelina Jolie lips. If she hadn't started going the way of Karen Carpenter, she would be a real beauty.

The other two passengers were both men. Across from the girl sat an obese man in his early thirties, who ran upwards of three hundred pounds. He was squeezed in his seat, and droplets of sweat trickled down his cheek. His washed-out orange hair, or what was left of it, was unruly and frizzy with a few stray wisps combed over his bald plate. He looked grossly uncomfortable, and he kept his eyes fixed out the window. He had zero interest in conversing with any of us. A few seats ahead of him was a short, compact fellow who made up for his height deficiencies with a killer physique. He, too, was balding, but unlike the heavy man, he kept the sides neat and trimmed. He wore a tight white T-shirt to showcase his muscles and crisp hip-hugging jeans. This guy was definitely not dressed for a wedding.

I decided to break the silence. "So, are you all friends of the bride or groom?" I knew full well they were all acquaintances of Juan Carlos, but it was an acceptable icebreaker. Charlie smiled. He loved watching me force people to socialize.

The girl spoke first. Her voice was as tiny as her body. "Groom."

More silence. I wasn't about to give up.

"So, did you have to travel far to attend?"

"Florida," she said flatly.

The short man's ears perked up and he flipped around in his seat. He and the girl made eye contact and there was both surprise and recognition in their eyes.

"What are you—?" she started to say to him, but thought better of it. He gave her a polite nod and they instantly turned away from each other.

"You two know each other?"

"No," they both said in unison.

I kept forging ahead. "Oh, is Florida where you met Juan Carlos?" I asked the girl.

"Yes."

She wasn't giving me anything. And the other two didn't seem very anxious to talk to me either. So I stuck out my hand. "I'm Jarrod."

She looked at my hand as if it were covered with abscesses, and then reluctantly took it for a moment. After a brief handshake, she quickly pulled away.

"Dominique."

"That's a pretty name," I said, trying desperately to win points somehow. I'm an actor. I have a need to be loved. It didn't work. She just grunted what I assumed was a "thank-you" and looked away.

"We're friends of Laurette's," I said, plowing on. "Have you met her yet? She's wonderful. You'll love her."

This got her undivided attention. She whipped around, her

eyes narrowing and her face tightening as she said evenly, "I don't have any interest in meeting *her*."

"Oh. Okay," I said. Charlie signaled me with his eyes to drop the subject. I smiled at him and then turned back to Dominique. "Why not?"

I heard an exasperated sigh come out of Charlie.

Dominique thought for a minute, probably debating whether or not she should say anything more. But her anger got the best of her, and eyes blazing, she said, "Because it should be me marrying Juan Carlos today."

"So you two were—?"

"Yes," she said.

"I'm surprised you got an invitation."

"I didn't." And with that, she turned back around, sending me the clear message that our conversation was over.

This was too juicy. But I was more than a little worried that an old flame of Juan Carlos's might ruin Laurette's big day. I wasn't sure how I should handle it, whether I should tell Laurette, or try to get Dominique to leave quietly, when Charlie, reading my mind, squeezed my arm and whispered, "It's none of your business." He was right. I decided to focus on someone else.

"You a friend of the groom's too?" I said to the short, muscular man upfront, but both men turned around.

The obese one nodded and then, with a miserable look on his face, gazed back out the window. I've never seen someone so unhappy going to a wedding. Except for maybe Dominique.

The other man was a bit chattier. "Yes, I've known Juan Carlos for some time now. Austin Teboe. We met in Florida as well. Working in a restaurant. I haven't seen him in a while. I'm hoping he'll be happy to see me."

This was too much. "So he doesn't know you're coming either?"

"Nope. Doesn't have a clue. It's going to be a big surprise."

The more he talked, the more nervous Dominique appeared. She started fidgeting in her seat, folding her arms, trying to stay calm.

"So are we the only two on the bus who have actually been invited?" I said to Charlie, as I kept one eye on the obese man to our left. But he never even bothered to acknowledge me.

The bus pulled in and deposited us at the Neptune Pool on the north side of the property, where the wedding ceremony was scheduled to take place. Made up of fragments of ancient Roman columns, bases, and capitals, and decorated with sculptured figures of Roman gods, the picturesque pool area was reminiscent of an Italian Renaissance villa. Laurette could not have selected a more visually exciting locale. With rain clouds hovering overhead, however, there was an unsettling foreshadowing of storms ahead.

Most of the guests were already seated, and I got the distinct feeling from the annoyed looks we were receiving that the ceremony was being held up due to our late arrival.

Charlie, the obese man, and I slipped quietly into a row of seats in the back so as not to draw any more attention to ourselves. Dominique and Austin, however, remained standing, making a concerted effort to be conspicuous.

The organist off to the side launched into those first notes that introduce the "Wedding March" processional, and Juan Carlos, his skin a perfect shade of bronze against his all-white tuxedo, strolled out to take his place in front of a makeshift altar set up near a breathtaking sculpture of the Birth of Venus. He broke out into a smile with enough wattage to light Dodger Stadium. He was in his element, enjoying everyone watching him and admiring him and envying him. Until his eyes fell on Austin. And then the smile faded. His face twitched a little. He was confused, almost disoriented. Austin was enjoying every minute of it. He sent back a slight wave and then folded his arms, satisfied he had made some kind of point. But Juan

Carlos's reaction to Austin's presence was nothing compared to his horrified reaction to Dominique's last-minute arrival. He stared at her, mouth agape, mind obviously racing. I could tell what he was thinking. What was she doing here? How did she find him?

For a minute I thought he was going to bolt. Get the hell out of Dodge. But then it was too late. The organist started banging out the familiar "Wedding March" melody, and Laurette Taylor, decked out in a bodacious satin off-white wedding dress complete with gauzy veil and an endless train carried proudly by four preteen first cousins, made her way down the aisle, ready for her moment in the sun.

That's when it started raining.

Chapter 3

God was undoubtedly sending Laurette a message when he opened up the skies and pounded her hastily planned wedding with an unrelenting torrent of rain. She chose to ignore it. Not budging from the altar, resolved to leave the Hearst Castle a newlywed, Laurette gripped Juan Carlos's hand tightly and strained to hear the sermon from the doddering old minister whose fogged-up glasses prevented him from sailing through his notes in a timely manner. And since she could afford the property for just over an hour, an unmistakable tension began creeping into Laurette's smile as the long-winded and soaked minister ate up a lot of time talking about love and commitment and the importance of trust. She pretended to listen, but I knew Laurette's mind was on the three-tier German chocolate wedding cake, and if the staff had thought to move it under the canopy to protect it from the rainstorm.

Several guests dashed for cover, but the majority of us stayed glued to our seats, resigned to the fact that we were going to leave this place drenched to the bone. Besides, we had to take our cue from the bride and groom and neither was acknowledging the fact that the wedding party and all their guests were practically drowning. None of us could hear a word the minister was saying, but when Laurette leaned forward and whispered something in his ear, I presumed she was advising the old man to wrap it up because he seemed to skip right to the "I do's."

The minister cleared his throat and tried talking above the now blustery winds. "Do you, Laurette Taylor—"

"Yes," she interrupted him. "Yes, I do. Thank you. And he does too, don't you, darling?"

"Yes," Juan Carlos screamed.

The minister was not good at improvisation. He desperately wanted to stick to the script, but Laurette was having none of it. He was at a loss.

"So by the power vested in you," she offered, trying to help him out a bit.

"Yes, yes, by the power vested in me . . ."

He took a pause for dramatic effect in a lame attempt to add some theatricality to the already drama-filled affair. But Laurette never gave him the chance. She turned and faced the crowd.

"He now pronounces us husband and wife. He gets to kiss me now." Laurette peeled the wet veil off her face and puckered up her lips. Juan Carlos grabbed her by the shoulders and devoured her face with his mouth in an obvious play of machismo that rivaled Al Gore's attempt to show his amorous side by sucking his wife's face at the 2000 Democratic Convention.

The crowd erupted in applause and I turned around in my seat to get a good look at Dominique. She watched the proceedings with a steely gaze, never flinching, just frozen in time, like one of the Roman statues behind her.

Laurette snatched a fistful of Juan Carlos's tuxedo jacket and pulled him down the aisle as the poor organist, sopping wet, began the standard "Wedding March" recessional.

Hurrying things along, Laurette bellowed, "Try to move it along, people! We have a lot to do, and we only have forty-six minutes!"

Mercifully, the reception was under a tent erected on the South Earring Terrace of the estate, built around an ancient Verona wellhead that the caterers almost used as a giant punch bowl before cooler heads prevailed. The nearly one hundred guests squeezed under the canvas cover, and there was very little room to move let alone browse the buffet and load up on chicken salad finger sandwiches and mini-éclairs.

In the interest of time, Laurette chose to forgo the usual wedding traditions of announcing the bride and groom, the first dance, the tossing of the garter, and a receiving line. But since she worshipped food, a devotion both she and I shared, the cutting of the cake was an absolute must. The head caterer did indeed have the foresight to protect the cake and move it under the tent before it began pouring, knowing the bride would blow her stack if one creamy frosted flower got hit with a single raindrop. She'd taken longer picking out the cake than she had picking out a husband.

Laurette pushed her way through the crowd, advising people to eat immediately because the staff had to commence with cleanup in a scant twenty-six minutes; otherwise she'd be charged an additional hour at a whopping cost of a cool five grand. A lot of guests felt so much pressure, they simply couldn't eat at all. I didn't have that problem. Charlie and I grabbed plates and dived right in, starting with the cheese and crackers. Before I had a chance to start sampling, Laurette was hovering behind me.

"Jarrod, my dumb ass sister got wasted and banged one of the groomsmen last night, big surprise, and now she's so hung over she doesn't want to make a toast. I know what she's doing. She's pretending to be sick so she can steal focus from my big day. So typical. Could you do it?"

"Do what?"

"Make a toast."

"But . . . but I haven't prepared anything."

"Oh, honey, please," she said confidently. "You're fabulous

with improv. You should have your own sketch show. And I know you'll be brief, unlike that loser of a minister. Could you believe him? I told him to keep his sermon down to three minutes. Doesn't anybody ever listen anymore?"

"What do you want me to say?"

"How much you care about me, how perfect you think Juan Carlos is for me, how happy we're going to be together. Blah, blah, blah . . ."

So she wanted me to lie.

"Laurette, I don't know . . ."

"He'd be happy to," Charlie interjected, squeezing my arm tightly, sending me a clear message to just shut up and do it so everyone could go home happy.

"All right, sweetie," I said. "Just tell me when."

"Be ready in seven minutes. If I can get that lame duck photographer who's always running out of film in place, we can cut the cake at the same time."

I was so happy Laurette was taking the time to enjoy her big day.

She hurriedly checked her watch. "I better grab a ladyfinger before the caterers start packing up." She lifted her dress to barrel her way to the dessert table when she stopped cold.

"Who's that?" she said.

I turned to see Juan Carlos engaged in a heated discussion with Dominique. Her eyes were bloodshot from crying and her hand shook as she pointed her finger in his face, on the verge of losing her composure completely. Juan Carlos stood fast, arms folded, a thin smile painted on his face, trying to downplay the seriousness of their conversation.

"Oh, that's an old friend of Juan Carlos's. We met on the bus up here," I said, also trying to downplay the seriousness. Laurette was too smart for that.

"I don't remember her on the guest list. Is she just an old friend or an old *girl*friend?"

"Um, girlfriend, I think."

"I see," Laurette said. "Excuse me."

She seized the hem of her wedding dress, and plowed through the crowd toward her new husband like a linebacker carrying the ball to an end goal. She was upon them in seconds, and stuck out her hand to introduce herself to Dominique.

"This is going to be good," Charlie said, smiling.

The blood drained from Juan Carlos's face as he offered up introductions. Dominique never cracked a smile. She was too upset, and quickly walked away after shaking Laurette's hand. There was nowhere for her to go. There were too many people packed into the tent. She found herself face to face with Austin. He grinned and gave her a hug, but she recoiled and hissed something at him. She was furious with him, and I half expected her to spit in his face. He seemed to be enjoying her fury, almost relishing her discomfort. Finally, she pushed past him and left the protection of the tent, racing toward the line of parked buses that waited to transport the guests back down the hill to their cars. Dominique and Austin were both from Florida, and obviously knew each other despite their quick denials on the bus. My curiosity was piqued. What was Austin Teboe's personal business with the groom all about? And what was his relationship with the groom's ex-girlfriend Dominique?

I was about to embark on a fishing expedition and strike up a conversation with him when angry shouts steered my attention toward the buffet table. Juan Carlos was yelling at the antisocial obese man from our bus trip up the hill. He slugged him in the stomach, but the man's massive bulk prevented Juan Carlos from doing any serious damage. Within seconds, several groomsmen appeared on the scene, and began manhandling the big guy. As the groom's posse physically hustled the man away from the party, Juan Carlos, flushed with anger, dusted himself off, took a brief moment to cool down, and then rejoined his bride. He was back to smiling and glad-handing within seconds.

Laurette waved us over, and Charlie and I wandered over to the happy couple.

"We're just about ready for the toast, Jarrod," she said.

"Is everything all right?" Charlie asked Juan Carlos pointedly.

"Yes, why?" Juan Carlos said as if the previous scene had been magically erased from his memory.

"I thought there was going to be a fight."

"Oh, you mean Rudy Pearson?" Juan Carlos said, his voice full of disdain. "He's just a little bug. Not even worth the effort to squash it."

To my surprise, Laurette jumped in with an explanation. "He's a writer for *Soap Opera Digest*. He's been following Juan Carlos around ever since he played that rapist/preacher on *The Hands of Time*. He's called my office every day for the past two weeks trying to get the exclusive of our wedding, but I told him no press. This was our private day, not to be shared with the public. Besides, Juan Carlos isn't doing soaps anymore. There's no reason he should be following Juan Carlos around. I think the guy just has a big crush on him."

"He's a sleaze ball. If he comes around again, I swear I'll rip his face off," Juan Carlos said, seething.

"Don't you just love that fiery Latin passion?" Laurette said.

I glanced at Charlie. Neither of us thought much of Laurette's new husband, but neither of us was willing to express that out loud. Yet, anyway.

It was the time for my toast. The rain had subsided and the winds had died down, so luckily I wasn't going to have to shout my sentiments. The clock was also ticking. The caterers had begun wrapping up the food and folding up the card tables. We were down to two minutes before we had to vacate the premises. The buses were already sputtering to life in anticipation of our journey back down the hill. The staff quickly poured plastic flute glasses of champagne and handed them out to all the guests.

Charlie gave me an encouraging pat on the butt and sent me up to the front of the tent, where I addressed the crowd.

"When Laurette asked me to say a few words, and believe me, few is the key word since we all have to be out of here in less than two minutes," I said as the guests laughed politely, "I wracked my brain trying to come up with something profound or moving or funny or—"

"One minute, Jarrod!" Laurette said, prodding me to edit myself and keep it moving.

"But in the interest of time, I will just say this. To Juan Carlos and Laurette, every day may you . . . light up each other's lives and give each other hope to carry on." Okay, so I plagiarized Debbie Boone. But it worked in a pinch. Charlie chuckled, instantly recognizing my source material. Laurette and Juan Carlos didn't get the reference at all. Laurette, teary-eyed, her mascara running, blew me a kiss then grabbed the man of her dreams and sucked on his face some more. The rest of the guests wisely chose to wash down my treacle with champagne.

Someone started coughing. I looked around and spotted Austin Teboe, having just downed his glass of champagne. He was gasping and choking and gripping his throat with his hand. Everyone stood, stunned for a moment, before one of the groomsmen, who had just returned from ousting Rudy Pearson, ran forward and grabbed Austin in an attempt to give him the Heimlich maneuver. But Austin wasn't choking on a chicken wing. This sounded different. A white fizzy liquid spilled out of his mouth as he broke away from the groomsman's hold and staggered through the throng of people. His eyes bulged, his face was ghostly white, and his wheezing and coughing came to an abrupt halt as he stopped in his tracks, the life swirling out of him. There was an absolute stillness as all eyes in the tent watched him. He then fell forward, belly flopping dead into Laurette's perfectly decorated three-tier German chocolate wedding cake.

Chapter 4

Laurette was wrong to worry about her drunken, trampy sister stealing focus from her big day. The dead body in front of the buffet table was going to do the job for her. By the time the local San Simeon police arrived on the scene, the guests had been herded into the Refectory, the hilltop's sole dining room located in the main house, usually cordoned off for tours but today reopened due to the unusual circumstances. Charlie and I huddled with several of Laurette's fellow talent agents, who were all buzzing about the identity of the deceased. No one seemed to have the slightest idea who he was.

"Austin Teboe," I offered, never one to refrain from a good dish session. "We rode up the hill with him today. He worked in a restaurant in Florida, but he never told us whether he was a waiter, or worked in the kitchen, or parked cars."

"So he was a friend of Juan Carlos's?" asked a tiny woman in a smart suit with frizzy hair so big I was surprised she could hold her head straight. I recognized her as another agent in Laurette's Sherman Oaks office.

"He said he met Juan Carlos at the restaurant. And that the two had personal business that he was here to take care of . . ."

Charlie interceded and gently took my elbow, steering me away from the enraptured group of gossipmongers. "I think the police are ready to talk to us now, Jarrod."

We walked over to the corner of the room where four police officers stood over Juan Carlos and a confused and dazed Laurette, who sat on an antique love seat from the nineteenth century, ignoring the clearly marked sign that said DO NOT SIT ON FURNITURE. The team of investigators were led by a grizzled, balding, pot-bellied detective, who might as well have walked right off the set of *Hunter*, the Fred Dryer action series from the eighties, where I once guest-starred as a convicted counterfeiter's wayward teenaged son in their memorable sixth season opener.

He shook Charlie's hand. "Lieutenant Cranston."

"Charlie Peters, LAPD. This is my partner, Jarrod Jarvis."

Cranston nodded, ready to welcome me into the brotherhood of peace officers. "You guys up here working on a case?"

"No," I said. "I'm his partner in life, not crime."

This took Cranston by surprise. But it was a new world so he simply grunted and declined further comment.

Charlie was right in his element. He compared notes with Cranston. "We met the victim earlier." Charlie recounted our bus ride up to the Hearst Mansion, and how Dominique and Rudy Pearson, who were both fiercely determined to attend today's nuptials, had left rather abruptly. One by choice. And one by force.

Cranston turned to Juan Carlos. "How did you know the victim?"

"I didn't," said Juan Carlos, as he sat comforting Laurette.

Either Austin Teboe was lying. Or Juan Carlos was. I'd put my money down on the slippery, opportunistic actor any day.

"Well, according to Mr. Peters here, Mr. Teboe claimed to have known you, and that the two of you had some personal business he was here to talk to you about," said Cranston in a slightly confrontational tone.

"I said I never met him," said Juan Carlos.

Laurette took her husband by the chin and gently turned his face toward hers. "What I want to know is, who is this Dominique person?"

Juan Carlos glanced in my direction, trying to judge whether or not I had any knowledge about his past with her. I decided to make it easy on him. "An ex-girlfriend."

"How come you never mentioned her?" Laurette said.

"We only dated a few weeks. She meant nothing to me."

"Then what was she doing here?"

"She's had a little troubling letting go. I think she may be a little obsessed with me."

"A *little* obsessed? Honey, she crashed our wedding."

"I didn't want to worry you."

"Why? Has she tried contacting you before?" Laurette said.

"Yes," he said. "For some time now."

"Why didn't you tell me?"

Cranston stepped forward, interrupting the newlyweds. "Look, the ex-girlfriend is not why we're here. As far as we know, she's alive and well. Our focus is on Mr. Teboe, who sadly is not."

"I'm sorry," said Juan Carlos. "I can't help you. I already told you I've never met the man in my life. And if he's saying I did, he's got me mixed up with somebody else."

Charlie and I exchanged looks, both silently agreeing that Juan Carlos wasn't a very good actor after all.

"That's an awfully big mix-up if he traveled all the way from Florida to track you down at the Hearst Castle, which is up here in the middle of nowhere," I quietly offered.

Laurette stood up, and glared at Charlie and me. Then she pushed forward in my direction. "Jarrod, may I speak to you privately, please?"

I nodded and followed Laurette into the adjoining Assembly Room, where William Randolph Hearst had once smoked stogies with Clark Gable and Jimmy Stewart. I didn't dare take a seat on the historic antique furniture that gave the elongated space its Renaissance flair. Laurette was just too angry to sit.

"Why are you and Charlie attacking my husband?" she said.

"We're not attacking him. But there are a lot of unanswered questions involving his relationship with the deceased."

"What relationship? He's already told the police he didn't know him."

I gave Laurette my best "let's not fool ourselves" gaze. "I just think we should look a little deeper into this and see who might have had reason to off the murder victim."

"How do we even know he was murdered? Maybe it was a heart attack or a stroke or something?"

Laurette had seen the white fizzy liquid come pouring out of Teboe's mouth herself. You didn't have to be William Peterson or Marg Helgenberger to assume it could have been some kind of poison. It was only a matter of time before the coroner would be able to confirm it.

"I can see what you're doing," Laurette said.

"What?"

"You're going to get your kicks again playing Nancy Boy Drew. Just like you did last year when Willard Ray Hornsby died."

"Yes, but if you recall, somebody did indeed murder Willard, and I got to the bottom of it."

"You're not a detective, Jarrod. You shouldn't be sticking your nose into things that don't concern you."

"Why not? Because I might stumble across some dirty laundry belonging to your husband?"

"How dare you? You barely even know him."

"And how well do *you* know him? For God's sake, Laurette, how could you marry a guy you only met a few weeks ago?"

"Because I love him!"

We both stopped before we said things neither of us would be able to take back. Our relationship had always been strong and solid, but I was reluctant to go traipsing into uncharted territory that could do serious damage to our decades-old friendship. And sometimes Laurette was more manageable when she was hearing things she wanted to hear.

"Honey, I'm sure he's everything you think he is." A little white lie never hurt anyone. But a big one like this could bring the roof down on us. "But a man has died, and I think we owe it to him to find out what really happened."

Laurette sighed. "I hate when you get like this."

"Like what?"

"Like a pit bull that's gotten a hold on an old shoe. I can see it in your eyes, Jarrod. You see Juan Carlos as that shoe, and you're not going to let go no matter what."

She was right, of course. I was certain Juan Carlos was lying about not knowing the murder victim, and I wasn't going to rest now until I unearthed the truth. Unfortunately, this time it meant straining my bond with Laurette. But in the end, I knew whatever I found would be beneficial to her. Either it would put her mind at ease about the commitment she had just made, or more realistically, it would give her enough information to extricate herself from a catastrophic mistake.

Laurette whipped around, gathered up her bulky dress, and headed for the door leading back to the Refectory.

"Fine," she said. "Sniff around all you want. Once the police are done questioning us, we're off for a fabulous honeymoon in Maui anyway."

Still stung by my suspicions, Laurette marched off back inside the dining room to join her husband and her other guests. I could tell there was a sinking feeling deep inside her gut that was gnawing at her, reminding her that she didn't know Juan Carlos as well as she thought. And perhaps maybe there were dark secrets swimming their way to the surface that might wash away the rosy hue on her rose-colored glasses.

To my surprise, the police released the newlyweds and most

of the wedding guests within an hour after writing down all of our contact information. The Hearst staff was anxious to clear us out so they could resume their meticulously scheduled tours of the expansive property.

Laurette declined to toss the bouquet. We weren't allowed to throw rice or anything, given the time it would take for the staff to clean it up, so the process of sending off the bride and groom lacked the traditional fanfare and was decidedly anticlimactic, especially given the dramatic events at the reception. Laurette simply waved to all her friends and family, then climbed into the back of a white stretch limousine. It quickly began its descent down the long, winding paved road. Within moments, the giant limo was the size of a matchbox car and it suddenly vanished behind a lush green hill. All the guests then quietly formed a single-file line to board the blue tour buses for the fifteen-minute ride back down the mountain to our cars.

As our bus dropped a group of us off in the parking lot at the bottom of the hill, my stomach rumbled, which caused Charlie to raise an eyebrow.

"Hungry?"

"Yeah, so?" I said, rather abruptly. The fact was I was always hungry.

In my defense, during all the excitement, I never even took a bite from my hors d'oeuvre plate. And hours had passed since the all-you-can-eat brunch at the Biltmore Hotel in Santa Barbara. So Charlie knew to find the nearest roadside diner pronto or my mood would inevitably darken during the long drive home, and he would be the one to pay the price. After turning left for the Pacific Coast Highway scenic route south toward Los Angeles, Charlie spotted the San Simeon Beach Bar and Grill just across the road from sweeping views of the glistening, hazy blue ocean. He instinctively jerked the wheel and pulled in and parked right in front of the entrance in order to cut down on the length of time it would take to get some food into me, and thereby make his journey back home more pleasant.

"This look good to you?"

I nodded, choosing not to reply with a verbal response that could be laced with sarcasm or a slicing edge. When I was ugly from hunger, just staying quiet was my preferred method of dealing with my mood. This foresight was one of the chief reasons Charlie and I were still together.

The sea-blue paint on the one-level, dilapidated structure was fading from the sun's intense daily beating. The restaurant probably did a good business owing to the fact that it was so close to the Hearst property and all that traffic, not to mention there didn't seem to be another dining establishment within ten miles. And it was probably safe to say that this bar and grill in the tiny seaside hamlet of San Simeon, California, wasn't going to make any top ten lists in *Bon Appetite* magazine.

Charlie and I strolled inside, and took a table next to the window so we could gaze out at the impressive view. A hefty waitress in her late fifties, with a seen-it-all scowl, ambled up with her pad of paper and asked if we were ready to order before either of us had even opened the menu. I was fine with that. I didn't need to peruse. I was ready to eat now. One quick two-second glance at the lunch offerings, and I was raring to go.

"Club sandwich, no mayo, extra cheese, with chips and a small salad, peppercorn ranch dressing on the side, a Diet Coke, and a glass of ice water."

The waitress stared at me. I could tell she was impressed. I knew what I wanted with no annoying questions or irritating special requirements. Her day just got a little bit easier. Charlie, however, was another matter. He hemmed and hawed as his eyes scanned up and down the menu. The waitress, who was almost ready to give us a smile after my precise ordering, went back to scowling as Charlie considered his options.

"Let's see . . . what do I feel like? The omelets look really good, but I might be in the mood for some French toast. Of course, that sandwich you're getting sounds pretty good too."

Since Charlie was willing to put up with my hunger-related mood swings, it was only fair I dealt maturely with his incessant waffling when ordering in a restaurant. The waitress didn't share a bed with him like I did, so she didn't have to be patient.

"Should I just come back?"

"Yes," he said with a weak smile. "Two minutes."

As she started to walk off, I gently grabbed her arm. "But go ahead and put my order in, okay?"

She nodded with understanding, closed her pad, and huffed off into the kitchen. I stared out at the crashing waves across the road and we sat in silence for over a minute as Charlie glanced at the menu, but then he put it down on the table and said, "So what do you think? Do you believe Juan Carlos somehow poisoned Teboe?"

I took a moment to consider, but it was pointless. I knew my answer before he even asked the question. "Yes," I said emphatically.

"Me too." His tone was even more certain than mine. And as he launched into his intention to stay on top of the case, get a copy of the autopsy report, and stay in contact with the San Simeon investigation, my attention was drawn to a man who had just walked in the door. He looked vaguely familiar from the back as he approached the waitress, who had just come out of the kitchen with my Diet Coke and ice water. She pointed to a table across the room perpendicular to ours, and he sauntered over to it. Just as he slid in his seat, the waitress blocked my view as she stopped to deliver my drinks.

She gave Charlie a wary look. "Got any decisions for me yet?"

Charlie gave her an embarrassed shrug. He had been so busy discussing the Austin Teboe murder, he hadn't yet had the chance to make any.

"One more minute," he said as he cracked open the menu. "No, wait. I'll have . . ." But the poor guy just couldn't commit. Luckily, unlike a lot of gay men, he was much better committing to relationships. "No, forget it. Just give me . . . another minute."

The waitress shook her head slightly and tossed me a look, knowing I shared her contempt of indecisiveness when it came to food. And then she disappeared back into the kitchen again, clearing my obstructed view of the new diner.

My heart almost stopped. I could feel the blood draining from my face. Charlie glanced up from his menu, and instantly knew something was wrong.

"What's the matter?"

"It's him. He's here," I said.

Charlie looked across the room, and his face froze at the sight of Wendell Butterworth, my insane childhood stalker, sitting across the room from us, calmly skimming the lunch specials at the San Simeon Beach Bar and Grill.

Chapter 5

Charlie was up out of his seat like a shot, and charged over to where Wendell Butterworth sat with a satisfied smile on his face. He barely acknowledged Charlie looming over him. His dead gray eyes were fixed on me.

"What the hell are you doing here?" Charlie said with controlled anger.

Wendell glanced up at him and, with an innocent shrug, replied, "Just having some lunch." And then he looked back at me, and gave me a flirtatious wink.

Charlie's imposing six-foot-two frame towered over Wendell as he reached down, grabbed him by his shirt collar, and hauled him out of his chair, which tipped over in the scuffle.

Charlie pulled him forward in his grip until their faces were mere inches apart. "I want you out of here . . . now!"

"I'm just here to get something to eat," Wendell said calmly, going limp in Charlie's grasp. He wasn't going to give Charlie the satisfaction of fighting back.

The seen-it-all waitress, who'd just come out of the kitchen carrying my club sandwich on a rectangular plastic tray, apparently hadn't seen anything like this. Charlie let go of Wendell's collar and hooked an arm around the back of his neck, securing him in a headlock. Then, he yanked him toward the front door. Wendell let his feet drag across the floor, making it even more difficult for Charlie to maneuver him out of the restaurant.

The waitress dropped her tray in surprise, and let out a squeak before she turned back to the kitchen and screamed, "Joey, Lanny, you guys better get out here now!"

Charlie kicked the door open with his right foot, planted the palms of his hands squarely in the middle of Wendell's back, and shoved him hard outside. He then was instantly back at our table, where I sat trying hard not to show him how scared I was. He put a comforting hand on my shoulder.

"You okay, babe?"

"Yeah, it just kind of freaked me out, that's all."

I lovingly placed my hand over Charlie's and we were both still for a moment, contemplating the surreal nature of what had just happened.

Joey and Lanny, the cook and busboy, and prime contenders for a tag team WWE Smackdown title, came bursting through the revolving kitchen doors. They charged up behind the five-foot-two waitress, their bulky size dwarfing her.

Without taking her eyes off us, she said, "The tall one just accosted one of my customers. Kicked his poor ass out the door."

Charlie reached into his back pocket to retrieve his badge, but I stood up and took his hand under the judgmental stares of the obviously straight brutes.

"Let's just go," I said, noticing the remnants of my club sandwich littering the scuffed, dirty floor. "We'll stop somewhere else to eat."

I tossed a ten-dollar bill down on the table. Lanny, hairy everywhere except on the top of his head, waddled over to the front door and pushed it open. He glared at us as we passed by in a vain attempt to intimidate us as we were leaving.

With Charlie's martial arts background and advanced weapons training, it would take a lot more than a three-hundred-pound goateed gorilla in a stained white cook's uniform to intimidate me. On the other hand, if Charlie hadn't been by my side, I probably would have peed in my pants.

Out in the parking lot, we both cautiously looked around for any sign of Wendell Butterworth. He had obviously been released from prison for over a week now. Plenty of time to drum up a handgun. But Wendell had disappeared as quickly as he first appeared, like a ghost. I never once deluded myself into thinking he wouldn't pop up again to haunt me.

Charlie and I climbed into his Volvo, Charlie behind the wheel, and we pulled back onto the highway, riding south toward home in silence. I stole a brief glimpse of Charlie as he drove. He was lost in his private thoughts, and there were worry lines creasing his forehead. He hadn't been there for the hell and pain that Wendell's wrath had brought upon my childhood. But he was acutely aware of the scars and nightmares it had left on me. And it troubled him. He noticed me watching him, so I offered him a reassuring smile. I didn't want him to think I was going to let this guy get to me again. After all, I was older now, stronger, and wiser. I could handle one loony tune. But the reality was, all the fear and anxiety that had paralyzed me as a child was starting to come back. And the idea of this monster kicking off a new campaign of terror made me shudder.

"Monkshood. Very lethal. They call it that because the plant it comes from resembles a monk's cowl."

Charlie and I listened with rapt attention to Susie Chan as she talked while devouring her blackened swordfish at The Little Door on Third Street in West Hollywood. This quaint French bistro, aptly named for its small wooden front door, was one of the top dining spots in LA, and, with even the Diet Coke imported from Europe, very expensive. But the splurge was worth it tonight because in exchange for a forty-dollar piece of fish and a couple of hundred-dollar bottles of wine, Charlie and I were gathering invaluable bits of information.

"It was used in ancient Europe and Asia to poison enemy water supplies during times of war. Hunters also used its sap to poison spears, arrowheads, trap baits, you name it," Susie said between bites of her swordfish.

After returning from Laurette's wedding, Charlie had called his ex-wife, who was the best medical examiner the county of Los Angeles had to offer. She was a five-foot dynamo, appearing on television as a coroner to the stars. She had made quite a name for herself. But despite her enormous career success, she never quite got over her husband coming out of the closet. And she blamed me for breaking up her marriage even though Charlie and I met years after they'd divorced and he'd declared himself gay.

Relations between Susie and myself had always been strained, but lately they had been particularly dicey thanks to a blowup we had when Susie intimated on television that I was directly connected to the murder of my friend Willard Ray Hornsby last year. Of course I didn't do it, and I subsequently unmasked the real killer. But an apology never came from Susie, and we had barely spoken since. Charlie, in the interest of diplomacy, had maintained a cordial relationship with his ex-wife, and they still met for dinner once a month to catch up on each other's lives. I rarely attended these evenings, but tonight was an exception. Susie had agreed to conduct an independent autopsy on Austin Teboe to clarify the cause of death. And owing to her celebrity status, the San Simeon police were more than willing to accommodate her. Some of the officers probably even secretly hoped they'd make the pages of her next book.

Nobody seriously believed Austin Teboe had died of a heart attack. He was still in his early forties and in reasonably good shape. No, there was something else at work here, and Susie was more than willing to help out because, well, let's be frank, she was still in love with her ex-husband.

Susie gulped down a mouthful of a pricey Chardonnay. We were almost down two bottles, and Susie, the lush she was, would undoubtedly order another knowing full well it was my acting residuals picking up the tab.

"Interesting fact. In ancient Greece, legend had it that the plant originated from the slobber dripping from the fangs of Cerberus, the three-headed dog Hercules supposedly brought back with him from the underworld." I didn't give a rat's ass about the Greek myth of a poisonous plant. But I nodded as if I were caught up in a riveting Discovery Channel documentary.

Susie poured herself another glass of wine and then batted her big brown eyes at me. "Should we order another bottle?"

"Sure," I said, clenching my teeth.

Charlie flagged down the waiter.

"So, you're sure this is the poison that was mixed into Austin's champagne?" I said evenly, trying to get as much out of Susie as I could before she got too drunk to speak coherently.

"Yes. It's very bad. Causes burning and tingling, numbness in the tongue, throat, and face, followed by nausea, blurred vision, and paralysis of the respiratory system. Mr. Teboe probably felt as if there was ice water in his veins. And with the amount we found in his glass, it's fatal within ten minutes."

"Was there anything we could have done had we known what it was?" Charlie asked.

"Nope. There's no antidote, at least not that we know about." She pushed her plate away with a third of her swordfish still left. "I don't want to get too full. I hear their dessert menu is fabulous."

"So he was definitely murdered," I said just to confirm it out loud.

"Absolutely. Even the ME in San Simeon, who does maybe one autopsy every two years, knew there was foul play involved before he even cut Mr. Teboe open."

"Where do you think the killer got the stuff?"

"In Nova Scotia, monkshood survives as a garden plant. It's not impossible to come by. So I don't think it's going to help narrow down your lists of suspects."

"You've been a big help, Susie, thanks," Charlie said with a smile.

I felt it was in my best interest to agree. "Yes, Susie, thank you. You never cease to amaze me with your crime scene investigation talents."

Susie knew she was the best, and was always open to fawning accolades. She simply sat back and enjoyed letting them wash over her.

The waiter returned with our third hundred-dollar bottle of wine, and Susie nearly clapped with glee as he twisted the corkscrew into the top of the bottle and popped it open. He poured a small amount into one glass, which Charlie tasted and approved, and we commenced with another full round. Susie signaled another waiter, who was carrying a tray with the evening's dessert selections, and he hustled over to her side so she could ponder over which sweet appealed the most to her. She just couldn't decide, and the poor guy, who had about seven other tables to attend to, was left standing next to her, holding a silver tray lined with seven different dessert selections. At least Susie and Charlie had had one thing in common when they were married: culinary indecisiveness.

As Susie debated between the crème brûlée and the chocolate mousse cake, my mind wandered to Laurette's wedding. The killer had to be somebody in attendance. Austin Teboe had apparently known only two people at the ceremony. There was a definite history between him and Dominique, though it was still a mystery what exactly it was. But she left early, long before the wedding toast, so it would have been impossible for her to mix the monkshood poison into his champagne. That only left one other person: Juan Carlos Barranco. Charlie had made a few calls to Miami Beach, and found out Teboe had worked at a trendy Lincoln Road eatery called the Nexxt Café, which was one of the more popular spots in South Beach. He'd served as a chef, having resigned just two weeks prior to the wedding. Still, we weren't sure that was the restaurant where he had met Juan Carlos; Charlie couldn't verify whether Juan Carlos had ever worked there, or even dined there.

But although I wasn't yet sure about the details, I was convinced Laurette's new husband was behind the murder. And with the happy couple returning from their Maui honeymoon the following morning, I knew this already precarious situation was about to get a hell of a lot more complicated.

Chapter 6

Brave soul that she was, Laurette rang me the morning she got home from her four-day honeymoon at a resort world-renowned for their sumptuous all-you-can-eat buffets, and suggested we rendezvous at a Weight Watchers meeting so we could both weigh in. She decided that if either of us had dropped even a fraction of a pound, we could immediately drive to Hugo's, a West Hollywood brunch spot, and split a plate of their delectable pasta alla mama, to celebrate. From what I could speculate from our brief conversation, the honeymoon did not go well. Her voice was hushed and strained, and when I asked her if everything was all right, she deflected the question by asking how many Weight Watchers points a McDonald's breakfast burrito would cost her.

I hopped into the car and drove to the nearest Weight Watchers location, which was on Beverly Boulevard, in the heart of Los Angeles's teeming Russian immigrant community. There was no reason for Weight Watchers to be in this particular location as far as I could tell. The Russians in the neighborhood didn't look any heavier than the Americans.

I parked on a side street, walked to the two-level glass building, and made my way to the back where a line formed out the door with nervous-looking dieters awaiting their weekly weigh-in on a sturdy, top-of-the-line scale you just can't buy at Sears. There was no getting around the numbers that would pop up on the digital display screen. These industrial, professional machines were designed for accuracy. Which was good or bad, depending on what kind of week you'd had. Today was bad since I had overindulged at The Little Door with Charlie and Susie the night before.

Laurette and I had tried every kind of diet there was, but Weight Watchers was the one that seemed to do the trick since it was very easy for both of us to get caught up in counting points. It became a game we could play together as we spent hours trying to figure out how it would be possible to eat a filet mignon and half a pepperoni pizza in the same day. Unfortunately, with only twenty-seven points to spend a day, and one slice of French toast with a dollop of maple syrup totaling a whopping eight points, I was done eating for the day after breakfast.

I had been standing in line for just a few minutes when I heard a commotion up at the front counter. It was Laurette. She had arrived just before me and was determined to stock up on the three-point chocolate bars you could gorge on between meals during the week. But there was only one box left on the shelf and a formidable three-hundred-pound newcomer was certain her hand had reached the box first. I loved watching Laurette in action. She was a force to be reckoned with, and most rue the day they foolishly choose to get on her bad side. I had come close on her wedding day. It scared me to think about life without Laurette. She was just too bright a light in my world. And despite my misgivings regarding her new husband, I didn't want to jeopardize our friendship.

To my utter shock, Laurette let go of the box and muttered to the obese woman, "Fine. You take it."

The obese woman grunted, a victorious smile on her face, and took her seat in one of the hard, gray folding chairs that had been set up for today's lecture.

Laurette was clearly upset. Otherwise, she would have chewed up this woman and spit her out, in spite of her enormous size. Whatever was bothering her had to be big. It was extremely unusual for her to give up without a fight. And the stakes involved chocolate. Suddenly I was worried.

She spotted me in line, and ambled over to give me a hug. Her eyes were red, as if she had been crying, and she wore no makeup. Laurette never left the house without makeup. She prided herself on always looking dazzling. The more I studied her, the more concerned I became.

"How was the honeymoon?" I said.

"I think Juan Carlos is cheating on me."

Well, at least I didn't have to pull what was wrong out of her. That was what made Laurette such a good talent manager. No bullshit. She always just cut right to the chase.

"What makes you think that?" I said.

"While we were in Maui, someone kept calling our room at the hotel and hanging up. Juan Carlos said it was probably just kids playing a prank. But I know it was her."

"Who?"

"Dominique, his ex-girlfriend."

"Maybe he was right. Maybe it was just kids," I offered weakly.

Laurette shook her head. "No. Juan Carlos kept leaving me on the beach, said he was going to take a nap in the room. Finally, I called the room and there was no answer. He wasn't there. I think he was meeting her."

"She was in Maui? Are you sure?"

"No. Not a hundred percent sure. But one morning we got up early and did one of those sunrise bike tours down the side of a volcano. Halfway down, our group stopped for breakfast at a small restaurant, and I thought I spotted her outside, just standing there, staring at us. Juan Carlos told me I was being ridiculous. He refused to take me seriously, which just made me all the more suspicious. I know it was her, Jarrod. I saw her."

By this time, Laurette and I were at the front of the line, and it was my turn to bite the bullet and step up on the scale. I tore off my belt and shoes, and dropped my keys and loose change on one of the folding chairs. I was a seasoned pro at this. I didn't need any random coins or metal weighing me down.

I turned and let out a sigh. Operating the scale was Richard, this rail-thin former fatty whom I affectionately referred to as the "Diet Nazi." Richard had lost a hundred and forty pounds on Weight Watchers, and so was a self-proclaimed expert on what was good for the rest of us. When I lost ten percent of my body weight after four grueling months in the program, Richard called me up in front of the class and hailed me as a hero. Until he discovered I had celebrated my monumental weight loss with a huge Thai dinner. He berated me in front of the class, and told me I was not an example to follow, and that earning a few activity points by walking Snickers around the block did not give me license to splurge on pad Thai noodle with peanut sauce. Tension had brewed between us ever since.

Richard gave me a cursory glance, and waved me up onto the scale. I closed my eyes and did as I was told. There was an agonizing moment as Richard waited for the digital numbers to settle down, and then a sly smile broke out on his face.

"It seems we've put on a couple pounds, Jarrod."

I opened my eyes to see the digital readout: 172 pounds. Not good. Not good at all. It was more than a couple of pounds. It was five. The Diet Nazi could barely contain his euphoria.

"And it's not even the holidays. Looks like someone needs to work a little harder. Better luck next week."

I wanted to punch him in the face. Normally I would have found solace in Laurette taking her turn. One smart mouth remark from Richard, and she would have done what I fantasized about doing. She would have socked him square in the mouth.

But instead, after witnessing my public embarrassment, Laurette was too distraught to even attempt a weigh-in.

"I'm not up for this," she said and we hauled ass out the door.

As I walked Laurette to her car, she began to cry. I stopped and took her into my arms. "I'm sorry, sweetheart, I really am."

She pulled away, placing a hand on her chest in a vain attempt to regain her composure. "I love him so much."

"I know you do. Is there anything I can do? Anything at all?"

"Yes."

When I said it, I thought it was one of those rhetorical questions that would have triggered an automated response such as, "No, just being my friend is enough." But I should've known with Laurette, I was being lured into a plan.

"What?" I said, unable to hide my hesitancy.

"Follow him."

"What do you mean?"

She wiped away the last tear from her cheek, and looked at me with fierce resolve. "I want you to follow him and prove that he's a no-good philandering son of a bitch."

Now every little voice in my head was screaming at me to say no. Just tell her I don't feel comfortable staking out my best friend's husband to catch him in the act of adultery. But to be honest, my own curiosity was peaked. I wanted to know his story, and by tailing him, I just might come up with some answers to the questions surrounding Austin Teboe's murder.

Although Charlie would undoubtedly need to be kept in the dark about what I was doing, it proved to be too enticing to pass up. "All right. I'll do it, honey. But remember, this stays between us. If Charlie found out . . ."

"I won't breathe a word."

I nodded and our pact was sealed.

"I can't start on an empty stomach," I said. "Hugo's? My treat."

"Meet you there."

Laurette opened her car door as I walked up the street toward mine, but before she climbed in, she called out to me. "Jarrod?"

I turned around.

"If you do find out he's cheating on me, then will you help me do one more thing?"

"What's that?" I said.

"Kill him."

She was joking. I think. There wasn't a trace of a smile on her face. Or a humorous lilt in her voice. We would just have to cross that bridge if we came to it.

Luckily Charlie was in the shower when Laurette called at five-thirty the following morning to alert me to the fact that Juan Carlos was on the move. He was on his way to Gold's Gym in Hollywood, and had an audition for a national Home Depot commercial at ten-thirty. He was particularly vague about his afternoon schedule, so Laurette was convinced that if he was going to meet Dominique, it would be sometime after lunch. I arrived at Gold's in a rather drab, nondescript neighborhood just south of the multimillion-dollar renovation projects in down-town Hollywood, including the upscale Cineplex, the Arclight, built around the historic Cinerama Dome; and Hollywood & Highland, a trendy mall full of shops, theaters, restaurants, and the spacious Kodak Theatre, the new home for the Academy Awards. But even with all the opulent new developments a few blocks north, the street where I parked outside of Gold's was washed out and depressing. I was stuck there a solid two hours. I should have known Juan Carlos was a gym rat, completely ob-sessed with his physique. He was obviously in there pumping every kind of iron there was, not to mention chatting up a few pretty faces too.

Finally, around eight, he strolled out the front door, convers-ing with a couple of other well-built actors showing off their sculptured pecs in form-fitting T-shirts. Juan Carlos waved good-bye to his buddies, hopped in Laurette's white SUV, and drove west. I pulled out behind him, but tried staying a few cars behind him so as not to arouse suspicion.

He pulled into a Starbucks just outside the Farmers' Market, and I watched as he had coffee with a man and a woman, both in sharp Italian business suits. Agents or managers. Definitely. I watched them through the window from outside, and Juan Carlos never stopped talking. He was probably talking about his career goals and himself in general. For over an hour. The agents looked relieved when Juan Carlos checked his watch, and jumped up to leave.

Then, it was off to his audition on the west side in Culver City. It was in a brick building, home to several casting agencies. He primped in the SUV a good ten minutes before donning his Armani sunglasses, adjusting one stray hair on his head, and then finally marching confidently inside. He was in there an hour.

When he finally came out, he looked excited as he spoke feverishly into his cell phone. My guess was he got the part. Or at least a callback. There was almost a skip in his step as he headed for the SUV.

After lunch with another out-of-work actor I recognized from an MCI commercial, I was beginning to think Juan Carlos was exactly as he came across. A self-absorbed player who used his looks to get ahead, but in the end, a faithful husband. That was before he headed over the hill to the San Fernando Valley. I thought he might be driving to a last-minute audition, but when he drove north to a middle-class neighborhood near the Burbank Airport, and parked on a quiet street called Screenland Drive, I perked up. Something was happening.

Juan Carlos got out of his car, and walked up to a one-story pea green house that would never see the pages of *Architectural Digest*. He rapped on the door, and a stunning young blonde, spilling out of a bright pink tank top, welcomed him inside. As she closed the door, I saw Juan Carlos lean in and kiss her. On the mouth. Jackpot.

I leaped out of the car, and ran up the walk to the house. The blinds were drawn so I couldn't see inside, but after maneuvering around some shrubbery, I came across an open window leading into the kitchen. I could hear them in the living room. Their voices were faint, but distinguishable.

"It's got to be tonight," the blonde said. There was an urgency in her voice.

"So soon? We can't make any mistakes. I could lose everything," Juan Carlos said.

"Don't worry. We'll make it look like an accident. Something quick and easy."

"What kind of an accident?"

"Oh, keep your voice down," the blonde said. "Do you remember that woman who tried to kill herself on Fire Island?"

"So?"

"I took it away from her, remember?"

"Took what?"

"What she tried to kill herself with."

"What good does that do us?"

"I got it. I saved it. I'll show you. See? Poison. And it works fast."

This couldn't be happening. It was all so surreal. Juan Carlos and this blond woman were plotting some kind of murder. And I was ready to bet my house on two things. The poison was monkshead. And the intended victim was my best friend, Laurette.

I whipped out my cell phone to call Laurette and warn her when I heard a low, steady growling. I looked down to see a pit bull, ears back and teeth bared, ready to lunge for my throat. I dropped the phone. My only weapon. Perfect. I slowly raised my arms to protect my face (an actor's first thought), when the shades in the open window rolled up.

"Badger, what are you growling at?"

The blond woman stared at me. And then she let out a scream. A long, piercing scream. Juan Carlos was at her side in a second.

"Jarrod?"

"Hi, Juan Carlos," I said.

"You know him?" the blond woman said, shaking.

"Yes. He's a friend of my wife's. What are you doing here?" He didn't look angry. Just confused. He had no idea I was on to him.

"Does that really matter? I heard everything," I said with an accusatory look on my face.

"Heard what?" he said.

"The accident. Tonight. Laurette."

It took a minute for him to process what I was talking about. And then it dawned on him, and his eyes went wide. I probably should have dived for my phone and dialed 911, but I stood my ground. Juan Carlos looked at the blonde, and then, they both laughed. Big, hearty, guffawing laughs. I didn't see the humor in the situation, so I remained stone-faced.

Juan Carlos disappeared back inside and then returned with a DVD. He tossed it out the window and I grabbed it. It was a classic fifties melodrama, *Sudden Fear*, starring Joan Crawford, Jack Palance, and Gloria Grahame. What this had to do with anything was lost on me.

"You ever see it?" Juan Carlos said.

"Yes," I said. It was actually quite a potboiler. Playwright Crawford rejects actor Palance for her play, he returns later to romance her and plot her murder with his ex-girlfriend Grahame . . . Oh no.

I slowly raised my eyes to Juan Carlos, who had a big grin on his face. I didn't dare ask. I didn't have to.

"We're doing a scene for our acting class."

The blonde piped in. "Our teacher's a Crawford fanatic. Everyone's doing scenes from her films. It's so funny that you thought . . ."

I shrugged. The joke was on me.

Once Juan Carlos and his scene partner stopped laughing, and Badger finally stopped growling, there was a deadening silence. I knew what was coming.

"So what *are* you doing here, Jarrod?" Juan Carlos folded his arms and his eyes narrowed. There was no getting out of this one.

Chapter 7

As I stood in the hedges, caught, embarrassed, and totally screwed, my mind raced with a number of scenarios I could attempt to use to explain my way out of this botched stakeout. But I decided the truth was probably the best way to go. Well, almost the truth. I had to protect Laurette at all costs. So I would just leave out the part where she asked me to tail her husband and find out if he was a lying, cheating cad.

The blond woman, whom Juan Carlos finally introduced me to as Tammy, rushed outside to retrieve her pit bull, Badger. She flashed me a look of warning, as if I were the one who was growling at her precious four-legged soul mate. Badger snapped at my leg as she pulled him by the collar back into the house, and I heard her murmur under her breath, "Good boy."

That left me alone with Juan Carlos, who looked down at me from the kitchen window, not budging, frustration rising the longer it took me to offer up an explanation.

I let out a deep sigh. "The thing is, Juan Carlos, I love Laurette with all my heart."

"As do I," he said emphatically, a hint of defensiveness in his inflection.

"Well, I've known her a long time, and she can sometimes be impulsive, and well, when she rang me up to tell me she was marrying you after only knowing you such a short time, naturally I became suspicious of your motives."

Juan Carlos didn't flinch. His brown eyes, almost empty of emotion, stared at me. I pressed on. "And, well, I just wanted to make sure you're sincere about your feelings for her because the last thing I want is for Laurette to get hurt."

"I would never hurt Laurette. She's my life now, my whole life," he said.

"But surely you can understand where I'm coming from," I said.

Nothing. Not even a slight nod. Apparently he didn't understand.

"With your ex-girlfriend showing up at the wedding and a dead body at the reception, I mean those are pretty big red flags."

"I already told you and the police. It's over between Dominique and me. It has been for a long time. And I don't even know that man who died at the wedding."

"He didn't just die. He was murdered."

Finally. A slight reaction from Juan Carlos. His eye twitched and he shifted in the window, a little uncomfortable hearing the word "murder."

"Poisoned. Didn't you hear?" I said.

"How could I? Laurette and I just got home last night." His patience with me was waning. "Look, Jarrod, as you can see, Tammy and I are just scene partners, not secret lovers. Dominique is long gone. I have no idea where. And I had nothing to do with that man who died . . . excuse me . . . was murdered at my wedding. You should be talking to the hundred other people who were there that day."

"You're right. I'm sorry," I said. "I've been very foolish."

He softened a bit, and even offered me a slight smile. It wasn't sincere. He was just the kind of guy who liked to keep his enemies close.

"I accept your apology," he said, rather condescendingly.

I needed to ensure that he didn't suspect Laurette of any wrongdoing.

"Please, Juan Carlos, don't tell Laurette what I've been up to. She'd never speak to me again."

He paused, and thought long and hard. He really wanted to make me squirm while he decided my fate. Finally, he gave me a wink. "Fine. This will remain between us."

"Thank you," I said. "Thank you."

He waved me off, and returned to continue rehearsing his dramatic scene with Tammy. What a prick.

I walked back out to the street, where the blinding valley sun made my eyes ache. I squinted as I climbed back into my car and donned my sunglasses. Starting up the Beamer, I pulled out from the curb to make my way over the hill back home, when I passed a Mazda 626 with an Enterprise rental car sticker on the rear bumper that was parked on the west side of the street. A tiny woman was in the driver's seat, watching the pea green stucco house I had just left. It was Dominique.

I turned the corner and drove back out onto the main strip just east of Screenland Drive, a major street called Hollywood Way, where I immediately U-turned in a strip mall parking lot, and double backed. I rolled to a stop on the opposite side of the street from Dominique's rental car. She didn't notice me. She was too busy studying Tammy's house.

About twenty minutes passed before Juan Carlos and Tammy emerged from the house. Dominique sank low in her seat, not wanting them to spot her.

Tammy gave Juan Carlos a peck on the cheek, and he flashed her a smile before hopping into Laurette's SUV and driving off. Dominique jammed her Mazda into gear, and roared off after him.

I followed Dominique. Juan Carlos, ignorant to the fact he was leading a caravan, steered onto the Ventura Freeway West toward the ocean. It was still early in the day, so traffic wasn't heavy. Juan Carlos exited onto Topanga Canyon, a loopy, rustic road that eventually spilled out onto the Pacific Coast Highway and the vast beaches of Malibu. It took over an hour to get there, and Juan Carlos kept driving north, to a remote spot just past the Malibu Colony, home to many of Hollywood's elite. He parked on the side of the road, jumped out, stripped off his shirt and jeans to reveal a tight black swimsuit, and padded down the sand to the surf.

Dominique pulled off the road, the car rolling over gravel until she was about twenty feet from the SUV. She turned off the car and stared down at the beach, where Juan Carlos bravely ventured into the cold, numbing water. When he was knee deep, he dove into a small wave and disappeared.

I was so busy watching Dominique eye Juan Carlos that I almost tapped the rear end of the Mercedes in front of me that was stopped at a red light. I slammed on the brakes, jerking to a halt, nearly causing the motorcyclist behind me to do a double flip over my roof. He screamed a couple of obscenities at me as he swerved out around me and passed by. I shrugged, mouthed, "I'm sorry," and took the hint to get off the road.

The sun was assaulting and the temperature must have been upwards of ninety degrees. Sweat dripped down my brow as I kept my eyes focused on Dominique, who had lost sight of Juan Carlos in the surf, and was starting to get antsy. She got out of the car, and wandered down to the beach, keeping one hand above her eyes to block out the sun. I had a pair of minibinoculars in the trunk I used when I could only get nosebleed seats for a concert at the Staples Center. I popped open the trunk, unhooked the lens protectors, and peered through them. After a few seconds of searching, I caught a glimpse of a pair of arms splashing through the water, circling around a buoy, and then starting back for shore. It was Juan Carlos.

Dominique waited for him. After another fifteen minutes, Juan Carlos surfaced and, muscles tired from his workout, slowly made his way up the beach. He didn't spot Dominique at first, never even looked her way. She finally called out to him, startling him, and he jerked his head around to see her. She was smiling, hopeful, as if she was expecting some kind of warm reunion. He gaped at her for a few moments, trying to discern if it was really her. And then she ran toward him, arms outstretched, yearning for an embrace.

When she reached him and threw her arms around his neck, he stiffened. When she began smothering his face with kisses, he pushed her away. I was too far from them to hear the conversation, but it was heated. He yelled at her, berated her, but she held on to his arm, her lips trying to desperately caress his bronze skin. He wrenched his arm free, and shoved her again. Hard. She fell down, her face in the sand, humiliated.

Juan Carlos spat out a few final words, and stalked back to the SUV. He was livid as he yanked open the door, grabbed his shirt to wipe himself off from the water and the smell of his ex's desperation, jumped in, and peeled away. Bits of gravel flew in all directions.

I didn't follow him. I knew he was probably heading home to Laurette. Instead, I kept my eyes fixed upon Dominique, who had now climbed to her hands and knees and was sobbing. Her eye makeup smeared her face like a clown as she rose to her feet. The blustery wind almost knocked her tiny body down again. But she pushed forward, hands covering her face, and rushed toward the ocean before her.

It took me only a few seconds to figure out what she was going to do. She bounded into the surf, her arms stretched out, as if offering herself to the turbulent, dangerous waters of the

Pacific. Before I sprinted down to the beach, she was already up to her waist, and by the time I had reached the water's edge, she had disappeared below the surface altogether. I blocked out the freezing sensation as I dove headfirst into the water and swam out with bold, choppy strokes. I stopped, treading water, my arms, legs, and torso paralyzed with cold. There was no sign of her. Nothing. All I could see was a family of four—mom, dad, and two kids, with their dog—having a picnic lunch down the beach. I wanted to call to them for help, but what could they do?

I inhaled sharply, and dropped down underneath the surface, eyes open, trying to focus on anything. But it was dark and murky, and after only forty-five seconds, I had to shoot up to the surface again, and take another deep breath. I dove once again, and this time I caught sight of something. A fish? No, it was a hand. Just a few feet away. I shot forward and grabbed it, tugging it toward me. A face appeared through the shadowy depths. It was Dominique, her eyes wide open, her mouth agape, filling with water.

I wrapped an arm around her waist, and hauled her to the surface. With all my strength, I dragged her limp body toward shore. I coughed and sputtered from swallowing a mouthful of saltwater. I wasn't sure if she was dead, or unconscious, or in a state of shock. Finally, my foot touched bottom, and I was able to carry her out, setting her down in the damp sand out of reach of the tide. I gave her mouth-to-mouth, and after a few tense moments, she gurgled, throwing up a quart of seawater, and crying uncontrollably.

I helped her to sit up, and we sat in silence as she held my hand and whimpered, unsure if she was happy or sad to have survived.

"Why did you do it?" I said.

She looked at me, vaguely recognizing me from the bus trip up to the Hearst Castle. She gave me a quizzical stare, and then shook her head and quietly cried.

"He wants nothing to do with me," she said.

"Juan Carlos?"

Her eyes fluttered, surprised that I knew who had broken her heart. "Yes," she said. "He told me he didn't care if I was alive or dead, just that he wanted me to leave him alone. He loves *her* now."

I knew exactly who "her" was. This was going to be good news for Laurette. But for this fragile creature, who took Juan Carlos at his word and decided her best option was simply to drown herself, I felt sorry. She struck me as a wounded bird, fallen from the nest, alone and afraid. Although Juan Carlos may have proven his intentions, his treatment of Dominique only reinforced my opinion of his character. And the thought of him sharing a bed with my best friend made me shudder.

Chapter 8

Dominique was in a trance-like state as I led her back to her car. Fearing she was in no condition to drive, I offered to chauffeur her anywhere she wanted to go, especially if it was to the nearest psychiatrist's office. But quickly snapping out of it, she assured me she was feeling better, and before I could convince her otherwise, she was back behind the wheel of her rented Mazda, and merging into the heavy traffic on the Pacific Coast Highway. She definitely had no desire to open up anymore to a complete stranger.

So I was left standing on the dusty, dirt shoulder of the highway, secure in the knowledge that Juan Carlos was at least faithful. That still didn't leave him off the hook as a murder suspect.

I got back into the Beamer, and headed east on the 10 Freeway, exiting the commuter-clogged La Brea Avenue north, which led me straight to the Hollywood Hills, and finally home.

As I wound up to the English Tudor–style house I shared with Charlie, I saw his Volvo parked out front. He was home early. Definitely a welcome surprise. Snickers was running in circles when I entered the kitchen from the garage, and I scooped her up and followed Charlie's voice into the den, which was my favorite room in the house. The walls were covered with Hitchcock and Wilder movie posters and an impressive DVD collection, all positioned around the wide-screen TV. In other words, heaven. Charlie sat on the couch, talking on the phone. He winked at me as I ambled in, and patted the cushion next to him. I plopped down, sinking deep into the soft, intoxicating lushness of the cushions (we spare no expense when it comes to comfort). He slipped a muscular arm around my neck, pulling me closer, and I closed my eyes, nestling my head against his chest as he talked.

"So man, how long has it been?" he said, smiling. "Jesus, that long? No, things here are good. I've got a boyfriend now, going on three years." He gently kissed the top of my head and I couldn't help but smile.

"No, seriously. What, you think I was going to wait for you?" Charlie said.

My eyes popped open. Who the hell was he talking to? Going to wait for whom?

"Very happy. He's an actor," Charlie said. And then, after a moment, Charlie laughed. "I know, I know, but I love him anyway."

Charlie tousled my hair, and gave me another wink. I wasn't as receptive anymore. I shot up, and stared at him as he wound up his conversation.

"You too, man, and thanks. You've been a huge help."

He clicked off the phone.

"Hey," he said, as he leaned in and kissed me softly on the lips.

"Hey," I said flatly. "Who was that?"

"Friend of mine in Miami."

"I don't remember you ever mentioning a friend in Miami." I knew I was being the unreasonably suspicious boyfriend, but after snooping around after Juan Carlos all day, it was in my blood.

"We met in Michigan. At the Police Academy. Good guy."

There was a long silence as I considered dropping the whole subject. But a lot of people have learned not to bet on me dropping anything. "So were you just friends, or were you, you know, more than just friends?"

"Yeah, there was a flirtation for a while. Pretty innocent though. Never got past the groping stage. But then he dropped out of the Academy and joined the military. We kind of lost touch."

"So what brought about this big reunion?" I said, my eyes boring into him.

Charlie was so used to my drama, he never flinched or blinked or lost his cool. He just chuckled to himself, and took my hand.

"You."

"Me?"

"Yeah. You've been so caught up in finding out if Laurette's husband had anything to do with that Teboe guy getting poisoned, I decided to make a few calls. I heard this guy was living in Miami, doing some side work for the police, so I got his number from the South Beach precinct, and rang him up to see if he knew anything about the victim."

I perked up. "Did he?"

"Did he ever." Charlie snaked his hand behind my back, and yanked me across the couch until our faces were inches apart.

"Well, what does he know?" I asked.

"Later," he said, and lowered me down on my back. He lifted my head in the crook of his elbow, and jammed his lips over mine. Our tongues danced and probed together, and he wrapped his legs around mine and locked them into place. Charlie didn't demand much from me, but when he got hot and horny, he hated to wait. We weren't going anywhere.

He was the best lover I had ever known, and if I had been

smart, I would have just gone with the flow, and put my curiosity into neutral, but once my mind starts racing, there's no turning back, and I just couldn't help myself.

I reached up, kissing his cheek, his forehead, making my way over to his right ear. Charlie's anticipation was building. This was always the part where I talked dirty.

"So what exactly did your friend know about Teboe?" I said.

Charlie let out a sigh, but chose to ignore me. He ripped open my shirt, and started caressing my chest with his hands. I slipped mine up underneath his sweater and did the same. Then, he grabbed ahold of my zipper and yanked it down, cupped a hand below my genitals, and rubbed furiously. I gasped, lost in the pleasure of his touch. Charlie was certain this would do the trick. No more questions until we were through.

"Did your friend know whether Teboe and Juan Carlos worked at the same restaurant?" I said.

Charlie stopped and pulled away. I could see the frustration on his pained face. But he knew it was a hopeless cause.

"Yes," Charlie said. "He confirmed it. The two met working at the Nexxt Café. Teboe was a chef. Juan Carlos a waiter. My friend was keeping tabs on Teboe because he was investigating Javier Martinez."

I had no clue who that was, so Charlie enlightened me. "Big head of a Miami-based crime family. Into money laundering, extortion, weapons smuggling, you name it. They're bigger than some multinational corporations. Teboe's last gig was working as a personal chef on Martinez's yacht. He left under mysterious circumstances, though no one knows why."

I sat up. "What about Juan Carlos? Did your friend say he was connected with the family too?"

"No. Juan Carlos never worked for them. But Martinez sure as hell knows who Juan Carlos is, and isn't a fan, to put it mildly. There was a rumor that Martinez put a hit out on Juan Carlos, which might explain why he left Florida in such a hurry."

"Why would a bad soap actor piss off a big-time crime czar? And why would Juan Carlos lie about knowing Austin Teboe?"

Charlie shrugged.

"Anything else?" I said.

"Nope. That was it."

To Charlie's chagrin, I started buttoning up my shirt.

"What are you doing?"

"Going over to Laurette's."

"Now?"

"Don't you think she ought to know that her husband is mixed up with the Tony Soprano of South Florida?"

He couldn't argue with my logic. But that didn't make him any less perturbed.

I jumped up, zipped my pants back up, and grabbed my car keys out of my pants pocket. I halted, then turned back, leaned down, and kissed Charlie hard on the mouth. "I know I'm insane, and obsessive, and really hard to handle, but just know that I love you, and I really hope you're here when I get back."

Charlie saw right through my quick fix. He wasn't going to let me off so easily this time. "Maybe," he said. "Depends on whether or not I can get a flight to Florida tonight or in the morning."

This floored me. My mouth dropped open and we stared each other down. And finally, after an agonizing thirty seconds, he gave me another one of his adorable trademark winks. "Don't be late."

"I love you," I said, as I raced for the garage.

"Yeah, yeah, I've heard it all before."

Chapter 9

"So, Juan Carlos told Dominique that he loved *me* and not her, is that right?" Laurette said, clutching an apple martini in her recently renovated backyard, which now boasted a kidney-shaped pool, a blue-tiled Jacuzzi, and several bamboo trees and rosebushes.

"Yes, but he lied about knowing Austin Teboe. They did work together in Miami Beach. Now why would he lie about something like that?" I said.

Laurette took a generous sip of her martini. I thought she was considering my question, but then, after a moment, she leaned forward and said, "So it's definitely over between them then."

"Yes," I said, unable to conceal my exasperation. "But this Javier Martinez sounds like a real dangerous character, and Juan Carlos has somehow ticked him off, and at the risk of sounding melodramatic, I think your life could be in jeopardy."

Laurette's eyes brimmed with tears. I thought I had finally broken through. She threw her head back and exclaimed, "Thank God! Thank God he's not cheating on me! Oh, I feel *so* much better!"

She never heard a word I said.

I snatched the apple martini out of her hand, holding it hostage. This finally spurred a reaction. As her arm snapped out to grab it back, I wrenched it farther out of her reach.

"Honey, this is serious," I said. "Juan Carlos is in with some big-time bad guys, and you need to deal with that."

"Please, Jarrod, whatever past he may have had in Florida is over. His life is in LA now. With me."

"But what if it turns out that he did have something to do with poisoning Austin Teboe? What then?"

"We've been over this and over this. He's not a murderer. The only time Juan Carlos killed anyone was when he played Brutus in *Julius Caesar* at the La Hoya Playhouse. Now enough. Promise me you'll leave him alone."

Maybe it was me. Maybe I just didn't like the guy. I knew if I kept up this relentless pursuit of the truth, I risked losing my best friend. It was time to pull back.

"Maybe I'm just being overprotective," I said.

"And I love you for it." Laurette squeezed my hand and leaned over and kissed me on the cheek.

Out of the corner of my eye, I saw movement inside the house. It was Juan Carlos. He tossed his keys on a side table in the living room, spotted us having a cocktail hour out on the patio, and sauntered out to join us.

"How was your day, honey?" he said as he leaned over his wife and gently cupped her face in his hands, stealing a soft, brief kiss.

He completely ignored me.

"Busy," Laurette sighed. "Seems with all these reality shows featuring D-list actors, my whole client roster is working." She caught herself, gently touched my arm, and with apologetic eyes, said, "No offense, Jarrod."

"Don't worry about it. I may be D-list, but I still have my dignity."

Laurette turned to Juan Carlos, who just stood there, glaring at me. "We got a generous offer for Jarrod to do *Child Star Hotel*, this new MTV show where a bunch of has-beens move in together and run a business, but he just won't even go there."

"A job's a job," Juan Carlos said.

I shrugged. "Call me Pollyanna, but I just think there's something better out there for me on the horizon."

"There is, sweetie, there is. You just hang in there," Laurette said as she reached out and took her husband's large, bronzed hand and brought it to her cheek as she gazed lovingly up at him. "How did your audition go today?"

"Got a callback for tomorrow."

Laurette leaped up and threw her arms around him. "Honey, that's fantastic!"

Juan Carlos never took his eyes off me. "Funny, I thought Jarrod might have told you already."

"Jarrod?" Laurette said, with all the commitment of Meryl Streep in *Sophie's Choice*. Her husband was hoping to expose me to his wife. Little did he know that it was his wife who'd sent me out snooping in the first place.

"It was the strangest thing. We kept running into each other today," he said.

"Really? How odd?" Laurette said, with big, fluttery, innocent eyes. She was overdoing it. If she wasn't careful, Juan Carlos was going to figure out she knew more than she was letting on. Subtlety was one skill God never had time to bestow on Laurette.

"Yes, I saw him in Burbank. At Tammy's house."

Laurette turned to me. "What were you doing there?"

I couldn't believe it. In her panicked efforts to hide her own complicity, Laurette was selling me out. She didn't mean to, but she didn't want to upset her new husband.

I just stood there, with my mouth open and my mind racing. "My dentist has an office on that street. I was getting a cleaning." How lame.

Juan Carlos grinned. He loved watching me lie. And he didn't care. He just wanted to see me squirm some more.

"After we rehearsed our scene, I drove out to the beach to do a little body surfing," he said.

Laurette ran her fingers over his hardened, sculptured biceps. "He exercises all the time. But why state the obvious?" She was proud of him. And had every right to be. He was a good-looking, sexy man. For a manipulative, cocky son of a bitch.

"It's weird. I was all the way out in Malibu, by myself, and I swear I saw Jarrod's car. That fancy Beamer he likes to cruise around town in."

"Well, it couldn't have been his if you had just seen him in Burbank," Laurette offered.

"No, I guess that would mean he was following me or something."

I was through playing Juan Carlos's little game. I stood up. "But since I've already said I was getting my teeth cleaned, I guess it doesn't mean anything."

"I guess not," Juan Carlos said, folding his beefy arms. "So what have you two gossips been whispering about while I've been out?"

There was a long, agonizing pause.

"That's agent-client privileged information," Laurette said with a forced giggle.

"I thought that only applied to lawyers." He was dead serious.

"Jarrod's NBC pilot died, so we were discussing what's next for him."

It was a good save. But Juan Carlos wasn't buying. Any of it. It was time to make a graceful exit.

"I better get home to Charlie," I said, downing the last of my own drink, handing Juan Carlos the glass, and heading for the door.

"Call me tomorrow. Give my love to Charlie," Laurette said as she gulped down the last of her apple martini.

I hated leaving Laurette alone with that brute, but I had to respect her wishes. If at any time she got in over her head, I was confident she would call me.

I slid into my car, hooked the seat belt in place, and turned over the engine. Suddenly blasting through the car stereo speakers was the original cast recording of *A Chorus Line*. Track Three. "At the Ballet." Look, I never claimed to be straight. As I started backing out of the driveway, the front door of the house flew open, and Juan Carlos stalked out. He circled around the hood of the car, and marched up to the driver's side window. I put my foot on the brake.

He tapped lightly on the glass, and motioned for me to roll it down. I complied, wondering what it was he wanted.

"Before you go, I just want to say something," he said in a low, gravelly voice.

"What?" I turned down the volume until the cast of *A Chorus Line* faded into silence.

Juan Carlos closed his eyes, took a deep breath, and then slowly opened them again. They were full of loathing. A shiver went up my spine.

"I don't like you following me around, Jarrod."

"Look, I thought you might be sneaking around on Laurette, and I was wrong. I already told you that. End of story."

"No. That's not the only reason. You think I had something to do with that guy Teboe's death. Well, I didn't."

I didn't answer him.

He put his hands on his hips, the frustration rising in his voice. "Why do you think I'm hiding something?"

"I don't think you're hiding something," I said evenly. "I think you're hiding a lot of things. Good night, Juan Carlos."

Before I had a chance to take my foot off the brake, he grabbed a fistful of my shirt and yanked me forward. The window was only halfway down, so my head barely made it through. The tip of the glass pressed against my neck, cutting off my air, and I gasped. The more I struggled, the harder it was to breathe.

Juan Carlos pushed his face up close to mine until our noses touched. "If you don't disappear, you and I are going to have big problems. I mean it, Jarrod. Your NBC pilot won't be the only thing dead."

Between gasps I managed to get out, "Let go of me."

"When I'm good and ready," he said, spittle forming at the corners of his mouth.

I grabbed the door handle, wrenched it up, and swung open the door with all my might. It slammed into Juan Carlos's groin, and he instantly released me. He fell back, falling into one of Laurette's immaculately kept rosebushes. I tumbled out of the car, grabbing my throat with my hand, coughing and trying to catch my breath.

Juan Carlos was on his feet in an instant, wild with fury. I was on my hands and knees. He reared back and, with a sharp boot, kicked me in the solar plexus. I rolled over, clutching my throbbing gut and curling up into the fetal position.

He stood over me. I could hear him chuckling under his breath. That really pissed me off. I lay there, sprawled on the ground, just like Richard Dean Anderson in this one particular *MacGyver* episode in the late eighties when I guest-starred as the son of a tough, bull-headed Army general who was physically abusive to me. When MacGyver befriended me, and began a crusade to free me from my father's beatings, the general decided to teach MacGyver a lesson for interfering in his private affairs. It was one of those very special episodes with a message, and the climax unfolded on a mountaintop with the general (ably played by Dean Stockwell) kicking the shit out of adorable Richard Dean Anderson. With the hero curled up and barely conscious, the general leaned down to inspect his handiwork. He rolled him over to make sure he was out. That's when MacGyver's fist shot out and slammed Dean Stockwell square in the face. If it worked for MacGyver, it could work for me. So when Juan Carlos knelt down to see if I was ready to give up, the back of my hand connected with his upper lip with a loud smack, and he screamed, reeling back. As I've said many times before, there's nothing more brutal than smacking an actor in the face. It's like cutting off the fingers of a painter.

I thought it would bring this brawl to a halt. It only served to enrage Juan Carlos even more. He threw himself at me just as I climbed to my feet, and the two of us hit the freshly mowed lawn hard. The blows were fast and furious, and I raised one arm to block them as I nailed him like a punching bag with the other.

Suddenly I felt a sharp jab in my lower back. And then another. And another. Someone else was hitting me.

I heard Laurette shrieking behind me. "Stop it! Stop it, both of you!"

Juan Carlos let go of me first. Whatever was whacking me was walloping him too. We both looked up, dazed, to see Laurette hovering over us, a crazed look in her eye, armed with a broomstick. "If you two don't leave each other alone, I'm calling the police myself! If the neighbors haven't done it already!"

Juan Carlos and I, both smarting from the unrelenting blows, slowly and with great effort stood up. Neither of us helped the other. And we didn't raise our heads to face Laurette. We kept them down, like two dogs that have just been caught making a mess.

"I don't want to know what started it," Laurette said, "or whose fault it was. I just want you, Juan Carlos, to get your ass inside and go to bed, and I want you, Jarrod, to get in that car and go home."

We both did as we were told. As I got back in the Beamer, I saw Laurette standing motionless in the doorway as Juan Carlos brushed the blades of grass off his pants. She was there to make sure I didn't try running over her husband on my way out of the driveway.

As I backed out, Juan Carlos disappeared inside. Through the kitchen window I saw him grab a cold Diet Coke from the fridge and place it over one of the welts I had left on his right cheek.

I had no idea how things had gotten so out of hand. And with my friendship with Laurette already on life support, I was afraid this little altercation might be the deciding factor for her to pull the plug. But I wasn't sure. I was only sure of one thing. This scuffle with Juan Carlos was only the warm-up. It didn't take my psychic friend Isis to tell me we would clash again. And one of us probably wouldn't walk away the next time.

Chapter 10

"Why didn't you call me? I would have been over in a flash and beaten the shit out of the bastard," Charlie said, popping a piece of chicken tikka into his mouth. We sat on the floor around our glass-top coffee table in the den surrounded by half-empty cartons of white rice, vegetable curry, and lamb vindaloo and crushed tin foil that had once been wrapped around meat samosas and onion bajji before we'd made short work of them. It was our weekly Indian food and DVD night. Just the two of us. We would unload our individual dramas of the week, make plans for the weekend, watch a popcorn flick, and more often than not, cap off the evening with some hot sex. Tonight was Charlie's turn to pick the movie so the James Bond movie *Die Another Day* starring Pierce Brosnan and Halle Berry played on our widescreen TV. After a week of chasing down LA's lowlifes, Charlie didn't want to tax his mind too much, so a light-action romp was the perfect way for him to unwind.

Halle had just wandered out of the surf in an eye-popping orange bikini revealing enough to stop even two gay men in mid-sentence. We stared in awe as she sashayed up the beach and began a conversation with 007.

Charlie finally tore his eyes off the TV and returned his attention to me. "It's not too late. I can go over there and haul his ass downtown for assault."

I shook my head. "No. Laurette's mad at me enough as it is. And it's not like he didn't have somewhat of a reason."

There was no point in hiding it from Charlie anymore. I told him all about the pact I had made with Laurette to find out if Juan Carlos was the dishonorable louse I feared him to be.

Charlie, ever the patient boyfriend, listened as I prattled on, and remained silent after I'd finished. I knew he was ticked off. But it was more out of concern for my well-being. It was always about that. And sometimes I felt I really didn't deserve such a catch.

"He could've really done a number on you," he said finally.

"I can take care of myself. Two years of scene combat classes, baby."

"That's fine if he takes a swing at you, but what if he decides to drop a little poison in your Diet Rite like he did with Austin Teboe."

"You know what?" I said. "We have no proof that he had anything to do with that. And for once, I'm going to let the police up in San Simeon do their job. I'm through with Juan Carlos. It's none of my business."

Charlie threw his hands up in the air and exclaimed, "Finally! A breakthrough!"

I playfully slapped him lightly on the cheek. "Bastard."

He tapped the back of my head with the palm of his hand. "Freak."

On the TV, Halle and Pierce were going at it big time. Lots of bare skin and thrashing about in a fluffy white bed somewhere in Cuba. That was all we needed. Charlie and I lunged at each other, both determined to try again after our aborted lovemaking attempt the night before.

Facing each other, both of us swelling with good old-fashioned lust, we ripped off our shirts as we locked mouths, anxious to make up for lost time.

The doorbell rang.

"Ignore it," I said as I worked to unhook my belt. "Probably just a Jehovah's Witness."

Snickers, who had been hovering near the coffee table, hoping one of us might drop a succulent piece of chicken tikka that she could snatch up in her teeth, tore out of the den, barking at the top of her lungs as she scampered to the front door.

This time, I pushed Charlie down on the couch, ran my fingers through his forest of chest hair, then tugged open the zipper on his jeans and set about devouring him.

The doorbell rang again. And again. And again. Snickers was in a frantic state, running back into the den to summon us, and then darting back to the front door. Between the unrelenting doorbell and our nearly rabid dog, we both knew our night of hot, passionate lovemaking was doomed to failure. Charlie zipped up. I threw on my shirt. We both headed for the door.

Laurette stood on the front stoop; her SUV was parked three whole feet from the curb and angled halfway into the street. She was obviously in a hurry.

"Laurette, I'm so sorry. I don't know what to say. Things just got out of hand," I said.

Charlie put a comforting hand on my shoulder from behind. "He feels terrible. Just now, we were discussing how he should apologize."

I glanced at Charlie, who stifled a smile.

"Oh, who cares about that?" Laurette said as she pushed her way in and headed for the kitchen. "You got any Scotch?"

After pouring herself a drink and settling down in the red

diner booth, Laurette got right to the point. "I got a call right after you left. From Larry Levant."

Nothing. Neither Charlie nor I had ever heard of him.

"The director. Made a big splash at Sundance last year for his documentary on the gay porn industry called *Give 'Em Head, Harry*.

"Sorry I missed it," said Charlie.

"Anyway," Laurette said. "He's been in preproduction on his new movie for months now. It's a low-budget horror movie. But smart, you know? Not one of those straight-to-Showtime pieces of shit. He had raised most of the money through independent sources, but was still about a million short, and just today the rest of the financing came through. Some big mucky-muck in South Florida who wants to be in the movie business."

"Is Larry Levant a client of yours?"

"No," she said, a teasing lilt in her voice. "I represent the actor who he desperately wants as his leading man."

My heart skipped a beat. I had been so down after my NBC pilot tanked in testing. Not one audition had come my way. Not even for an under-five-line bit part on *7th Heaven*. And now, was Laurette excited because she had finally done her job and snared me a leading role in a promising independent film?

"Me?" I said.

"No. Juan Carlos."

This was either a mean-spirited joke on her part or bitter revenge for brawling with her husband on her front lawn. "You came all the way over here to tell me that?"

"Of course not," she said. "Larry's a big fan of yours. And there's a supporting role we both think you're perfect for. Frankly, I think it's more interesting than the lead."

Agents always said that. I wasn't about to fall for it.

"You'd play a single dad camping with your son," she said. "Going through a bitter divorce. Fighting for custody. At your wit's end. Things couldn't get any worse. And that's when you're stalked by a homicidal maniac in the woods."

Actually it sounded like a meaty part. One I could make a meal out of if someone let me. "I've never played a wounded single parent."

"You die twenty minutes into the movie, but you're in almost every scene up to the point where you get an axe in the back of your head."

"Sorry, Laurette. He's not going to do it."

I froze. Who had said that? It sounded like my boyfriend Charlie. But he knew I would psychologically torture him senseless if he denied me a richly deserved acting gig.

Laurette and I both stared at Charlie, waiting for some kind of explanation for such a sweeping, dictatorial decision.

"You heard what she said, Jarrod," Charlie argued. "Juan Carlos is playing the lead, and I think we've strongly established that you two don't get along."

"In this business, that's not a deal breaker," Laurette said.

"Well, I don't think it's a good idea for you two to spend three months on a film shoot together."

"But you heard Laurette," I said. "I die after the first twenty minutes. I'll be there two, three weeks tops."

"Why put yourself through that?" Charlie said.

"Because it's a job," I said, pouring myself a Scotch. "And we both know how few and far between those have been lately."

"I just don't think it's a good idea." Charlie was adamant. But I had no intention of letting this opportunity slip through my fingers.

"But the director is a fan. He really wants me to play the part. How can I compromise his vision by saying no?" I was the King of Bullshit when I had to be.

Charlie chuckled. "Come on, babe. Can't you see Laurette is playing you? I think you're a terrific actor, but seriously, do you really believe this big director only wants *you* for the role? There's something else going on here."

Actors, especially former child actors, live to be the center of attention. And sometimes they can float above the realm of reality, and simply exist inside their own heads. As much as it angered me that Charlie was yanking me back down to earth from my blissful fantasy of being indispensable and one of a kind, he had a point. Larry Levant insisting I play an important role in his new film was akin to Steven Spielberg crowing that he could do *Saving Private Ryan* only with Corey Feldman. Laurette was scheming, and she had just been exposed.

Charlie and I looked at her, and she caved immediately. "All right, all right. Larry owed me a few favors, so I talked him into giving you a part in the movie."

"Why?" I asked.

"Because you haven't worked in a while, and I was feeling guilty about not getting you more work."

I was ready to buy it, but Charlie wasn't. "And?"

"And because Juan Carlos got a phone call while he was on the computer, and when I went into the office to get my checkbook so I could pay a few bills, there was an e-mail up on the screen from a woman in Florida."

"Dominique?"

"I don't think so. It was someone else. But obviously a woman. And they've clearly known each other awhile. She didn't write her name or anything, but the note had a very strong sexual connotation."

"What the hell does that mean?" I said.

"There was a lot of dirty talk," Charlie answered.

"Oh."

"This woman clearly has feelings for Juan Carlos," Laurette said. "And she's still very much in his life. But to what degree, I don't know."

"What does that have to do with me playing a part in Larry Levant's movie?"

"Isn't it obvious? She wants you to be on location to make sure Juan Carlos doesn't fool around behind her back with this mystery woman," Charlie said, folding his arms, satisfied the case was closed.

I turned to Laurette. She had no fight left in her. Everything was on the table, and there was nothing she could do about it. She was just betting on the fact that my ego would outweigh my common sense. Good bet.

"I'll do it."

"What?" Charlie said, stunned.

"A part is a part. And this is a feature. I haven't done a feature film since I was twelve years old and played Huck Finn in that hideous *Tom Sawyer* remake with Jason Bateman. Who knows what this could lead to? If I don't take it, I'll always wonder if it could have turned things around for me."

"I don't believe this," Charlie said. "You're actually going to do this."

Laurette knew to keep her mouth shut, and let me handle Charlie. I gently touched his arm, and smiled. "It's only for a few weeks. Besides, my parents have been bugging me to come see them, and they're only a couple hours north of Miami. And don't worry about Juan Carlos and me. I'll buy him a beer, make nice, we'll be buddies by the end of the first day. Besides, it'll make it easier for me to babysit him when we're not shooting."

"You're going to be great, Jarrod. And this is going to do wonders for your career," Laurette crowed. "Larry Levant is hot, hot, hot."

Charlie stood there, steadfast in his resolve. But even he knew this was a no-win situation. In the end, I would go where the work took me. He knew that about me on the first day we met. But he still didn't have to like it.

"Fine," he said, and stalked out of the kitchen to the den, where he resumed watching *Die Another Day*.

"I didn't mean to cause a fight," Laurette said.

"Don't worry. He'll be fine."

Easier said than done. This was going to take more political wrangling and sensitive diplomacy than the Israeli-Palestinian peace talks. But I was up for the challenge. Charlie would come around. Eventually. And as for me, I was excited about working again. Despite the gnawing fear that Juan Carlos might slit my throat in the wilds of South Florida.

Chapter 11

The only way I could convince my shopping buddy and personal clairvoyant Isis to drive me to the airport for my flight to Miami was if I promised to make a pit stop at a Costco discount warehouse on the way. Isis was one of those extreme bargain hunters, willing to bungee-jump off the Golden Gate Bridge if it would save her a few pennies on a refill bottle of Ivory Liquid Soap. She had lost her membership card, and while she was waiting to get issued a new one, she needed my Costco card in the interim to gain access to Mecca.

When Isis arrived in her weathered, dented, smoke-billowing 1986 Chevy Caprice Classic, Charlie and I were in the middle of a terrible row. We rarely fought, but somehow the tension surrounding my imminent departure to Florida had ignited an inferno that was burning holes through the fabric of our once fireproof relationship.

Charlie was already late for a court appearance downtown where he was testifying in the trial of a two-hundred-and-twenty-pound Latina gang member named Tiny who had hurled an empty bottle at one of his fellow detectives when they were dispatched to investigate a homicide in the neighborhood. But I guess his boyfriend costarring in a low-rent shocker with a real-life suspected murderer took precedence.

"Sometimes I get the feeling you take your career far more seriously than you take me," Charlie said, arms folded, hovering over me in the kitchen as I tossed a few candy bars in my carrying case for the flight.

"That is not true, and you know it, and I'm tired of you always making me choose between the two," I said.

"Just once I would like to see you make a decision based on what's best for us, as opposed to what's best for you."

I zipped up my bag, stood erect, and threw the strap over my shoulder. "If that's what you really think, then maybe me going away for a while isn't such a bad idea."

There was a loud honking from outside. It was Isis in her Caprice. I glanced out the kitchen window that overlooked the street in front of the house. She was checking her watch, and craning her neck to see how ready I really was. I could tell she was calculating just how much time we would have to buy Green Forest toilet paper in bulk before we had to head on to the airport for the tightened security checks.

I started for the door. Charlie gripped my arm, stopping me. "Look, babe, I know things haven't been perfect between us lately, and maybe I just need to blow off a little steam, but you're not thinking straight."

"I never have," I said, unable to resist a little humor.

Charlie didn't smile. Hell, he didn't even smirk. He always found me funny. This was not good. "Maybe I'm just a little pissed off that you're not respecting what I think."

"What do you think?"

"I think Juan Carlos Barranco is bad news, and he's got it out for you, and buying him one beer is not going to smooth things over between the two of you. And . . ."

"And what?"

"And I'm worried I'm not going to be there to make sure he doesn't try to harm you in some way."

I should've dropped the bag right there and threw my arms around him. I should've said, "Screw the movie. I want to stay right here in LA and be with the man who loves me more than anyone else in the world." I should've said all that. But I didn't.

"Just because I don't have a badge like you doesn't mean I can't take care of myself," I said.

More honking. It was as if Isis's left hand was surgically attached to the car horn on the steering wheel. She could see us arguing in the kitchen, and with her right hand clutching the four-page shopping list, she wasn't going to indulge us with her patience.

Charlie threw his hands up in the air. "Fine." He grabbed his wallet and holster off the table, and walked to the door off the kitchen leading to our two-car garage. He turned his head slightly, barely making eye contact. "Call me when you get there . . . if you find the time." And then he opened the door, marched through, and closed it with a big slam.

I almost went after him. But Isis was now hitting more notes on her car horn than Beethoven's Fifth. With only three hours until my flight, and heavy traffic building on the 405 Freeway, Isis's time at Costco was limited. I grabbed my bags and headed out the front door.

As we bombed down the hill toward Franklin Avenue, Isis sat behind the wheel, her tiny body slumped down in the seat, her eyes barely making it over the dashboard. Her foot was pressed on the accelerator, and she continually flicked her eyes to the digital clock in front of us. We had gotten a late start, and she was not happy about it.

We sat in silence for a few minutes before I cleared my throat and decided to say something. "I'm afraid Charlie and I might break up."

"Don't be ridiculous," she said, slamming on the brakes, hurling us both forward as we stopped in the middle of an intersection for a red light. "It's just the seven-year itch. All couples go through it."

"But we've only been together for three."

"Oh," she said quietly.

More silence.

"So tell me. Do you see us breaking up?" Isis was my psychic. My spiritual guru. Like the Egyptian gods of her homeland she studied so prodigiously, Isis had adopted ancient Eastern philosophies and possessed many mind-blowing powers of acute observation, many of which were astounding glimpses into the future. Even though lately the farthest east she'd ever been was to a Bruce Springsteen concert outside of Boston.

Isis hit the gas when the light turned green, and we sprang forward.

I sat in the passenger seat, watching her, as her mind kicked into gear, and a torrent of psychic energy washed over her. I couldn't stand it anymore.

"What do you see? What are you thinking?" I said.

"I'm thinking that maybe La Cienega might be faster at this time of day. I don't want to get clogged up in traffic on Fairfax. As it is, we'll only have twenty to thirty minutes at Costco."

"What about me and Charlie?"

"I see a lot of conflict."

You didn't have to be a psychic to pick up on that.

"But the power lies within both of you to weather it and move on together," she said. "There are worse things than to be with someone who worries about you, Jarrod."

She was right. And I was feeling guiltier than the time I told Charlie I borrowed three hundred dollars from our Alaskan cruise vacation fund to buy a new suit for a callback for a recurring role on *The West Wing* when I actually used the money on a deluxe treatment at the Burke Williams Day Spa in West Hollywood.

I rummaged through my bag for a cell phone to call and apologize, but Isis put a gentle hand on my thigh. "Give yourselves some breathing room. Take some time to think about what you're going to say. Call him when you get to Florida." She was right again. I was never in top form when I impulsively spewed a stream of apologies and reasons for my sometimes abhorrent behavior. It was best to rehearse the speech, work on my character motivation, and deliver such a tour de force performance that Charlie would find it utterly impossible not to forgive me. God, it's no wonder some people can't stand us actors.

When I thought about it, it dawned on me that Isis's sound advice had its own hidden motivations. She was afraid if I called Charlie down at the courthouse, and we got wrapped up in a conciliatory conversation, I would seriously cut into our shopping time at Costco.

When we reached the Costco on Washington Boulevard in Culver City, a scant twenty minutes from Los Angeles International Airport, the parking lot was jammed. Isis hurriedly did a few loops, before she spotted one narrow space, and squeezed her Caprice between the lines reserved for compact vehicles. We both had to squeeze out our respective doors so as not to bang into the cars parked on either side of us.

Isis immediately snatched my trusty Costco card out of my hand, grabbed a cart almost twice as big as her tiny frame, and rolled it inside. I did everything I could just to keep up. She was like a NASCAR racer, speeding through the meat and produce section, squealing into a sharp turn that led her to the mass quantities of boxed cereals and cans of coffee. Her eyes blazed with determination as she filled one cart, and dispatched me to round up another.

When I returned with a second cart, she was carefully scanning her list to see what else she needed.

I was still hung up on my fight with Charlie. "Do you think Charlie is right to worry? Should I be concerned about working in such close proximity to Juan Carlos?"

Isis sighed. I was starting to irritate her. She was on a mission and I was hampering her efforts. "Of course he's right," she said. "You said yourself that the two of you duked it out on Laurette's lawn like a couple of middleweight boxers. Juan Carlos isn't going to forget about all that just because you're now acting to-gether in a movie."

"So do you see me in physical danger down in Florida?"

Isis studied the prices on two brands of paper towels, not sat-isfied with either. "They've both gone up four cents since last month," she muttered to no one in particular. "Unbelievable. This place is supposed to be a cheaper alternative."

I stepped forward, grabbed the cheaper of the two brands, and tossed the eight-roll package into the empty cart. "I'm going to miss my flight if we don't get through your list faster."

Isis tore the list in half, and handed me one of the pieces. "Here. You get the items on this, and I'll concentrate on these. We'll get out of here a lot sooner."

"Deal," I said, checking my list. Lots of soaps and detergents. Isis spun around, and pushed her cart toward the next aisle. I called after her. "You didn't answer my question. As my psychic, tell me, am I in danger?"

She stopped her cart, and spun back around. She nodded. "Yes, you are. There's danger everywhere. It's around you right now. Now leave me alone so I can concentrate."

Not the most comforting observation. But good to know never-theless.

After stockpiling enough provisions for another Waco stand-off, Isis was ready to check out. She sent me back for one more extra large package of Pillsbury cookie dough while she found a place in the checkout line.

When I returned, I saw her immersed in an argument with a big, lumbering man who had obviously cut in front of her. His back was to me, so I couldn't make out his face. Even though he towered over her, Isis was spunky and aggressive, and she was not going to back down.

"I would've let you go ahead of me if you had asked politely," she said. "But you just pushed me aside." The man was unresponsive. For a minute I thought he might be deaf.

I decided diplomacy was the best tactic since time was of the essence. My flight was in a little over an hour and I had bags to check. "Excuse me, sir, normally we wouldn't mind you going through first, but we're in a bit of a hurry. I have a flight to catch. So we'd appreciate it if—"

The man slowly turned to face me. And my blood ran cold. It was Wendell Butterworth. He broke out into a wide smile. "Of course, I'm sorry. Go right ahead." He yanked his cart back, giving Isis enough room to move ahead of him in line. With a huff, she positioned her cart at the belt, and started unloading her groceries.

I stood frozen. I didn't want to take one step nearer to Butterworth. He waved me forward, as if taunting me. He wanted to know if I had the guts to step closer to him.

Isis, who had never seen Wendell Butterworth, had no idea who he was. And her psychic powers were not suggesting he was anything but a rude shopper lacking people skills.

We stared at one another for what seemed like an hour, but it couldn't have been more than a few seconds. Finally, a frizzy-haired Irish lass with a cherubic smile and wearing the traditional Costco uniform of a red vest and blue pants logged on to her cash register and called out to Wendell. "Excuse me, sir, I can take you over here."

Wendell grinned from ear to ear as he maneuvered his cart around mine and wheeled it over to the open register.

Isis, completely clueless and having given up on me helping her, pulled my cart forward and started unloading the items herself.

Wendell Butterworth was stalking me again. And I felt powerless to do anything about it.

Just a few feet away from me stood the man who tried to kill me. To the naked eye, he appeared harmless enough. Just a big cuddly bear of a middle-aged man out stocking up on a few canned goods. But to me, he was a living nightmare.

He glanced over at me, and gave me a wink as he plunged his hand into his cart and withdrew a twelve-pack of Reese's Peanut Butter Cups. When I was ten, I told Johnny Carson that was my favorite candy, and the following day Wendell had four giant boxes delivered to the set. He made sure I got a good look at what he was buying. And then he started whistling. The tune was instantly recognizable. It was the theme song from my long-running sitcom, *Go to Your Room!*

Chapter 12

After leaving Costco, I had my eyes fixed on the side-view mirror to see if Wendell Butterworth was following us. After hustling through the checkout line, and loading up Isis's Caprice, I spotted him waving at us as we peeled out of the lot. I was convinced he was following us, and would book a ticket to Miami to join me on my film shoot. Isis, having learned how to drive from her parents, who were used to maneuvering through the suicidal highways of Cairo, zipped in and out of traffic with the precision and focus of Paul Walker in the *Fast and Furious* movies. If anybody could lose Wendell, she could. But there was no sign of him as we slid into the steady stream of cars filling up the departure lanes leading into the airport. I thought about contacting the parole board and updating them on Wendell's recent activities. But what could they do? They had already granted him parole.

Once Isis had deposited me in the white loading zone at United Airlines, I took one last look around at the sea of travelers lined up with their bags for curbside check-in. I half expected to see Wendell's eerily serene yet maniacal face staring at me. I walked into the terminal, momentarily disoriented by the late-morning chaos, and dragged my bags to the endless line of economy passengers waiting for their boarding passes. Since this was a low-budget production, first-class travel was not an option, especially for a supporting player in the cast like me. The last time I had done a feature film I hadn't even started shaving yet.

I stood there, people watching to pass the time. And then I saw him. Wendell. He was in a wheelchair being pushed by an airport employee. No, wait. He was over to the right. In a USC football jersey and cutoff jeans. No. Behind the counter in a blue jacket and tie, checking in first-class passengers. Wendell Butterworth was everywhere. In my head. I needed a sedative, or at the very least, a stiff drink.

What I really needed was my boyfriend. I needed Charlie. And it finally dawned on me that I could not get on that plane without clearing the air. I didn't want to give us both some breathing room as Isis had suggested. No. I wanted to see him now. I gathered up my bags, left the line, and bustled back out to the curb, where I glimpsed a cab dropping off another traveler. Wendell stepped out of the back. Or it could've been Wendell if he'd had gray, wispy hair pulled into a bun, a hunched back half concealed by a bulky blue overcoat, and was a four-foot-eight-inch-tall grandmother. I was really losing it.

After helping the old woman deliver her bags to a curbside check-in attendant, I hopped into the cab and instructed the driver to take me downtown to the Los Angeles County Courthouse, where I knew Charlie would be just about finished testifying at the gang-related assault trial.

As we raced along the 105 Imperial Freeway, connecting to the 110 Harbor Freeway that stretched north toward the shiny, pristine skyline of downtown LA, I imagined the perfect movie moment ending with me showing up in the courtroom in a surprise last-minute appearance. Charlie would be sitting on the stand, relating the events of the night in question. I would sweep in, momentarily distracting him. He would fumble in his testimony, fight back a smile, and continue on, ever the consummate professional police officer. Once the judge allowed him to step down, we would meet outside in the hallway for an embrace, and then retreat to an empty courtroom for some hot, passionate sex on top of a hard wooden table usually reserved for the defendant and his attorneys. I was flushed just thinking about it as I sat in the back seat of the taxi.

When I arrived at the LA courthouse, the line to pass through security took forty minutes. I had to take off my belt, shoes, and jacket, and my three pieces of luggage I was hauling had to be carefully sorted through. Who showed up at the courthouse with a month's wardrobe? Once cleared, I took the elevator up to the fifteenth floor of the criminal courts building and to the room where Charlie had mentioned he would be testifying.

I opened the room, and quietly entered, expecting to slide into an empty seat off to the side and wait for the judge to call a lunch break. But to my surprise, the room was empty. This was odd. It was a four-day trial that had just begun yesterday. I couldn't understand where everybody had gone. I looked around for a stenographer, bailiff, anybody to enlighten me. But nobody was around. I walked back out into the hallway, where a tiny woman in her late twenties, wearing a suit jacket with a matching short skirt, her face hidden in a massive array of light brown curls, jotted furiously in her notebook. I glanced down and recognized Charlie's name in her scratchings.

"Are you one of the lawyers for the assault trial that's supposed to be going on in there?" I asked.

She nodded, not bothering to even look up.

"I'm looking for Charlie Peters."

"We're on a break. Judge Yellin asked to see him in his chambers."

"Could you tell me where I can find Judge Yellin's chambers?"

"Down the hall to your right," she said, and then snapped her notebook shut, annoyed at my intrusion. She stood up and clicked down the hall in her high heels. Definitely a big fan of the canceled *Ally McBeal* show.

"Thank you," I called after her, but she didn't respond. She just disappeared around a corner. I followed her directions, and found a door marked JUDGE YELLIN. I knocked softly, but got no answer. I tried again. I pressed my ear to the door, hoping to hear if he was on the phone or something, but all the commotion in the hall made it impossible to hear anything. I tried the door. It was unlocked. Should I just barge into a judge's chambers unannounced? I should've tried Charlie's cell phone instead, but I didn't want to cheat myself out of all the bells and whistles of an emotional reunion. Alerting him by phone would diminish the impact. So I opened the door and stepped inside.

It was dark. The shades were drawn, blocking the sunlight from the gorgeous day outside. I turned to leave, when I heard a rustling sound across the room. And heavy, intense breathing. I reached over and felt for a light switch. When I flipped it up with my index finger, I had a sinking feeling I was in the wrong place at the wrong time. And as the fluorescent lights struggled to reach maximum capacity, I knew I had made a tragic mistake. On the couch, off to the right side of the door, I saw a man in a judge's black robe, lying on top of another man. They were making out on the couch. The sudden flood of lights startled the judge, who despite being well north of fifty, was impressively distinguished with an immaculate head of silver hair and a tanned, handsome face. He leapt to his feet, in a state of shock and confusion.

"I'm sorry," I said, embarrassed and mortified. "I didn't mean to . . ."

My eyes fell on the man still sprawled out on the couch. His tie was askew, his dress shirt ripped open, his slacks had been hurriedly unzipped and wrenched halfway down to his lower thighs. It was Charlie. My Charlie. Detective Charlie Peters. Sucking face with a judge and about to do a whole lot more. As they used to say on *Laugh-In*, "Here cums da judge!"

"Ladies and gentlemen, we have begun our descent to Miami. Please make sure your tray tables are in the upright position, and that all portable electronics have been turned off. We will be landing in approximately ten minutes."

The soothing female flight attendant's voice stirred me out of a deep sleep. Another flight attendant, this one male with a severe look and a prissy demeanor, scooped up the knocked-over plastic cup that sat wedged between my legs. I yawned, and the spittle caked onto both corners of my mouth cracked. Catching Charlie in a compromising position with a judge had just been a dream. But I knew if I didn't make amends soon, it could become my reality.

I hadn't rushed to the courthouse. Like the good SAG member I was, I had boarded my plane to Miami. With makeup and hair tests scheduled for the morning and wardrobe fittings in the afternoon, I didn't have a choice if I wanted to keep in good stead with the independent film community.

After we landed and I retrieved my bags, I stepped out into the balmy air of south Florida and looked around for my ride. I immediately spotted a maroon van with a cardboard sign jammed into the dash that read, CREEPS—TRANSPORTATION CAPTAIN. A bouncy, chatty production assistant rolled down the window and called out to me, "Jarrod Jarvis?"

She didn't wait for me to answer. She jumped out and threw open the back doors of the vehicle. She was short and had a cute little body tucked into an aqua blue T-shirt with *Creeps* emblazoned on the front and tight jeans that accentuated every delicious curve of her hips and legs.

"I'd recognize you anywhere," she chirped. I knew it was coming. "Baby, don't even go there!" She exploded with laughter. "God, that cracked me up when I was a kid."

"You seem a little young to have been a fan of the show," I said, guessing she was no more than nineteen or twenty.

"TV Land. They play all those moronic shows," she said, and then caught herself. "Not that your show was moronic. I mean, it wasn't Shakespeare or anything, but it had its moments." She wisely chose to change the subject. "I'm Amy Jo."

"Hi, I'm Jarrod," I said. She grabbed my bags and tossed them in the back, and then was behind the wheel in an instant. I was winded just trying to keep up with her. As we drove south toward Miami Beach, Amy Jo decided I was due to hear her long-range career goals in the film business. Despite her knowing the trademark line from my long-running sitcom, Amy Jo insisted she'd never watched much television growing up. Her parents had raised her as an artist, and after a brief stint at the Academy of Dramatic Arts in New York (she wasn't asked back for vague reasons best described as political), she decided her future was behind the camera, and this gig as a PA would be the perfect way to kick off her foray into writing and directing and composing and editing. I loved the misguided idealism of youth. It just made me feel better about myself, being a bitter old pro in my thirties.

When Amy Jo began a dissertation on her life-long devotion to Quentin Tarantino and how his films affected her on a deeply fundamental level, I whipped out the cell phone, begged my driver's pardon, and tried to call Charlie. I got his voice mail. Maybe he really was banging the judge. No, I wasn't going to go there. It had just been a silly, ridiculous dream. So we fought, and whenever we fought, Charlie always had to go blow off some steam, and what better way to blow off steam than to ... No. I had to stop it. Otherwise, I was going to have Amy Jo turn the van around and drive me back to United, which would leave my career in tattered ruins. Or at least in more ruins than it already was.

Amy Jo dropped me off at the Ritz Plaza, one of the many hotels lining Miami's historic South Beach. Although the film was shooting in a small wooded park in Coral Gables, the production was putting the cast up in downtown Miami Beach. I was ecstatic. There were lots of diversions here, and the Latin-heavy population was just gorgeous to look at. Unfortunately the hotel, surrounded by the more opulent and ornate establishments such as the Delano and the Marlin, was a decidedly lackluster affair. The box-like rooms with scuffed white walls and simple, uninspired furniture did nothing to excite one's aesthetic sense. In fact, it downright depressed it.

I debated switching rooms, but I didn't want to cause a fuss. I understood that I was not part of a Warner Brothers multimillion-dollar production starring Jennifer Lopez. So I kept mum and unpacked my clothes.

Amy Jo told me she would be back at 7 A.M. to pick me up for makeup and hair tests, which left me the rest of the evening to grab some dinner and stroll along the boardwalk of Ocean Avenue, which boasted dozens of outdoor cafés, shops, and bars. I showered, shaved, and changed into a light white shirt, white pants, dark blue blazer, and sandals, which seemed appropriate for a night out in South Beach.

When I stepped off the elevator into the lobby, I recognized the man checking in at the reception desk. It took me a moment to place him out of context, but then it came to me.

"Rudy? Rudy Pearson?"

He turned and looked at me. Sweat poured down his chubby cheeks. His skin was ruddy and pale. His linen suit was stained with sweat. Rudy, the soap journalist who had been ejected from Laurette's wedding, had suddenly popped up in Miami.

Rudy knew exactly who I was, but in an attempt to put me on a more level playing field, he feigned ignorance. "I'm sorry . . . you are?"

"Jarrod Jarvis. We met at Laurette and Juan Carlos's wedding."

"Oh, right. I had to leave early that day for another appointment," he said, rewriting history and completely blocking out the fact that he was tossed out of the Hearst Castle on his ass.

"What are you doing here in Miami?" I said.

"Officially, my magazine sent me down to cover a *Days of Our Lives* fan convention being held here this weekend," he said, his eyes darting back and forth. I didn't need a lie detector to tell that wasn't what had brought him here.

"So if that's the official reason, is there an unofficial reason?"

This caught him off guard. But he went with it. "Yes," he said. I wasn't expecting him to elaborate, but Rudy was a soap journalist after all, and all journalists are shameful, relentless gossips. "I've come across some interesting information about someone who is down here shooting a movie, and I'm going to make sure it gets out so the whole world knows."

"I'm down here shooting a movie, so I sure hope it isn't about me," I said, nudging him gently.

He stepped back, surprised. Rudy apparently wasn't used to people touching him. And from where I was standing, I'm sure they're weren't a lot of takers anyway. He just stared at me and then, in a soft voice, replied, "No, it's not about you."

This guy had not hit the jackpot in the lottery of social skills.

"What the hell are you doing here?" a voice bellowed behind us.

We both spun around to see Juan Carlos charging toward us.

"I'm . . . I'm in the movie," I said. "Didn't Laurette tell you?"

"Not you," he barked, pointing a thick finger at Rudy. "I mean him!" If it hadn't been obvious before, the subject of Rudy's hatred was painfully obvious now.

Rudy, his ire up, straightened his drenched linen coat and lifted his nose as high as it could go. "It's a free country. I can be wherever I want."

"Not here," Juan Carlos said, pushing me aside, and towering over the much shorter Rudy. "I want you out of here right now."

"Make me," Rudy squeaked, as he had probably done countless times on the playground when harassed by one of the many bullies who'd undoubtedly paraded through his miserable life.

Juan Carlos shrugged, then bunched up his fingers into a fist and let it fly smack into the middle of Rudy's fleshy, pockmarked nose. Rudy stumbled back, his eyes wide with astonishment.

The hotel staff began congregating behind the reception desk, quietly debating on whether or not they should call the police, or handle the situation themselves.

Rudy rubbed his nose. A stream of blood trickled down his left nostril.

Juan Carlos took a step closer to him, and pointed to the door. "I'm not telling you again! Get out of here!"

Rudy, humiliated, tried sniffing the blood back up into his nose, but to no avail. It kept flowing. His hand was smeared with it, and some more had wiped off on his light-colored suit. But instead of retreating, Rudy let out an anguished roar, and with arms outstretched like an angry bear, he rushed at Juan Carlos. Rudy had at least a hundred pounds on him, so when they collided, I could feel the air whoosh right out of Juan Carlos's body. I felt like I was watching a repeat of my own altercation with the fiery former soap star.

But what Rudy had in size, Juan Carlos made up for with street smarts. As I had already learned, Juan Carlos had a whole repertoire of dirty tricks at his disposal. He gouged Rudy's right eye with one of his fingers, and bit hard into one of his fat cheeks.

The concierge grabbed the phone and punched in 911. My hand shot out to stop him. "No! I'll take care of this!" This was not a heroic act on my part. I just didn't want an arrest to hold up production on my big comeback movie.

I jumped in between Rudy and Juan Carlos. "Stop it right now, both of you!" But they were in the zone, too immersed in their battle to even realize I was attempting to pry them apart. Which was why I could never blame Rudy for socking me square in the right eye.

I sank to the ground. The room spun around me like some bad AFI student's opening shot in his first short film. My eye throbbed with pain, and I managed to look up to see both Rudy and Juan Carlos, staring down at me as if noticing me for the first time. At least I got them to stop fighting.

Chapter 13

"Hi, this is Charlie Peters. You've reached my voice mail. You know what to do."

Beep. This was the fourth time in an hour I had tried calling Charlie. Why wasn't he picking up his messages? Was he embroiled in a big case I didn't know about? Was he really screwing the judge presiding over the trial he was involved in? I couldn't let my paranoia consume me. I returned to the matter at hand.

Stella, a gloriously big-boned, brassy blond makeup stylist, was applying some pancake base to the corners of my right eye as I sat still in a director's chair in the tight quarters of the makeup and hair trailer. It was obvious she was using the cheap stuff, because no matter how much she rubbed onto my face, it wasn't enough to cover the dark bruise that made me look like half a raccoon.

Stella stepped back and inspected me. "Oh, honey, we're going to need a little more."

"But you've used almost the whole jar already," I wailed. "We're never going to be able to cover it up. Do you have something else?"

"This is all the budget allowed me to buy. Hell, this production is so cheap, I had to bring my own brushes and eyeliner pencils."

"Maybe I can run out to the nearest Sav-On and find something," I said, starting to stand up.

Stella pushed me back down in my seat. "There's no time. They're nearly done with the lighting out there. You're probably going to be called to the set any minute now."

The door to the trailer flew open and Larry Levant, the documentary wunderkind who was about to shoot his first narrative feature film, stuck his head in. He had obviously read his "How to Look Like You're an Up-and-Coming Hollywood Film Director" handbook. He had taken great pains to dress the part. A baseball cap, T-shirt, brown leather jacket, blue jeans, and Reebok sneakers. He was a small guy, not much over five and a half feet, had a hawkish nose and tiny hands, and the cap covered what I was sure was premature balding.

"Hey, Jarrod, how's the eye?"

"Can't even tell," I said hopefully, knowing full well I looked like a battered Farrah Fawcett in *The Burning Bed*.

Larry inspected me closely, unable to hide his obvious revulsion, and thought for a moment. He pressed a fist to his chin, and lowered his head like a Rodan statue. After a few painfully long seconds, he raised it again and this time had a twinkle in his eye.

"Why don't we write it into the script?" he said, snapping his fingers for emphasis.

"Brilliant idea," said Stella, an obvious kiss-up who wanted to be hired on future Larry Levant films.

"We've already established that your son Stevie is a troubled kid. Gets into lots of fights on the playground and that kind of shit. Where does he get it from? Dad! You're a drunk who gets into all kinds of bar brawls, and one of the reasons you went on this camping trip was to recover from getting the shit kicked out of you by some yahoo redneck you mouthed off to when you were liquored up!"

He looked at me for a reaction. I paused. "I thought Stevie and I were on the camping trip to get over the fact my wife deserted us to go find herself."

"Yeah, yeah, I know. I stole that from *Kramer vs. Kramer*. Great movie! Changed my life! I *was* that kid. But this is far more fucking original, don't you think?"

"Um, sure," I said, not wanting to argue with my director on the first day.

"I love it!" Stella chirped as she started scraping the mounds of makeup off my face. "It totally works with his black eye."

"Perfect. I'll get you some rewrites by tonight. See you on the set," he said as he flew out of the trailer.

As Stella worked her magic on my face, I wondered if Juan Carlos had arrived yet. After I had been knocked down in the lobby of the Ritz Plaza, Rudy Pearson had beaten a hasty retreat. He was afraid I might press charges or something. Juan Carlos watched him scurry away, and then reached down and hauled me to my feet. He looked at the swelling around my eye.

"Jesus, that's gotta hurt," he said. Not exactly a warm truce, but at least he didn't sock me in the other eye so I'd have a matching set. Juan Carlos steadied me, and then strolled out the glass door toward Ocean Avenue to kick off his own night on the town. Dizzy and disoriented, I swayed a bit as the concierge, a tall, slim Colombian, raced to my aid and escorted me back up to my dismal and depressing room. A bellman arrived with an ice pack, and I crawled into bed, calling it a night.

It seemed as if only a few seconds had passed before Coldplay was blaring through the CD alarm clock. I stumbled back downstairs, where the impossibly perky Amy Jo quickly greeted me and then, before I could request coffee, whisked me out to her maroon transport van, and we began our twenty-minute journey to the set of *Creeps* in a wooded park just outside Coral Gables.

Stella finished dabbing up the sweat that had formed on my brow, and then wheeled me around so I could get a good look at her handiwork. I was pale, haggard, my hair was matted and dull, and my eyes were bloodshot. But none of it was noticeable because all attention was drawn to the large purple-and-black shiner that was now taking up a quarter of my face, and was getting bigger by the minute.

"I look terrible," I said weakly.

"Well, you heard Larry. You're a mess. Your wife just ditched you and you were in a bar fight."

"But don't you think this might be overkill? Maybe you went slightly overboard with the whole death-warmed-over look."

Stella bristled at my pointed criticism of her artistry.

"Honey, I didn't do a damn thing," Stella said. "This is the real you." She saw the horror in my face and decided to mollify the situation by adding, "Besides, this is an independent film. We want to go for realism."

I pulled myself up out of the chair and left the trailer. Outside, the mood was a bit ebullient as the crew prepared for the first shot on the first day of production. People were a lot more cheerful on Day One when inclement weather, blown-out klieg lights, injured actors, and overexposed film were still days, perhaps even weeks, away from having to be dealt with.

The first scene on the schedule was a simple-enough one to kick off the five weeks of principal photography. At this point in the story, the intrepid hero, a park ranger played by Juan Carlos, has gathered a group of campers to warn them that a homicidal maniac may be loose in the forest, and that it is vital we stay together as a group until he is caught. Of course, in the following pages, various circumstances occur that split us all up so the methodical killer can pick us off one by one.

In addition to my character and the boy playing my son, the other endangered campers included college students paired off into three couples, a retired Army general and his son, and the script's leading lady, a psychoanalyst, who would later prove useful in providing a disturbing psychological profile of our adversary. With her was her mother, a doctor, who would later on offer medical assistance to those lucky few who escaped the killer with their lives but nevertheless nursed dangling limbs and knifed torsos.

My only line in the scene, which I had already committed to memory, was, "Forget it. I'm going to take my chances and try to get out of here with my son!" At which point, the ranger (Juan Carlos) would shake some sense into me, and impress upon me how important it was we all stick together, or risk certain death. I refuse to listen until my son, a child with wisdom well beyond his years, looks at me with his big brown eyes and says, "Daddy, please. Do as the nice man says. I don't want to die." I stop cold. Look at everybody. And then my eyes fall back down to meet my son's pathetic gaze. After a long beat which I planned to milk of every last ounce (and to ensure extra screen time), I muss my son's hair with a smile, deeply affected by his words, and nod silently. The boy throws his pudgy little arms around my waist and sobs, "I love you, Daddy." Not a bad scene for a first day.

I spotted Larry hugging a brunette, presumably our leading lady, who had just arrived on the set. My involvement with this picture had happened with such speed, I still had no idea who my costars were besides Juan Carlos. When the brunette pulled away, I was in for a big bombshell. It was Dominique.

Larry clutched her hand and dragged her over to me. "Jarrod, I want you to meet Dominique. She's playing Sarah the psycho-analyst."

Dominique looked at me with empty eyes. She had no memory of who I was.

"We've met," I said.

"We have?" she said incredulously.

"Twice. Once at the Hearst Castle and once out in Malibu," I said, refraining from adding, "When I fished your ass out of the surf following your attempted suicide drowning."

Her eyes flickered at bit, trying to come to life, like a pair of waning headlights sucking the last juice out of a dead car battery.

"Oh, right," she said.

"I have to set up the master shot with the DP. I'll let you two get acquainted," Larry said as he hustled off toward his Panavision camera, the one top-of-the-line piece of equipment on this shoot.

"I didn't know you were an actress, Dominique," I said, studying her face for any signs of animation.

She nodded.

"So, are you doing well? The last time I saw you, you were a bit . . . down." That was putting it mildly.

She perked up ever so slightly. "I'm fine. I've put the past behind me, and I'm moving on. I want to put my career first for a while."

I was ready to believe her until I saw her notice something. Her face fell, and she let out an audible gasp. I turned to see what had caught her so off-guard, and spotted Juan Carlos sweep in, his arm around a stunning older beauty in her mid-forties. She carried herself like a queen and was blessed with a porcelain face, immaculately styled hair, and a slim, statuesque figure. She was in a smart white pantsuit, and laughed while resting her head on Juan Carlos's broad shoulder. They were sharing a private joke.

The stunning woman's eyes met Dominique's, and she gave her a halfhearted wave. Juan Carlos, barely able to contain himself, bussed the older woman's cheek with his hot passionate Latin lips. And then he slapped her playfully on the behind as she scampered over to the hair stylist and commandeered a hand mirror to check her appearance.

Juan Carlos managed to give me a half smile as he sauntered over to the craft service table for a bagel. He gave a quivering Dominique even less attention.

"First team in, please," bellowed the first assistant director through a bullhorn as the stand-ins who filled in for us while the lighting was set up filed off the set. I had one last chance to call Charlie. I hit the speed dial. It rang twice.

"Hi, this is Charlie Peters. You've reached my voice mail. You know what to do."

Damn. I shoved the phone into my coat pocket, not allowing my-self to imagine where he could be. I had already done enough of that.

I stepped on my mark next to the cherubic blond boy playing my son. He looked nothing like me. His mother, a squat, harried woman with what looked like a nervous tick, stood off to the side, watching her offspring intently.

Larry was circling the cast one last time, making sure he was happy with his blocking.

Dominique fought bravely to keep her cool. The sexy older woman sashayed on the set, walked right up to Dominique, and squeezed her arm.

"Mommy's here," she said with a laugh. She was clearly the actress playing Dominique's mother in the film.

Stella rumbled onto the set for final makeup checks. She stopped at me last, her nose crinkling up with distaste at the sight of me, but then she caught herself.

"Great," she said.

Before she could run off, I whispered, "So who is that actress playing the mother?" If anyone knows the lowdown on a film set, it's the makeup and hair people. Nothing gets by them.

"Her name's Viveca something," Stella said, relieved to know there was another gossip on the set. "I think she's married to one of the investors, which is how she got the part. Like they say, it's who you know."

"She and Juan Carlos seem chummy," I said.

"That's the understatement of the year. Amy Jo told me she dropped her off at the hotel last night, and helped her up to her room with her bags. Before the elevator came back up, she saw Viveca dash down the hall to Juan Carlos's room with her tooth-brush. This morning when she picked them up, they came down together. You do the math." Stella bounded off the set, and watched from the sidelines.

"Okay, quiet, everybody. We're rolling," screamed the assis-tant director.

"And action!" Larry hollered, thrilled to have this much authority.

Juan Carlos, wearing a green park ranger's uniform, launched into his cautionary monologue about the dangers of camping while a killer lurks about. He displayed all the gusto of a bad soap actor desperately trying to branch out. He was awful. But the rest of us reacted gamely, as if we were listening to one of Martin Luther King's speeches, and waited for our turn to speak and steal the spotlight.

That's when we all heard an incessant ringing. Juan Carlos kept going, not about to be deterred by some muffled annoyance.

Larry's face went beet red, and finally he screamed, "Cut!"

Everybody fell silent. All we heard was that damn ringing. I looked around, an exasperated look on my face, anxious to identify the idiot who forgot to turn off his cell phone. That's when it hit me. It was coming from my coat pocket. Oh God. The first shot of the movie. And I'd ruined it. I debated on whether I should ignore it, and keep the exasperated look on my face in place. Maybe no one would notice it was me. But all eyes were fixed upon my coat pocket, and I finally had to fess up.

"I am *so* sorry," I said.

Larry tapped his foot angrily as I yanked the phone out and pressed the talk button. I would've just turned it off, but I was afraid it might be Charlie.

"Hello?"

"Hi, Jarrod, it's me," Laurette said. "Is this a bad time?"

"Um, yes, actually it is," I said, as I slowly became unglued under the glares of my fellow cast and crew.

"Then just tell me quickly. How's Juan Carlos? Is he behaving himself?"

"Yes," I lied. Now was not the time to divulge the truth. There would be plenty of time to fess up, since every fiber of my being was telling me things were about to get much worse.

Chapter 14

After my rather inauspicious first day on the set, I decided it was best to leave my cell phone in the trailer I shared with two other supporting actors in the cast while shooting my scenes. My relationship with Larry Levant, our esteemed director, improved dramatically after that. As for the rest of the cast, I got along famously with almost everyone. Even Juan Carlos and I managed to keep things professionally civil. We just stayed out of each other's way. Juan Carlos wanted the film to be a success. It was not in his best interest to stir up conflict with other cast members, so he cut a wide berth around me.

However, there was one notable cast mate I did not get along with right from the start. I despised Simon, the little spawn of Satan who was playing my son in the picture. On the first day of shooting, he demanded that I surrender the last Jell-O Pudding Pop, so he could suck on it between takes. Not accustomed to being ordered about by an overindulged child actor, and having always respected my fellow adult costars when I was in his shoes, I adamantly refused. He screamed at the top of his lungs for his mother, the director, and his agent. The first to arrive on the scene was Caitlin, his thirtysomething stage mom. Once alerted to what was bothering her little star, she tried appeasing him with a measly box of raisins. The screaming just got louder, piercing the air with such force I thought for a moment I'd blown out an eardrum. No wonder the mini-asshole's mother had a nervous tick.

"How about if you shared it with him?" Caitlin said with a pleading look. I was about to lay into her about her decidedly lax parenting skills when I spied a production assistant summoning Larry on the walkie-talkie. After ruining the first shot of the movie with my ringing cell phone, I thought it best to drop the matter. I didn't need to tick off the director twice in one week. I peeled off the plastic wrap, and handed the Jell-O Pop to Simon. He swiped it away from me with his piggish little hands and started devouring it without even a thank-you. I looked to his mother, who shrugged, as if to say, "What can you do?"

I was going to say, "I can strangle the little bugger until his fat ugly face explodes," but didn't want to risk social services swarming down on the set armed with whistles and restraining orders.

Crisis averted, I wandered over to watch Larry shoot the last take of the day with Juan Carlos and Dominique. It was a pivotal scene in the picture where they both profess their love for each other right before setting off into the woods together to vanquish the killer. Viveca watched from the sidelines. She gazed at Juan Carlos lovingly as if picturing herself in the scene with him as opposed to Dominique.

Although Juan Carlos was stiffer than Steven Seagal in an Adam Sandler comedy, Dominique showed real promise as an actress. As she clutched the forest green ranger's jacket Juan Carlos was wearing, the look in her eye betrayed real feelings, real emotion, and real desire. She made the stilted dialogue resonate because the delicate little flower really did love him.

Larry sat in his chair, his big round saucer eyes glued to his actors, practically orgasmic over Dominique's performance as he mouthed the dialogue along with her.

As they neared the end of the scene, a lone tear streaked down Dominique's face. She shyly wiped it away and said, "If we don't get him before he gets us, I want you to know, even if that mad killer carves out my heart with a hunting knife like he did to those other campers, it will still belong to you."

Okay, really bad dialogue. But she sold it. And a euphoric Larry screamed, "Cut! That's a wrap for today! Everybody have a nice weekend!"

Larry sprinted over to embrace Dominique. She accepted his accolades with graciousness, but kept one eye on Juan Carlos, who bounded off the set and over to Viveca. Juan Carlos, though obviously wanting to shower the older woman with affection, restrained himself when he realized I was watching. The last thing he needed was his wife's best friend calling her to report his on-set shenanigans. He settled for a soft sweep of his lips across Viveca's still beautiful but aging and definitely pulled-back face.

Dominique excused herself from Larry, who was still fawning over her, and dashed off to her trailer. Once she was gone, Viveca was less apprehensive about where she put her hands. Right on Juan Carlos's butt. She yanked him closer, whispered something in his ear, and then with a flourish, grabbed her fur coat, threw on her oversized Christian Dior sunglasses despite the fact that it was already dark outside, and said her good-byes to the crew.

Juan Carlos watched her go with an adoring smile on his face. It faded when he noticed me watching the whole scene. With a scowl in my direction, he grabbed his leather jacket, tossed it over his shoulder, and marched off the set and down a trail to the parking area, where his Kawasaki motorcycle awaited him.

I gathered up my things, and followed him. I figured since Juan Carlos and Viveca had made such a production of leaving separately, then they were undoubtedly planning a secret rendezvous later. When I'd reached the end of the trail leading to the large paved lot at the foot of the park, Viveca was not there to greet him. But Dominique was. He marched up to her and enveloped her in a hug. They spoke softly, completely oblivious to me. I walked nonchalantly toward the Ford Taurus that Amy Jo had so kindly rented for me the day before in case I wanted to do some sightseeing over the weekend.

Juan Carlos brushed aside some of Dominique's hair to get a good look at her face. He smiled, and then kissed her gently on the lips. She quivered at his touch. This girl had practically been stalking him, and now he was acting as if she was on *The Bachelorette* and he was the last guy holding a rose. What was going on here? It was clear to me that Juan Carlos was two-timing Laurette. But I just couldn't figure out whom he was cheating with. Viveca or Dominique? Or both? That was too much to think about.

I slipped behind the wheel of the Taurus, and shut the door as quietly as possible. I didn't want Juan Carlos to know I was watching. He held Dominique in his arms, and they rocked back and forth, her head resting on his broad chest. He seemed to be whispering gentle apologies in her ear.

Finally, when Larry and his assistant director loudly pounded down the trail to the lot discussing the dailies from yesterday's shoot, Juan Carlos pulled away. He kissed the tip of his right index finger, and then pressed it to Dominique's lips. As she ran off giddily to her car, Juan Carlos peeked around to make sure there had been no witnesses, then put on his shiny black helmet and straddled his Kawasaki. Revving it up, he squealed out of the lot, heading, from what I was guessing, straight toward a hot night of unbridled sex with Viveca. I turned the ignition key, threw the Taurus into drive, and peeled out behind him. He headed straight for the 95 Freeway north, hit the on-ramp, and at that point I almost lost him. He effortlessly weaved the cycle in and out of traffic, getting farther and farther ahead of me.

Luckily, as we hit the Fort Lauderdale exits, traffic slowed and he cut down on the fancy maneuvering. Once past the city, the highway opened up, and it was easier to hit the gas and keep him in my sights while maintaining a safe distance.

We drove on 95 for over two hours. Where the hell was he going? Was he so afraid of getting caught that he had to drive to a remote part of the east coast of Florida? Or did Viveca have a quiet little getaway on the Sebastian River? She had a few minutes' head start, so she was probably putting on a little mood music and pouring a couple of glasses of Merlot. I could still see the bright red glow of the Kawasaki's taillight as it veered right off the freeway, ten minutes past the town of Vero Beach. It dawned on me exactly where I was. The little hamlet of Sebastian situated roughly midway between Orlando and Miami. I had been here many times before. This was the home of Clyde and Priscilla Jarvis. My parents. Like many Florida zip codes, Sebastian was populated primarily by East Coast retirees who had discovered the joys of golfing and square dancing. For my parents, it was paradise. They had bought a quaint two-story riverfront house at an affordable price after I turned eighteen and no longer needed them to manage my career. They had despised the Hollywood scene, and were more than happy to leave it behind. They had both grown up on the East Coast, and were blessed with grounded East Coast sensibilities. They loved the simple life of Florida, where they could lounge with a cocktail on their deck that overlooked the river and watch the space shuttles take off from Cape Canaveral a short distance away. Viveca was just shy of their age range, so it didn't surprise me that she had bought in the area as well.

Juan Carlos sped down Highway 111, and for a brief disquieting moment, I thought he was heading straight for my parents' house. But just a mile short, he pulled into the parking lot belonging to a flat, plain-looking structure. In front, a weathered hanging sign barely illuminated by a dull street lamp rocked in the heavy wind. It said SAND DRIFT MOTEL. Viveca had certainly presented herself as a woman of means with her fur coats and flashy jewelry. This was well beneath her. Maybe I was wrong. Maybe Juan Carlos was meeting Dominique, and at any moment, she would pull in behind me. As Juan Carlos pressed the kickstand of his bike down with the heel of his boot, I drove pass him so as not to raise any suspicion. I parked on the far end of the lot, facing him, turned off my engine, and shut down the lights.

Juan Carlos checked himself out in the rearview mirror of his Kawasaki, straightened his jacket, and popped a breath mint into his mouth. He ambled down the row of doors lining the one-story motel. When he reached door number six, he rapped on it twice with his fist. After a moment, the door opened, and I saw a young man step out. He was about Juan Carlos's height and slender of frame, with dark olive skin and wavy jet-black hair. He broke out into a sexy, winning smile when he saw Juan Carlos. The kid was about twenty-four. He had on a ripped pair of jeans, no shirt, and he was barefoot.

I had expected Viveca or Dominique and was surprised by this new character in the picture. I was even more surprised when he grabbed Juan Carlos's jacket and drew him close, covering Juan Carlos's mouth with his lips. They stood there, devouring each other, before Juan Carlos got self-conscious, glanced around to see if they were being watched, and then pushed the kid back in the room, following him inside and slamming the door behind him.

I sat motionless in my Ford Taurus. The question was no longer, "Who is Laurette's new husband sleeping with?" The question was, "Who *isn't* Laurette's new husband sleeping with?"

Chapter 15

I staked out the Sand Drift Motel for the whole night. Juan Carlos and the young shirtless stud who had greeted him at the door never left the room once. When the sun rose hours later, I sat in the Taurus, bleary-eyed and exhausted, knowing full well that the night hadn't been nearly as satisfying for me as it had been for the occupants of room six. My scratchy throat ached for hot coffee, my mind imagining the jolt of caffeine that would help spring me to life. But if I left my post, I risked missing something that could shed some light on the salacious secrets of Juan Carlos Barranco.

With overwhelming proof, I was certain at this point that Juan Carlos was a stinking, lying cheat who never really loved Laurette, and used her heart and kindness to get ahead as an actor. But a murderer? With the San Simeon police not any closer to handing out an indictment in the murder of Austin Teboe at the Hearst Castle, my firm belief that Juan Carlos was somehow behind it all was a shaky proposition at best.

My cell phone battery was dead, so I plugged the jack into the cigarette lighter and started the car to give it some juice. Luckily I was on the Verizon America's Choice plan that gave me unlimited calling access anywhere in the country. I hit the speed-dial button for home, and waited for a grumpy, groggy Charlie to pick up. I got our machine. It was eight-thirty in the morning in Florida. That meant it was only five-thirty on the West Coast. Where the hell was he? Why couldn't I reach him? Was he on some all-night stakeout like me? I tried his cell number and got his voice mail. I was beginning to regret accepting the job in Florida. Charlie and I always worked things through, but maybe this time I had gone too far. Maybe he had reached his limit with me, and there would be no coming back from this one. As I pondered the state of my relationship, I spied a sleepy, long-haired desk clerk in his late twenties stirring inside the registration office. Since the shirtless kid in room six had arrived before Juan Carlos, chances were he had registered himself.

I stepped out of the Taurus, stretched my legs, and bounded across the parking lot, keeping one eye on the door to room six to make sure no one came out while I was in plain view.

The bells above the door clanged as I entered the office and startled the laconic clerk with the half-closed eyes.

"Can I help you?" he said with a slow, Southern drawl, barely offering me a cursory glance.

"Yes," I said, mustering up a chipper, friendly voice. "I was wondering if you could tell me who is in room six?"

"Can't. It's like a rule or something." His gaze suddenly caught mine, and his half-closed eyes popped opened all the way.

"Oh," I said with proper disappointment. I reached behind for the wallet tucked into the back pocket of my jeans. I was not above a little bribe since it looked like the kid, wearing a torn, stained Counting Crows tour T-shirt and faded cutoffs, barely made enough for beer money.

He was still staring at me. "You're . . . you're that guy. From the TV show."

Sometimes my past proved to be an invaluable asset.

"*Go to Your Room!*" I offered with a smile.

"Yeah, I watched you all the time when I was just a rug rat. You had that saying, the one that was on all the T-shirts," he said, straining to remember. "What was it?"

"Baby, don't even go there!"

He shook his head. "No, that wasn't it. It was something like 'Baby, don't you be messing with me.' "

I wasn't going to correct him. Let him think he was right if it got me what I needed.

"That's right," I smiled.

"Man, you've gotten old."

My smile faded.

Oblivious to his social faux pas, the kid prattled on, "So what the hell are you doing way out here in the boondocks?"

"I thought I spotted a friend of mine from the good old days. One of the kids from *Head of the Class*."

"You're shitting me, man! No way! Which one?"

I had to think fast. I had gone clubbing with pretty much all of them at some point during the heyday of our various sitcoms. There was one in particular, though, I had always thought was adorable. I went with him. "The one who played the preppy, snooty kid."

"Fuck, yeah! I remember him! That show was awesome, man!"

"Totally awesome," I lied. When my show was canceled, my agent tried to float the idea of adding me as a new student in the show's third season, but they didn't bite so I forever hated the show.

"So where did you see him?"

"Right here. At the Sand Drift."

I thought the clerk was going to drop dead from shock. Not one, but two big stars at this obscure, crumbling motel were almost too much for him to take. He snatched up the registration book off the desk, and began skimming through the pages.

"I saw him go into room six," I said, praying he wouldn't ask me the actor's name because I was drawing a blank.

The clerk ran his finger down the page and studied the name. He looked up at me hopefully. "David Miller?"

I shook my head and sighed. "Nope. Not him. Damn. He looks just like him."

"Fuck, man, what a bummer. I was going to offer him a free continental breakfast and get him to be the first one to sign our VIP guest book."

I glanced out the window and saw David Miller heading straight for the office. I turned to the clerk and said quickly, "Oh, well. Thanks anyway."

"Hey, would you sign it?" the clerk said. "I know you didn't stay here or anything, but who the fuck's gonna know?"

I figured it was quicker to do as he asked rather than argue, so I scribbled my name illegibly in his scuffed blue notebook, dropped the pen, and held open the door as David Miller swept inside.

"I'm here to check out," he said gruffly, tossing the keys down on the desk. He never looked my way and I took the opportunity to slip outside.

Juan Carlos stood by his bike and put on his helmet. I turned my head the other way as I passed him, hoping he wouldn't recognize me, but he was lost in his own thoughts.

As I crossed the parking lot, I noticed a black Lincoln Town Car situated across the street and facing the motel. Two giants, one Caucasian, one Hispanic, were stuffed into the front seat. The one in the passenger seat held binoculars up in front of his face and watched me as I headed toward the Taurus. When he noticed that I was watching him watch me, he quickly turned and spoke to the driver. The Town Car roared to life, spun out of the gravelly road across from the motel, and sped off down Highway 111.

I hopped into my car just as David Miller ambled out of the

registration office. Juan Carlos sat on the bike, twisting the handlebar accelerator so the bike's engine revved loud enough to accentuate his macho posturing. Juan Carlos was obviously proud to have such a powerful machine wedged between his muscular, toned thighs.

David stopped, caressed Juan Carlos's cheek with the back of his index finger, whispered a good-bye, and then headed to his own car, a sleek red BMW from the five hundred series. Whoever this kid was, he had money. So why meet at the dumpy Sand Drift?

Juan Carlos zipped out of the lot and headed back toward the 95 Highway. I knew he was returning to Miami. He had already gotten what he'd come for, and there was no reason to hang around on this desolate stretch of road anymore. I debated following the kid to find out more about him, but I was afraid someone in the area might recognize me. And if it got back to my parents that I was in town and didn't at least stop in to say hello, Jarvis family relations would undoubtedly be dealt a severe blow.

It was a five-minute jaunt to River Oak Drive, and as I pulled up to the white two-story house with its breathtaking river view, I saw my father, Clyde, fussing in his tiny vegetable garden that sprouted one cucumber a year if he was lucky. Oh, well, it gave him something to do between golf games and square-dancing competitions.

The Ford Taurus pulling into the small paved driveway caught his attention, and as I waved with a bright smile, his face lit up. My father was a retired Navy captain, who'd spent most of his life touring ports around the world. He cut a striking figure at six feet four inches tall, and had a barrel chest that would have made him physically intimidating were it not for his sweet, kind demeanor. His silver hair was thinning, and he wore thick glasses that suggested his age, but his broad face darkly tan from nine months a year in the Florida sunshine was nearly wrinkle-free. Although seventy, most people would put him somewhere in his mid-fifties.

When Dad retired from the Navy, I had just landed my first commercial. I was five years old, and it was a thirty-second spot for Cap'n Crunch cereal. Although all I had to do was salute a cartoon character and say, "Ahoy, matey!" before diving into a bowl of cereal, seeing me on television made him cry. For a Navy captain, my dad cried a lot. He cried when I got my sitcom. He cried when I guest-starred on his favorite show, *JAG*, as a Navy admiral's homicidal son. He cried when I broke up with my first boyfriend. He was always proud of me no matter what I did or whom I was dating. His years of military service did little to diminish his loving acceptance of me. I was his son and I was gay. Big deal.

As I stepped out of the Taurus, he rushed at me and enveloped me in his big, comforting, tanned arms. "Well, hello, stranger!"

"Hi, Dad," I said breathlessly as he squeezed the last gulps of air out of me with his bear hug.

"How's the movie going? How's Charlie?"

Before I could answer, my mother, Priscilla, came sauntering out of the house. A foot and a half shorter than my father, she was your typical fiery redhead, a ball of energy and full of uncensored attitude. She carried a crossword puzzle and pen, and pushed her husband aside to steal a quick hug for herself. "He just got here, Clyde. Don't hit him with so many questions!"

Although my mother had once run my career, she was not a fan of Hollywood. She was much happier now, mingling with real people outside of the spotlight. And although she'd lived among the gays while residing in LA and counted many of them as her close friends, in a stunning twist of irony she was not as accepting as my Navy dad. Her reaction was similar to Cher's when her only daughter, Chastity Bono, had her coming-out party. "I love the gays, they've made my career, but please God, not *my* kid!" She cried, too, when I broke up with my first

boyfriend, although upon closer inspection, I was able to identify them as tears of joy. In the early days of our relationship,
Charlie had worked his magic, and she instantly adored him,
treating him like her own son. She chose to ignore what went on
between us behind closed doors and loved us both uncondition-
ally. But she made it very clear she didn't understand what had
made me this way.

Mom and I decided to keep our relationship on a superficial
yet loving level. She didn't ask questions about my personal life,
nor did I offer up any answers unprompted. Dad, on the other
hand, would have drawn his own PFLAG posters to march in a
gay pride parade if he'd felt it would bring us even closer. The
bottom line was, however, that I loved them both. And to see
their happy faces at my surprise visit dispelled any issues I had
with the depth of my relationship with my mother.

After the initial flurry of kisses and hugs and updates on all of
our activities, we piled into my parents' Roadtrek motor home,
which they'd purchased for a cross-country excursion that never
happened, and drove to the nearest Olive Garden for an early
lunch. Over pasta, garlic sticks, and the famous bottomless salad,
my mother asked about Laurette's wedding. She had heard
through my sister in Maine that someone had died at the reception and she was champing at the bit to hear the details.

"He was a chef. He worked for some kind of mobster based
out of Miami. Javier Martinez."

"I've seen that guy on the news," Dad said. "Feds have been
trying to nail him for years," he added gleefully, thrilled to be
discussing something other than which restaurant chain they
were going to target for an early-bird special later. "You think
Laurette's husband poisoned him?"

"I don't have any proof of that, but I've got a gut feeling he's
involved somehow."

"Motive?" Dad could barely contain himself. When I became
embroiled in the murder of former child star Willard Ray

Hornsby last year, my notoriety reached new heights. My Dad, a huge fan of *CSI: Crime Scene Investigation*, reveled in my involvement. He was a closet detective and an avid reader of mystery novels. He yearned to discuss the fine points of police work with Charlie whenever he could corner him in a room, and now that I was this amateur sleuth who'd cracked a real case, he found it harder and harder to suppress his own desire to be the next Lieutenant Columbo.

My mother wasn't very tolerant of her husband's fascination with murder. She preferred lighter topics such as the latest movie releases and what kind of salary I was pulling down for this small independent film shoot in Miami. Even though her time in show business was peripheral and now a distant memory, Priscilla Jarvis loved talking money.

"Just give me a hint. Is it at least five figures?"

"It's not about the money, Mom," I said defensively. "Sometimes it's about the art."

"I thought you said it was a cheap horror movie," she said, her eyes raised with suspicion like most mothers who are on the brink of catching their child in a lie.

"That's right. And sometimes it's not about the art, it's about just working on something. The director is really hot right now, and if I do well, he could use me again when he gets his first big job at a studio. This could be an amazing opportunity."

"What does Charlie think?" Dad asked innocently.

I should have at that point confessed that my relationship was teetering on the edge of extinction, and that I hadn't been able to reach him by phone from the moment I arrived in Florida, and that I feared he was banging a judge, but instead, I popped the last garlic bread stick into my mouth and, between chews, replied, "He thinks it's great."

After a brief tussle over who was going to pay the whopping twenty-two-dollar bill, we piled back into the Roadtrek, and drove north toward the senior center where my parents square danced every afternoon at one o'clock sharp. My father pulled off Highway 111 and zipped along a narrow back road, the motor home taking up most of the pavement. I prayed we wouldn't collide with a car coming from the opposite direction.

Gripping the wheel, Dad glanced back at Mom and me as we sat at the tiny kitchen table booth in the back of the vehicle. "So, you want to know what I think?"

"No," Mom said emphatically. But Dad was years beyond listening to her.

"I think Juan Carlos has somehow crossed this gangster Martinez, and Martinez sent this Teboe fella to the wedding to rub out Juan Carlos. But before he had the chance, Juan Carlos spiked his drink with a fast-acting poison. How does that sound?"

My mother rolled her eyes, and jabbed a finger at Dad. "Keep your eyes on the road!"

Dad grimaced, and then swiveled back around.

"I swear he's going to get us killed someday. If it's not from poking his nose where it doesn't belong, it'll be from his driving," she said.

Dad sat quietly in the RV's captain's seat. He desperately wanted a response to his theory, but he didn't want to ask me for fear of another tongue-lashing from his wife.

"Sounds like a reasonable scenario, Dad. Except for the fact that the poison was something called monkshead. Very rare and not indigenous to California. Someone had to bring it to the wedding with the intent of using it. It was pretty clear Juan Carlos wasn't expecting Austin Teboe to show up."

"Damn. I thought I had the case wrapped up." He thought some more. "How about this? You said Juan Carlos is cheating on Laurette. What if she found out and was wild with fury, and decided to take him out at the wedding. But instead, she poisoned Teboe by accident—"

"Oh, for heaven's sake, Clyde. Shut up! You don't know what

you're talking about! Laurette is not a murderer!" my mother screamed, whacking him on the back of his head with her crossword puzzle book.

"They say it's always the least likely suspect," he said softly.

"Well, then you might as well accuse Jarrod. Or what about me? I was down here in Florida with you. Thousands of miles away from the wedding. That makes me the least likely, wouldn't you say?" She was mocking him now, and he hated it.

I was about to intervene when I noticed a black Lincoln Town Car behind us. I left my mother at the table and walked up to sit next to Dad. I casually glanced out the side-view mirror for a better look. It was the two linebackers I had seen earlier scouting out the Sand Drift Motel. And they were closing in on us.

Chapter 16

"I don't want anyone to panic," I said quietly and evenly. "Don't turn around."

"What?" my mother said, spinning her head around faster than Linda Blair in *The Exorcist*. "Is it the police? How fast are you going, Clyde?"

"Jesus, Mom, what did I just say?"

"What is it, son?" Dad asked, an excited lilt in his voice.

"We're being tailed."

My mother's face fell.

Dad's eyes danced with glee as he tightened his grip on the wheel and broke out into a wide smile. "Want me to outrun 'em?"

"For crying out loud, Clyde, we're in an RV!" my mother wailed before grabbing my shirtsleeve in desperation. "Do they have guns, Jarrod? Are they going to shoot us?"

"I don't know," I said. "I have no idea who they are."

"Then that settles it," said Clyde Jarvis, former Navy captain and hero of the high seas. "They're going to eat my dust!"

And with that, Dad slammed his foot down on the accelerator.

As the Roadtrek shot forward, the sudden jolt sent my mother and me flying to the back of the RV, and we both landed on the plush plaid comforter decorating the queen-size bed just off the narrow kitchen area. After untangling our limbs, I glanced out the back window to see the Town Car speeding to catch up with us.

I studied the license number and committed it to memory as my mother grabbed the wood-trimmed dining table for support, and hoisted herself forward toward her husband.

"For God's sake, Clyde, slow down before you get us all killed!"

Ignoring his wife's pleas, my dad could barely suppress his euphoria over his first experience with a real-live car chase. "Those fuckers still on my ass, son?"

I wasn't used to hearing my dad swear. He was usually such a gentleman, but the adrenaline of the moment was turning him into his favorite macho movie star, Clint Eastwood. Dad was suddenly in his own *Dirty Harry* movie and loving every minute of it.

"Still there, Dad," I said.

Dad jerked the wheel, and the Roadtrek screeched into a sharp turn off the paved road. My mother and I collided, and fell to the floor as dishes and glasses from the cupboards rained down on us, smashing and shattering all around us.

"Clyde, my Fiestaware!"

But Dad had tuned her out, and was intently steering the RV down a narrow dirt path through a wooded area. The vehicle shook and rattled as it plowed over the bumpy terrain and managed to drown out my mother's own colorful language.

I grabbed the steel handle on the utensil drawer and used it to regain my balance and climb to my feet. But Dad threw us into another sharp turn, and the drawer flew completely out of the cupboard. A hail of forks, knives, and spoons fell clattering to the floor, much to my mother's horror.

Dad checked on us through the rearview mirror to make sure we weren't bleeding or unconscious. Then, with another gleeful smile breaking out on his face, he gripped the wheel of the RV tighter and barreled forward through the woods.

"Dad, where are we going?"

"Don't worry, son. I know these roads like my own backyard. Those ass wipes won't be able to keep up with us for long!"

The Town Car had fallen a bit behind but we were still in its sights. How we were going to lose them was a big question mark in my mind.

My mother was on her knees, carefully picking up the broken shards of her dinner plates and silently cursing my father.

We broke through a thicket of trees, and hit a gravel road that stretched across an empty field. In the middle were some train tracks. And a red light in front flashed at us to stop. But we didn't.

"Dad, I think you better slow down."

"Clyde, a train's coming," my mother said, her voice trembling, knowing in her heart he had no intention of stopping. After thirty-five years of marriage, she had developed an instinct.

A train approached from the east, clocking in at close to sixty miles an hour. The Town Car didn't see it. Dad slammed down on the accelerator until his foot pressed against the floor. We hurtled onward, and careened over the tracks just as the black-and-white-striped guard pole came down fast within an inch of our taillight.

I looked out the back window to see the two goons in the Town Car erupt in panic. As the driver hit the brakes, the car spun to the right, its passenger side door crashing into the metal guard pole. The mile-long Amtrak train zipped by, serving as a wall to separate us, and ensuring our escape.

Dad let up on the accelerator and, with a big, broad grin on his face, turned around and said, "Everybody okay back there?"

My mother was so filled with fury, she couldn't even open her mouth to yell at him.

I, on the other hand, was duly impressed. "Nice going, Dad. Thanks," I said.

"No problem, son." He tried to stay cool, but he couldn't stop beaming. The guy was proud of himself for making short work of the bad guys.

My cell phone rang. I checked the caller ID. It was Charlie. Finally. I hit the talk button, and sounding a bit too much like my mother for comfort, I said, "Where the hell have you been?"

Charlie's voice was calm. "Been working on a new case. I haven't been home much."

"I've been trying to call you. You're never home."

"I've been working a stakeout. It's been brutal," he said, and then after a long pause, added, "Isis has been nice enough to come over and walk Snickers while I've been at work."

Uh-oh. Isis was a talker and I knew what was coming next. "How come you didn't tell me you saw Wendell Butterworth again at Costco?"

"I tried, but I couldn't reach you."

"You could have called me at the precinct and left a message. I can't protect you from that psycho if you keep things from me."

"Well, I'm thousands of miles away from him now, so it's a moot point."

"I hate when you get like this. You don't want to face the fact that this guy is stalking you again, so you slip into a state of denial."

He was looking for a fight. He was still angry with me. I had two choices. Engage or retreat. It was better to retreat. At least for now. "You're right. I'm sorry."

He wasn't used to me backing down so quickly. But if we lapsed into a fight, then I wouldn't have been able to sweet-talk him into securing me some information.

"So I was wondering if you could run a license plate for me," I said.

"Why? What's going on down there?"

"Oh, it's nothing, really. Just a car I've spotted a couple of times while I've been out. I just want to make sure Wendell didn't find out I'm in Florida and follow me here."

My mother's ears perked up at the mention of Wendell. I had tried to keep Wendell's recent parole under wraps for fear they would be sick with worry.

"He's out?" she said, her voice tense.

I nodded, and then cupped the phone with the palm of my hand. "Yes, but it's nothing to worry about."

I took my hand away and said into the phone, "Florida plate. CASA CON 6."

"Hold on," Charlie said. "I'll run it through the computer."

While I waited, my mother stopped picking up her broken Fiestaware and hovered over me with a worried look on her face.

"When was he released?" she said.

"A few weeks ago," I said as nonchalantly as possible.

"You see him skulking around any?" my Dad asked, glancing through the rearview mirror as we barreled back toward my parents' house on the Sebastian River.

"Oh no," I lied. "He knows to keep his distance."

"I should hope so," my mother said.

"I'm just playing it safe," I said.

"I got a good look at those goons in the Town Car," my dad said. "Neither one looked anything like that creep Butterworth."

I instantly clamped my hand back over the phone's mouthpiece and prayed Charlie didn't hear.

"But you never know. He may have made some friends in prison," Dad said.

My mother shuddered at the suggestion.

Dad was still in Clint Eastwood mode. "I'll mow those fuckers down if they dare try anything."

"I'm probably just being paranoid," I said.

Charlie came back on the line. "Car's registered to a building contracting company in Fort Lauderdale. Casa Construction. It's one of twelve company cars."

"Why would somebody from a construction company chase us?"

"Chase? I thought you said you just spotted it a couple of times?" Charlie said.

All my little white lies inevitably came back to haunt me. "It followed us for a bit, but Dad lost them."

"I didn't know you were visiting your parents," Charlie said, his voice brightening. He was a big fan of Clyde and Priscilla.

"Just for the day. I have to get back to Miami for shooting on Monday."

"Promise me you'll call if anything weird happens," Charlie said.

"I will."

There was another long pause before I said hesitantly, "I miss you."

"I miss you too. Bye, babe."

Click. He was gone. And even in the company of my loving parents, without Charlie, I felt very alone.

Chapter 17

When I returned to the set on Monday, the cast and crew were abuzz over the reputed affair between Juan Carlos and his much older costar, Viveca. As Stella applied a pound of makeup to the slowly fading bruise on my right eye, she could barely contain herself.

"I heard they spent all weekend locked in a room at the Delano. I'm sure she paid. He couldn't afford a place like that on what he's making on this movie," she said.

I could have clued her in to the fact that Juan Carlos was also screwing around with a handsome young lad two hours north of Coral Gables, but decided it was wiser to play my cards close to the vest.

A mousy PA armed with a walkie-talkie poked her head into the messy makeup and hair trailer. "We're ready for you on the set, Jarrod," she said tentatively.

"Okay, thanks, Lucy," I said.

Furrowing her own brow, Stella studied my face and shrugged. "About as good as it's going to get, I'm afraid."

I yanked off the paper bib protecting my freshly pressed

wardrobe, and stood up. "You sure know how to talk to actors," I said.

Stella guffawed, and slapped my behind as I headed out of the trailer.

The outdoor campground set was bustling with activity as I made my way to my mark. A lighting technician gauged the shadows in the shot, and then repositioned a klieg light set up just outside of camera range.

Larry was engrossed in conversation with his director of photography, while over at the craft services table, Viveca picked up a Payday candy bar, unwrapped it, and playfully stuffed it into Juan Carlos's mouth. He let his hand slip down until it cupped her still firmly toned butt.

Caitlin dragged her devil child Simon onto the set, and spoke to him in urgent hushed whispers. I assumed she was bribing him. If he completed the scene without a tantrum, she would indulge his sweet tooth with all sorts of goodies. It was a pointless effort. Even if he did cry and make demands, she'd still give the little bugger anything he wanted.

"Good morning, Simon," I said with as much cheer as I could muster.

He snorted. No real words. Just a short, derisive snort. I hated him so much. It was going to take every last ounce of my acting ability to portray this little shit's loving father.

Larry bounded on the set. "Okay, this is a pretty straightforward scene," he said, talking with his hands. He turned to Simon. "You're pretty scared at this point. There have been rumors around the campground that four tourists have been found brutally slaughtered just half a mile away. You want to go home. But you know how much your dad's been looking forward to this quality time with you, so at the last minute you decide to stick it out. Serial killer be damned!" Larry then turned to me. "Jarrod, this is basically Simon's scene so just react accordingly."

Great. I was a glorified extra to this tiny terror. But I smiled and nodded enthusiastically. No one could ever accuse me of not being the utmost professional.

Larry ran back behind the camera, leaned over the shoulder of his DP to check the shot, took his seat in the director's chair with his name embroidered on the back, and yelled, "Action!"

Simon launched into his monologue, and as much as I loathe admitting it, he was pretty good. The kid had talent. I stayed in the moment, playing the doting parent who took great pains to understand what his frightened son was trying to tell him. Just as Simon reached the climax of his speech, making the choice to stay in the woods and risk a run-in with a madman, someone's cell phone rang.

"Cut!" Larry screamed, hurling his baseball cap to the ground in frustration. "Who the hell forgot to turn off their phone?"

Of course this time I knew it couldn't be mine. Since that disastrous first day, I had always left my cell phone in my gym bag, which I kept stored in the wardrobe trailer. The ringing continued. It was very close by. Everyone looked around frantically, trying to locate the source of the disturbance.

"It's coming out of his ass!" Simon screamed, pointing at the back pocket of my jeans. Oh God! I had taken it out to check my messages when I'd arrived on the set, and got so interested in watching Juan Carlos and Viveca paw each other at the craft services table that I had completely forgotten to put it back in my bag.

"Larry, I'm so sorry," I offered weakly.

"Just answer the goddamned phone! It's driving me nuts!" he said. "Everybody, take five!"

Simon glared at me and then ran after Larry. "I can't work like this, Mr. Levant! That was my best take on the whole picture and he ruined it!"

I was mortified, and looked around at everybody with an apologetic smile, but they scattered to keep their distance as if I were a walking virus.

I finally answered the phone. "Hello?"

"It's me," said Charlie. "Can you talk?"

Glancing around at the deserted set, I shrugged and said, "Sure. I've got five whole minutes."

"I did some digging on Casa Construction. Found out it's a legitimate business owned by none other than Javier Martinez."

"The Miami mob boss?"

"Yeah. I called my friend in South Beach and he said it's probably a front for all sorts of illegal activities. The question is why has a guy like Martinez suddenly taken an interest in *you*?"

I should have told Charlie that Martinez's henchmen probably spotted me staking out Juan Carlos, who was busy hooking up with a young stud at a dilapidated motel, and decided to find out if I was somehow connected to whatever business it was that had soured Martinez on Juan Carlos. But instead, I simply said, "Beats me."

"I don't like this one bit, Jarrod," Charlie said. "Martinez has a history of making people disappear, and if you're suddenly on his radar, that can't be good."

"I agree. So don't worry. I'll be really careful."

"Maybe I should book a flight down there."

"Charlie, I'm around people all the time on the set. I'm completely safe." Charlie wasn't a fan of my amateur sleuthing, so I didn't want to raise any hackles by confessing my recent Hardy Boy adventure.

"All right. But I have a very bad feeling, so if you get the slightest hint that someone's following you . . ."

"I'll call the police and then call you."

"Okay. What about Juan Carlos? Laurette's been calling three times a day to see if I've heard from you, and if you have any news."

I wasn't ready to fess up to the fact that Laurette's new husband was shacking up with more Floridians than the number who voted in the state's ill-fated 2000 presidential election. I needed to find out more about Juan Carlos's illicit affairs, his relationship with Austin Teboe, and the deadly business he had gotten mixed up in with Javier Martinez. The last thing I needed was Charlie reporting back to Laurette.

"I haven't seen much so far," I said. "But I can say he's got his fingers in a whole lot of pies."

Larry stalked back onto the set, his face covered in powdered sugar from the half-eaten donut in his hand. If looks could kill.

"Charlie, I've got to go. We're about to start shooting again."

I shut off the cell phone and was about to stuff it back into my jeans pocket when the mousy PA ran up to me, stuck out her hand, and said, "Larry wants me to hold on to your phone." Her eyes pleaded with me not to make a fuss.

I surrendered the phone without a word.

Caitlin brought her son back onto the set as an exasperated Larry screamed, "Are we finally ready to do this again?"

Trying my hardest to be contrite, I turned to Simon, who stepped on the piece of black tape designating his mark. "I'm really sorry I disrupted the take, Simon," I said.

He just snorted. And I clasped my hands behind my back until the urge to strangle his fat little neck subsided.

My scene with Simon wrapped just before lunch, and after grabbing a turkey and Swiss sandwich and a Diet Coke to go, I jumped in the Taurus and drove to Fort Lauderdale in just under twenty minutes. If I was ever going to unearth the mystery of why there was such bad blood between Juan Carlos and Mr. Martinez, the best course of action was to talk to the Miami mobster directly. After placing a call to Casa Construction, I was told by the very curt receptionist that Mr. Martinez was on-site today supervising an oceanfront construction job. She refused to disclose the exact address, but since the city's downtown area was relatively small, I decided to just drive around until I spotted a couple of guys in orange vests and a few cement trucks.

A viable alternative to the glittery, fast-paced South Beach, the city of Fort Lauderdale had reinvented itself by pouring over twenty-six million dollars into refurbishing its dreary and dated oceanfront. Now completely revitalized, the city was thriving in the tourist trade. And no doubt companies like Casa Construction were reaping the benefits.

It took all of ten minutes to lock in on a building under construction. And before I could even find a parking space across the street, I saw a big sign posted out front boasting the newest job by Casa Construction and a telephone number to call if you needed the city's number one building contractors.

I stepped out of the Taurus, locked it up tight, and made my way across the street to the site. There were a few workers sitting in folding chairs eating takeout from Taco Bell. I started to approach them when I spotted the two goons pull up in the familiar black Town Car. I ducked behind a giant green earthmover that had been parked about a hundred feet from the half-constructed building. They walked toward a white aluminum trailer that had been set up to serve as a makeshift on-site office. They rapped on the door, waited a few moments, and then entered. Just as the bigger one went to close the door behind him, I spotted Javier Martinez sitting behind a desk, sipping a Starbucks coffee. He had a strikingly handsome face marred by a scar down his left cheek. He was in his late forties and very fit from what I could tell. The door closed. I knew his goons Laurel and Hardy would never let me get close to the boss, so my best point of attack would be to sneak around to the back of the trailer, wait for his henchmen to leave, and then talk my way in, pretending to be some kind of representative of a company interested in acquiring the services of Casa Construction. That would only work, of course, if Martinez had yet to see a picture of me. I was banking on him knowing I was out there following Juan Carlos, but not knowing what I looked like.

I left my earthmover cover and circled around behind the

workers on their lunch break. I tiptoed behind the trailer, carefully making sure not to step on any rocks and debris that littered the site. Once I was positioned in the back, I picked up a discarded pail and set it down underneath a window. Stepping up on it, I raised my head high enough to peer inside. The two goons were both talking at once, presumably filling in their boss on their own surveillance activities. I had little doubt I was a part of the discussion. Martinez's back was to me, so I had no idea what his reaction was. After a few minutes, Martinez put down his Starbucks cup and waved Laurel and Hardy away. They both nodded, and then turned to leave, bumping shoulders in the small, enclosed space. They both tried going through the tiny door at the same time, almost crushing each other in the process. Finally, with a big sigh, the white guy allowed the Hispanic to pass through first. I couldn't tell if Martinez had even noticed this little comedy sketch.

Now was my chance. Martinez was alone. I stepped down off the pail and moved quickly to the edge of the trailer. I peeked out and spied Laurel and Hardy getting back in the Town Car. They drove away. I had to move fast. I thought up a fake name for the company I worked for and a nonexistent building project to bluff my way into Martinez's office, but before I could take a step toward the small aluminum door, a beefy hand clamped tightly over my mouth and yanked me back behind the trailer.

Chapter 18

Whoever it was who grabbed me spun me around and shoved me hard up against the chain link fence that separated the office trailer from the construction site. He kept his hand pressed firmly over my mouth as he hissed in my ear, "Not a word, or we're both dead."

When he was confident I was going to keep quiet, he removed his hand and stepped back so I could finally get a good look at him. He was a big guy, well over six feet, with a shaved head and a dragon tattoo on his left bicep. He looked like a studly action hero cut from the Vin Diesel mode, and even wore a tight Army green tank top, camouflage pants, and black scuffed boots. His handsome stubbled face was dark and tan, a perfect testament to his obvious Latin heritage. He was the sexy, strong, silent type, and boasted a killer body underneath his casual military attire. If I hadn't known better, I would have sworn I had just walked into the middle of a gay porn video.

"Who are you?" I whispered.

"Later. Right now I'm going to get you out of here."

"Not until I talk to Mr. Martinez."

He looked at me as if I were an idiot. And at the moment, that was exactly what I felt like.

"You say the wrong thing to Martinez," he said, "and you might wind up on a one-way cruise to Cuba as fish food."

I had heard that line before. It was probably from when I'd guest-starred on *Miami Vice* in the eighties as a child prodigy chess champion who competes in a high-stakes international tournament against the thirteen-year-old son of a Havana-based drug dealer Crocket and Tubbs were investigating.

"Trust me," he said. "Not a smart move. Now come with me."

I wasn't used to being told what I could or could not do. Charlie would certainly attest to that. But my instincts told me to trust this guy.

He gripped my arm with his enormous, thick hand and steered me toward an alley leading away from the site and to a vast empty parking lot on the other side of a neighboring building. He pulled a set of keys out of his pants, clicked a button, and unlocked a custom-made sleek blue van that was more buffed and built up than he was. He released my arm and crossed to the driver's side door.

"Get in," he said in a gruff, impatient voice.

"What about my car?"

"Forget it. Martinez's meatheads recognized it parked across the street when they came out. They're just waiting for you to come back so they can pounce. Now are we going to stand here and jabber all day or are you going to get in my van?"

I stopped just short of climbing in the passenger's seat. "You're not some serial killer, are you? I just had this vision of you knocking me over the head with a crowbar, and me waking up in some carved-out ditch in your basement handcuffed to a water heater."

He treated me to a barely perceptible smile. "Relax. You're safe with me."

I decided to go with it and jumped in the van next to him. As he thrust the key into the ignition and fired the van up, he turned and added with a swift wink, "Of course, if you don't stop looking at me with those ocean blue eyes of yours, I may have to pounce."

I was starting to like him. A lot.

We pulled out and drove south toward Hollywood, Florida, a tiny hamlet wedged between the two larger, more famous cities of Fort Lauderdale and Miami. We drove in silence for a few minutes. I was still reeling from his flattering remark regarding my eyes. Maybe it was a tactic to throw me off balance so I wouldn't give him any more trouble. I guess the *Hairspray* T-shirt I was wearing, from the Broadway show, had given my loosely guarded sexual orientation away.

"So what were you doing sneaking around Martinez's site?" I asked.

"Same as you," he said, keeping his eyes fixed on the road. "Trying to find some answers. I'm a private detective. Name's Bowie. Bowie Lassiter."

I wasn't sure how much I should reveal. He could be lying. He could be on Martinez's payroll and just pretending to be on the same side to find out how much I knew about Martinez's illegal operations. And once he had drained all the necessary information out of me, he would just slit my throat with the hunting knife that was sheathed in the leather pouch tied to his belt. Man, he was butch.

"I'm not pulling your chain. Check the glove box," he said.

I twisted the knob, and the compartment popped open, revealing a Florida private investigator's license with a laminated photo. It was definitely him. The picture didn't begin to do him justice. I tossed the identification back in the box and snapped it shut.

"Your turn," he said.

"I'm Jarrod Jarvis. I'm here working on a movie, and I have

reason to believe that one of my costars on the picture has some-how gotten mixed up with Javier Martinez."

"Too bad for him," Bowie said.

"I think he's crossed him in some way."

Bowie shook his head slowly. "Man, pissing off Martinez is like contracting a fatal disease. It's not a question of if you die, it's a question of when."

"How do you know so much about Martinez?"

"I grew up in the area. Everybody knows the family. They're famous for outfoxing the police, the lawyers, the city, and who-ever dares to stand up to them. Javier controls half the busi-nesses in South Florida. I've managed to stay out of his way until recently," he said.

"Why poke your nose into his business now?"

"A cousin of mine, Calvin, met Martinez's daughter at a night club about six months ago. Had no idea who she was. They started dating. She fell hard for him. But then, it slowly dawned on him who her father was, and it scared the hell out of him. He didn't want to be dragged into the mob, so he pulled back. And it broke her heart. Once Daddy found out that some local kid upset his only daughter, he made it his mission to be damn sure he'd never do it again."

"You mean he had him killed?"

Bowie shrugged. "Don't know. Calvin just up and disappeared one day. That was three months ago. But there's a long list of unsolved homicides that the cops are convinced are tied to Martinez's operations. So it's a good bet."

"I guess your family is counting on you to give them some closure," I said.

Bowie nodded, but didn't say anything else.

When we arrived in South Beach, I was about to instruct Bowie to drop me off at the drab Ritz Plaza where I was staying, but he veered off to the right and headed down the congested Ocean Boulevard and finally to a dock housing several retro houseboats from the swinging sixties. He pulled the van into a reserved parking space in front of a wide, flat, white houseboat in desperate need of a paint job. There was a deck on top for sunbathing. Stenciled on the bow was QE3. If his gratifying comment about my eyes hadn't betrayed him, a houseboat named after Queen Elizabeth would have certainly clued me in that all was not completely butch in boy land.

"Come on in," he said, waving me inside. "I'll make us a drink."

I dutifully followed, and once I crossed the threshold into the unknown, I found a messy, disheveled, old-fashioned bachelor pad with an unmade pull-out couch bed, empty pizza boxes and beer bottles, and a wide-screen TV that had been left on ESPN. As he crossed to the wet bar, Bowie scooped up the remote and hit the mute button so he could check out the scores while making us cocktails.

"Scotch okay?"

"Sure," I said, looking around and spotting a weathered, creased manila folder that rested on top of the worn, stained couch bed. On the front, someone had scribbled MARTINEZ FILE in pencil that was now smudged. I picked up the folder, flipped it open. There was a small stack of surveillance photos of Martinez leaving his various properties and businesses, dining out at some of South Beach's finest eateries, meeting with a few prominent city officials. When I reached the bottom of the pile, one picture caught my eye. I froze. A man and a woman in their early twenties playfully frolicked in the Miami surf, blissfully unaware of the shutterbug in their midst. Pulling it out of the folder, I crossed to the bar and shoved it in front of Bowie as he diluted the scotch with a splash of soda and then stirred the drinks with his index fingers.

"Who is this?" I asked.

Bowie studied the picture for a second and looked up at me. "That's Calvin. My cousin."

I pointed at the young woman. "And her?"

"That's Martinez's daughter."

I stared at the picture. There was no mistaking it. Martinez's daughter was Juan Carlos's fragile, emotionally distraught ex-flame Dominique.

Chapter 19

After three more scotches, the shock of Dominique's family tree began to wear off, and I was swimming in a sea of confusion. I may have uncovered some dirty secrets involving Juan Carlos's ill-fated love affair with the daughter of a Miami crime czar, but I still wasn't any closer to solving the murder of Austin Teboe. Charlie's friend had told him Teboe was once a chef on board Martinez's yacht, but had left his employ under a cloud of secrecy. Juan Carlos and Teboe met working at the Nexxt Café on Lincoln Road. Was it just a coincidence that Juan Carlos's coworker had worked for the father of his one-time girlfriend? Was it Teboe who had introduced them? The only thing I was pretty sure of at this point was the reason behind the rumored hit Martinez put out on Juan Carlos. Dominique was an emotional powder keg, and the blame for her recent breakdown rested squarely on Juan Carlos's shoulders. If I were Martinez, I'd hire an assassin to rub him out too.

Bowie folded up his mess of a sofa bed, and the two of us sat side by side on the dusty, worn, patched-up converted couch, our feet resting on the cracked and scuffed coffee table. I polished off the last of my scotch.

"So why would Juan Carlos be stupid enough to accept a movie role down here in Florida knowing Martinez and his men are just lying in wait to off his ass?" Bowie asked.

"Someone must be protecting him," I said.

"Dominique?"

"Maybe. But one minute he's made her suicidal and the next they're cooing and kissing like newlyweds. It's hard to get a good read on her. Although he's certainly got some kind of guardian angel looking after him," I said. "Actually, he's got a lot of little angels around him. The guy gets more action than the backroom of a Bangkok massage parlor."

Bowie laughed, drained the last of his own scotch, and grabbed the nearly empty bottle of Johnnie Walker Black Label off the coffee table. I covered the rim of my glass with my hand.

"Please," I said. "One more and I won't be responsible for my actions."

"Works for me," Bowie said as he playfully tried to fill up my glass again.

He was smart and swarthy and funny and sexy, and I knew it was time for me to get the hell out of there. I set my glass down and stood up. "Think it's safe to go retrieve my car now?"

A disappointed look flashed over Bowie's face, but he quickly replaced it with a smile. "Should be. But I'll take you there just to make sure everything's cool."

"You okay to drive?" I said.

Bowie nodded, grabbed the keys to his van off the cluttered wet bar, and we headed out.

I felt a pang of guilt as we drove north back to Fort Lauderdale. Bowie and I had hit it off, and I could tell there was some simmering chemistry between us. He was definitely interested. So why didn't I mention I was already involved with a terrific guy back in Los Angeles? Charlie and I had been enjoying a wonderful, fulfilling monogamous relationship for the past three years, and I never once had the urge to jeopardize it in any way. But it gnawed at me that I didn't bring him up. Not once. What did that mean? Fortunately I was sober enough not to do something stupid that I would live to regret despite the not-so-subtle hints from my handsome, musclebound host.

I was paralyzed by my attraction to Bowie and how bad it made me feel, so he did most of the talking on the twenty-minute drive back to my car. I learned that he'd been born into a large Cuban family in the heavily Latino-populated city of Coral Gables. He figured out he was gay when he was fifteen and on the football team and wasn't too anxious to let go after tackling an opponent. When he got out of high school, he dabbled in a couple of careers before joining the Navy to ease some of the burden his parents had in supporting such a big brood. He wound up joining the Seals and partook in a number of top-secret missions worldwide before he fell victim to the military's "Don't Ask, Don't Tell" policy. He got involved with an officer and felt no obligation to hide it from anybody. The officer, though, turned out to be married with four children, a fact he kept hidden from Bowie. To save himself from a discharge, the officer reported Bowie as a homo, and he was promptly drummed out despite a stellar record. So much for a wobbly, ineffective policy to protect our gay military personnel. Most critics claim it's even worse now than before "Don't Ask, Don't Tell." Bowie moved back home, got his private detective's license, sank his life savings into buying the *QE3*, and opened up his own shop. His gumshoe work had been paying the bills for five years. Except when he took on cases for free like finding his cousin Calvin, who may or may not have fallen victim to Martinez's dirty doings.

When we reached Fort Lauderdale's oceanfront, Bowie shut off the headlights as we rolled to a stop half a block from my rented Taurus. It was dark and windy with just one lone street lamp illuminating the quiet and deserted construction site.

Bowie and I sat quietly scanning the area for any sign of Laurel and Hardy. They had obviously long given up on me returning to my car. It seemed pretty safe now.

"Thanks for everything, Bowie," I said and reached for the door handle.

"You know where to reach me if you need anything," he said, and then patted my knee with his hand. "I mean it. Anything."

He let his hand linger a moment on my knee. I froze, having no idea what to say. So I giggled. Like a damn schoolgirl. God, I hated when I did that. It was a nervous response and I did it all the time. Some casting directors used to call me "Dr. Giggles" after an obscure horror flick starring the actor who played the retarded office boy on *L.A. Law* in the eighties. It was a humiliating name, and I learned fast to control my annoying little giggle fits during auditions. But during moments like this, when a hot-looking ex–Navy Seal had his hand on my knee, well, there was just no holding back. It was like a bad case of the hiccups.

"Good night," I said, practically diving out of the car. He watched as I unlocked the Taurus and got behind the wheel. Before I turned the key, I imagined a stack of dynamite strapped to the bottom ready to blow me up at the turn of the ignition, but decided Martinez wouldn't try something like that before he found out my connection to Juan Carlos. I took a chance. The car roared to life before settling into a steady hum. I waved to Bowie, who sat in his van watching me, and hastily peeled away, heading straight for the Ritz Plaza in South Beach.

When I arrived back in the Ritz's "desperate to be as hip as its neighboring hotels" lobby, I took the elevator to my own floor, the same floor Juan Carlos was on. I marched down to his suite and rapped on the door. It was just after midnight. After a moment, I heard a familiar voice answer from inside.

"Who is it?"

"It's me, Juan Carlos, Jarrod. I'd like to talk to you."

"It's late. Can't it wait until tomorrow?"

"No. I'd really like to say this now."

I heard him unhook the safety latch and open the door halfway. He was naked except for a white cotton towel draped around his waist. He had a half-eaten green apple in his hand and a sharp pocketknife to slice it with.

"What?" he said huffily.

"I know who she is."

"Who?"

"Dominique. I know she's Javier Martinez's daughter."

I turned to go.

"Wait. Who's Javier Martinez?" His face feigned innocence.

"Don't," I said.

"Don't what?"

"Don't pretend you don't have a clue what I'm talking about. I know you have a history with Austin Teboe at the Nexxt Café. I know you had an affair with Dominique and broke her heart and pissed off her father, who unfortunately for you is a violence-prone mob boss. And I know you're cheating on Laurette with both men and women."

His face darkened. I was becoming more of a problem than he had anticipated. He took a big bite out of his apple and let the juice run down the corners of his mouth. Then he casually waved the pocketknife in front of me as he spoke.

"You think you know everything, don't you?"

"No. I still don't know why you killed Austin Teboe."

"How many times do I have to tell you? I didn't kill anyone!" he said, gripping the handle of his knife so hard, I thought his knuckles would pop out of his skin.

"Well, then who did?"

"I don't know. I'm as much in the dark as you."

I nodded, not saying a word, wanting to let the deafening silence hang in the air. Juan Carlos, ever the actor, couldn't let the silence go for too long. It might force him to reflect on his actions.

"I don't know who is gossiping about who I may or may not be sleeping with, but it's bullshit, you hear me? Bullshit!"

"I saw you at the Sand Drift Motel. He was a cutie."

His face went pale.

"And I wasn't the only one," I said. "A couple of guys on Martinez's payroll were there for the show too."

I thought he was going to faint. He fell against the door, and grabbed the knob to steady himself.

"They . . . they saw me with . . . him?"

"Yeah, they did," I said with a twinge of insincere sympathy. "Bummer."

Juan Carlos dropped the apple, and his hand shot out and grabbed my arm, pulling me closer to the door. In the other hand, the sharp tip of the pocketknife was a quarter of an inch from my belly.

"Don't mention any of this to anybody, do you hear me?" Juan Carlos said, his voice full of desperation. "Promise me, Jarrod."

"Laurette is my best friend," I said as I kept my eyes focused on the knife's blade. I now felt it straining against my skin just to the right of my belly button. It was about to puncture through and draw blood.

I looked up into his eyes. They were wild with fear. He was on the edge. And for a minute I was afraid I had overplayed my hand. As the knife pressed into my gut, I suddenly had the sick feeling I was about to befall the same fate as Austin Teboe.

Suddenly a woman's voice came drifting out from the bathroom inside Juan Carlos's room. "Darling, is it room service? Did you order more wine?"

It was Viveca. I caught just a glimpse of her as she strolled toward the door in a Victoria's Secret red lace bra and panties. For a woman in her late forties, she still looked like she could easily grace the cover of their summer catalog. I was impressed.

Panicked, Juan Carlos withdrew the knife and seethed, "Good night, Jarrod." He slammed the door in my face.

I just stood there. The more I baited Juan Carlos, the more nervous he got. And with Juan Carlos ready to snap under the pressure, there was no telling whom he would take down with him. As I lifted my *Hairspray* T-shirt to see a trickle of blood slide down my belly and stain the elastic band of my Calvin Klein briefs, I was pretty sure I would be the first one on his list.

Chapter 20

After sticking a Band-Aid on my slight flesh wound in my room, I checked my messages on the cell. I only had one, from my parents. My mother cooed about how nice it was to see me if only briefly, and my father offered a few more well-thought-out theories in the Austin Teboe murder. I picked up the TV remote and started channel flipping. I was restless and couldn't sleep, and finally after shelling out twelve bucks for a pay-per-view showing of the Martin Lawrence stinker *Big Momma's House*, with Martin in drag, I was able to catch a couple of hours of sleep before the phone startled me awake. I reached out from under the covers, snatched the receiver from its cradle, and grunted.

"Good morning, Jarrod! Rise and shine!" a cheery voice chirped. It was Amy Joe, the perky production assistant.

I rubbed my eyes, shook my head, and tried focusing on the clock: 5:32 A.M.

"Amy Jo, it's really early," I said, trying to maintain my cool, even though I wanted to rip into her for waking me up after I had finally gotten to sleep.

"I know. We're running late. I'm waiting for you downstairs in the van."

"But I don't shoot today."

"Yes, you do. Today's your big death scene."

"No. I'm pretty sure that's tomorrow," I said.

"I think you better check your production schedule, Jarrod," she said.

"Hold on." I put the phone down, crawled out of bed, and crossed to the cheaply made acrylic desk near the window. I had laid out the week's production schedule sheets. I picked up the first one and examined it. Just as I had thought. Today was a few simple exterior scenes with the extra they had hired to play the homicidal maniac. Underneath it was tomorrow's schedule, which listed my last scene in the movie. A particularly bloody affair involving a meat cleaver and my skull.

I walked back over and picked up the phone off the night table. "I'm looking right at today's call sheet, Amy Jo, and I'm not scheduled to work."

"Check the date."

"March fifteenth."

"That's tomorrow's date, Jarrod. Look at the other page. The one where you *are* scheduled to work."

"March fourteenth."

"Bingo!"

My heart stopped. I had somehow inverted the pages when Amy Jo had slipped them under my door. Today was my most important day on the entire shoot, and I was operating on two hours' sleep. Not to mention the fact I hadn't even memorized any dialogue. I was screwed.

"Well, what do you know? You're right. Um, I'm going to need a little time up here," I said with a nervous giggle.

There was a long pause on the other end. And then, with just a hint of panic in her tone, Amy Jo said, "Are you trying to tell me you're not ready? Your call time is in ten minutes and it's a twenty-minute drive to the set."

"I'll be right down."

I slammed down the phone and raced into the shower, suppressing a scream as the ice-cold torrent hit my bare skin. I washed as fast as I could with some cheap no-brand soap supplied by the Ritz Plaza, scrubbed a dollop of Nioxin Bionutrient Scalp Therapy into my locks (an aging actor in his thirties needs a good hair stimulant), and quickly dried off. As I bolted for my closet, I jammed my left foot into the sliding glass door and howled like a three-year-old at Disneyland who didn't get his picture taken with Ariel. But I didn't slow down. I pulled on some jeans, threw on my soiled *Hairspray* T-shirt, stepped into a pair of Docksiders, and was good to go.

When I bounded out of the lobby and spotted Amy Jo's maroon van, I could tell from the look on her face that the hint of panic I had detected in her voice had now grown into a full-blown meltdown.

"Hurry up! Let's go! Let's go!" she barked.

I hopped into the passenger's seat, and we squealed away before I had a chance to even buckle up.

"I'm really sorry, Amy Jo," I said.

"No problem," she lied. "But if I get fired over this, would you put in a good word for me on your next movie?"

"They're not going to fire you. I'll make sure they know this is my fault," I said, knowing full well that at the bottom of the totem pole, she would bear the brunt of everybody's wrath. I kept thinking, "They can't fire her, because after this movie I'll probably never work again so I won't ever be able to give her any kind of recommendation."

We broke speed records to reach the Coral Gables campground set. Amy Jo was impressive maneuvering expertly in and out of traffic. As we pulled up to the makeup and hair trailer, I noticed Stella standing outside, sucking on a Virginia Slim and tapping her foot angrily.

"You are so fucking late," she bellowed.

"I know, I know. Don't blame Amy Jo. I didn't know I was shooting today," I said.

She hauled me into the trailer and started slapping globs of base on my face as I picked up some sides off the counter and read them over. Luckily there wasn't a lot of dialogue in my pivotal death scene. Just a lot of screaming and lines like, "Run, Joey, run!" as I sacrifice myself to save my son. I wondered if the "Run, Joey, run!" line was an homage to that old seventies ballad by David Geddes. That was before I realized there would actually have to be a modicum of depth required in the script, and depth was one thing this opus sorely lacked.

Amy Jo poked her head inside the trailer. "They're ready for you on set, Jarrod," she said.

"Jesus, I haven't even done your hair," Stella said. "Forget it. I'll do it in final touchups. You better go, Jarrod, before Larry starts yelling."

I dashed out of the trailer and over to the campground set, where the crew waited for me. Viveca, in a flattering yellow sundress, flirted with the crew as I said my good mornings and walked over to my mark. The lighting technician and a couple of his assistants immediately buzzed around me to make sure I was lit properly.

Viveca turned and offered me a bright smile. "Good morning, Jarrod."

I was sure this was the first time she had ever deigned to speak to me. "Good morning."

"Sleep well?" she cooed.

"Not really, no."

"Me neither. I was up *all* night," she said with a playful wink. We both knew where she was last night, and she seemed mighty proud of it. I guess it was our little secret. I didn't know much about Viveca, nor was I anxious to find out more. She struck me as too flighty and girlish for a woman in her late forties or early fifties. Her behavior annoyed me, and it took every last ounce of self-control not to offer her my opinion. But I wasn't about to start yet another feud with a costar. I was in enough trouble already.

So I plastered a conspiratorial smile on my face. "That's too bad you didn't get any sleep. Must have been something you ate," I said, returning her wink. "You go, girl."

She erupted in laughter. "You're so naughty. I love you." I had called her a "girl" so in her mind we were now the best of friends.

Larry ambled onto the set, gave me the once-over, and then turned his head and yelled, "Stella, get over here and do something with his hair! And can we get some drops for his eyes? They're all bloodshot. He looks like shit." Larry looked back at me suspiciously. "What's the matter? You just get up?"

"Of course not. I just thought after the turmoil and trauma my son and I have been through up to this point in the story, I would be looking awfully run-down and exhausted."

"Christ, don't tell me you're one of those method actors," Larry said, making a big show of rolling his eyes. Stella was all over me now with her eyeliner pencil and a wooden brush that she wrenched through my hair.

"No," I said, "I just want to be truthful."

"Okay. Whatever. Let's shoot this." Larry left momentarily to inspect the shot.

Stella gently placed her hand above my eyes and let loose with a shot of Alberto VO5 hairspray to hold my freshly combed locks in place. "You sure pulled that one out of your ass," she said, smirking.

"Do you think he bought it?"

"For him not to, he'd have to stop thinking about himself for one second. And we both know that's never going to happen."

Stella stepped back and nodded, satisfied with her handiwork.

We were ready to roll. I looked around for the tiny terror playing my son, but he was nowhere to be seen. "Where's Simon?"

Larry shuffled back over to me. "We don't need him for this scene. We'll have Maggie, the script coordinator, read his dialogue off camera. This is all about you and the killer, finally face to face." Larry glanced around the set. "Where is he, by the way?"

A grip pointed to a large man sitting in a spare director's chair. He wore a red and black plaid hunting jacket, Army-issue green pants, and a pair of black boots. A cartoon mask of Elmer Fudd covered his face. That was a last-minute touch added by Larry. He didn't want the killer's identity to be revealed until the end, but he didn't want the headache of hiding his face throughout the movie. So in the tradition of *Friday the 13th* and *Nightmare on Elm Street* (a couple of Larry's childhood favorites), he gave the killer a mask. And Elmer, in Larry's mind, was an inspired choice. After all, Elmer Fudd was a hunter who spent most of his time chasing after Bugs Bunny. But he was never able to catch him. Larry explained to us all in the hotel bar one night early on in the production that all of our characters represented all the other rabbits in the woods, and Elmer Fudd, who had spent years unsuccessfully hunting Bugs, was now going to take his frustration out on all of us. He'd kill and kill again, skin a whole slew of bunnies, but he would never be satisfied because none of us was truly Bugs Bunny, the elusive prey he could never beat. Larry saw the mask as the perfect symbol for the story he wanted to tell. I saw it as too many Jell-O shots after a long day of shooting.

"You ready to do this, big guy?" Larry called to the masked actor.

He nodded, stood up, and lumbered over to us. He carried a machete made of rubber. Larry turned quickly and whispered frantically in my ear, "The guy we hired in LA went AWOL on us, and we just hired this guy yesterday locally, but I can't remember his name, so I just call him big guy, okay?"

"Okay," I said as I reached out to shake Elmer Fudd's hand. "Hi, I'm Jarrod. Nice to meet you."

"I'm Elmer Fudd," he said in a deep, scratchy voice. Everyone laughed appreciatively. Larry slapped him on the back.

"You feeling confident about what we're going to do here?"

Elmer nodded. Larry clasped his hands together and addressed us both. "Good. Now, your son's been lost in the woods for almost a day. The whole campground has risked their lives searching the area, knowing a maniac is loose somewhere out there. You finally find him. Kneel down to hug him. Big reunion. Blah, blah, blah. The kid screams bloody murder. You turn to see Elmer standing over you. You tell the kid to run. He does. Elmer pushes you down on the ground with his boot. You do your "No, please, no!" line, and then he starts whacking chunks off your face with the machete. Everybody cool with that?"

"Sounds simple enough," I said.

"Excellent. We can wrap this scene up by lunch," Larry said as he jogged back over to the camera and slid into his director's chair. As the makeup and hair people rushed in for final touchups and the cameras began rolling, I tried again with my new costar.

"I'm sorry, I didn't catch your name?"

He didn't answer me. The goofy face of Elmer Fudd simply stared at me. And the open slits in the eyes weren't big enough for me to see anything behind it.

"Quiet on the set, please!" said the assistant director.

"We're rolling," said the cameraman.

"And action!" roared Larry.

Maggie the script coordinator, a been-there, done-that, bored veteran in her late forties, who had worked on countless productions, read Simon's lines.

"Daddy, look out, he's right behind you," she said flatly, with all the enthusiasm and dedication of a DMV lifer.

Looking at empty air in front of me since the boy playing my son was absent, I shot out my hand and shrieked, "Run, Joey, run!"

"No, Dad, not without you," Maggie read directly from the script. A coma patient would have given more of a performance.

I turned to see Elmer Fudd raising the rubber machete over his head.

"No, please don't!" Shoot. As the words came out, I realized the correct line was "No, please, no!" and I hated disrespecting the writer's words, but Larry didn't yell "Cut!" so I kept going.

Elmer pressed the heel of his boot on my chest and shoved me down so I was on my back, struggling and wriggling like an upended cockroach. The guy pressed harder with his boot to the point where I could barely breathe. Either he was truly in the moment or he just didn't like me. I did what the script called for and covered my face with my hands and released a guttural wail. Elmer slashed down seven times with his rubber machete. He was supposed to stop a couple inches short of my head, but instead he managed to whack me five out of seven hits. Since this was a master shot, Larry had decided not to use the blood squibs that would illustrate my head coming apart. He was saving those for the close-ups.

"And . . . cut!" Larry said. He leapt up and excitedly ran over to us. "Beautiful! Just beautiful."

I was happy he was pleased. It would make up for some of my blunders so far, such as my disruptive cell phone and my call time tardiness.

Larry threw his arms around Elmer Fudd. "I love you, man. You're so fucking scary."

I waited for Larry to compliment me, but he was too preoccupied showering praise on my costar. "Man, I believed you were a nut job. I really did. You're a natural."

I tugged on Larry's sweatshirt. "Need me to make any adjustments for the next take?"

Larry threw me a cursory glance, suddenly aware of my presence. "No, Jarrod, that was fine."

I had come to the set totally unprepared so it shouldn't have bugged me that I was all but ignored. But it did. Actors live with so much rejection they crave any kind of positive reinforcement. We want everything we do to be adored and we have a need to be constantly showered with accolades as if every day we were the special guest on James Lipton's *Inside the Actor's Studio* series.

"I want to watch the playback on the monitor and then we'll go again," Larry said as he hustled back over to the phalanx of cameras and film equipment.

I turned to Elmer. "Nice job."

"Thanks," he said in his low, barely audible, raspy voice.

"For a minute there, I thought you were really having fun killing me."

Elmer removed his mask to finally reveal himself. Wendell Butterworth stood there, leering at me. His grotesque face was decorated with a sick, disturbing smile.

Chapter 21

Wendell Butterworth just stood there grinning as I sent all the furry little creatures of the forest scattering with my yelling. The startled crew descended upon us, and after I explained just who the man in the Elmer Fudd mask was, Larry marched up to him, poked a finger in his face, and with a quiet authority said, "You're fired. I don't ever want to see you near this set again, or I'll call the cops."

A couple of burly grips escorted him off the set.

"Can't we have him arrested?"

"For what?" Larry asked.

"I don't know. For impersonating an extra or something."

Larry put a comforting arm around my shoulder. "I don't think so, Jarrod. He gave us his correct name and social security number when we cast him."

I nodded, completely shaken. Now that he was sprung from prison, Wendell was never going to leave me alone.

"Jarrod, I'm so sorry," Larry said. "I thought he was a local. I hired him because of his intimidating bulk."

"It's okay, Larry, you couldn't have known."

Juan Carlos had arrived on the set just in time to witness the whole messy scene. He took great pleasure in watching my melt-down. Not even Viveca's little kisses on his shoulder or playful butt squeezes could draw his attention from me. After the initial flurry of drama had died down, Juan Carlos sauntered over and said with a self-satisfied smile, "Well, well, well. Jarrod has a stalker." He took a long sip of his coffee. "Maybe now *you'll* get a little taste of what it feels like to have someone following you around, watching your every move. How ironic."

"You know what amazes me the most, Juan Carlos?" I said, red-faced but remaining calm.

"What's that?" he said.

"That you actually know the definition of ironic, and can use it in a sentence."

He didn't like that one. He almost hurled his cup of coffee in my face. But he thought better of it, and strutted off in a huff.

Larry declared the campground a closed set for the duration of the shoot, and security guards were hired to patrol all access routes into the wooded park. Shooting resumed without inci-dent, I finished my death scene with a strapping young grip fill-ing in as Elmer Fudd, and we were wrapped by five-thirty in the afternoon. Larry was impressed with my performance (I didn't have to dig deep to find a lot of fear to play), and as the cast and crew dispersed for the day to various restaurants and bars, I was left alone in my trailer to change clothes and head back to the Ritz Plaza alone.

My cell phone rang. I pressed the talk button and cradled the phone between my left shoulder and ear as I stuffed my script and spare shirts into a gym bag.

"Hey, babe, just checking up on you," Charlie said. "Have a good day?"

I didn't want to run crying to Charlie every time something scared me. I had been standing up for myself since I was a little kid on the playground cornered by a gang of bullies, and I cer-tainly was not about to become one of those whiny, victimized boyfriends who always rely on their better half to get through everything. On the other hand, this was the third time Wendell Butterworth had shown up, and I couldn't take it anymore.

"He's here, Charlie. He's here in Florida."

"Who?"

"Wendell Butterworth."

"Are you kidding me?"

I told him the whole ugly scene on the set with Wendell pretending to split my head open with a rubber machete while wearing an Elmer Fudd mask.

"Christ, Jarrod, why didn't you call me the minute it happened?"

"Because I didn't want to disrupt shooting. We're half a day behind schedule as it is."

"Where is he now?"

"I don't know. They tossed him off the set immediately. He could be anywhere."

Charlie took a deep breath, and then said, "Okay, I don't want you going back to that hotel by yourself. I want you to stay with someone tonight."

I wasn't sure who that someone could be. I had been so single-minded in my mission to expose Juan Carlos as a philanderer and connect him to the Austin Teboe murder that I hadn't exactly made a lot of burgeoning friendships on the set. Amy Jo was ticked off at me for being late this morning. Stella had already mentioned she was going up to Palm Beach to pal around with some friends. Juan Carlos despised me so it was safe to assume his two female lovers, Viveca and Dominique, were in the same camp. Larry was my boss, and not about to do me any favors after I'd mucked up two takes of his movie with my cell phone. And Simon was the spawn of Satan and more dangerous in my mind than Wendell Butterworth. My parents were too far away. After racking my brain, there was really only one person whom I would feel safe staying with tonight and who would be open to putting me up.

"You got somebody you can crash with?" Charlie asked.

"Yes," I said. "Yes, I think I do."

"Good. I want you to call me when you get there so I know you made it."

"Okay."

"The chief is on the other line. I've got to go. Call me."

"Charlie . . . ?"

But he was gone. And I was alone again.

I finished packing up my gym bag, and hurried down the wooded path toward the parking lot. The Taurus was the last vehicle left. I was surprised no one had offered to stay with me until I was ready to leave given the dramatic events that happened earlier, but I wasn't about to win any popularity contests on this job.

I jumped behind the wheel and drove straight into the glittery lights of South Beach. I didn't stop until I reached a parking space marked VISITOR in front of a boat slip off Ocean Avenue occupied by the *QE3* houseboat.

As I approached the front door, I suddenly felt foolish. What was I doing? I was a grown man who could take care of myself, and here I was about to ask a complete stranger to put me up because I was too afraid to spend the night alone. Despite Charlie's orders, I wasn't going to be some kind of damsel in distress. No. I would go back to my hotel room, order a nice big juicy steak so I would have a sharp knife to defend myself with, and tough it out. I walked back to the Taurus and was about to get in when the door to the houseboat flew open. Bowie stood there wearing a pair of shorts and nothing else. The lights from the marina illuminated every contour of his muscular torso. Damn. It was going to be a lot harder to leave now.

"I thought that was you. I was making some dinner and saw

you through the kitchen window," he said, a warm smile on his face.

"I . . . I don't want to bother you. Go back to what you were doing."

"I've made enough for two. Why don't you come in?"

I wanted to. I really did. But it didn't feel right. No. I had to leave now.

But then again, I would just be doing what Charlie wanted me to do. Right? He was adamant. He didn't want me by myself tonight. I would be openly defying the wishes of my boyfriend. And what would that say about our relationship? I had gone against Charlie enough lately. It was time I started to listen to him. At least that was how I convinced myself it would be okay to spend the evening with Bowie Lassiter.

"Thank you," I said. "I'd love to."

Bowie opened the door wide, welcoming me inside.

After a feast of seafood pasta, spinach salad, and warm choco-late cake, Bowie and I settled down on his couch to polish off the last of our third bottle of Chardonnay, our bellies stuffed and our eyes drowsy. Over dinner I had told him about the Wendell Butterworth drama, and he was happy to know I trusted him enough to put myself in his hands. Figuratively, of course.

As we sat on the couch, our knees slightly brushed against each other's. I felt woozy and naughty and none of that was good. I had to go to bed. Alone.

"Bowie, I really appreciate you letting me stay here," I said, as I yanked my knee away from his so they were no longer touch-ing.

"I have to admit," he said with a sly smile, "I was pretty stoked when I saw you loitering outside the houseboat."

"Loitering?" I said, feigning indignation. "I wasn't loitering."

"Yes, you were. You were debating with yourself about whether or not you were going to come in."

How humiliating. He was completely aware of my attraction to him.

"But I'm glad things worked out the way they did," he said as he reached out and planted a hand on my knee, drawing it back closer to his. Then, using my knee to steady himself, Bowie leaned in slowly. His lips were about to touch mine when suddenly I jerked back, spilling my wine all over his couch.

"Oh, damn, I'm so sorry," I said, wiping the already stained upholstery with my hand.

"Don't worry about it. It's white wine. And the couch is pretty much trashed already if you hadn't noticed," he said with a chuckle.

Our eyes met, and he took my hand. "Hey, I'm sorry if I was moving too fast for you. I just really like you a lot."

"Bowie, I'm so sorry. But I have to tell you, I'm in a relationship."

"Oh," he said.

"I'm not going to say you got the wrong impression. I gave you the impression I wanted you to have. I didn't mention it before on purpose, and I feel lousy about that."

"It's cool. Don't worry about it." He was trying hard not to look disappointed, but was having a difficult time of it.

My cell phone chirped from inside my coat pocket.

"Excuse me," I said.

"Sure." He stood up and carried the empty bottle of Chardonnay into the kitchen. I fumbled through the pockets of my coat before finding the one storing my cell phone.

"Hello?" I said.

"Hey, babe," Charlie said. "Did you get to your friend's safely?"

"Yes," I said. "I'm here now."

"Good. You don't know how much better that makes me feel."

"I'll call you tomorrow from the set."

"No need to do that. I'll be there by then."

"What do you mean?"

"I'm at the airport now," Charlie said. "I'm taking an overnight flight to Miami that arrives in the morning. I'll be there by six."

"Charlie, really, you don't have to—"

"I know I don't have to," he said. "I want to. I want to see you. And I want to be there with you if that freak pops up again."

I glanced over at Bowie. He was scraping a few stray noodles from the seafood pasta off our plates into the garbage can before stacking the dirty dishes in the sink. He caught me looking and I swiftly averted my eyes.

"So where are you?" Charlie asked. "I'll just come there to pick you up."

"No," I said much too quickly. "Let's meet back at the hotel. The Ritz Plaza. You have the address."

"Okay, sounds good, babe. Sleep well."

"Good night, Charlie."

I was about to hang up when I heard his voice pipe up again. "Wait. What's the name and number of your friend so I can call in case the flight's late or something?"

I hesitated, but in the interest of full disclosure, I said. "Bowie Lassiter."

"Are you serious?" he said.

"Yes. He lives off Ocean Avenue—"

"On a houseboat called the *QE3*."

"How did you know?"

"Jarrod, that's my friend. The one in Miami who I've been calling for information."

I could almost hear God laughing.

Chapter 22

"You're *that* actor? Charlie's boyfriend?" Bowie said as he grabbed his wineglass, swished the last of his Chardonnay around, and then swallowed it in one big gulp.

"Small world, isn't it?" I said, instantly embarrassed by the lameness of my response.

I was still reeling from the shock. So was Bowie. After hanging up with Charlie, I knew I had to disclose everything. I didn't want any secrets coming back to haunt me. Secrets inevitably have a way of doing that.

"It makes sense now that I think about it," Bowie said. "Charlie called me to find out the dirt on Martinez, and then I run into you spying on him. Kind of funny we didn't figure it out before."

"Yeah, it's a laugh riot," I said. I wanted to get out of there. I was so consumed by guilt and confusion, and now with Charlie winging his way south, I had a desperate need to regroup. "Bowie—"

"Hey," he said, stopping me. "No worries. You were up front with me. You told me you were involved before anything happened. Everything's cool."

"So you and Charlie are old friends?"

"Yeah," he said with a smile. "*Just* old friends."

"He's on his way to Florida," I said. "I told him I'd meet him at the hotel when he gets here in the morning."

"What about this Butterworth dude?" he said.

"If I'm lucky, right now he's waiting for me in my hotel room with a loaded pistol, ready to put me out of my misery."

Bowie chuckled. "Seriously, you want me to escort you back there to make sure it's safe?"

Handsome *and* chivalrous. Charlie was on his way. Charlie was on his way. I had to keep telling myself that. "No. I'm a big boy. I can take care of myself." Yeah, right. The first sign of trouble, and I hightailed it over to a Navy Seal's houseboat to hide out. "Thanks for dinner. I had a great time."

"Me too," he said.

He walked me to the door. I resisted the urge to give him a hug good night. Hugs can lead to a kiss. And one kiss can lead to more kisses. And kisses can lead to . . . well, then you're screwed. Literally.

"Good night," I said.

"Good night, Jarrod."

I slipped behind the wheel of the Taurus, and as I drove back up Ocean Avenue toward the Ritz Plaza, I glanced through the rearview mirror and saw him standing in the doorway of the houseboat, watching me. He was still there when I turned right onto a side street, heading for Collins Avenue.

I got back to my hotel room without incident. Apparently Wendell had suspended his stalking activities for the night. Even delusional nutcases need their beauty sleep.

I climbed into bed, picked up my *Creeps* script off the night table, and turned to an earmarked page a third of the way through it to study the scene of me arriving at the campground with my son. We were scheduled to shoot it the day after tomorrow, and I needed to memorize the dialogue. Movie scenes are almost always shot out of sequence. The order is designed to accommodate a wide variety of considerations such as location availability and actors' schedules. So it was not unusual that my death scene was in the can before my first appearance in the movie. After reading it through a few times, my eyelids became heavy, and I fought to keep them open, but within moments I had drifted off to sleep.

I shot up at the sound of the phone ringing. No. It couldn't be Amy Jo to pick me up. I had gone over the production schedule five times to make sure I wasn't shooting today. "Please, God, don't be Amy Jo!" I thought as I reached across for the phone.

"Hello?"

"Hi, babe, it's me," said a reassuring voice. Charlie.

"Hey, how was your flight?"

"Good. We're downstairs. What room are you in?"

"Eight-oh-six," I said.

"Okay, we'll be right up."

Click. Wait a minute. "*We'll* be right up?" Charlie wasn't alone? Had he gone to his old pal Bowie's place first to pick him up? Were we going to be the happy threesome sightseeing around South Beach? I felt queasy, and those lingering pangs of guilt only exacerbated my upset stomach.

I threw on a black and white *Creeps* sweatshirt that Larry had handed out to the cast and crew on the first day of production, and slipped on a pair of gray sweatpants just as there was a knock on the door. When I opened it, Charlie stood there beaming, and then enveloped me in a big bear hug.

"Man, it's good to see you," he said, squeezing so hard I thought my bones would crack. He let up on his grip and then kissed me gently on the lips. Maybe there was something to that whole "absence makes the heart grow fonder" theory.

"Surprise!"

It wasn't Bowie. The voice was decidedly more feminine. And more direct than a bulldozer. It could be only one person.

"Laurette!" I said, with as much fake enthusiasm as I could muster. This was not good. The jig was up for Juan Carlos. With his multiple affairs the talk of the set, it was only a matter of time before Laurette got wind of them.

She pushed her way into the room, inspecting the décor. "What a dump."

"Maybe you can get a suite or something that has better furniture," I said.

"Oh, please, I'm not staying here. I'm a couple of doors down at the Delano. Five stars. Very chic. Somebody saw George Clooney in the lobby checking in about a half hour before I did." It would only be a matter of time before Laurette befriended the entire staff and would know Clooney's room number.

Laurette plopped down on the bed, her purse in her lap. "I'll have Juan Carlos's things moved over. What room is he in? I want to surprise him."

Bad idea. Very, very bad. "I don't know," I lied. "But I'm sure he's already left for the set. I think he had an early call."

"Well, let's all drive over there. I want to see my husband," Laurette said.

Charlie noticed my visible hesitation. So did Laurette.

"What?" she said. "What aren't you telling me?"

"I think . . ." I wanted to spill everything. Dominique. Viveca. The young stud at the Sand Drift Motel. Possible mob ties. But I froze up.

"Come on, Jarrod," she said, clutching her purse tightly. "I can take it."

"Juan Carlos has gotten himself in some trouble. A dangerous guy named Javier Martinez wants to see him dead."

"Do you know how many people in Hollywood want to see *me* dead?" Laurette said.

"Martinez makes Tony Soprano look like Mr. Rogers. And his daughter is Dominique."

"The actress? The one from the wedding? The one who . . . ?"
I nodded.

Laurette's eyes brimmed with tears. Charlie put a comforting hand on her shoulder.

"And that's not all. There are more. Another actress in the movie. An older woman . . . and . . ." I really hated divulging all the sordid details. Laurette was so strong, but she sat on the bed, speechless and shaking. "And there's somebody else. A . . . a man . . ."

Laurette slapped her hands over her face and cried. I dashed over and threw my arms around her. Charlie's hand remained on her shoulder.

"I'm so sorry, honey," he said.

Laurette hunched over, sobbing, and said, "I don't believe it . . . I just don't believe it . . ."

"I know, I know . . ." I said.

"He told me I was the only older woman he's ever been attracted to. He made me feel so special."

"Laurette," I said softly, "didn't you hear what I said? He's also been sleeping with a man."

Wiping away her tears, she sniffled and said, "Oh, please. Half my boyfriends have been bisexual. You have to expect that when you date actors. But an older woman? That's such a betrayal!"

Laurette stood up, threw the strap of her purse across her shoulder, and marched for the door. "Come on, we're going over to the set right now to confront him."

"But, Laurette, he's shooting today. We can't disrupt the production."

"Movies come and go, Jarrod. This is my life we're talking about."

I glanced over at Charlie to garner some support, but he just shrugged. We both knew there was no stopping Laurette once she'd made up her mind.

* * *

When we arrived on the set, we were greeted by complete pandemonium. Juan Carlos was a no-show, and nobody knew where he was. The entire day had been structured around him, and now with him AWOL, Larry had nothing to shoot. As Juan Carlos's manager, Laurette was instantly embroiled in the controversy, and had to kick into her business mode in order to deal with the crisis. The production company was threatening to sue for the cost of the lost day, and Laurette was on the horn to her team of lawyers back in LA, keeping them apprised of the situation.

I was worried that Javier had made good on his promise to wipe Juan Carlos off the face of the earth. And deep down, I wasn't too distraught over it. But with Juan Carlos gone, any hopes of finding Austin Teboe's killer would probably disappear with him.

Charlie and I went to Juan Carlos's trailer to see if we could drum up any clues as to his whereabouts. It was locked up tight. I told Charlie to wait by the door while I fetched the keys from a production assistant. As I rounded the back of the trailer, I ran smack into a giant of a man, in a familiar plaid hunting jacket and wearing an Elmer Fudd mask over his broad face. I stood before him, paralyzed, my mouth open.

The big guy flipped the mask up. A kind face with an eager smile was underneath. And it didn't belong to Wendell Butterworth.

"Hi, I'm Eddie. I'll be playing the killer."

A rush of relief washed over me as I stuck my hand out and shook his. "Nice to meet you, Eddie."

My cell phone rang. I excused myself from Eddie, pulled it out of my pocket, and flipped it open. "Yeah?" I said impatiently, my eyes scanning the campground set for anyone who would have a key to Juan Carlos's dressing room trailer.

"Jarrod, it's Bowie. I think you better meet me."

"Why?" I said.

"It's Juan Carlos."

"Is he . . . dead?"

"No," Bowie said, his voice low and serious. "But I think you better see this for yourself. Can you meet me at the houseboat in twenty minutes?"

"Sure," I said and hung up. I grabbed Amy Jo as she scuttled past me. We were both in our matching *Creeps* sweatshirts.

"Amy Jo, I need to get into Juan Carlos's trailer."

She looked at me blankly. "I can't let you in there. It's against the rules."

"Look, he's missing and we're all going to lose our jobs if we don't find him. The best way to do that is to search his dressing room for some answers."

She stared me down defiantly. After all, I was the loser who slept late and almost got her fired. But the set was a madhouse because of Juan Carlos's disappearance, and if I did manage to find him, she'd be a hero for helping me get inside his trailer. She pulled it off her bulky ring of keys and handed it to me.

"Don't lose it," she said.

"Thanks," I said and ran back to find Charlie.

I searched around the set but didn't spot him. I asked around but nobody could tell me where he was. He was probably looking for Juan Carlos somewhere in the woods. Bowie was waiting, and it seemed important, and I had to make a quick decision.

So against my better judgment, after scanning the set one more time and not seeing my boyfriend, I hustled off to meet Bowie, the hot Navy Seal.

Chapter 23

I knew if I had found Charlie and told him where I was going, it would open a floodgate of questions. And right now I had my hands full enough already with Austin Teboe's murder, Juan Carlos's extramarital escapades, and psycho Wendell Butterworth's sudden appearance in Miami. As I drove the Taurus through heavy midday traffic toward the boat slip housing Bowie's home, I knew it was only a matter of time before I would have to deal with the inevitable reunion between just old friends Charlie Peters and Bowie Lassiter.

When I reached the *QE3*, Bowie was waiting for me out front. He was decked out in a tight black tank top, khaki shorts, and a pair of sandals. A cheap pair of sunglasses shaded his eyes from the oppressive glare of the sun. I jumped out, and before I could even open my mouth to speak, he waved at me to follow and said, "Boat's ready. Let's go."

I decided not to ask him where we were going. I figured I'd find out soon enough.

I padded behind him silently as we circled around to the back of the houseboat, and walked down some metal steps to a small floating dock connected to the slip. Waiting for us was a sleek white 1990 Hydrostream Vegas XT twenty-one foot speedboat. Really cool. Bowie jumped in, turned the ignition, and the boat roared to life. I had barely stepped down inside of it before we were pulling back from the dock and hurtling out to the open sea. Sea spray splashed against my face, and I kept wiping it away to see where we were heading. Just ahead, only a few minutes from South Beach by boat, was the luxurious, world-famous Star Island. Rosie O'Donnell lives there. So does Gloria Estafan. It's a jetsetter's paradise boasting expansive, stunning multimillion-dollar homes, with tropical punch-colored flowers and towering palm trees swaying in the soft breeze and white caps from the electric blue-green ocean crashing gently onto the immaculate sandy beige beaches.

We circled around to the north side of the island until we were about two hundred feet out from a large mansion nestled into the foliage. Much of the property was hidden safely behind the trees and gardens, but wide picture windows gave the inhabitants a magnificent view of the bay.

Bowie cut the engine, and we floated up and down, riding the curve of the waves.

"So who lives there?" I asked.

"Javier Martinez. At least some of the time."

"You think Juan Carlos is in there? That maybe Martinez is holding him prisoner?"

Bowie shook his head. "No. Martinez and his wife are staying at their penthouse in the Delano. Except for a few of the household staff, the place is supposed to be empty. But it's not."

He picked up a pair of binoculars and handed them to me. "Go ahead. Check it out."

I peered through the binoculars. It took a few seconds for my eyes to adjust to the powerful lenses. I located the picture window on the back of the house and saw Juan Carlos inside, lying flat on a plush white leather couch. He was on his belly, totally nude, his left arm stretched out as his fingers mechanically stroked the fur on an enormous yellow-striped cat curled up on the floor.

"What's he doing there? Is he on some kind of suicide mission? What if someone catches him?"

"Keep watching," Bowie said.

Dominique. He must be there with Dominique. He was still seeing her. Mafia Daddy be damned. I had to admit, the guy had balls.

I saw a pair of hands slither down over the top of the couch and begin to massage Juan Carlos's shoulders, moving south down to his lower back and butt. Juan Carlos stopped patting the cat, wriggled happily at the sensuous touch, and smiled.

I steadied the binoculars. As the hands kneaded deeper into Juan Carlos's flesh, the mystery masseuse's face finally lowered into view. It wasn't Dominique. It wasn't even a woman.

I spun around to Bowie. "That's David Miller, the kid from Vero Beach who Juan Carlos has been sneaking around with!"

Bowie nodded evenly. "His name's not Miller. It's Martinez. That's Javier Martinez's son. Dominique's younger brother."

Oh . . . my . . . God.

I was drawn back to the scene inside the mansion. Looking through the binoculars, I saw Juan Carlos roll over on his back, reach up, and wrap his hands around David Martinez's neck, pulling him down over the couch on top of him. They laughed playfully, David hoisting himself up just enough to strip off his T-shirt. The two men locked lips, and began devouring each other before sliding off the couch and falling out of my eye line.

"They've been at it all day," Bowie said.

"But there are servants around," I said. "Won't they see? What's stopping them from telling their boss what's going on?"

"Are you kidding?" Bowie snorted. "Would you want to be the guy who tells a mafia kingpin that his only son is screwing around with another guy? The same guy who broke his daughter's heart?"

"I guess there's that risk of him wanting to kill the messenger," I said.

"He'll want to kill more than the messenger if he finds this out. And everybody in that house knows it."

I was awestruck by Juan Carlos's outright brazenness. He knew Javier Martinez had it out for him, and yet he openly and quite publicly returned to Miami to shoot this movie. He was practically flaunting himself right in front of the mobster's face. Even using the guy's own home as a little love pad. Maybe he was just insane. Or maybe he had someone high up in the Miami mafia protecting him. But who? And why?

In any case, Juan Carlos didn't appear to be the least bit concerned about his safety. At the moment, he was clearly more concerned about how long it would take for him to climax.

If Dominique found out that Juan Carlos was sleeping with her own brother, she would have been inconsolable. That might have been what brought her out to California. The reason she crashed the wedding at the Hearst Castle. She wanted to confront him with what she knew. Maybe even threaten him. Or threaten to tell her father. But she also wanted him back. So there was also the possibility that she tried to blackmail him. She could have told him she would keep quiet if he dumped her brother and came back to her. But Juan Carlos must have flatly refused. He knew Dominique loved him no matter how badly he treated her, and she would never knowingly put him in any kind of danger. Distraught, she tried drowning herself in the Pacific Ocean.

It all seemed plausible. But there was one big fat nagging question. What did Austin Teboe have to do with this whole scenario? Dominique obviously knew him. He worked for her family as a chef for years before he mysteriously quit. Had he and Juan Carlos met earlier than when they both worked at the Nexxt Café? Had they been introduced when Juan Carlos got romantically involved with Dominique? And what was the nature of their relationship? Maybe somehow things went sour between the two of them and Teboe sprung up in California with the intent of causing some kind of harm to Juan Carlos. Dominique found out about it and poisoned him to protect the man she loved. But where would a mafia princess get a lethal hit of monkshead? All I really knew was that Juan Carlos was playing a very dangerous game of Russian roulette, and sooner or later his luck would run out.

Chapter 24

Bowie shifted the gear of the Hydrostream Vegas XT, and we cut through the waves heading back toward Biscayne Bay and the dock housing the *QE3*. As we circled back around Star Island, I spotted another dilapidated boat with its motor off, bobbing up and down in the choppy water. A tanned, chubby fisherman with no shirt and wearing a Miami Dolphins baseball cap sat at the stern, chugging the last gulp from a bottle of Corona. Up front was another man, much heavier, his red flowery Magnum, P.I.–like Hawaiian shirt drenched from sweat. He clutched a Fujifilm digital camera and vigorously snapped pictures of the Martinez compound. I signaled Bowie to pass around in front of the boat so I could get a good look at the photographer. As we roared up and around the old wooden fishing vessel, the obese man at the bow stumbled back, startled by the sudden appearance of another boat, almost dropping his camera into the surf. It was Rudy Pearson. I ducked down fast, and Bowie powered us past the old barge before he had a chance to recognize me.

Why was Pearson so single-minded in his determination to dig up dirt on Juan Carlos? And for whom exactly was he working? *Soap Opera Digest* or the *National Enquirer*? Pearson's hatred for Juan Carlos was palpable, and there was obviously more history between them than either was willing to admit. I doubted Pearson was behind Austin Teboe's murder simply for the fact that neither acted as if they had ever met when I first saw them on the bus together driving up to the Hearst Castle. Still, my curiosity about this vengeful soap journalist was peaked, and I decided it was time to find out what his role was in the *Juan Carlos Show*.

When Bowie and I pulled up to the dock housing the *QE3* houseboat, it was going on four o'clock in the afternoon.

Bowie tied up the Hydrostream to a brass rail, and gently placed a hand on the small of my back. "Want to come inside for a drink?"

"No, thanks," I said, forcing a smile. "I better get back to the hotel. Charlie is probably there waiting for me."

Bowie raised an eyebrow. "Charlie's here in South Beach?"

I nodded, trying to conceal the flicker of guilt that undoubtedly flashed across my face. "I left him behind when you called. He's not too keen on me playing Mike Hammer."

"Well," Bowie said, swallowing hard. "I'd love to see him while he's down here . . . if you two have the time."

"I'm sure he'll want to see you too."

There was a long silence. Neither of us knew what to say next. The chemistry was crackling. Bowie finally took the lead. "Okay then. I'm going to head back out and keep a watch on the Martinez compound. I'll let you know if I see anything interesting."

Good. Back to the case. "Man, do you Navy Seals ever take a break?"

"I got a call from my uncle today. He was desperate for any news I might have about Calvin. It was tough telling him I had a big fat nothing. I've got to keep at it until I can give the poor guy some peace of mind about his son." Bowie averted his eyes to hide a show of emotion. His missing cousin was having a big impact on him, but he wasn't about to advertise it.

When I got back to the Ritz Plaza lobby, I picked up a house phone and dialed the reception desk. I watched as a lovely Cuban girl in a blue blazer answered my call.

"Reception, may I help you?" she said in a cheery voice.

"Yes, I'd like to leave Rudy Pearson a message, please."

"I'll connect you to his room right away," she said as her hand went down to transfer me.

"No! I know he's out covering a *Days of Our Lives* convention. I'm his editor at *Soap Opera Digest*."

She was probably wondering why I was offering so much information, but I was afraid if I stopped talking, she'd transfer me anyway.

"Just tell him to call the office when he gets a chance," I said, watching as she typed the message into a computer and hit the print button. It spit out into a tray, and she handed the piece of paper to an equally cute young Cuban male bellhop, who carried it toward the elevator.

"I'll be sure he gets it," she said.

"Thank you." I hung up the phone and dashed across the lobby to the bank of elevators where the cute bellhop was stepping into an available car. I joined him just as the doors closed.

"How are you today?" I said, smiling.

"Fine, sir. And you?"

Sir? Sir? I wasn't *that* much older than him. I suddenly liked him a lot less.

"What floor?" he said, finger poised.

I glanced at the floor numbers. Ten was lit up. I turned and nodded. "I'm going to ten too."

"Very good, sir."

When we reached the tenth floor, he stuck a hand out to hold open the door for me. I didn't want to go first. The plan was to follow him.

"After you, sir."

Okay, enough with the damn sirs.

This guy wasn't going to budge. So I stepped off first. I could go left or right. There was a fifty percent chance of getting it right. I went left. After walking a few feet, I didn't sense him behind me so I glanced back to see him heading down the opposite end of the hall. I should've gone right. I walked briskly to catch up with him, but slowed down as he stopped at a room and slipped my phone message under a door. Room 1032. He stood back up and saw me approaching. There was a slightly confused look on his face. I knew I had to offer some explanation.

"Dyslexic. Takes me an hour just to find the right room," I said, laughing.

"I see. You have a good day, sir."

Bastard.

After he turned the corner to get back on the elevator, I loitered outside the room until I saw a tired, overworked maid in a drab gray uniform complete with white apron slowly push a housekeeping cart up the hall. I marched up to her.

"Excuse me, I'm Mr. Pearson in room 1032. I've locked myself out of my room and was wondering if—?"

She looked up at me, and her mouth dropped open. "Sweet Jesus!"

"What?" I said.

"You're not Mr. Pearson! You're that little white kid from *Go to Your Room!*"

Sweet Jesus.

She howled and poked me in the ribs with a sausage-like finger. "Baby, don't even go there! I loved when you said that! I busted a gut every time!" She then swiveled her head around. "Is this one of those hidden camera shows?"

"You caught me . . . what's your name?" I said.

"Estelle."

"You caught me, Estelle. No, this isn't a hidden camera show. I just wanted to play a joke on my friend Mr. Pearson. I haven't seen him in a while and—"

"You know, I always had a crush on you. I wrote to that show on E! called *Star Dates*, where they hook you up with some has-been loser celebrity from way back. I told them if they ever tried to get a date for you, I was their girl! I wouldn't make fun of you afterwards like some of them do."

I was close to crying. Talk about hitting where it hurts. But I had to get in that room so I couldn't just walk away and lick my wounds.

"You know, I've thought about going on that show," I said.

"No shit. Really? You'd be a hell of a lot better than some of the jackasses they get. I mean, Eddie Munster? Come on! No. They need bigger names like you and Urkel. You know, real stars."

"Well, I'll make sure they contact you if I go on," I said.

Her eyes nearly popped out of her head. "Oh my word. Are you serious? Me on *Star Dates*?" I think she was more enthusiastic about being on TV than actually going out on a date with me.

"You're my pick. *If* I go on."

"You like to bowl?" she said, brimming with excitement.

"Love to."

She clapped her hands, envisioning our night together. And then, almost absent-mindedly, she pulled out her passkey and opened room 1032. "What about Italian food. You eat spaghetti?" she said.

"Every chance I get. Thanks for letting me in my friend's room."

"Please. You're a big star. I don't suspect you'll be stealing anything," she guffawed. I guess she hadn't seen the rap sheets of several of my fellow child stars.

"You're a peach, Estelle," I said as I headed in the room.

"You smooth talker," she said and she pinched my ass. Hard. I liked Estelle. A lot better than the bellhop who called me sir.

Once inside Rudy's room, I shut the door and looked around. I heard a hissing sound. No, more like the sound of running water. It was coming from the bathroom. Someone was in the shower. It couldn't be Rudy. There was no way he could've beaten me back to the hotel. No, Rudy was probably still floating out in the bay, snapping pictures of Juan Carlos and the Martinez boy in a wide variety of X-rated poses. Someone else was in the shower. I figured as long as I heard the water running, I had time to search the place. I went about opening suitcases and drawers in search of clues.

On the desk were two large scrapbooks. I opened the one on top. It was chock full of clippings and press photos of Juan Carlos. Soap articles written by Rudy about Juan Carlos. Any shred of news related to his comings and goings. A couple of candid photos of him leaving the studio. For all his obvious contempt of the soap actor, Rudy was acting like a fan. I picked up the second scrapbook and opened it. My heart stopped. This one wasn't a shrine to Juan Carlos. It was a shrine to me. Every page was filled with *TV Guide* articles, *People* magazine profiles, and Polaroid pictures of me when I was twelve years old, holding my mother's hand as we walked along the street in our neighborhood. There was one of me signing autographs for my adoring fans outside the sound stage where we taped the show. There was a signed script from *Go to Your Room!* that had been auctioned off for charity. There were even recent photos of me hiking in the hills with Charlie and Snickers. A shiver went up my spine. Was Rudy Pearson some kind of freakish fan?

With Rudy's mysterious roommate still in the shower, I poked around some more. On the night table next to one of the two queen-size beds I found Rudy Pearson's passport. I flipped through it and stopped suddenly. On the last page was a stamp from Canada. Nova Scotia. Rudy had been there just last month.

The best place to buy monkshead poison. I headed straight for the closet, pulled out two travel bags, and unzipped all the compartments. I found nothing but a few toiletries and paperback novels in the first, but as I sifted through the second one, I discovered a small vial in one of the tiny pockets. It was unlabeled except for a tiny black skull and crossbones emblem on a sticker in the back. I didn't need a label. I knew exactly what it was and where Rudy had got it.

My mind was racing. Rudy must have killed Austin. But why? Should I go directly to the police at this point or try and gather more evidence? Charlie would know what to do. Maybe this person in the shower could shed more light on what was going on. I crept toward the bathroom door with the intent of opening it a crack and getting a peek, but that's when the water stopped running, and I heard someone slide open the glass door and step out of the tub. Probably toweling off. I had run out of time, and didn't want to risk getting caught, so I quickly and quietly left the room. I would have to wait to find out who was shacking up with Rudy Pearson.

When I got back to my own floor, I was halfway down the hall to my room when the door to Juan Carlos's room flew open and Viveca marched out in a huff. Laurette flew out behind her.

"I don't want to see your face anywhere near this room again, do you hear me?" Laurette screamed, her eyes wet with tears.

Viveca kept her face tight, and it wasn't all from plastic surgery. She was stressed out.

Laurette didn't see me in her state. She withdrew back into the room and slammed the door shut. As Viveca passed me in the hall, I gently touched her shoulder. "Are you all right?"

"Of course I'm all right. I knew Juan Carlos was married all along," she said. She was lying. She was fighting back enough tears to fill Niagara Falls, but she wasn't about to cry in front of me.

"Juan Carlos is a boy," she said. "You can never invest much in a boy. I had a bit of fun, and now it's over." This was one steely broad. I had to give her credit. "I'll see you on the set tomorrow, Jarrod."

She kept walking toward the elevators, her heels grinding into the carpet as she went. I pulled out my key and entered my room.

Charlie sat on the bed, his arms crossed, his eyes narrowed and suspicious. "Where the hell have you been?"

Chapter 25

"I was with Bowie Lassiter," I said. No point in prolonging the inevitable.

Charlie nodded, a knowing look in his eye, as if he already knew the answer to his question before he asked it.

"Why couldn't you have just told me you were going to meet him?" he said.

"I couldn't find you," I said, flushed with guilt. "Nothing happened, if that's what you want to know."

Charlie didn't take his eyes off me. He was reading my face. He knew me better than anyone, and he would know if I was going to try and perform a little song and dance. Full disclosure was my best and only course of action.

"I didn't tell you I was going to meet him because I didn't want you to get the wrong idea."

"And why would I get the wrong idea?" Damn. He just wasn't going to let it go.

"I don't know," I said. "He's a good-looking guy, and we weren't exactly on the best of terms when I left to come down here, and . . ."

"And?"

"And maybe a part of me was a little bit attracted to him, but that doesn't mean I would ever act upon it . . ."

There was an unsettling silence. Had I just ruined the best thing that had ever happened to me in my entire life? Was Charlie going to throw his hands up and finally call it quits? My heart stopped, waiting for him to speak.

"Okay."

"What?"

"Okay, fine," he said.

"That's it?"

"Yeah. I get it. Bowie's hot. I'm not blind. Look, I can't expect you not to be attracted to other people. Hell, I am all the time."

"You are?"

"Sure. Look at all the buff guys in uniform I deal with day in and day out. I wouldn't be human if I wasn't attracted to some of that," he said.

"Which ones are you attracted to?"

"Does it matter?" he shrugged.

"Of course it does. I've been wracked with guilt over this, and now you tell me you ogle half the LAPD!"

He gave me a wink. "It's not like I'd ever act upon it." Point taken.

"You were right about one thing," I said. "Bowie's hot."

Charlie grimaced. He may have declared the obvious, but he hated me agreeing with him.

"But you are so much hotter," I said, crossing over to the bed and kissing him lightly on the lips. And the fuse on this potentially explosive situation was temporarily snuffed out.

Still seated on the bed, Charlie wrapped his arms around my waist and pulled me close to him. "Just remember, though, in order for us to stay healthy, we have to be honest . . . about everything." He wasn't scolding me. It was more matter-of-fact. Years of failed relationships talking.

I was really glad he was there.

* * *

Larry Levant shuffled around the shooting schedule and moved up some night scenes in an effort to salvage some of the day after Juan Carlos went AWOL. We were all called back to Coral Gables that evening to film a sequence early in the film where the campers converge after the first sighting of the masked Elmer Fudd madman. Charlie and Laurette accompanied me to the location, where I was rushed through makeup and immediately called to the set to join little Hitler Simon, Viveca, Dominique, and a rather contrite Juan Carlos, who took great pains to explain that he had misread the call sheet. Fat chance. Like anybody would be stupid enough to misread the call sheet. The other inconvenienced cast members had plenty of room to gripe, but I didn't have a leg to stand on.

When Juan Carlos returned to the Ritz Plaza, he never even saw Laurette. Amy Jo was on call to whisk him back to the set the second she laid eyes on him. So everyone was present for the uneasy reunion. Laurette tried her best to put on a brave face, but after a perfunctory hug and kiss, Juan Carlos withdrew from her, clearly uncomfortable by her sudden arrival. He mumbled some feeble excuse about spending the day sightseeing on his own. To her credit, Laurette didn't launch into a litany of accusations about Viveca when she first saw her husband. She was the utmost professional, playing her role of talent manager to the hilt, working overtime to patch up the rift between the production and its star. But Laurette was my best friend, and I knew she would let loose once she got him alone back at the hotel.

Larry was just happy his movie was back on track, and that there was still time to get a few feet of film in the can after a disastrous, wasted day. So he spent little time chastising his leading man. Instead, he barreled forward as if nothing had happened. He offered a quick speech explaining our motivation for the scene, which could basically be summed up in one word: fear.

And then, he bounded back behind the camera with his director of photography, and yelled, "Action!"

I was a glorified extra in this scene, holding my son's hand and listening as Juan Carlos explained the importance of watching out for one another, sticking together, and not allowing this maniac to pick us off one by one. It was the third scene in the picture that said the exact same thing. I was losing any hope that this sinking ship could be anything but a direct-to-video bust. But Juan Carlos was giving it his all again, and doing a bang-up job for once. I had to credit David Martinez. His talents in the bedroom undoubtedly gave our star an extra dose of confidence and charisma on this particular day.

"Cut!" Larry screamed. "Not bad. Let's reload and go again in five." The cast dispersed for makeup checks. Simon howled at his mother, Caitlin, to bring him some apple juice. Viveca grabbed the nearest mirror to check out her face. Dominique kept her eyes pinned on Juan Carlos, who sauntered over to Laurette with a boyish pout, his tail firmly between his legs. Laurette was on the phone to LA and ignored his arm, which had snaked around her back in an obvious ploy for attention.

I turned and looked for Charlie. He was nowhere to be seen. I snagged Amy Jo as she rushed by with her walkie-talkie. "Have you seen my boyfriend?"

"I think I saw him heading into the woods over there. He's probably taking a leak. It's too damn far to hike back to the port-a-johns from here if you really have to go." She kept moving, and with five minutes to play with, I decided to walk down the trail to find him.

It was dark now, and the trees took on a life of their own, blowing in the breeze, sweeping down over me as if I were a lost cherub in a spooky illustrated children's book. I saw some movement ahead, and as I drew closer, I saw the figure of a man, his back to me. I assumed it was Charlie zipping up his jeans. But as the wind blew through a thicket of trees to the right, enough light from the moon seeped through to illuminate the man in front of me. It wasn't Charlie. This man had a much wider frame and was about a foot and a half shorter. When he turned around, I saw the sad-sack face of Rudy Pearson.

"Well, funny how fate keeps bringing us together," I said, surprising him.

"What do you mean by that?" he said, fingering the camera looped around his neck.

"First I see you boating around Star Island taking all sorts of interesting pictures and now I run into you skulking about in the woods," I said.

"I'm not skulking! I'm just getting a story."

"I know. Juan Carlos. You're going to ruin him. Big yawn. The real story is Austin Teboe."

"Who?"

"I think you know who I'm talking about. The poor man who choked down some pretty awful poison at your buddy Juan Carlos's wedding?"

"Oh, right," he said, his eyes darting around to see who else was around.

"How was your trip to Nova Scotia?"

His eyes stopped darting and stared straight at me. "How did you know I went to Nova Scotia?"

I wasn't about to admit searching his room so I decided to play it vague. "I've got spies everywhere."

"I was there covering a soap convention. They're held all over the world, you know."

"No kidding," I said. "So what do you do at one of those things? Take pictures of the stars with their fans? Raffle off *As the World Turns* memorabilia? Buy a couple hits of monkshead poison?"

His eyes went dead and his voice was monotone as he spoke. "What are you trying to say?"

"It's just interesting to me that Nova Scotia is one of the few places you can find that particular poison, and that's exactly what Austin Teboe died from."

"I didn't kill him. I didn't even know him!" He was clutching his camera so tight, I thought he was going to crush it.

"Okay, then what aren't you telling me, Rudy?"

He opened his mouth to speak. Despite the night chill, he was sweating. And then another man, much bigger than Rudy, stepped out from behind the tree a few feet from where Rudy stood.

"Charlie?" I said.

It wasn't Charlie. It was Elmer Fudd. Or Eddie, the big lug playing the killer in the movie in costume.

I smiled. "You gave us quite a start, Eddie. You too lazy to walk to the port-a-johns too?"

Elmer Fudd nodded, and then pulled a long sharp knife out of the sheath attached to his wide, thick brown leather belt.

Rudy froze, unable to move as Elmer Fudd stepped slowly toward him.

"Eddie?" I said.

Rudy shivered as Elmer hovered over him. And as I watched in horrifying slow motion, Elmer grabbed Rudy from behind, hooking one arm around his neck and raising the knife up over his head with the other. And then, in one fast, sweeping motion, he brought it down, plunging the blade into Rudy's chest.

Blood spurted everywhere.

Rudy's eyes bulged, his body convulsed, and as Elmer released his grip, Rudy's body sank to the ground in a crumpled heap.

"Omigod!" I screamed. "Omigod!"

The man removed his Elmer Fudd mask. It wasn't Eddie. It was Wendell Butterworth.

Chapter 26

As Wendell stepped over the dead body of Rudy Pearson toward me, I whipped around and ran as fast as I could through the woods, yelling for help at the top of my lungs. My voice echoed through the night breeze as I kept my arms in front of my face while barreling through an endless barrage of swaying tree branches. I became disoriented from the darkness, unsure if I was even heading back in the direction of the movie set. I ran until my legs ached and I was out of breath, and then I crouched down behind a bush and looked back. There was an uneasy stillness. No sign of Wendell. After a moment's rest, I stood back up and turned around to keep running when I collided with a big man who grabbed me by the arms.

"No!" I screamed. I pummeled his chest and face with my fists, momentarily stunning him. But then, he pushed me away, and raised his hands up to deflect my vicious assault.

"Whoa! Jarrod, stop! It's me!"

Charlie. Thank God. It was Charlie.

"Wendell . . ." I managed to get out between heavy breaths. "Back there . . . he killed a man . . . with a knife!"

Charlie just stood there for a moment, making sure he heard

right, and then with a fierce resolve, he turned to head back, looking deep into the woods in the direction where I pointed. I lunged forward and grabbed him by the shirtsleeve.

"No way are you going near that maniac unarmed! We have to call the police!"

"He could get away!"

"I don't care," I said. "I'm not going to risk him getting you too. He's big and strong and crazy!"

Adrenaline pumping, Charlie was ready to take on this madman all by himself, but I gripped his arm tightly enough to press my point even further, and finally he stopped resisting me, and nodded. "Okay, let's go get some help."

Charlie knew which direction to go, and within two minutes we pounded onto the set, interrupting a take with Viveca. Before Larry could erupt in a tantrum, Charlie had commandeered Amy Jo's cell phone and was dialing 911. I quickly explained what had happened, and a small band of bulky teamsters grabbed some hammers and drills and a couple of lights, and we charged into the woods in pursuit of my childhood nightmare. I led the determined little army to the spot where I had witnessed Wendell stab Rudy Pearson. As we came upon the clearing, there was no sign of Wendell. Or Rudy Pearson's body. There was nothing. One of the grips on the crew shined a portable klieg light from the set on the entire area, and we scanned the leaves on the ground for any traces of blood. But there were none.

By the time the police arrived forty minutes later, the interest of the film crew in my story was waning, and a few started whispering to one another, speculating on whether or not I was drunk and making the whole thing up. You know those attention-seeking actors. Charlie stood firmly by my side. He knew my history with Wendell Butterworth, and his recent creepy appearances in the diner up in San Simeon, at Costco, and on the set of this movie. When investigators finished combing the area, the lead investigator, a handsome African-American man in his mid-forties with a close-cropped beard and a barrel chest, walked over to Charlie and me.

"Your killer must have moved the body in the time it took for you to come back with the cavalry," he said with a shrug.

"Well, can we put out an APB on Butterworth?" Charlie asked.

The investigator shook his head. "No, I'm sorry. We're having a tough enough time establishing that there's even been a crime."

"But I saw him kill a man!" I yelled. Charlie placed a gentle hand on my back, silently suggesting I rein it in a bit.

"Without a body, there isn't a whole lot we can do," the investigator said, trying hard to be sympathetic but anxious to move on to a real crime scene.

"Butterworth has a history of stalking Jarrod," Charlie said calmly. "He followed him down here and weaseled his way onto the set. He's a menace, a danger to society, and I think it's in everybody's best interest that we find him."

"If he's such a danger, why did the parole board up in Vacaville release him?" the investigator asked. He had a point. Without any proof, it was a waste of time trying to enlist the police to help us. Sooner or later, Rudy Pearson's body would have to turn up. Some hiker or a couple of hunters would stumble across his corpse, or a piece of it, or something. And then we'd be in business. But until then, I felt completely exposed. It was as if Wendell Butterworth was anticipating my every move, taunting me, and it scared the hell out of me.

As we walked back to the set, I caught a few looks from the crew. They weren't accusing looks, but they betrayed a sense of skepticism. They had all witnessed my world-class freak-out when Wendell turned up on the set in the Elmer Fudd mask, and they were contemplating my current mental state. Maybe I was so discombobulated from all the stress, I was starting to see things. After all, it was dark in the woods, and swaying branches from a tree can create the illusion of a person, and wouldn't there have been just a tiny spec of blood if Butterworth had indeed stabbed Rudy Pearson repeatedly and then dragged the body away? How could I blame the crew for eyeing me suspiciously? A small part of me was beginning to question what I'd seen out there myself.

Larry wrapped for the day, having completed only half a scene. We were now two whole days behind schedule thanks to Juan Carlos going AWOL and my fantastic murder-in-the-woods adventure. For a young guy, Larry looked as if he was on the verge of a stroke. He was pale, gaunt, and grim. I was about to wish him a good night, but decided the last voice he wanted to hear was mine.

Laurette and Juan Carlos had left for the hotel long before all the drama blew up, and most of the actors had cleared out the minute the police were contacted. Nobody, not Viveca, Dominique, or even the little brat Simon, wanted to be associated with a possible tabloid scandal that could adversely affect their career. There was only a handful of crew members left to clean up and close down the set for the night as Charlie and I made our way to the trailer I shared with several of my costars.

"My bag's inside. Let me just get it, and then we can go," I said to Charlie. Charlie sauntered over to an ice cooler, bent over, and perused the soda selections as I opened the door to the trailer and entered.

"You gave me quite a fright," a deep voice said. I nearly jumped out of my skin before I spun around to find Bowie sitting in a folding chair, his hands clasped behind his neck.

"Jesus, Bowie, what are you doing here?" I said.

"Got a friend in the Coral Gables Police Department. He gave me a ring after your 911 call came in. Came out here as soon as I could," he said.

"Well, I don't think they'll be giving me a Good Citizen Award anytime soon. I'm not sure they believe my story."

"They don't. They think you're making it up to get Butterworth off the street and out of your hair."

I nodded. Big shocker. "Do you believe me?"

"Of course."

"Good. Because I want to hire you."

Bowie raised an eyebrow curiously. "To do what?"

"I want you to prove Wendell Butterworth killed Rudy Pearson. I want you to find the body, tie that freak to the murder, and send his ass to prison. And this time I don't want him ever getting out."

I was shaking. I had kept it together for so long. But now, in front of a man I had known for only a few days, I was coming apart. Ever since the parole hearing in Vacaville, I had been haunted by all those disturbing images from my childhood. Over and over I would see the contorted, wild face of Wendell Butterworth trying to snatch me from my home while I was eating breakfast or attempting to shoot me while I sat in a car with my mother. I had never truly gotten over those traumatic events, and now they were coming up again as Wendell continued to insert himself into my life. I couldn't take it anymore. I just wanted it all to go away. I was tired of worrying, tired of running, tired of waiting for my past to finally catch up to me.

Bowie stood, quietly walked over to me, and put his arms around me. He squeezed me tight and whispered in my ear, "Don't worry, Jarrod. I'll do whatever it takes to make him go away."

"Thank you," I said, feeling weak and helpless, and hating myself for it.

I felt a cool rush of air from outside. Someone had opened the door to the trailer. I looked up to see Charlie's crestfallen face staring inside at me as his old friend embraced me.

Chapter 27

Bowie immediately sensed me tensing up, and let go, turning to see Charlie hovering in the doorway.

"Charlie, man, how long has it been?" he said as he walked over and gripped his hand.

Charlie shook it, but his face remained hard and unresponsive. "Been a while, Bowie. Been a while."

The two friends just stared at each other awkwardly, neither knowing how to break the stifling tension.

"We should get together while you're in town," Bowie offered. "Kick back a few, talk about old times at the academy."

"I'm not sure how long I'm going to be down here," Charlie said. The chill in the air was enough to frost over the smudged, grimy windows on the trailer.

There was a long, agonizing silence. Finally, Bowie said, "Well, you've got my number. Give me a call." And then Bowie turned to me. "I'll get to work right away on that matter we discussed." He wasn't willing to talk about the details of a case in front of anyone but his client. Bowie was the utmost professional. He nodded to Charlie, who had to move to the side to let him pass.

When we were alone, I sighed, and said, "Charlie, he was here when I came in, and I was a little shaken up over the whole Butterworth mess, and he just agreed to—"

"I really don't want to hear it, okay, Jarrod?" Charlie fought hard not to explode. In a way, I wished he would. Get it all out. I could reassure him that nothing had happened, and we would be done with the whole matter. But that wasn't going to happen. He clearly didn't want to deal with me at this moment, and he turned to leave.

"Make sure one of the crew walks you to your car in case Butterworth's around," he said, and then he was gone.

I started to chase after him, but stopped when I saw him climb aboard the last transportation van back to the hotel. He never even turned to see if I was watching as they drove away from the set. I was on my own, not about to stick around for any length of time on the off chance that Butterworth was lurking about. The psycho had already proven he could mysteriously appear anywhere at will, like some ghostly apparition fiercely determined to haunt me. I ran down the wooded path to the parking lot, jumped into the Taurus, locked all the doors, and drove back to the Ritz Plaza in South Beach.

When I got back to my room, the red message light was blinking on the telephone next to the double bed with the tacky red floral print spread. God, I hated this room. I scooped up the receiver and punched the voice mail button, praying it was Charlie wanting to meet me and talk everything out and resolve all this drama over my budding friendship with Bowie.

"Jarrod, it's me. I'm at the Delano in the bar. I need to speak with you right away. Get over here as soon as you get this," Laurette said, her voice frantic. There was a click. The message had been left twenty minutes ago.

The much fancier, hipper Delano Hotel was right next to the Ritz Plaza and it took all of four minutes to get there. When I entered the restored Deco lobby, bathed in milky white draperies hanging from soaring white columns, I quickly crossed to the bar, where I found Laurette hanging off the arm of George Clooney. Damn. She was right. He was staying at the hotel. Laurette had pinned him against the bar and was working on what was probably her fourth or fifth Cosmopolitan. The bartender, dressed from head to toe in white, the signature color of the Delano, watched her with amusement as she prattled on to Clooney about their shared Kentucky heritage, which she'd read about in *People* magazine.

"I understand people from Kentucky, George, being from Lexington myself," she said, her words slow and slurred. "I could really help jump-start your career, get you moving in the right direction."

George flashed his megawatt smile. He was enjoying this. "Yeah, things have been pretty bleak lately on the work front."

"Are you sure you're from Kentucky?" Laurette said, trying to focus on his face.

"Yeah, why?" George said.

"Because when you smile, you've got all your teeth." Laurette guffawed and slapped her knee. Thrilled she'd made a funny.

It was time to intervene. I touched Laurette gently on the arm. "Excuse me. Sorry to interrupt."

Laurette was not happy someone was screwing up her quality time with George. She swiveled around on her bar stool with a scowl, and for a moment, I thought she was too drunk to recognize me.

"I came as soon as I got your message," I said. "What's the emergency?"

Laurette sat up straight, and made an attempt to be lucid and professional. "George, this is one of my top clients as well as my best friend, Jarrod Jarvis." She then leaned into George and whispered loud enough for the whole room to hear. "He's really not one of my biggest, but he is my friend, so I have to say that."

George shook my hand and smiled. "Nice to meet you, Jarrod."

"You probably don't remember, but I played an Amish burn victim in the first season of ER. But I had a lot of makeup on . . ."

"Of course I remember," George said. "Noah Wyle was so stoked to have you on the show. He was a big fan of *Go to Your Room!* He wouldn't shut up about it."

"Really?" I said.

"Oh yeah, he didn't want to embarrass you by making a big deal about it, but every day, he'd pop into my trailer and go—"

George and I did it together. "Baby, don't even go there!"

Wow. I was bonding with George Clooney. Maybe he'd put me in his next movie and I could bid adieu to these cheap horror films. Now I was dreaming.

"Well, I'm meeting some friends so I better go," George said.

Laurette slapped a business card in the palm of his hand and winked at him. "Call me. We'll talk."

He held the card up and, ever the consummate actor, pretended it was like a winning lottery ticket. "Thank you, Laurette." And George Clooney waltzed out of our lives. We both let out an audible sigh.

"He's just one of those people who gets better looking with age," Laurette said, before grabbing the bar rail to keep from falling off the stool.

"People say that about me," I said, hoping she would agree. She didn't. So I took a seat next to her at the bar and ordered a vodka tonic from the bartender.

Laurette grabbed the neck of her Cosmopolitan glass and lifted it unsteadily to her lips, splashing the drink over the sides and onto the floor. She took a small sip, and put it down again. "Juan Carlos ditched me."

"What do you mean ditched you? Did he ask for a divorce?"

"No, nothing like that. We were walking along Ocean Avenue, and we were right in the middle of a serious discussion about our marriage, and how trust is important to me, when suddenly he spotted these two men following us. He got really nervous and ducked inside a sidewalk bar to go to the bathroom, but he never came out. I went inside and looked everywhere. He was gone. I was so upset. And so were the two men who had been following us."

"What did they look like?"

Laurette shrugged. "I don't know. Big guys. One white. One Hispanic."

Javier Martinez's goons. No doubt about it. "Did they follow Juan Carlos inside?"

"No, they hung around out by the street, a few feet away from me. I guess they thought he wouldn't just leave me standing there like a fool. Their mistake."

"Laurette, I can't stress enough the kind of danger Juan Carlos is in. Those men work for Javier Martinez, and he could do some serious damage to both him and you."

"Please, I've dealt with bigger sharks in Hollywood," she said, staring straight ahead toward the entrance to the hotel bar.

"I'm afraid he may already have gotten to Juan Carlos," I said.

"Omigod."

"What?"

"Over there," Laurette said. "The two guys who were following us. They're here."

I whooshed around and saw the two giants, wearing a couple of print silk shirts, white slacks, and sandals, amble in and survey the room. Satisfied, they turned and signaled behind them. Javier Martinez, in a light beige linen suit, swept in with a gorgeous woman in her forties on his arm. She was poured into a tight yellow dress, and boasted a fortune of sparkling Harry Winston jewelry on her neck and wrists. I immediately recognized her as Juan Carlos's paramour and costar, Viveca.

A host, also covered in white, scurried up to them and said in the most pleasant voice he could muster, "Good evening, Mr.

and Mrs. Martinez, I have a private table waiting for you in the back."

I was floored. Viveca was Javier's wife. No wonder Juan Carlos was in such big trouble. He was sleeping with almost the entire Martinez family. Viveca. Dominique. David. Forget Bob Dole. Juan Carlos was the perfect spokesman for Viagra.

"What a slut. She's already married and she's fooling around with my husband. I'll scratch her eyes out," Laurette said, making a halfhearted move to stand up, but one little tug on her sleeve from me, and she was firmly planted back on the bar stool, swaying a bit, but settled.

"As much as I'm a fan of *Dynasty*-style catfights, I'm not sure confronting a mobster's wife is such a good idea."

Laurette's eyes began to well up with tears. "I've been so stupid, Jarrod. So stupid." She laid her head on my shoulder, and I wrapped my arms tightly around her.

"You can't help who you fall in love with," I said. I thought about Charlie. And where he could be.

Laurette opened her purse and pulled out some Kleenex. She blew hard and then wiped some tears away. Out of the corner of her eye, she saw Javier and Viveca disappear around a corner to a private space in the back of the bar.

"That bitch shouldn't have even been in the movie. But her husband was financing the picture, and he only agreed to cough up the money if they gave his wife a big part," she said.

It hit me that Viveca and Dominique were using different last names to conceal both their mother-daughter relationship and their connection to Javier Martinez.

"Javier financed the movie starring a man who was sleeping with his wife and daughter and son? Oh boy. No wonder Martinez hates him so much."

"That dirty cheating louse!" Laurette sobbed. "How could he do this to me? I gave him the best weeks of my life!"

Laurette's cell phone chirped from inside her purse. She pulled it out and snapped it open. Sniffling, she said, "Hello?" After a moment, her face darkened and she turned to me. "Bad news," she said. "He's still alive."

"Where is he?" I said.

Laurette listened and nodded and then hung up the phone. She downed the last of her Cosmopolitan, and slid off the stool. "Come on. We're going to meet him."

"You want me to come with you?"

"Yes. I want you there to make sure I don't kill the bastard."

Juan Carlos had told Laurette to meet him at his former place of employment, the Nexxt Café, a trendy hotspot for the locals located squarely in the middle of upscale Lincoln Road. It was a short ten-minute walk from the Delano, and when we arrived, the outdoor tables were nearly filled to capacity.

"He said he was at a table off to the side," she said as we both scanned the crowd of diners. I spotted him first. He sat alone at a marble table wearing a blond wig, dark glasses, and a heavy brown overcoat. Given the sweltering eighty-degree weather, the sloppy disguise made him stand out like a Hassidic rabbi in an Easter parade.

"There he is," I said, guiding Laurette's gaze with my finger. "I recognize the wig and coat from the movie's wardrobe department."

Laurette gripped my hand as we maneuvered through the myriad of tables to get to Juan Carlos. I whispered into her ear, "Now just stay calm. Let's hear what he has to say. Don't freak him out by laying into him too quick."

"You're right," she said. "We'll just let him talk."

As we circled in front of Juan Carlos and sat down in the pair of empty seats at the table, Juan Carlos didn't move. He just stared straight ahead, his eyes hidden behind the dark glasses.

"You imbecilic asshole!" Laurette screamed. "How dare you

drag me into this mess! What kind of stupid moron are you, seducing the whole family of a sadistic mafia killer? Do you have some kind of death wish?"

So much for letting him talk.

"Don't just sit there, you lying piece of shit! Answer me! Do you hear me? Answer me!" she said, grabbing a fistful of his overcoat and shaking him. He teetered a bit, and then dropped face first into his plastic black bowl of Chinese chicken salad. Juan Carlos Barranco was dead.

Chapter 28

Laurette screamed, panicking the other diners and alerting the wait staff that something was seriously wrong. The wide-eyed hostess picked up the phone and dialed 911 when she spied us hovering around a slumped-over body in a bulky overcoat and a blond wig askew, revealing wavy jet-black hair underneath.

I grabbed Laurette and hugged her tightly as curious patrons craned their necks, most probably wondering if it was the food he was eating that did him in. With one arm draped around Laurette's back comforting her, I reached down with my other and casually lifted Juan Carlos's wrist and felt for a pulse. Nothing. He was definitely history. I wished I could muster up some kind of emotion, maybe a passing sadness, but what I wound up doing was suppressing elation. Every instinct was telling me Laurette was much better off without him.

"I can't believe he's gone," she cried, the words barely audible between sobs. I was not about to point out that three minutes ago she was ready to poison him herself for his multiple infidelities.

Even with a restaurant full of witnesses, I was not about to leave Juan Carlos's corpse alone for even a second. I had learned my lesson after witnessing the brutal slaying of Rudy Pearson, and with his body still missing, it allowed Wendell Butterworth to roam around free to stalk and murder me at his convenience.

The police arrived within minutes, followed by paramedics in an ambulance. The hostess with the big wide eyes pointed at Laurette and me accusingly, as if she had seen us do away with him ourselves, and the cops descended upon us to ask a barrage of questions. Charlie always told me to tell the cops everything during an interrogation. Don't leave anything out. You don't want something coming back to haunt you later. So Laurette and I spilled it all. The murder in San Simeon. Juan Carlos's extramarital activities. And most importantly, his making an enemy of Javier Martinez. The cops froze. They didn't like hearing that name. The last thing they seemed to want to do was rattle Martinez's cage. No telling what kind of trouble a man with his connections could stir up. Did Martinez own these guys? After I mentioned the Martinez name, the cop asking the questions briskly changed the subject.

"Any other enemies he had you can think of?" the cop asked Laurette.

"He was an actor with the lead in a feature film," she sniffed. "Half of SAG would like to see him dead."

The CSI investigator arrived to examine Juan Carlos's body. He was a hefty bald man in a blue windbreaker with a distracting mole on his left cheek. He wore plastic gloves and ate walnuts from a zip-lock bag as he scanned the corpse for any clues. He'd touch the head looking for bruises and then pop another nut in his mouth. Then he'd check the cold, dead arm, and follow it with another nut. I was completely grossed out. He caught me watching him and snickered.

"Doing the Atkins Diet. These walnuts are very low in carbs."

"That's a terrible diet," Laurette managed to get out between sobs. "In fact, the doctor who came up with it died of a heart attack."

"No, he didn't," I corrected her. "He fell on the ice and went into a coma."

"Please," she said. "That's what they wanted you to believe. Weight Watchers is the way to go." Even a grieving widow can be allowed a quick evaluation of the best weight loss programs.

The CSI investigator crumpled up his empty zip-lock bag and stuffed it into his coat pocket. "No outward signs of foul play. Could be a heart attack, or stroke, something like that."

"He wasn't even thirty!" Laurette said.

"I'm just speculating here. I need to conduct an autopsy for any definitive answers. Then we'll see if there are any traces of poison in the bloodstream."

Poison? Monkshead? That raised an interesting question. What if Juan Carlos had been taken out with a hit of monkshead? There were certainly enough people who wanted to see him dead. Javier Martinez. Viveca. Dominique. Maybe even David. Not to mention half the cast and crew of *Creeps*. The only one I could safely rule out at this point was Rudy Pearson. I saw him murdered with my own eyes. Unless his ghost did it. But Rudy could have been in cahoots with any one of the other suspects. He at least knew one person here in Miami. I heard him or her taking a shower when I cased Pearson's room. And he could have easily shared the poison with his accomplice before Wendell fatally stabbed him. I had to find out who that person was.

With the cops ignoring my bombshell about Javier Martinez's hatred of the deceased, I didn't trust them anymore so I decided to modify Charlie's helpful advice when interrogated. I neglected to mention the Rudy Pearson murder and the whacked-out psychosis of Wendell Butterworth. It would only incriminate me. If any one of them had a pipeline to the Coral Gables Police Department, they would find out my habit of showing up at a crime scene and start to suspect me of being some kind of serial killer who calls the cops for kicks after committing a murder.

Although Laurette did admit she wanted to hang her husband up by the balls after discovering his multiple infidelities, the cops had no concrete proof tying either of us to Juan Carlos's death. The CSI guy wasn't even prepared to list the death as a homicide at this point. So after a two-hour marathon of questioning, we were told we could leave, but that it would be wise of us not to leave the Miami area.

As we hiked back to the Ritz Plaza, Laurette stared straight ahead, as if in a trance. The shock of all the revelations she had encountered since arriving in Florida were starting to have an effect on her, and I felt she was close to a complete breakdown. I lured her up to my shabby room with the promise of a couple of stiff drinks from room service. When we walked into the room, we found Charlie on the bed, reading the paper.

"I'm glad you're back," I said. "You're not going to believe what we've just been through."

He lowered the paper, and glared at me. The vision of me hugging Bowie was apparently still fresh in his mind. There was a palpable tension lingering in the air. Laurette wasn't about to indulge us because she was having the worst day of all. She recounted everything to Charlie, whose anger subsided as she related all the dramatic details. He was mesmerized. And when she'd finished, he stood up, crossed over to her, and grabbed her in a warm hug.

"Honey, I'm sorry you've had to go through this," he said as she laid her head on his big shoulder.

"Somebody up there doesn't want me to be happy," she said, sniffling.

Charlie lifted her chin up with his thumb and forefinger until she was looking directly into his eyes. "Juan Carlos never would have made you happy. I'm sorry he died, but in time you'll see you deserve so much better."

He had her attention. And mine.

"He lied to you. He cheated on you. And he would've drained you financially and emotionally. Laurette, you're a beautiful, vibrant woman, and I know there's a man out there who is looking for you, and will appreciate you, and love you for who you are, not what you can do for him."

He squeezed her tighter, resting his chin on the top of her head, and said, "You and Juan Carlos, it never felt right. There wasn't a lot of trust there. And trust is the foundation of every relationship. Trust and communication."

He was looking at me when he said this. His piercing eyes were like a sword through the heart. But now was not the time to worry about us. Laurette was hurting too much.

"You're too good to me," Laurette cried as she pulled away from Charlie and held out a hand to me. "Both of you. I'd be lost without you."

I smiled, took her hand, and we hugged. The phone rang. Charlie slowly backed away to give us our best friend moment, and answered the call.

"Hello?" he said. I saw his face get hot and red, but his voice remained steady. "He's a little busy right now." Bowie. It had to be Bowie. God, this was getting more out of hand by the minute.

Charlie sighed and scribbled something on the pad of paper on the nightstand.

"All right, I'll tell him," he said and then slammed down the phone.

"Who was it?" Laurette asked.

"It was for Jarrod," he said as he tore the piece of paper off the pad and handed it to me. "Bowie wants you to meet him at this address."

"Did he say what it was about?" I asked meekly.

"No," Charlie said.

"I'm one of his clients now. Maybe he has some information about Wendell Butterworth's whereabouts or maybe he found Rudy Pearson's body . . ." I said.

"Look," Charlie said, walking back over to Laurette and putting a strong, muscled arm around her shoulders. "I don't feel right about you running all over Miami while Butterworth is on the loose, but I certainly can't stop you from doing what you're going to do. So go."

"You can come with me if you want," I said meekly.

"I think one of us should stay here and be with Laurette, don't you?" he said.

He was right. I wanted more than anything to stay and patch things up with my boyfriend and be a supportive shoulder for my best friend to cry on. But if I didn't find Butterworth and prove he was a homicidal maniac, then I would never be able to sleep at night ever again.

"I'm sorry," I said, and then I quietly turned and slipped out the door.

Chapter 29

When I arrived at the *QE3* houseboat, it was already dark. The moon illuminated a shimmering carpet across the bay, and for a city the size of South Beach, it was unsettlingly quiet.

I tapped on the door of the boat and waited. I wished Charlie had come with me. That would have been one way to allay his fears that I was having some kind of secret affair with Bowie. On the other hand, he was right. Laurette was upset and fragile, and it was best that one of us stay with her tonight.

Bowie opened the door, and motioned for me to come in. He was sweating, his face was tight, and his eyes betrayed a distinct uneasiness.

"What's going on? Did you find Wendell?" I said as I followed him inside. I jumped with a start when I saw my stalker, Wendell Butterworth, tied to a chair in the middle of the room, a piece of duct tape over his mouth.

"Omigod!" I said, spinning around to Bowie, who quickly shut the door to shield the scene from any passersby. "What happened? How did he get here?"

"I've been quietly tailing you since you asked me to help," he said as he circled around me and headed straight for the wet bar. "Since he kept popping up to scare you, I figured he'd turn up again eventually. And he did. I caught him loitering outside your hotel."

Wendell was slumped over in the chair, his eyes shut tight. I cautiously moved toward him to see if he was breathing.

"He's alive. Don't worry. He's just pretending to be asleep so I don't harass him with any more questions," Bowie said as he poured himself a generous glass of scotch and downed it one gulp.

Now I was sweating. "I don't understand. Why are you holding him prisoner? I didn't ask you to—"

"Look, I approached him outside the Ritz Plaza. When I got too close, he pulled a knife on me. Luckily during my military training they taught me how to kill a guy with a quarter, so he wasn't too hard to take down," Bowie said.

"But this isn't exactly legal, is it? I mean, he may belong behind bars, but that doesn't give us the right to—"

"I don't care," Bowie said as he lifted his fatigue green tank top up to reveal a deep cut sliced across his torso. "The son of a bitch got me. Hurt like hell. But not nearly as bad as the hydrogen peroxide I used to clean it out with. Damn."

"Why didn't you call the police?"

Bowie marched over to Wendell, grabbed a fist full of his hair, and yanked his head back. Wendell's eyes popped open, full of fear.

"Because then we'd never find out what he did to that soap reporter's body. By keeping him here, we can work on him until he tells us what we want to know. Isn't that right, Wendell?"

Wendell struggled in the chair, but it was halfhearted. He knew it was useless. Bowie knew how to tie a knot. After all, he was a Navy Seal. And probably a Boy Scout to boot.

Bowie ripped the duct tape off Wendell's mouth, knelt down, and spoke quietly into his ear. "Where is he, Wendell? Tell me and I'll let you go."

Wendell turned his head away defiantly. Bowie grabbed his chin and jerked his head back toward him. "Talk to me, Wendell. I'm not a patient man."

"Maybe we should turn him over to the police . . ." I said, my stomach flip-flopping. This wasn't what I'd had in mind at all.

"I'm not going to ask you again," Bowie said, slapping Wendell hard across the face. Wendell groaned, but remained steadfast in his silence. Bowie slapped him even harder.

"Bowie, stop!" I yelled, rushing over and grabbing his wrist to stop him from going another round. "I don't want this."

"This loony tune has been stalking you since you were a kid. How many nights' sleep did you lose thinking he was right outside your window? And now you want to show him some mercy?" Bowie said, his eyes blazing, his muscles taut. He stared me down.

Wendell gazed at me with pleading eyes, his mouth open in a state of shock. And then it hit me. I had him. Right in my corner. Bowie had provided the perfect setup. I leaned down to Wendell and gently stroked his face and smiled at him. He had never received such an affectionate gesture from me, the object of his obsession. He didn't know quite how to react.

Bowie clamped a big paw on my shoulder to pull me away from him, but I shook him off. "I'm sorry he hurt you," I said, staring straight into Wendell's eyes.

Wendell went limp. He looked at me and smiled. A tear slowly streaked the side of his face. He couldn't believe what he was hearing.

"I guess I always knew, but there were so many people in my life who couldn't accept it. They filled my head with all sorts of horrible thoughts to keep us apart. But I can't deny your love for me anymore. You do love me like any true soul mate would. And I love you too."

I threw my arms around him and squeezed tight. At first he tensed up, but as the reality of what was happening sank in, he burrowed his head in my chest and sobbed. In his mind, I had finally come around.

I glanced back at Bowie, who had quickly caught on to what I was doing. He gave me an encouraging wink.

I carefully lifted Wendell's head off my chest and tenderly raised it up so we were face to face. I offered him a warm smile. He sniffed and cleared his throat and squinted his eyes to rid them of the onslaught of tears.

"The truth shall finally set us free, Jarrod," he said, beaming.

"I know, Wendell, but this guy here, this evil man, will never let you go until you tell him what he wants to know."

"I don't know . . . He wants me to go back to prison. I don't want to ever go back, do you hear me? I wouldn't make it, " he said, his voice shaking.

"We'll tell him what he wants to know, and then we'll go away. We'll leave the country. Make a new life somewhere else," I said, ready to shoot my hand out to accept that elusive Emmy Award that I had been chasing after for so many years.

Wendell scanned my face, not a hundred percent ready to believe I was sincere. I had to seal it with a kiss. I softly brushed my lips across his cheek and whispered in his ear, "I just want to be with you, away from all this like we're meant to be."

Wendell took a deep breath, and released it, allowing years of frustration to escape his body. After all this time, his soul mate had finally come home. He then turned to Bowie and said, "A tool shed."

"Where?" Bowie barked.

"I didn't have to drag him far. It's right near—"

A burning smell wafted up, and I stood up and looked around. "What is that?"

Bowie took a whiff and then, with a start, flung his body forward. "Jarrod, watch out!"

I caught sight of the lighter pressed into the palm of Wendell's hand too late. It must have been in his pocket, and he managed to get ahold of it and burn right through the ropes binding him. He freed himself, and shoved me aside as Bowie pounced on him like a cougar. Wendell head-butted Bowie with such force, he flew back, smashing against the wet bar, jostling it enough so that bottles of scotch, tequila, and vodka tipped over and fell, smashing Bowie over the head. Glass shattered everywhere, and Bowie, half-conscious, drooped down to the floor.

Wendell was out of the chair like a shot, and took advantage of the opportunity to flip Bowie facedown on the floor, and quickly bind his hands together with the singed rope.

"I'm tired of listening to you," he said as he picked up the roll of duct tape off the coffee table, tore off a nice long piece, and pressed it over Bowie's mouth. Wendell stared at Bowie for a moment, debating on what to do next, and then he marched over to the kitchen area, scrambled around in a drawer, and studied the blade of a sharpened steak knife. He walked back over to Bowie's prone body and hissed, "Don't you worry, Jarrod. He won't be bothering us anymore."

Straddling Bowie, he raised the knife in the air. I sprang across the room and grabbed ahold of his arm. "No!" I yelled, trying to pull him off Bowie. He swatted me aside like an annoying housefly.

"Boy," he said sternly. "Stay out of my way."

He raised the knife again. This time I hurled myself between Bowie and the blade, hoping to dear God he would stop short of stabbing his "soul mate." Luckily he did.

I had to give the performance of a lifetime. "Wendell, listen to me, please," I said. "We don't need more police chasing us. If you keep killing, we'll never have any peace. And isn't that what we both want? To be left alone in peace?"

Wendell's stone face relaxed into an admiring smile. "You're right, Jarrod. You're a good boy. Smart boy. I'm so proud of you."

"The people on the other boats may have heard all the commotion. Someone might have called the police. We should leave," I said, motioning him to join me. I just wanted him to step away from Bowie before he changed his mind and plunged the knife deep into his back.

We walked outside, and Wendell veered toward my rented Taurus. He had been following me for so long he knew exactly what kind of car I was driving in Miami. Wendell opened up the driver's side door to get in, but noticed me hanging back.

"Come on, boy, what are you waiting for? Let's go."

I hesitated. Every childhood fear was rising up inside of me. I was about to get in the car with the man who had stalked me for over two thirds of my life and had tried to kill me twice.

Wendell could smell my fear, and he melted. "Being scared is nothing to be ashamed of, Jarrod. We've all got things we're afraid of," he said with an understanding smile. "And I know you're worried about all the people who are going to chase us and try to separate us again."

I nodded, playing along for lack of a better plan.

"Chances are we will get caught eventually and they will take you away from me. But there's one surefire way to make sure that never happens."

"What's that?" I asked, not sure I wanted to hear the answer.

"The only way we'll be safe and together is if we leave this world. Right now."

I shuddered. This was the Wendell Butterworth I knew and loathed.

"I'll kill you first. Nice and quick. You won't feel a thing," he said as he reached into his pocket and pulled out the steak knife. "And you wait for me at the light. I'll be right behind you."

Chapter 30

Wendell took a step forward, raising the knife over his head. I slowly began backing away.

"Don't be scared. You won't feel a thing. I promise," he said. And that's when I turned and hightailed it out of there. I bolted down the sidewalk running along the marina, yelling at the top of my lungs for anyone who could hear me. I wrenched my head around and caught sight of Wendell, huffing and puffing, as he chased after me.

"Jarrod, come back!" he bellowed before he had to stop and catch his breath. It was my dumb luck that Wendell hadn't spent his long years behind bars working out at the prison gym. I was in much better shape from my many hikes in the Hollywood Hills with Snickers. I stayed well ahead of him.

I spotted a pair of headlights in the distance and debated whether or not I should run out into the road, but the car was coming too fast and shot by before I had a chance to get the driver's attention. I heard Wendell wheezing a few hundred feet behind me as he closed the distance between us. Instinctively, I sprinted to my right, but quickly discovered I was running down a dock slip housing a line of expensive yachts. When I reached the end, there was nothing but Biscayne Bay ahead of me. I could hide on one of the boats. Wendell would be hard pressed to find me. Screaming for help at this point might not be the smartest move. Most of the owners were out dining at the finest restaurants South Beach had to offer, and it would only lead Wendell to me. I spotted a darkened white cruiser with the name CHARLIE'S ANGEL stenciled in blue across the bow. It was enormous and easily worth a couple of million. It probably had a lot of compartments and closets for me to hide. I made a dash for it, but stopped suddenly when the moon illuminated the big, bulky form of a man gripping a steak knife. Wendell stood motionless at the other end of the dock, trapping me.

"Why are you running from me, boy?"

I whipped my head from side to side, searching for some way, any way, to escape. Wendell cautiously started to walk toward me. The only sound I could hear was the rocking of the wooden dock against the gentle waves lapping into shore and the steady approach of my stalker's footsteps.

There was nowhere to go. I knew it. Wendell knew it. I turned and sprinted straight off the dock in a swan dive, silently praying Wendell had never learned how to swim. I hit the bone-chilling water and swam for my life, as far out as I could. Other than fishing Dominique out of the surf, I hadn't swum since I played the son of a Midwestern tourist who accidentally steals a cache of diamonds from the Hawaiian mafia in a *Magnum, P.I.*, episode in 1984. One of the native gangsters tries to drown me off Waikiki Beach as a warning to my father, but I manage to swim away from him. It took nine takes to get right. I nailed it every time. The guy playing my attacker had had too many mai tais at lunch and had trouble hitting his mark.

My arms and legs ached after a few minutes, and I stopped and treaded water while I tried to rest up. I looked back at the dock, maybe a hundred feet away. Wendell stood forlornly at the edge, staring out at the moonlit bay.

"Jarrod? Jarrod?" he wailed.

I bobbed up and down in the waves, trying to keep my breathing steady. Don't panic. Just stay here, and pretty soon he may give up and leave and I can swim back to shore. I worried my legs wouldn't be able to tread much longer. I was spent. What a choice. Stabbed by a stalker or death by drowning.

A light hit my eyes, blinding me. I squinted and tried to focus. Had I already drowned and this was the light where I was supposed to meet Wendell? I heard the rumble of an engine and smelled gasoline as a motorboat pulled up in front of me. A hand reached out, hauling me up over the side and into the boat. I had been rescued.

Coughing and sputtering from the salty seawater, I said, "Thank you so much for picking me up. There's a guy on the dock who—"

For the first time I was able to see my rescuers. Two giants. One Caucasian and one Hispanic. Martinez's henchmen. I spun around to jump over the side, but the Hispanic grabbed a fistful of my shirt and yanked me back, shoving me down on a hard wooden seat in the back of the boat.

"Relax, will you?" he barked. "Enjoy the ride."

I sat silent, staring at them, wondering how far out we would go before they tied a cement block around my ankle and sent me hurtling to the ocean floor. But after a brief ten-minute ride, we drove up alongside an impressive cruiser, nearly twice the size of all the other boats docked in the marina. On the bow, I saw the name VIVECA II in big bold lettering. He'd named a boat after her, and she still felt the need to go sleep with a sleaze like Juan Carlos. But who was I to judge? The two henchmen wore loud flower print shirts and khaki shorts. Not exactly the butchest bad guys you would ever run across. But what they lacked in fashion style, they made up for in pure bulk. They hustled me up the ladder, and I braced myself for my first face-to-face meeting with Javier Martinez.

I was led into the private quarters and through to a back office deep inside the boat. I didn't see any other people aboard except for us. Viveca and the kids were probably in town wondering what had happened to their beloved paramour. The Caucasian rapped on a shellacked wooden door with a gold plate that said PRIVATE, and a gruff voice said, "Bring him in."

The door opened to reveal a brightly lit space with a glass-top table and high-back chair, four televisions, computer, phone, fax, everything. Rupert Murdoch could run his corporation out of this place. Javier Martinez in an open floral print shirt and white slacks, a look only an intimidating mafia don could ever get away with, stood up and offered me a warm smile.

"Well, Mr. Jarvis, at last we meet," he said. "Can I offer you a cocktail? I make an excellent margarita. My entire family swears by it."

"I'm fine, thank you," I said, a little confused by his hospitality. "First of all, Mr. Martinez, I want you to know I appreciate your . . . associates . . . picking me up when they did. They saved my life." I went on to explain my history with Wendell Butterworth and his endless pursuit of me leading up to the last few hours. Martinez listened to my story, wide-eyed and fascinated. When I'd finished, he took a big gulp of his tequila sunrise and set the glass down.

"Sounds like a very nasty business," he said dryly.

"Oh, I'm sure it doesn't even compare to what you're used to," I said, instantly regretting it. Here I was on his turf, surrounded by his thugs, and I was being flippant like Bruce Willis in his umpteenth *Die Hard* sequel.

"You'd be surprised," Martinez said with a smile, his eyes downcast. "I'm not as brutal and ruthless as most people think. Nobody's going to do a show on HBO about me anytime soon."

"Why did you bring me here?"

Martinez looked up at his goons and waved them away. They turned and walked out, closing the door behind them. "You've been following me. You and that private eye, what's his name, Bowie something . . ."

"Lassiter," I said.

"Right. And I want to know why."

"Okay, um, well, I'm not sure really where to begin, but a dear friend of mine recently married someone you might know . . . Juan Carlos Barranco."

Martinez picked up his glass and squeezed it so hard, I waited for it to crush in his hands. But he caught himself, and finished off the drink with one swig. "Yes, I know him. Too well, I'm afraid," he said.

"Well, another man connected to you, Austin Teboe, died of poisoning at Juan Carlos's wedding, and the trail has led me here . . . and to you."

"You think I'm behind Teboe's murder?"

I awkwardly shifted position. "Well, um," I said, "he did work for you. And he did betray you by leaving. And you do have a reputation for . . ." I stopped myself. This wasn't exactly my smartest hour accusing a mobster of murder. But I had to know the truth.

"I had no reason to get rid of Austin. Yes, he left me high and dry to go work in some restaurant. But he came crawling back, wanting his old job. I said no. It was a question of loyalty. He had disappointed me once. I was not going to let him do it again. But I never held a grudge. Now the other one, the actor, now that's another story."

"He's dead too."

Javier raised a brow, genuinely surprised. "Really? How?"

"Poisoning. My guess is it was the same kind used to kill Austin Teboe."

A sly smile crept across his face. "Well, I may be guilty of a lot of things, but lately my biggest crime has been just trying to make my family happy."

"What do you mean?"

"My daughter Dominique was dating that Barranco character. I never liked him, or the effect he had on her. He got her all excited about the movie business to the point where she had stars in her eyes. She wanted to be an actress. She heard some low-rent horror movie was in town looking for funding, and she came and begged me to invest. She figured it would ensure she get a part in the picture. It's hard to say no to your only daughter. In fact, I've never said it to her, so I agreed. Then, before I knew it, my wife came to me and told me not to write the check until the director promised to cast her in a role too. It was turning into a damn Martinez family production."

"Did you know Juan Carlos was playing the lead?"

"Of course not. I hated the bastard. I would've shut the whole damn movie down if I had known. Viveca and Dominique went to great lengths to hide that key piece of information from me."

"So when did you find out?"

"That self-promoting son of a bitch couldn't resist announcing in one of the local papers that he was back in town starring in a new film. A member of my household staff saw it and brought it to my attention. He had already broken Dominique's heart once, and I was afraid he would try again. I told him if he ever came near my daughter again, I would cut off his head, so I had my boys follow him around to make sure he didn't try to contact her . . ." His voice trailed off. He stared out a portal at the vast ocean.

"They saw him up north," I said. "At the Sand Drift Motel, with—"

"David," Martinez choked out. "My son."

We stood silent. Martinez poured some more tequila, stirred it around with his forefinger, and raised the glass to his lips. "I was ready to kill him right then and there. But things only got worse . . ."

"Viveca?"

Martinez nodded. "She left clues all over the place. And there was a lot of tension between her and Dominique, so it was only a matter of time before I put two and two together. At that point, the sick mother fucker had signed his death warrant."

"So you had him killed?"

Martinez shook his head. "No."

"Mr. Martinez," I said. "You have a history of offing men who cross your family."

He stared at me blankly. "I don't know what you're talking about."

"Your daughter Dominique's ex-boyfriend Calvin. He mysteriously disappeared after breaking it off with your daughter. Are you telling me . . . ?"

Martinez laughed. "I didn't kill him. I just threatened him. Told him if I ever saw his face again, I would slaughter him and his entire family. He ran off scared. Last I heard he was working as a bartender in Havana."

"But why hasn't he tried contacting his family? They're worried sick."

"He will eventually. When he thinks it's safe. I can have a certain effect on people," he said proudly.

"So you had nothing to do with Juan Carlos's murder?"

"I'll be honest with you. I had every intention of doing it. And I wanted to do it all by myself. I wanted him to see *my* face as I squeezed the last bit of breath out of his skinny, weak body." He snapped out of his fantasy and looked at me. "But I guess someone else got to him first."

I believed him. There was no reason for him to lie. He could've confessed and then just fed me to the sharks.

"Jarrod, I respect your need to find out what happened to Austin and the actor. I have no problem with that."

"Okay," I said warily.

"But let's set the record straight. Feel free to poke around all you like, and solve your little murder mystery. But when you dig for your information, just be sure you don't come across anything that could prove hazardous to your health."

"Like what?"

"Like anything related to me. I'm telling you right now, I had nothing to do with either of those deaths. But I am embroiled in certain activities that need to be kept under wraps. If you unwrap them, then we have a problem."

"I get the message. Loud and clear."

"I suspected you would."

"Am I free to go now?"

"No," Martinez said, standing up and coming around the desk. "My wife and children should be arriving at any moment. I believe you know them all. I'd like you stay for dinner."

"Oh, I don't know if they really want to see me . . ." I said.

"If they've heard about Juan Carlos, I'm sure they all must be in mourning. I'll need your help in cheering them up," he said as he gripped my arm, signaling to me that I didn't have a choice.

I would've preferred being fed to the sharks.

Chapter 31

Martinez was kind enough to allow me to freshen up in one of the guest staterooms. I used the opportunity to pick up a shore-to-land phone and immediately call the *QE3*. I was afraid Wendell Butterworth might have doubled back and finished off Bowie, whom we'd left tied up and gagged on his houseboat. The phone rang and rang and I finally got his machine. I hung up and dialed the Ritz Plaza. When the operator put me through to my room, Charlie picked up the phone on the first ring.

"Hello?" he said. I could tell he was worried.

"Charlie, it's me," I said. "Look, I don't have time to explain, but I need you to go over to Bowie's houseboat and make sure he's all right."

"Why?"

I quickly explained everything, and when I'd finished, he said, "Where are you now?"

"On Javier Martinez's boat. Somewhere out in the marina."

"What?" Charlie said, more than a bit concerned.

One of the crew rapped on the stateroom door. "Mr. Martinez is requesting your presence in the dining room, Mr. Jarvis."

"In a minute," I called out.

"Mr. Martinez isn't used to being kept waiting," the crew member said.

"Okay, be right there," I said, then spoke fast into the phone. "Charlie, I have to go. I really don't want to piss this guy off. Please, just go make sure Bowie is all right."

The crew member outside the door inserted the key and turned the knob. I didn't want him catching me on the phone, so I hung up, and smiled at him as he stepped inside. He was short and squat, a balding Latino in a crisp white uniform, his pressed shorts showing off some hairy, knobby knees. He stared at me sternly.

"I love the little duck soaps in the bathroom. Can I take some home with me?" I said, hoping I would be able to actually go home at some point.

He wasn't amused. He just held the door open for me, and I passed him with a shrug. He escorted me to the dining room, and made sure I went inside before quietly retreating. I had entered the lion's den.

Javier sat at the head of the table, Viveca to his immediate right, Dominique and David on his left. Javier watched with glee as his wife and children finally noticed me. Viveca nearly spit out her peach schnapps. Dominique stared daggers. And David strained trying to place me, probably having a vague recollection of seeing me at the Sand Drift Motel.

It was obvious Javier hadn't mentioned I would be tonight's special guest. He had a sick sense of humor, and enjoyed catching them off guard like this.

Dominique spoke first. "What's he doing here?"

"He's my friend and I've asked him to join us for dinner," Javier said, barely able to contain himself he was having such a good time.

"I didn't know you and Dad were friends," Dominique said,

barely even looking at me. "Is that how you got cast in the movie?"

"No," I said. "We've only recently met."

"We've discovered we have something in common," Javier said as the same crew member that brought me to the dining room rushed in to refill his boss's glass of bourbon.

"And what's that?" Viveca asked.

"A mutual loathing of your dearly departed Juan Carlos," Javier said. There was a deafening silence, finally broken by Javier's almost merry voice. "Jarrod, can I offer you a drink?"

"Just some water, thank you, Mr. Martinez."

"We're friends, Jarrod, call me Javier," he said with a wink.

So this is how Miami crime bosses got their kicks. Stirring the pot at home. I never saw someone have such a good time.

David finally spoke up. "Have we met?" He looked me up and down.

"No," Javier answered for me. "At least I don't think so. But Jesus and Abe first saw him up in that little town north of Vero Beach. Sebastian. Where you were last week. With Juan Carlos."

Another long, painful silence. David looked down at his clean, shiny, empty plate guiltily. I knew Viveca and Dominique both knew that the other was sleeping with Juan Carlos, so I tried reading their faces to ascertain if they knew about David's involvement with him as well. Both remained still, and stone-faced, and silent. They definitely knew. Talk about a family affair.

The wait staff arrived with a sumptuous feast of pan-fried scallops as an appetizer, shrimp salad, a delectable pecan-crusted catfish, and a very expensive French white wine with a name I couldn't pronounce. Javier was clearly a lover of seafood given the rather one-sided menu, and mother, son, and daughter dove in with relish, obviously relieved that the food could serve as a distraction from the excruciatingly uncomfortable circumstances.

None of them had any idea how much I knew about their individual escapades, though Viveca flaunted it on the set every chance she got. Of course, how could she ever imagine that I would at some point be joining the family for dinner on their yacht? Javier stuffed huge bites of catfish in his mouth, and chewed with his mouth open. Smack. Smack. Smack. I could easily understand why Javier had such deplorable table manners. Who in their right mind would want to mention it to him? Viveca and Dominique exchanged furtive glances. David sat sullenly, poking at the shrimp on his salad plate with a tiny stainless steel fork.

He then took a small bite of scallop, and hurled it back onto his plate. "It's overcooked . . . again," he huffed. "I wish we could get Austin back."

"Well, we can't because Austin's dead," Javier said, shooting an annoyed glance at his son. "And dead people are useless in the kitchen."

"Maybe if you had let him come back, he wouldn't be dead," said Viveca.

Javier's face reddened. "Austin left us high and dry for greener pastures. Loyalty means everything to me, Viveca. You know that," he said, and then glared at the entire family. "You should *all* know that."

"I miss him," Dominique said quietly. "He was a good man."

"Good man. Good man. Austin Teboe was a traitor." Javier spit out his catfish. I jerked my head to the right to avoid a bull's-eye. "None of you ever took the time to really know him. You just liked the way he prepared your food. The three of you have proven time and time again that you're not particularly good judges of character."

Nobody dared to respond. They all looked down at their food and continued eating. Nothing made much sense anymore. Austin Teboe had quit working for the Martinez family. But did that necessarily provide the motive for a family member to poison him? And Dominique had been the only Martinez present at the time Austin Teboe was murdered. So everybody not there was pretty much cleared. So who did kill him? And why? And what about Juan Carlos? Javier said he didn't do it, and I was predisposed to believe him. If he had done it, he probably would have bragged about it after all the humiliation Juan Carlos put the poor guy through, sleeping with his entire immediate family. No. I was pretty sure Martinez was innocent, at least of the Austin Teboe and Juan Carlos Barranco murders. But what about the rest of the family? Juan Carlos had broken Dominique's heart, toyed with Viveca's affections, and slept with David while also banging his mother and sister at the same time. Probably recycled his sweet nothings too. No, there were plenty of motives to choose from. But as I looked around the table, I didn't see a smidgeon of guilt or remorse, just pure unadulterated grief. These people were in mourning. They should have been rejoicing. Juan Carlos wouldn't be around anymore to lie, steal, cheat, and play a sad little ditty on their heartstrings. But none of them were willing to look at that side of him. They chose to focus on his positive attributes, whatever they might be. Just as Laurette had. All I could imagine was just how good he must have been in bed.

I decided that although this family was wildly dysfunctional, there wasn't a murderer among them outside of their mobster father. So if no one in the Martinez family killed Juan Carlos, then who did? I was no closer to solving this puzzle than I was when my plane touched down in Miami a few weeks ago.

The knobby-kneed crewmember burst into the dining room, his face tense. "Excuse me, sir," he said to Javier.

"Yes, what is it?"

"We're under attack."

Javier stood up, and threw his napkin down. "What?"

"Two men are on board. Our security cameras caught them climbing over the deck railing. And they're armed."

"Stay here," Javier said to all of us, and hastily followed the crew member out. We all sat frozen for a moment, and then jumped up at the same time and dashed out of the room and up the narrow steel stairs to get a good view of the action. By the time we'd reached topside, a swarm of Martinez's men were searching the boat. The intruders had yet to be found. Javier barked orders and nervously paced the deck. He caught sight of us peeking out from the door leading to below deck.

"I told you all to stay put! I want you to go to your staterooms now!" The family knew better than to defy orders from the master of the house twice, so they all solemnly retreated. Since I didn't have a stateroom, I figured he didn't mean me. So I took the opportunity to poke around. Who were these men? A rival mob family? The feds on a raid? And how on earth did I get caught in the middle? As I passed a midsize rubber dingy, a pair of hands grabbed me from behind and hauled me over behind it. The attacker wrenched my arms behind my back, and before I could call out to my good friend Javier, someone else in front of me cupped a hand over my mouth.

"Quiet, Jarrod, it's me," Charlie said, looking very sexy in a black skintight wet suit unzipped far enough to show off his broad, furry chest.

"What are you doing here?" I whispered urgently.

The man holding me from behind let me go, and said, "We came to rescue you." It was Bowie.

"Rescue me? I don't need to be rescued," I said in a hushed voice.

"When you called me to tell me you were on Martinez's boat, you sounded nervous," Charlie said.

"I was late for dinner," I said. I turned to Bowie. "Are you okay?" I could feel Charlie tense up the minute the words came rolling out of my mouth.

"Yeah, Wendell never came back. I was hogtied in my living

room until Charlie thankfully showed up," Bowie said, also looking sexy in the same black wetsuit.

"You guys better get out of here before Martinez finds you. They saw you on the security cameras, and it's only a matter of time before—"

A flood of lights blinded all three of us as Martinez and his men, armed with flashlights and pistols, swooped down on us. We all threw our hands up in the air to surrender. We were too outnumbered to try anything.

"Who are you?" Javier asked Charlie and Bowie brusquely. "What are you doing on my boat?"

"They're friends of mine," I said, with an upbeat smile. "I was hoping there might be room for them at dinner."

Chapter 32

Unfortunately Javier wasn't in the mood to resume dinner after the dramatic invasion. And it was lucky for us he decided not to kill any of us for ruining his meal and nearly causing him a heart attack. He knew three bodies washing ashore was a headache he didn't need at the moment. Instead, he had his crew escort Charlie and Bowie topside and to the small speedboat they had tied to a post just a few hundred yards from the yacht.

As I was heading back up to the deck of the boat to join them, a stateroom door creaked open, and a voice said softly, "Jarrod, come in here. I need to tell you something." It was David Martinez. We hadn't exchanged two words ever, and now he had a burning need to confide in me. I looked around to make sure Daddy wasn't spying on us, and then slipped inside his stateroom.

"What is it?" I said.

David shut the door and locked it. "I know Juan Carlos was a shit. Deep down I've always known it. But I couldn't help myself. He had a power over me."

"And a lot of other people," I added.

David nodded. "I know. But I want to know who killed him. It's tearing me up inside now that he's gone, and I have to know."

"I'll do my best."

"Do you really think there might be a connection between Juan Carlos's death and Austin Teboe's?"

"Yes."

"Then maybe this will help you somehow. After my dad refused to rehire him, Austin fell into serious debt and really needed some cash. He showed up at the house one day when he knew Dad was away to ask me if I could help him somehow, maybe talk to Dad for him, and he walked in on me and Juan Carlos fooling around in the sack."

"Did he already know about Dominique and your mother?"

"Everybody knew about Juan Carlos dumping Dominique. It was very messy and very public. It's what drove Juan Carlos out of town. I'm not sure if Austin knew about Juan Carlos and my mother though. But the fact that Juan Carlos was bisexual and sleeping with me and my sister, well, he figured he had enough."

"Enough to do what?"

"Austin was hiding out from loan sharks by the time word leaked out that Juan Carlos was marrying some TV agent out in California. He was penniless and desperate. So he went out there to blackmail him. If Juan Carlos helped him out financially, he'd keep quiet and my father would never have to know that his gay son was sleeping with the same man who destroyed his daughter's heart. Dad would never have to know any of what was going on behind his back."

"How do you know that was what Austin was planning?"

"Because Dominique saw him at the wedding. She figured out what he was going to do, and confronted him about it. He certainly didn't deny it."

"So did your sister poison him to protect Juan Carlos?"

"No. She says she didn't and I believe her."

"Then what about Juan Carlos? He could've retaliated and

poisoned Teboe at the wedding. You were as close to him as anybody. Surely you might have some idea if it was him."

"Juan Carlos was a lot of things, but he was not a murderer. I think if you find out who killed Austin, you'll find out who killed Juan Carlos."

"What about you, David? You certainly had a lot to lose if your father found out. Maybe you sent someone out there to do the job for you."

"Would I be telling you all this if I had? I'm hoping this gives you the information you need to find out who murdered Juan Carlos."

He had a point. Why implicate yourself to such a degree if you were guilty? My initial hunch was right. No one in the family was responsible. But this key piece of dirt opened up a host of new possibilities. A blackmail scheme. But Juan Carlos must have refused to play ball. Teboe threatened to put in a call to Martinez. And an hour later Austin Teboe was dead. It sure sounded like a textbook case of murder. Juan Carlos knocked him off before he could talk. But Juan Carlos was never away from Laurette's side at the wedding. There was no way he could have poured the poison in Austin's champagne. No, it was impossible for Juan Carlos to have pulled it off. Besides, no one else but Rudy Pearson had possession of the lethal monkshead poison. But why would Rudy Pearson have reason to murder Austin Teboe? It was clear on the bus ride up to the Hearst Castle that the two didn't even know each other. Unless Rudy meant to poison someone else. Yes! Austin could have swallowed the poison by mistake. Rudy despised Juan Carlos for some reason, and wanted him dead. When Austin keeled over instead, Rudy decided to follow Juan Carlos to Florida and finish the job once and for all. It made perfect sense. But since Rudy was already dead by the time Juan Carlos died in his Chinese chicken salad, someone else must be behind that murder.

I left David in his grief and went topside where the knobby-kneed crew member waited to show me the plank, or ladder rather, that led me down to the speedboat where Charlie and Bowie waited for me. As Bowie revved the engine, and we began the short trip back to shore, Charlie put a hand on my knee.

"By the way," he said. "I had the guys back in LA call in a few favors with the Miami Police Department. They let me take a look at the toxicology reports that just came back from the lab."

"And?" I said.

"It's official. Juan Carlos died from a hit of monkshead poison."

Bowie stole a glance at Charlie's hand resting on my knee. He grimaced. It was clear he had developed some feelings for me. And I felt wholly responsible. But I couldn't iron out those problems now. This new surprise just raised more unanswered questions. Who other than Rudy had access to the stash of monkshead? There was that mysterious roommate taking a shower in Rudy's room while I was searching it, but I had no idea who that might be. Maybe he or she took over for Rudy after Wendell killed him?

When we reached the dock, I told Bowie what I had learned from Javier about his cousin Calvin. Bowie was taken by surprise by my news. It was the first solid lead he had heard in months. It was clear he was anxious to get on it. He mumbled his good-byes and quickly disappeared inside the *QE3*. Charlie and I got into the Taurus and headed back to the Ritz Plaza.

I turned to Charlie. "Thank you for rescuing me," I said.

"No problem," Charlie said.

"I love you," I said, and meant it.

Long, long pause. He really wanted me to suffer a little bit before finally relenting. "I love you too."

When we got back to the room at the Ritz Plaza, Charlie sat me down on the bed. "I meant what I said in the car," he said.

"I know. So did I."

He stared at me sharply, trying to read my face for any signs of insincerity.

"From the moment we met, until now, and forever," I said.

"So you're not leaving me for some muscle-bound ex–Navy Seal with his own boat?"

"Never was, never will," I said.

Charlie slowly nodded, considering, and then he said, "Well, I'm leaving you. Your director, Larry Levant, came out to me on the set, and we really hit it off, and one thing led to another and well—"

I whacked him with the pillow. We both laughed. I started to unzip his black wetsuit all the way down to the lower regions when the phone suddenly rang, disrupting the mood. Sighing, I scooped it up and said impatiently, "Yes, what is it?"

I heard a bright, cheery, familiar voice. "Hi, Jarrod, it's me, Amy Jo."

"Hi, Amy Jo. What's up?"

"Well, given the recent tragedy, the producers have decided to shut down production indefinitely." I had forgotten that some people might consider Juan Carlos's death a tragedy.

"I see. Well, I'm sure it's for the best."

"So we need all of the cast to clean out their trailers ASAP," she said. "Like right now."

"It's kind of late, isn't it?" I said.

"Most of the cast did it this afternoon. You were nowhere to be found. I kept calling and calling. You really should tell us when you're going to take off like that." Mean, vicious Amy Jo was suddenly reemerging.

"I'll get my stuff first thing in the morning."

"We really need you to do it now, Jarrod. The crew wants to pack up all their equipment and caravan it back to California in the morning. And we promised the city of Coral Gables we would leave the park cleaner than when we found it, and that won't happen if your belongings are littered all over the place."

"Fine. I'll go out there now."

"Good. I sure do appreciate your cooperation," she said, her mind already onto her next job. I was about to hang up when Amy Jo said, "Oh, Jarrod, by the way, some guy left a message for you at the production office about an hour ago."

"Who was it?"

"He didn't say. But he said he left you something in the tool shed on the set, and you really need to go pick it up."

"What tool shed?"

"You know, the one out in the woods a few feet from the set. Stella from makeup keeps some hairbrushes and hand mirrors, stuff like that in there for safekeeping. But she couldn't find the key this morning, and that thing's a bitch to open. So bring a crowbar."

"Did the person say what it was he left me?"

"No. Just that it's someone you've been looking for." She paused and then giggled. "The receptionist must have written this down wrong. It has to be 'something,' not 'someone.' She makes it sound like there's a person in there."

"Thanks, Amy Jo," I said robotically as I hung up the phone and looked at Charlie, my face drawn and pale.

"What is it?" Charlie said. "What's wrong?"

"I think I know where Wendell Butterworth stashed Rudy Pearson's body."

Chapter 33

After I told Charlie what Wendell had said about the tool shed and not having to drag Rudy's body far, he unzipped his suitcase, rummaged through it, and drew out his gun. He stuffed it into his shoulder holster. "I'm going with you this time," he said.

"Believe me," I said, "I'm not about to go out there without you."

We headed out the door and down the hall.

"Do you know where the shed is?" Charlie said.

"I'm not sure I remember ever seeing it. But it has to be in the vicinity of the set."

We reached the bank of elevators, and I pressed the "down" arrow button. After a few moments, the bell rang and the elevator doors slid open. Laurette and Larry Levant stepped off. Larry had his arm around Laurette's waist. She was bleary-eyed and giggly.

Larry smiled weakly. "I found her in the bar. She was drowning her sorrows. She's had a rough time of it."

"He's so sweet," Laurette slurred. "Isn't he sweet?" She turned to Charlie and me. "Well, don't you think so?"

"I'm sorry," I said. "I thought it was a rhetorical question. Yes, he's very sweet."

"And probably gay too," Laurette said. "Just my luck. Or bi. Like my husband. I mean, my dead husband. The jerk." Laurette teetered, but Larry's hand on the small of her back steadied her. Laurette fought to focus, and squinted to get a good look at the two of us, or from her blood alcohol level, all six of us.

"I've told her four times I'm not gay, but she won't believe me," Larry shrugged. "What do I have to do to prove it?"

Laurette stroked a finger down his cheek. "I've got a few ideas." Then, she burst into tears. "What am I doing? I've been a widow for less than two days."

"It's okay, sweetheart," I said. "Juan Carlos wasn't exactly a role model for fidelity, and I know a woman should take her time after the end of a relationship, but after what that bastard put you through, I say go for it."

"Thanks, Jarrod," Larry said. "She's a cutie, isn't she?"

I smiled. Laurette glared at me through her blurry vision.

"Yes," I said quickly. "She is. I'm sorry, Laurette, I thought it was another rhetorical question."

"You're my best friend, Jarrod," she mumbled as she started sliding down the wall. Larry had trouble holding her up. Charlie and I swooped in to give him a hand. Once Larry had her in his grasp again, Charlie and I stepped back as the bell rang again, and another elevator arrived. Charlie reached out and held the door open.

"Jarrod, we better go," he said.

"Where are you two off to?" Laurette called out as Larry attempted to maneuver her down the hall.

"Back out to the set," I said. "I think we may have found Rudy Pearson."

Laurette stopped cold, grabbed the wall for support, and sobered up a bit. "Excuse me?"

"We'll explain later. After you've had some coffee," I said and got on the elevator. Laurette wrested herself free from Larry, and charged back up the hall and to the elevator. She stuck her hand in to stop the doors from closing.

"I don't want you two going out there tonight. It could be dangerous. Call the police, and have them come with you," she said.

"I called the police the last time, and when they showed up, I couldn't prove anything had happened. They think I'm some screwy actor making up stories. If we find anything, then we'll call the police."

Charlie opened up his jacket far enough for Laurette to see his holstered gun. "We'll be fine, Laurette," he said.

I gently pried Laurette's fingers off the elevator door. "I'll call you as soon as we get back. I promise."

"Be careful," she said as the doors closed on her worried face.

When we reached the set in the wooded park just outside Coral Gables, most of the props and equipment had been packed up and the area cleared. There were a few trucks and trailers locked up tight in the parking lot, but no one from the crew was around. It was completely dark now, and Charlie and I stuck close together as we surveyed the area for any sign of the mysterious tool shed.

The temperature had dropped to the low fifties. It was cold for Southern Florida and there was a biting breeze that made me shiver. It also could have been the macabre circumstances of searching for a butchered body that gave me chills. I led the way, Charlie right on my heels, as we walked down a path leading away from the set. It was the spot where I had witnessed Wendell Butterworth stab the life out of Rudy Pearson. When we reached the clearing, the trees swayed ominously around us, blocking the moonlight, making it that much darker.

"You see anything?" Charlie said.

"No," I said. The truth was I was seeing a lot of things. When I was a little boy, I watched the John Carpenter horror classic *Halloween* on late-night TV. Jamie Lee Curtis played a nubile young babysitter stalked by a vengeful escaped mental patient named Michael Myers. He wore an eerie, white mask over his face, and stalked unsuspecting teenagers in the neighborhood accompanied by a disturbing, bone-chilling film score. It had an undeniable impact on me, and for several weeks after that, I saw the masked face of Michael Myers everywhere. On the street, outside my bedroom window, in my closet. Everywhere I turned there he was. And on this night, after all I had experienced at the hands of Wendell Butterworth, I saw his face. Everywhere. Peeking out from behind the trees, waiting for us down the path, hovering above us in a tree branch. I couldn't shake his image, and it began working the knots in my stomach.

"Jarrod, down here!" Charlie said as he pounded off down a hidden trail I had missed. I ran after him, not wanting to lose him from my sight. When I caught up to Charlie, he was standing still in the middle of the path, his gaze fixed on a small wooden shed, about six feet in height, not more than four feet wide. There was a steel padlock around the rusted door handle.

I looked at Charlie, my eyes wide with anticipation, and the knots in my stomach twisting tighter. "You think this is it?"

Charlie shrugged. "I guess there's one way to find out." He picked up a rock and banged it against the padlock. Nothing. Not even a scratch. He tried again. No luck.

"Amy Jo was right," I said. "This is going to be a bitch to open."

"Stand back," Charlie said, drawing his gun out of his holster. I did what I was told and Charlie aimed the barrel right up against the lock and pulled the trigger. There was a loud pop, and it made me flinch. The padlock snapped off. Charlie put his gun away and lifted the broken lock off the door handle.

"You ready?" he said.

I nodded, and watched as he gripped the handle with his right hand and slowly opened the door. The first thing I saw were Stella's beauty supplies lined up on a small shelf that ran across the top of the shed, and then I saw him. Rudy Pearson sat almost in a lotus position on the floor, covered in dried blood, his eyes wide open in terror. Wendell had told the truth. His body had been right under our noses the whole time.

I stepped back to get a good look. "Oh, shit."

"Come on, Jarrod, let's call the police. This is all we need to get Wendell off the streets for good."

Charlie started back up the path. I took a moment to stare at the dead body. Who else would have to die before the authorities realized what a menace Wendell Butterworth was to society? I took a deep breath, and turned. Charlie stood still, halfway up the path. Why had he stopped? And then, just beyond him, I saw the face of Wendell Butterworth. Was this my mind playing tricks on me again like it did when I was a kid with Michael Myers? A part of me prayed it was just my imagination, but I knew better when Charlie went for his gun. Before he could snatch it out of the holster, Wendell rushed forward with a shovel raised over his head and cracked it down on Charlie's skull. Charlie crumpled to the ground.

"Charlie!" I yelled, and ran to him. Not even concerned with Wendell at the moment, I knelt down and saw a trickle of blood stream down Charlie's forehead. He moaned softly. Thank God he was alive.

"Why did you betray me, boy? We had a chance to escape to a place where no one would ever bother us again, and you ran away! Why?" Wendell stepped forward, still gripping the shovel.

"Because you've been bad. Very bad. You've hurt my friends. First Bowie. Now Charlie. Who else have you hurt, Wendell?"

Wendell glanced down at the still body of Charlie and pointed an accusing finger at him. "He was the one who wanted to hurt *me*. I was just protecting myself. Same with the other one. And Juan Carlos."

"What about Juan Carlos?"

Wendell didn't answer. His fingers tightened around the wooden handle of the shovel.

"Did you poison Juan Carlos?"

Wendell's eyes were blank, as if I were talking to a robot. He didn't respond. He just stared off into the distance.

"Did you somehow get your hands on some of Rudy's poison and use it to kill Juan Carlos?"

Wendell looked at the ground and shrugged, like a schoolboy brought to task for shooting a spitball.

"I don't understand, Wendell. Why? Why would you go after Juan Carlos? The facts just don't add up."

"Because Wendell didn't kill him," a voice said from behind me. I spun around and gasped at the smiling corpse of Rudy Pearson. He was on his feet, and very much alive. "I did."

Chapter 34

Rudy Pearson lifted his heavy body up out of the shed using the wooden door for balance. He pulled a white handkerchief out of a pocket in his trousers and began scrubbing off the dried blood on his face.

"Pretty nifty, huh?" he said. "Blood looks so real."

I stood a few feet away from him, my mouth agape, still somewhat in a state of shock. "I don't understand, Rudy. Why did you go to all that trouble to make it look like Wendell killed you?"

"Too many people knew I hated Juan Carlos, especially you. I would've been the first person the cops came looking for."

Wendell stepped over Charlie's inert body, and lumbered up behind me. I felt his presence, his hot breath on my neck, but stayed calm. The last thing I was going to do was make a sudden move and spook him.

"You knew I was hot on your trail after I found the monkshead poison in your room," I said. "So you manipulated Wendell into helping you set all this up."

Rudy grinned and nodded. He was rather proud of himself. I didn't dare to turn and see what Wendell was doing.

It was clear now that Wendell was Rudy's mysterious roommate at the hotel. He was the one taking a shower when I found the monkshead poison. All the facts kept spinning around in my head. It was an incredible rush of information, and I felt I was reaching up and grabbing pieces one at a time to fit into the puzzle.

"Why? Why would Wendell help you?" I said.

"Because I promised to help reunite him with his soul mate if he did as he was told. And look, I did," Rudy said as Wendell pressed his giant hand around my bicep in a steel-like vise grip. "See how happy he is, Jarrod? Just don't disappoint him by running away again. He suffers from separation anxiety, not to mention a white-hot temper."

I glanced up at Wendell, who squeezed my arm so tight, the pain shot through my entire body. I winced.

"Look at the big lug," Rudy said. "He was like a kid in the candy store when we were setting this whole thing up. He loved all the fake blood and makeup we stole from the set to make my murder look real. And the crew never even missed one of the retractable prop knives we lifted while you were shooting your death scene. Once we had you convinced Wendell had stabbed and killed me in the woods, I was free to poison that bastard Juan Carlos."

"Now you can just disappear and start over, and Juan Carlos can never hurt you again," I said.

"That's right," Rudy said, a euphoric grin slinking across his face.

"Why, Rudy? Why did you hate him so much?" I said.

Rudy clenched his fist, and stared at the ground. Just the thought of Juan Carlos sent him spiraling into an internal rage.

"Did he sleep with you too?" I said.

"No!" Rudy snapped. The thought of it disgusted him. "I'm not some love-starved, pathetic, needy, blithering idiot like that Dominique girl. I would *never* allow myself to manipulated by that piece of shit."

"You two obviously have some kind of history," I said.

"Yes, we did. When we were struggling actors, we both went up for the same parts time and time again," Rudy said, eyeing me for my reaction.

This was indeed a surprise. I had no idea Rudy Pearson had ever acted before. And given his rather slovenly appearance, I was hard pressed to believe he and Juan Carlos had ever competed for the same roles.

Rudy gauged my reaction and sighed. "I used to look a lot different."

I didn't want to set him off so I remained silent, still very much aware of the giant hand squeezing my left arm and the formidable presence of a much taller Wendell Butterworth standing behind me.

"It was the late nineties," Rudy said. "I gotta tell you, I was a real hunk. Worked out every day. Surfed on the weekends. My acting teacher kept telling me I was leading man material in my scene study class. But I just couldn't catch a break. My manager wasn't sending me out on any auditions. My prospects looked pretty bleak. I was about to quit the business and start looking around for something else to do, when a friend of mine came to me and said he heard they were looking for a good-looking, sexy guy around my age to play a professional rugby player from England to romance Tori Spelling for a story arc on *Beverly Hills 90210*. Man, I was perfect. I had just finished a short run doing a Noël Coward play at one of those small equity waiver theaters on Santa Monica Boulevard. I had perfected an English accent, and I knew how to play rugby. But my manager was useless. She said she couldn't even get me in to see the casting director. So I took matters into my own hands. I bluffed my way in. And I blew her away. I remember her saying, 'Where the hell have you been?' She took me straight to the producers and they loved me. I even tested with Tori. We flirted. I could tell she thought I was cute. It was pretty much a done deal."

Rudy let the stained handkerchief slip from his fingers and drop to the ground. He kept staring at the ground, remembering. "I had it in the bag. My manager, who actually took me out to dinner after she got the call, was busy negotiating the contract. I was going to appear in seven out of the first thirteen episodes of the new season, with an option for more. I had such a good feeling about it. I kept having dreams that I'd make such a great impression, they would reshoot the opening credits so they could put me in with the other cast members. You know, shots of me on the beach messing around with Luke Perry and Jason Priestly, pinching Jennie Garth's ass. That kind of stuff."

Rudy's eyes welled up at the memory, the lost opportunities, another Hollywood dream shattered.

I knew the rest. The rumors about Juan Carlos sleeping with the married executive producer to land the role of the sexy rugby player.

"Juan Carlos was runner-up for the same part," I said. "If they couldn't close your deal, they were going to go with him. He found out they were going to cast you, so he decided he had to do something about it. One of the executive producers had the hots for him, and he knew it. He used that to his advantage. Started up a big romance. That poor woman probably never knew what hit her."

Rudy nodded. "She should've known better. Actors will do anything for a part. She was a fucking executive producer! How could she not know that?"

"People, no matter how cynical, can often be blinded by love, or lust," I said, wondering at what point it was that I had suddenly turned into Dr. Phil.

"They gave it to him," Rudy said, almost spitting out the words. "He gave her multiple orgasms so she made sure they gave it to him. That fucking lowlife user. I was supposed to be the big cheese! Not him!"

"That's Hollywood," I said, instantly regretting it. Rudy

stared at me with contempt. I shrugged. "We've all got a story like that."

"My one big shot, and he stole it away from me. I spiraled after that. My manager used the botched deal as an excuse to drop me. I couldn't even get hired to be a cowhand extra on a fucking *Dr. Quinn, Medicine Woman*. I started eating too much, gained about a hundred pounds. I started drinking too much, smashed up my car, and got arrested for DUI. It was downright tragic. I was three months behind on my rent. I didn't know what I was going to do. I just sat at home watching soap operas all day and downing bottles of gin. I was becoming a fucking cautionary tale!"

Wendell loosened his grip, and for a moment, I had a chance to run. I could have made it out of the clearing, and into the woods, but I just couldn't leave Charlie. There was no telling what they might do to him. I had to make sure he was safe, even if it meant giving myself over to Wendell.

"Finally, the girl who lived next door to me was going out of town to visit her folks in Iowa or somewhere. Her mom had some kind of a stroke and she had to get home fast. She wrote freelance articles for *Soap Opera Digest*, and offered to pay me a hundred bucks if I finished up a couple for her while she was away. Hell, I figured it would be a cinch. I knew everybody on all the shows. I'd been watching them every day for the last six months. So I wrote them for her and they loved what I did. Then she recommended me to the magazine, and they started giving me my own work. An article here, an article there. And before long they offered me a staff position. Can you imagine the humiliation of writing fluffy profiles on those people? I was supposed to be one of them! They should have been writing profiles about me!"

"But things got better for you," I said. "You moved on and forgot all about Juan Carlos."

"That's right. Until they cast him as that rapist/preacher on

The Hands of Time and the magazine asked me to do a fucking cover piece on him. I did it, but then he started to get bigger and bigger. He was popping up everywhere. Commercials. TV movies. I couldn't get away from him. It was driving me mad!"

"So you decided to get rid of him once and for all. You got your hands on some obscure poison while you were covering that soap convention in Nova Scotia, crashed the wedding at the Hearst Castle, and spiked some champagne intended for Juan Carlos. Trouble was, he had you booted off the premises before you could make sure he drank it. Poor Austin Teboe gulped it down instead. The wrong man died. So you had to try again. You couldn't stop until you killed the man who cost you your ticket back into the big time."

Rudy's eyes grew wide. He stared numbly at me. "*Back* into the big time? What are you talking about?"

"Oh, come on, Rudy," I said. "I knew the minute you recited your trademark line. 'I was supposed to be the big cheese!' I'm figuring Rudy is your real name, and you no longer go by your stage name . . . Cappy Whitaker."

I sized up his portly frame, the receding hairline of orange hair, a few freckles spread out over his fleshy cheeks. He had changed so much. But the eyes were a dead giveaway. They still had that same twinkle from those long ago Kraft Macaroni and Cheese commercials. I was face to face with Cappy Whitaker. The one who made a lasting impression in a Disney adaptation of *The Prince and the Pauper*, the one who played Debbie Reynolds's grandson on a short-lived situation comedy, and the one who landed on the cover of *People* magazine after Wendell Butterworth tried abducting him from a Santa Monica beach. He was also the Cappy Whitaker who wrote to the parole board in Vacaville, California, to request Wendell's immediate release from prison.

"So, Rudy, did your grandmother make you change your name in order to stand out at auditions?" I said.

He nodded. "You know, it's funny, Jarrod, when we were kids, we basked in so much attention. Everybody loved us. They did anything for us. Gave us everything. And then, when a lot of us hit puberty, they took it all away. And what were we left with? Pretty much nothing. My grandmother didn't have much use for me after the parts dried up once I turned thirteen. I was all alone. Not you, of course. You got *Go to Your Room!* That kept you going another few years. And I've seen you on TV now and then. You've managed somewhat of a comeback. Congratulations."

Charlie moaned softly a few feet away from us. I wanted to run to him, get him some medical attention, but it would do neither of us any good if Rudy or Wendell snapped.

"But nobody wanted me anymore," Rudy said. "Nobody but Wendell Butterworth. Without fail, he wrote me a letter from prison every damn week. Never missed one. And not only that, he sent me cards for Christmas and every year on my birthday. He was the only one, Jarrod. After years of fame, he was the only one. I was so lonely, one day in a weak moment, I wrote him back. I knew he was whacked out and crazy, but hell, I didn't even care at that point. I just wanted somebody to talk to."

We both glanced at Wendell, who stood silently, his eyes blank, as if in a trance.

I looked at Rudy. "So you became pen pals?"

Rudy laughed. "We sent each other all kinds of puzzles and games. Can you imagine that? I befriended the man who tried to kidnap me. My childhood stalker. My grandmother blew every cent I had ever made as a child actor. Wendell was the last tie to that whole life of fame and fortune. I found him to be a fucking comfort, if you can believe that."

"So when the authorities up in Vacaville were going to release him, you wrote a letter of support."

"Damn straight. Why wouldn't I want my only friend to be free? It worked too. Look at him. He's a free man. Free to do anything he wants."

"The only problem is," I said, swallowing hard, and trying not to panic. "What he wants to do is to kill me and then kill himself so we can be free together on the other side."

Rudy considered this for a long moment before looking at both of us and smiling. "Well, Wendell was there for me, so in all fairness, I need to be there for him. And if that's what he wants, then I don't want to stop him."

Rudy called out to Wendell. "It's time, Wendell."

Wendell snapped out of his trance. He bent down, roughly turned Charlie over on his back, reached into the holster strapped across his chest, and pulled out his gun. He stood back up and pointed it at me, a loving smile on his face.

Chapter 35

"We've hung around here long enough, Jarrod," Wendell said warmly. "It's time for us to go." He released the safety on the gun and pressed back on the trigger.

"No!" a voice hollered. It was Charlie. He was conscious. He seized Wendell's right leg, and jerked it back with all of his remaining strength. Wendell tumbled just as the bullet fired. It nicked my left ear, drawing blood. As he went down, Wendell shot at me again, but this time his aim was way off. I heard an agonizing scream from behind me, and whirled around to see Rudy clutching his right arm, real blood seeping through the sleeve of his coat over the dried fake blood.

"He shot me! The fucker shot me!"

It was only a flesh wound. I heard a scuffle and turned back around to see Charlie on his feet, his arm wrapped around Wendell's neck, trying hard to subdue him. But Charlie was dizzy and weak from the blow to the head, and was no match for the much stronger, much bigger man. He flung Charlie off him like a piece of lint. Charlie hit the ground hard, and rolled down a hill of leaves until he smacked into the trunk of a tree. Wendell pounded down toward him. I couldn't let him get near Charlie. I couldn't allow Wendell to hurt him anymore.

"Wendell, come back. We can leave. Right now. You and me."

Wendell stopped in his tracks, and slowly turned to look at me. His face was full of hope but mixed with mistrust. I had betrayed him before, and he wasn't sure if I was being straight with him. But at least it took his mind off killing Charlie.

"Don't you worry, Wendell, I'll make sure your boy here doesn't play any more games with you," Rudy said as he came up quick behind me, twisting my arm up behind my back and pressing the cold, sharp blade of a knife against my throat.

Wendell stared at the two of us, in a state of utter confusion.

Rudy hissed in my ear, "Just so you know, this isn't one of those retractable prop knives, Jarrod. This is the real thing." He pressed the blade harder against my skin to prove his point.

"He's hurting me, Wendell," I gasped, trying desperately to appeal to Wendell's paternal side.

Wendell threw out his hands at us and cried, "Let him go, Cappy. He belongs to me. Not you."

Rudy didn't move.

"I said let him go!" Wendell bellowed so loud it echoed in the night breeze.

"You always preferred Jarrod to me," Rudy said, scowling. "I did so much for you. I sent care packages to you every week in prison, I wrote letters to the governor pleading for your release, and I was a better soul mate to you than *he* ever could be! So why, Wendell, why did you always prefer him to me?"

Wendell opened his mouth to speak, but no words came out.

"Tell me, Wendell," Rudy said, grabbing my shirt collar and pressing the blade so hard a small drop of blood slid down over my Adam's apple. "Tell me now or I cut his throat!"

Wendell, with downcast eyes, said softly, "Because Jarrod had a hit series and, well, you never did."

That was it. Rudy just couldn't face any more rejection. He

was going to kill me. I had to take action now to save myself or at least die from trying. Cappy and I had long ago gone up for the same guest-starring role on *The A Team*, and I had won the part. I played a general's son kidnapped by a ruthless band of mercenaries that the much-decorated officer had abandoned in the jungles of Vietnam. They were out for revenge and I was the target. At one point, Mr. T tries to rescue me, and I mistake him for one of the bad guys, so I elbow him in the solar plexus, knocking the wind out of him. Had Cappy been cast instead, I never would have learned that move. And it wouldn't have saved my life at this moment. I slammed Rudy as fast and hard as I could. I felt the rush of air escape from his mouth, the shock of the blow forcing him to loosen his grip on my arm. The knife sliced across my neck as he stumbled back, but not deep enough to puncture my wind pipe. Rudy was only momentarily stunned. As I sprung forward to get away from him, he tackled me around the waist and we landed facedown in the dirt. He snatched a handful of my hair and started pounding my face into the dirt. I scrounged around with my hand for the knife he'd dropped, and finally my fingers felt the sharp blade. I circled my fingers around the handle, and raised it up to defend myself, but Rudy must have seen me out of the corner of his eye. He stopped driving my skull into the mud long enough to grab at my arm holding the knife. We wrestled and rolled for possession of it, clubbing one another with our free hands and kicking each other with our legs. Rudy tried prying my fingers off the knife handle one by one, but I had a tight hold on that sucker and I wasn't about to let go. That's when he kneed me in the groin, and I felt the strength rapidly drain from my body. I roared in pain, instinctively dropping the knife to protect myself from another blow, and it gave Rudy enough time to snatch up the weapon, shove me down on my back, and straddle my waist. He raised the knife high over his head, cackled with relish, and sneered, "And . . . action!"

As he brought the knife down, I shot my arms out to stop him from plunging it through my heart. Everything seemed in slow motion. Our eyes locked together, our bodies entwined, both our hands struggling to gain possession of the knife in a desperate last-minute murderous standoff.

Suddenly a burst of light blinded both of us. The whole woods lit up as if daylight had sprung upon us. Wendell looked skyward, probably expecting a UFO to land in the clearing. Rudy squinted, covering his eyes from the oppressive light. I recognized what it was right away—a powerful, megawattage klieg light used to illuminate a set. Whoever had turned it on had just rescued me from certain death.

I used the distraction to shove Rudy off me, and scramble to my feet.

"Who is it? Who's there?" Rudy screamed.

Larry Levant stepped into the light. He had a handheld Panavision film camera strapped to his shoulder and was aiming it at Rudy. "Drop the knife, Rudy. You don't want us filming you committing a murder, do you?"

Rudy stared into the camera lens, almost wistfully. Probably somewhere in the back of his mind, he was saying, "I'm ready for my close-up, Mr. Levant." He let the knife slip from his fingers and drop into the leaves. Larry kept approaching him slowly, cautiously, until he was right up in his face with the camera.

"You've got a very expressive face, Rudy," Larry said. "You really should be in features."

"Really?" There was a slight smile on Rudy's face. He loved being back in the spotlight.

Wendell, mystified by the goings-on, made a sudden break for it. The person holding the klieg light flashed it in his face, and he stopped suddenly, blinded and disoriented. Five police officers swooped in and wrestled him to the ground, cuffing his hands behind his back. The light shut off, and I saw the smiling face of Laurette as she set the bulky light down on the ground and ran over to hug me.

"Do you honestly believe I would let you two come out here all alone at night without backup? Are you all right, honey?" she said in her usual motherly tone.

I nodded as I watched more cops swarm into the clearing and surround and arrest Rudy Pearson. He didn't put up a fight. He just kept staring at Larry's camera, smiling, as the police carted him away.

"Did you hear Larry Levant?" Rudy said to one of the officers. "He thinks I should be in features."

I swiveled my head around frantically. "Charlie!"

He was sitting upright, against a tree, as a paramedic stitched up his head wound. Laurette and I ran over to him.

"Charlie, are you okay? I was so worried!" I said.

He reached out and squeezed my hand. "Paramedic says I need something like fifteen stitches. You know what that means?"

"What?"

"Lots of recovery time at home. With you tending to me. You've played a lot of parts in your career, Jarrod. It's time you played a nursemaid. And I mean twenty-four/seven. For as long as it takes for me to feel better. Making sure the patient gets everything he wants." He patted my butt with his free hand. "And I do mean *everything*."

"Absolutely," I said. I was just so damn happy he was alive and well, and still willing to put up with me, that I would have agreed to anything. He deserved it.

Laurette clasped her hands over ours and beamed. "Who would have thought that both of us would be lucky enough to find the love of our lives, Jarrod?"

Charlie and I exchanged baffled looks and then turned to Laurette. "I'm not sure I get what you mean, Laurette," I said gently. "Juan Carlos didn't exactly turn out to be your fantasy man."

"Oh, I know, I'm sorry he's dead and all, but good riddance to that good-for-nothing asshole," she said, crinkling up her nose in utter distaste before returning to her excited smile and motioning with her head. "I'm talking about Larry."

"You just met him," Charlie said.

"I know, I know, but sometimes you just know. I think he's the one."

"Laurette . . ."

"Look, I know I've said that before . . ."

"At least four times."

"Well, if you're going to keep a record of my romantic life, then okay, sure, but Larry's different. And I know I've said that before too. And I know you've questioned my judgment in the past, but I think this time I'm really turning a corner! No more bad choices in men. From here on in, it's all about Larry."

"He's an egotistical film director, Laurette," I said.

"And you know how I'm a sucker for creative types. Now I'm not going to rush things this time. I'm going to take things slow, let things unfold naturally."

Charlie and I knew Laurette was past the point of no return, and our best course of action was to just smile and nod to appease her.

"But there's a three-year wait to book the Hearst Castle for a wedding. I can't count on a last-minute cancellation like last time. So it probably won't hurt to book it now." Laurette fished out her cell phone from her coat pocket. "Excuse me, I won't be able to focus on anything until I at least know my name is on their calendar." And she headed off to make her call, winking and cooing at a poor unsuspecting Larry as she passed by him.

The paramedic stitched up what he could, but suggested Charlie drop by the hospital to consult with a doctor and make sure there wasn't a concussion.

Charlie drew our clasped hands to his mouth and kissed my

fingers with his soft, gentle lips. "Can we go home now, babe?" he said.

"Yes," I said as I helped him to his feet. "Just as soon as the doctors give their okay."

"I want to sleep in my own bed. I want to play ball with Snickers," he moaned. "I'm done with Florida."

I slid my arm around his waist, and with my support, he hobbled back toward the Taurus. He was still woozy from the head injury, so I held on to him tight to make sure he didn't lose his balance. I don't remember ever holding him that tight. And at that moment, I knew I was never, ever going to let go of him again.

Following is an exciting sneak peek
at Rick Copp's next Jarrod Jarvis mystery
THE ACTOR'S GUIDE TO GREED!

Chapter 1

As I raced through the thick, foreboding woods, entangled in a maze of sharp tree branches and knee-high shrubs, I gasped and sputtered in a panic, disoriented and lost in my surroundings. It was dark and the air chilled my bones. I couldn't stop shivering. I darted my eyes back and forth, searching, so desperately trying to get my incessant wheezing under control. The last thing I needed was my lack of an effective exercise program to give me away. Taking cover behind an overgrown bush, I bent down and hugged my knees, praying he wouldn't find me. I took a gulp of air and held my breath. I heard some rustling branches as if someone were walking steadily toward me. A twig snapped. He was so close.

After a few tense moments, he mercifully retreated and all I could hear was the restless gust of the wind. He was gone. And I was still alive. Exhaling an exhausted sigh of relief, I stepped out from behind my hiding place and turned toward the direction of the campsite, where the others were waiting. Suddenly I stopped. There he was. Looming over me in a cartoon Elmer Fudd mask and wielding a sharp hatchet in his white-knuckled fist. He raised it above his head, and before I could let out a scream, he brought it down. Hard. So hard it cracked open my skull like a melon. Blood spurted everywhere. I stumbled back, shaking my head in utter shock and disbelief, grabbing my head and then staring numbly at my blood-soaked hands. I sank to my knees and raised my eyes in time to see Elmer Fudd swing the axe down again. I prayed that at any moment I was going to wake up from this horrible nightmare. But it wasn't a nightmare. It was real.

How could I ever have let this happen? How did I allow Laurette to talk me into making this dreadful movie?

Charlie and I sat in the fourth-row aisle seats at the New Beverly Cinema, a run-down revival house near the Fairfax district of Los Angeles, for the world-premiere screening of *Creeps*, an exploitative slasher flick I shot last year in south Florida. I knew the project was completed on a shoestring budget, but actors always hope that sharp editing, some realistic sound effects, and a suspenseful score will somehow make it look a little better at the end of the day. No such luck. This piece of schlock was an unmitigated disaster. People were chuckling at my death scene. It was so silly and unbelievable. And it wasn't just the script or the way it was shot. It was me. I was awful. Completely over the top. Like Susan Hayward's wacky performance in *I Want to Live!* But Susan won an Oscar and went on to play juicy supporting roles in camp classics like *Valley of the Dolls*. This celluloid Titanic was going to sink my career. Or what was left of it.

Charlie knew I was on the verge of a breakdown. He gently placed one hand on my knee while stuffing a fistful of popcorn into his mouth with the other. I knew what he was doing. He was afraid I was going to ask him what he thought of my performance and figured a mouthful of movie popcorn would keep him from having to give me an honest answer.

The camera lingered on my crumpled, twisted, broken body for much longer than necessary, finally panning and stopping for a close shot of my separated skull. What a memorable big-screen debut. A ten-foot-high corpse in Technicolor. Mercifully, the film finally cut away from the flies buzzing around my dead body to a new scene as my ten-year-old son in the movie (played by a four-foot-high, Satan-possessed child star) wandered through the woods, worried about his dad, who had suddenly gone missing. The film's strapping, stoic, hard-bodied hero accompanied him.

I wanted to run screaming out of the theater, but the film's director was sitting directly behind me. Larry Levant was a rising young *artiste* full of creative promise that would instantly be washed away upon this clunker's release. He was in his early thirties, on the short side, with dark features and an intense gaze. With him was my manager, Laurette, a gorgeous, plus-size beauty who dwarfed him whenever they were together. They had found love on the set even though Larry never found a story for his movie. I wanted to yell at both of them for getting me involved in this mess. But when I spun around and was met with their expectant smiles, I simply gave my nervous director and my best friend an enthusiastic thumbs-up.

The film lasted another excruciating sixty-two minutes. Charlie shifted several times, especially at the gory parts. My boyfriend, Charlie, was a cop and saw blood and violence every day while investigating LA's underbelly. Accompanying me to the premiere of this movie was above and beyond the call of duty. And I loved him for it.

When the credits finally rolled, there was a smattering of applause. Most of the audience bolted from their seats and out the door before there was any chance of running into Larry and having to comment on the film. The cluster of executives from Sunbelt Films, a small, independent releasing company that unwisely chose to pick up this movie nightmare for distribution, offered a few perfunctory pats on the back to Larry, then clamped their cell phones to their ears and made their escape.

Charlie and I were stuck. We had agreed beforehand to accompany Larry and Laurette to the postpremiere party being held a few blocks from the theater across Beverly Boulevard at Starbucks.

Yes, Starbucks. Not the Skybar. Or Chinois on Main. Or Mortons. Or any other high-end LA hotspot the studios flock to for their numerous celebratory events. Sunbelt cried poverty when it came to hosting a party. Of course, this was after they saw a rough cut of the film. So Laurette, who refused to let the evening go by without some kind of festivity, organized a gathering at the nearest coffeehouse. She even sprang for pastries.

The handful of moviegoers who hadn't already dashed for their cars marched across the street. There was a somber mood in the air on this crisp, late-spring night. We were all thinking the same thing. What would we say if Larry and Laurette pressed us for our opinions on the film? Laurette and I had shared a years-long friendship based on honesty and I promised her very early on that I would always be up front with her, never hold back, never sugarcoat anything. And I expected the same from her. We had both zealously stuck to our pact. Well, almost. There was the time I traded in my BMW for a Prius in an effort to make an environmental statement and Laurette blindly leased a new Cadillac SUV that she had to fill up every time she made a two-mile trip to the nearest Nordstrom. Why make her feel bad? And then there was the time she made noises about her desire to adopt a toddler from China. I was concerned because the last thing she had to care for was a hamster she got when she was twelve that she forgot to feed for three weeks while she was busy mourning A Flock of Seagulls' failure to win a Best New Artist Grammy. I never said a word to her. Okay, so maybe fibbing about my true reaction to her boyfriend's new movie wouldn't be the first time I didn't stick to our honesty agreement.

As the small group of us poured into Starbucks, the workers with their black pullover Izod shirts and coffee-stained green aprons steeled themselves for a rush. Charlie and I were first in line, and I rattled off my usual iced venti sugar-free vanilla non-fat decaf latte. I know, I know, what's the point? Charlie spied an inviting maple-nut scone that was calling out to him and ordered a house blend to wash it down with. I declined a pastry because I'm an actor and we spend half our day comparing body-fat measurements. Charlie was on his feet all day, active in his work as a detective, and never worried about what he ate. It just made me feel better to know I refused to give in to my sweets craving. Of course, Charlie would inevitably offer me half his scone, and I would happily accept it. So in the end, it would all work out for me. I would demonstrate self-restraint *and* get half a maple-nut scone.

As we stepped aside to allow the next person in line to place their order, I heard a familiar voice behind me.

"Baby, don't even go there!"

That was the catchphrase I made famous during my five-year stint as a precocious troublemaker on a hit 1980s sitcom called *Go to Your Room*. It felt like a million years ago, but those five words would probably wind up on my gravestone right next to Gary Coleman and his signature catchphrase, "What you talkin' about, Willis?"

I plastered on a fake smile and spun around to see who just couldn't resist dredging up my cheesy past.

Wallace Goodwin, a bespectacled, balding, slightly paunchy sitcom writer in his mid-forties, beamed at me. Wallace had been a staff writer on my show for its entire run. He loved to claim credit for that snappy retort I used time and time again on any given episode. It was always so important for Wallace to let the world know he had come up with that immortal line that made such an indelible impression on American pop culture. He was convinced that some day it would be the deciding factor in his possible induction into the TV Academy Hall of Fame.

"I came up with that, you know," Wallace said, puffed up with pride.

"I remember." That's all I could think of to say.

Sitcom writers are a strange breed. They spend their lives cooped up on a studio lot in a bland, claustrophobic conference room with scuffed walls and stained rugs, eating most of their meals out of take-out Styrofoam at two in the morning as they pitch to improve bad jokes that rarely ever get better. They are also extremely competitive and hyperaware of how well other writers are doing. Who's the funniest? Who's the dead weight? Their entire self-worth is based on whether or not they can succeed in getting the show runner to laugh so hard he blows Diet Coke out through his nose.

After the show was canceled, Wallace went on to write for a string of successful shows, albeit no Emmy winners. He reached his peak in the late eighties by winning a NAACP award for a very special episode of a sitcom starring Marla Gibbs from *The Jeffersons*. Not bad for a middle-aged, white Jewish writer from New Rochelle. After that career high, his luck ran out. He snared freelance assignments on a few syndicated shows and at one point developed a pilot recharging the old *Knight Rider* franchise with a team of talking cars. He brought me in to audition for a gay minivan. By then, I was completely out of the closet thanks to a *National Enquirer* cover photo of me and a buddy making out at the LA Gay Rodeo. Wallace was hoping I could infuse my innate homosexuality into the personality of a screaming queen vehicle manufactured by Ford. He was polite when I came in to read for him, if not a little embittered by his circumstances. He wasn't exactly writing *Seinfeld*. After the audition, he assured me I did an admirable job, but in the end, wound up casting his fey personal trainer, who offered him a lifetime of free workouts if he gave him the part.

I never heard from him again until tonight.

"It's good to see you, Wallace." I wasn't lying. I had fond memories of those golden years of my childhood stardom. *Go to Your Room* was a seminal period in my life, and those of us involved in the show were like a tight-knit company of war-torn soldiers. We faced many battles together, lost some of our men, came back with a few scars, but were thankful we at least made it home alive.

"Great performance, Jarrod. I really enjoyed the movie a lot." Wallace obviously didn't get the honesty memo. His neck was beet red, a clear sign he wasn't telling the truth.

"You die very well," a woman's voice purred as Katrina Goodwin marched up with a bottled water and slid her arm through her husband's. Katrina was a raven-haired beauty, a former actress about nine years younger than Wallace was. She had guest-starred on *Go to Your Room* as the cheerleader friend of my older sister. Wallace had penned that week's script, and during our first run-through for the studio, she complimented him on his fine comedic writing. Wallace's script had been overhauled by the entire staff before the first reading, and there was only one line left from his original draft. "Hi, Mom." But nevertheless, Wallace accepted Katrina's gracious accolade and was smitten all week after that. The two became inseparable, but many naysayers suspected Katrina's motives. Especially after Wallace insisted the show bring her back as a semiregular due to her overwhelming chemistry with the rest of the cast. Everyone else on the writing staff failed to see her potential, but Wallace was undeterred. Every story line he pitched and every script he turned in featured that sweet-natured, batty, and mammary-stacked cheerleader friend. And amazingly, the viewers responded. Mostly the teenage boys, but hey, that's exactly who the show was designed for. Then Katrina started hanging around the set during the weeks she didn't even appear in the script, and it soon became clear she and Wallace were an item. The crew placed bets that she would bolt by the end of the season, but she stuck around, and even after the show was scrapped, they stayed together. And remarkably, after all these years, Wallace and Katrina Goodwin seemed as happy and in love as the first day they met.

Katrina touched my arm, and with the utmost sincerity, said, "You look happy, Jarrod. You don't know how happy that makes Wallace and me."

Wallace nodded vigorously in agreement. Of course, he automatically agreed with anything his beloved wife said.

"I am happy." I smiled. "I may not be so happy after reading the reviews of this movie, but hey, we've all been associated with a lot of crappy projects. You've got to pay the mortgage, right, Wallace?"

Wallace stared at me blankly. In his mind, everything he ever did was art that was simply misunderstood. I remember him telling me at my audition that his *Knight Rider* redo was a quirky, intelligent reimagining of the franchise, and critics be damned if they weren't smart enough to see that. Wallace wasn't about to group himself with me, whose only critically hailed project since the good old days of *Go to Your Room* was a memorable turn as an earnest rookie cop gunned down in the line of duty in an Emmy-nominated episode of *Homicide: Life on the Street*.

Katrina bristled at my unintentional slam aimed at her husband. She was very protective of him. I had to backpedal fast.

"So what show are you working on now, Wallace? Any sitcom would be lucky to have you."

Katrina relaxed. I had tactfully sidestepped the land mine.

Wallace scoffed. "I haven't done a sitcom in years. I got tired of the grind. It was time to stretch myself as an artist." Writer speak for "No one will hire me, so I have to scramble and find something else to do."

"Writing movies?" I said.

"No. Why waste my time in features? Writers get no respect in movies. Studios go through more on one film than a stuffy nose goes through Kleenex."

Maybe if Wallace worked on his analogies, he would get more work as a writer.

"If you come out of sitcoms, the movie execs look down on you. It's tough out there for writers," Wallace said, almost growling.

"It's even worse for actors," I said, trying to offer my own perspective on the hardships of carving out a lasting career in Hollywood. "You get pigeonholed from one role. For years, I tried to break out of that child-star box they put me in, and then, when I finally prove I can do drama as a young adult on that *Homicide* episode, all the casting agents say, 'We saw him as the cop, but can he do comedy?' Everybody forgets I had my own sitcom!"

Wallace was looking blank again. He had been enjoying his rant, and as actors are prone to do, I had shifted the attention from him onto myself.

Katrina pouted, annoyed that I would so blatantly steal the focus from her husband.

More backpedaling. "I'm just saying, I know how frustrated you must be."

Wallace shot a glance at his wife, as if to say, "Can you believe this guy?" Then plowed on. "I socked some cash away after the *Knight Rider* fiasco. Took some time to regroup, consider what it was I really wanted to write, and you may not believe this, Jarrod, but—"

"Wallace wrote a play," Katrina chimed in, excited and proud of her husband.

There was an awkward silence. Clearly Wallace wanted to tell me this exciting news himself. He glared at Katrina, but her enthusiasm was bubbling over with such intensity, she didn't even notice.

"It's a murder mystery. Wallace's agent absolutely loved it. He said Wallace is going to be the next Ira Levine."

"Who?" I said, recognizing the name as my dentist on the West Side, not a famous playwright.

"Ira Levine," Katrina said, obviously put off by my stupidity. "The guy who wrote *Deathtrap* and *Boys in the Band*."

"Levin," Wallace hissed. "Ira Levin. And it wasn't *Boys in the Band*, it was *Boys from Brazil*."

"Whatever," Katrina laughed. "It was about homosexuals in Rio."

I bit my tongue.

Wallace sighed. "*Boys in the Band* was about homosexuals in New York. *Boys from Brazil* was about breeding young boys to be Nazis."

"Were the Nazis gay?" Katrina said, completely serious.

"No!"

I quickly intervened. "What's your play about, Wallace?"

The tension immediately drained out of Wallace's face. He loved talking about his work. "It's set at a bed-and-breakfast in Manchester, England. A rainstorm traps the guests in the house for the weekend, and one of them is an escaped killer. No one knows who it is, and the bodies start piling up, and there is a detective from America who ultimately exposes the killer—"

"Turns out it's the Danish countess with a split personality," Katrina said.

Wallace's face flushed with anger and he turned to his wife. "You just told him the ending."

"Well, you can pretty much guess it by the end of the first act," Katrina said.

"No, you can't!"

Somehow I remembered these two much happier. In one more attempt to defuse the situation, I said, "Sounds very Agatha Christie."

It didn't work. Wallace spun around and barked, "No! She was all about the puzzle. My play is a deep psychological portrait of a mind gone mad!"

"It was fun to research too," Katrina cooed. "We traveled to England, met with some psychiatrists, even took lessons at the shooting range so Wallace could conceive a plausible murder."

"I learned I don't like tea and crumpets, despise head shrinks, and I can't shoot a rifle worth shit. Katrina fared much better," Wallace said with a thin smile.

Katrina reached into her bag and pulled out a copy of the script. "Wallace was hoping we'd run into you tonight," she said. "He wants you to read his new play."

"Why should he bother?" Wallace huffed. "You already told him the ending."

I snatched the script from Katrina. "I'd love to read it," I said, hoping to make a fast getaway soon. I glanced over to Charlie. He was half done with his scone and about to dive into the other half. This was a disaster. I was stuck with these two lunatics, and I was going to miss out on him offering me half of his scone!

I was just about to pry myself free when Katrina said, "We'd like you to be in it, Jarrod."

This stopped me in my tracks. "It's getting produced?"

Wallace beamed. "Yes. We got the financing last week. Rehearsals start a week from Monday."

"Here in town?" I said.

Wallace shook his head. He wasn't about to tell me. He wanted me to guess.

"Broadway?" I said, straining to hide my incredulity.

He shook his head again.

"London! The West End!" Katrina said while clapping her hands excitedly.

Wallace narrowed his eyes so hard they almost disappeared. "I wanted him to guess, Katrina."

"Sorry," she said without a hint of remorse. I got the feeling Katrina wasn't as dumb as she pretended to be. She just liked pissing off her husband.

"Are you serious?" I said.

"I brought your name up to our producer, and he went wild," Wallace said. "He thinks you're prime for a comeback. London audiences adored *Go to Your Room*. They all want to see what you look like now. They'd flock to the theater in droves."

Macauley Culkin did a play in London, and it reignited his whole career. A flashy role in an edgy independent film. A funny turn on *Will & Grace*. He was back on the map. This play could do the same for me.

"Who would I play? The American detective?"

Wallace almost laughed but caught himself. "No. His gay valet."

"Wallace said he was visualizing you in the role the whole time he was writing it," Katrina said, resting her head on Wallace's shoulder. After an uncomfortable moment, he flinched and she moved her head upright again.

The gay valet? It sounded like Wallace wanted to cash in on my tabloid notoriety. But honestly, I didn't really care. I had always dreamed of appearing on stage in the West End. The same dusty old theaters graced by the likes of Sir Laurence Olivier, Sir John Gielgud, Dame Judi Dench, and supermodel Jerry Hall. All the greats!

I noticed Charlie raise an eyebrow as I talked in hushed tones with Wallace and Katrina. He knew we were conspiring about something and was curious as to what I was getting mixed up in now.

I told Wallace I would read the play tonight and give him a call first thing in the morning. A part of me didn't even have to read the play. I knew I was going to England. This was fate. I didn't know which notion was more outlandish. Me on a London stage or Wallace Goodwin's name on the marquee.

As I left Wallace to scold Katrina for giving away his precious ending, I bounced back over to Charlie, snatched the last piece of scone out of his fingertips, and popped it in my mouth.

"You really think you deserve that for leaving me here alone all this time?" Charlie said.

"Wallace wrote a play. And he wants me to be in it."

"I thought you said Wallace was a hack."

"I never said that. He just needed to stretch himself creatively

THE ACTOR'S GUIDE TO GREED

to demonstrate his real potential." Of course, I probably did tell Charlie at one time that I thought Wallace was a hack. But actors are adept at rewriting history when there is a part at stake.

"So is it going up at one of those little theaters on Santa Monica Boulevard?" Charlie said.

I shook my head. Like Wallace the sadist, I wanted him to guess.

Charlie's eyes lit up. "Broadway?"

"London!" I couldn't contain myself. "I'm doing a play in London!"

Charlie smiled, genuinely pleased. "That's great, babe." But then, the issues involved in this decision began sprouting up. "How long will you be gone?"

"I'm not sure yet. I haven't even read the play. I may hate it."

But we both knew I'd love the play. No matter how bad it was. In my mind, I was already on that plane with my passport and a London walking-tour guide.

I swiveled around and spotted Laurette and Larry at a corner table, sipping extra foam lattes and sharing an oatmeal raisin cookie. Laurette had her hand over Larry's, and I presumed she was reassuring him that his new movie had some artistic merit and was not going to be a career killer.

I leaned down and kissed Charlie on the forehead. "Be right back."

Racing over to Laurette, I blurted out, "I've been offered a play in London!"

Laurette glanced up at me as if she didn't hear me correctly. "I'm sorry?"

"Wallace Goodwin wrote a play—"

"That hack wrote a play?" Laurette said.

"Keep your voice down," I hissed. "He's right over there."

Laurette left Larry to sulk over his film's reception, promising to return soon. She grabbed my arm and dragged me outside so we could have a little privacy.

I filled Laurette in on all the details, and she squealed with delight. She knew how much this meant to me. She knew what a great opportunity this would be for my career. And she knew in a matter of weeks she would be on a shopping spree at Harrods.

"Sweetheart, this is sensational news," she said. We both looked back inside to see Wallace and Katrina in deep conversation with another couple. Wallace was grimacing as Katrina spouted stories animatedly. I wondered if Katrina was revealing the ending of Wallace's play again just to get his blood boiling.

"I never thought he had it in him," Laurette said. "You never know, I guess. He could be the next Ira Levine."

Unlike Wallace, I chose to let it go.

"You'll be great," Laurette said. "Just great."

"Now, I don't want this conflicting with any jobs you may be working on lining up for me."

Laurette stared at me, not sure how to respond.

"You know, there might be another film on the horizon or a recurring role on a series that you were going to send me out on . . ." I was losing steam. I could see it in her eyes. "Nothing, huh?"

Laurette didn't want to hurt me, so she tried to be diplomatic. "It's really a bad time for everybody. Pilot season is months away. Movies are going after big names right now . . ." It didn't work.

"So flying off to London is probably a good idea?"

"Absolutely," she said. "Besides, Larry and I are leaving for Maui in a few days. We'll be gone for three weeks. So I won't be lining up auditions for you anyway."

"Three weeks? But he'll miss the opening weekend of his movie!"

Laurette leaned in, and whispered in my ear. "That's the idea."

Poor Larry. When I met him he was indestructible. And after a mere twenty-seven-day shoot in south Florida, he was now a pariah. I knew what he was about to go through. I had weathered the ups and downs of a stormy Hollywood career myself. You just keep trudging on, never giving up, and one day, destiny might shine on you and you're rewarded with a second chance to recapture the glory of the past. Most people give up and move on to a new path. But a few of us diehards remain steadfast gluttons for punishment.

"This play couldn't have come at a better time for you," Laurette said. "It'll perfume some of the smell you're going to get from this stinker of a movie."

She was right. Wallace Goodwin's stage thriller was looking to be not only a dream come true, but also a much-needed career move.

Wallace Goodwin's play *Murder Can Be Civilized* wasn't half bad. I didn't find it to be a searing psychological portrait of a mind gone mad by any stretch of the imagination. Wallace's artistic claims were a bit exaggerated. But as a light romp that poked fun at the clichéd Agatha Christie murder-mystery conventions, it worked brilliantly. Sometimes perennial unemployment can really hone a writer's craft. The secondary role of the gay valet was also a surprise. It wasn't a stock role by any means. Damien Sheffield was a blisteringly sarcastic, ruggedly sexual, and dangerously cunning concoction full of bravado and swagger. He was hiding a multitude of juicy and scandalous secrets, which bubbled over at the worst times. And he didn't even get knocked off until late into the third act. So I was looking at a wealth of time onstage.

I finished reading the script just after midnight, keeping Charlie awake by spouting aloud some of my character's more colorful lines. When I finally put the play down, Charlie had already dropped off to sleep. Our Pekingese, Snickers, was curled up at the foot of the bed snoring softly. I was going to be up all night, my mind racing at the exciting prospects of a new career in the theater. This was the break I had been waiting for.

The following morning, I rang up Wallace and told him how much I loved the play and wanted to do it. He had already been in contact with his London producers to alert them to my interest. Within an hour, Laurette had received an offer, and by lunchtime, the deal was closed. I was to report to the old Apollo Theatre on Shaftsbury Avenue in London on the following Monday. Laurette and Larry postponed their Maui getaway a few days to allow her some time to finish up the details of the contract.

I had committed to four weeks of rehearsals and a three-month run. The producers would put me, my fellow castmates from abroad, and the Goodwins up at the swanky Savoy Hotel in Covent Garden during the duration of the play. I was ecstatic. This was shaping up to be my best job ever. I couldn't imagine anything going wrong. Of course, whenever I say that, something usually goes wrong. And this time, it shook my entire world.

Praise for Chris Kenry and
UNCLE MAX

"Zippy . . . Kenry has a knack for spinning clichéd, banal material into endearingly comical, featherweight entertainment. The great leap to more substantial literary terrain feels but a book or two away for this talented author."

—*Publishers Weekly*

"A modern-day mix of *Oliver Twist* and *Auntie Mame* set in Kenry's beloved Denver."

—*The Weekly News* (Miami, Florida)

"When it comes to gay beach reading, nobody does it better than Kensington. Its best books are escapists, humorous and upbeat."

—*Gay Today*

Praise for Chris Kenry and
CAN'T BUY ME LOVE

"Kenry manages to charm and hold readers with his witty, fluid prose . . . a lighthearted, wonderfully silly, laugh-out-loud farce. . . . This is one author whose potential will make his next book worth looking out for."

—*The Lambda Book Report*

"A rollicking debut . . . the author's talent for catchy, catty dialogue and innovative (and often quite humorous) sexual interplay buoys his storyline. . . . "Kenry shows promise with this first effort and his moxie shines through . . . a satisfying confection."

—*Publishers Weekly*

"With his clever comic observations and rapid-fire dialogue, Chris Kenry is a smart and funny writer."

—*The Advocate*

"Well written with bold humor and witty asides."

—*Library Journal*

"A romp through every gay subculture imaginable. The lead character charges by the hour, but the book will give you a charge every minute."

—Michael Musto, *The Village Voice*

Books by Chris Kenry

CAN'T BUY ME LOVE

UNCLE MAX

Published by Kensington Publishing Corporation

Uncle Max

CHRIS KENRY

KENSINGTON BOOKS
http://www.kensingtonbooks.com

KENSINGTON BOOKS are published by

Kensington Publishing Corp.
850 Third Avenue
New York, NY 10022

All Kensington titles, imprints, and distributed lines are available at special quality discounts for bulk purchases for sales promotion, premiums, fund-raising, educational or institutional use.

Special book excerpts or customized printings can also be created to fit specific needs. For details, write or phone the office of the Kensington Special Sales Manager: Kensington Publishing Corp., 850 Third Avenue, New York, NY 10022, Attn. Special Sales Department. Phone: 1-800-221-2647.

Kensington and the K logo Reg. U.S. Pat. & TM Off.

ISBN 1-57566-848-3

First Hardcover Printing: May 2002
First Trade Paperback Printing: April 2003
10 9 8 7 6 5 4 3 2 1

Printed in the United States of America

For Bill Weller

Acknowledgments

Thanks to Chuck Mallory, Sean Wolfe, Craig Dietz, and Dave Leger for helpful and insightful critiques; to Nancy Karpan, Jennifer Marx, and my mother, whose never-ending redecorating kept food in my belly; thanks to Jeff Elliott for his help with antiques; and thanks to John Scognamiglio and Alison Picard for their insight and guidance with this manuscript. Most of all thanks to the powers that be for creating the central branch of the Denver Public Library, in which the majority of this book was written.

I never came across anyone in whom the moral sense was dominant who was not heartless, cruel, vindictive, log-stupid, and entirely lacking in the smallest sense of humanity. Moral people, as they are termed, are simply beasts. I would sooner have fifty unnatural vices than one natural virtue

—Oscar Wilde

The man seemed to know his way around households of this kind, he knew where everything was. He had made himself at home. This gift of being everywhere at home belongs only to kings, light women and thieves.

—Honoré de Balzac

Chapter One

If you don't know what you're looking for, Nguyen's is not easy to find. Unlike the hundreds of other antique stores that compete for space on the crowded Antique Row, Nguyen's does not have a flashy sign proclaiming its presence. Nor has the building in which it is housed been painted garish attention-grabbing colors. No, Nguyen's is in an unremarkable, two-story building of blond brick with a large storefront window facing Broadway.

In this window, there are no artfully arranged displays of furniture, no silver tea sets, or chandeliers (its owner being too concerned with theft and sun damage to ever display any of her treasures to the public). In this window, there is nothing more than a floor-to-ceiling black velvet curtain. A curtain that acts both as a sunblock and as a backdrop for her sign—an artist's easel on which rests a matte black canvas in an elaborate gold frame. On this canvas there are small, raised, gold letters spelling out *Nguyen's*, and then below, in identical, although somewhat smaller script, is the exclusionary phrase *by appointment only*. There used to be a telephone number on the sign, which the curious could call to gain entry; but lately even this has been removed and replaced with an e-mail address, since the owner, who is impatient with most of the buying public, now does most of her buying and selling online.

Nguyen's deals in high-end antiques, mostly of French or Asian origin, and is owned by Jane Nguyen, who is as minimal in appearance as her first name and storefront imply. On any day, in any season, she is invariably dressed in a simple, sleeveless black dress, the hemline of which, regardless of the current fashion, she keeps just above the knee. A simple strand of pearls or occasionally a gold brooch adds variety to what is otherwise a uniform. She is short, perhaps only five feet tall, and thin, and her long straight black hair is usually held back in a ponytail by a simple black band. Her one concession to whimsy is a pair of cat's-eye glasses, the corners of which are encrusted with small, almost imperceptible, rhinestones. In addition to her encyclopedic knowledge of French antiques, she is known about town, and with the dealers and clients around the country, for these glasses, whose lenses (unbeknownst to all but a select few) have as much prescriptive value as a window pane. They are completely useless as anything other than an accessory, and somehow I knew, even before she confessed it to me, that the glasses had been my uncle's idea.

Max was like that: always coming up with simple ways to make ordinary things extraordinary. His love of all things marinated or pickled is a perfect example of this. Okra, watermelon rind, cheap cuts of meat—anything that people usually wouldn't consider eating, would actively avoid or even discard—Max could dress up in some colorful vinegar with a few floating herbs, *et voilà!* The mundane would become a delicacy.

"The French are wise that way," I remember him saying (according to Max, the French were wise in just about every way). "They could pickle a piece of shit and make it edible. It's all about potential, Dil. Never mind what things *are*, the important thing is what they can become."

My name is Dillon, but he always shortened it to Dil, which is perhaps appropriate since I was nothing more than one of his very large pickles. An awkward, ugly, all-too-ordinary suburban adolescent who he marinated into something much more one summer almost a decade ago.

But, on this particular summer morning, it was to Nguyen's shop that I eagerly made my way. I work there on the weekends and on some evenings or on the days when I'm not in class. I was not scheduled to work for another hour, but something I'd come across in the newspaper that morning while paying for my order at the coffee shop had caused me to rush over, paper in hand, to show Jane.

"It's him!" I cried, breathless with excitement, dropping the paper on the desk in front of her, open to the page I'd been reading. "It's got to be him."

Calmly, Jane pushed the paper aside and neatly stacked the invoices on which she'd been working. She emitted an annoyed sigh and slowly put on her glasses. She was not yet forty, but her somber world-weary manner made her seem much older. She picked up the paper, scanned the articles, and then finally discovered the one I'd intended her to see. I watched her dark eyes behind the glasses as they darted across the text.

It was a small article on page two in the slender column devoted to celebrity news, which is, I have to admit, the first section I look at in the morning.

FORMER DENVER TYCOON AND WIFE ROBBED AT GUNPOINT IN SOUTH OF FRANCE, the headline blared. The article went on to detail how Lloyd and Beverly Boatwright-Stark, former Denver residents, had left St. Tropez early Friday afternoon en route to Monaco, where they planned to spend the winter. Roughly midway on their journey, their car was forced off onto a side road by another car and two motorcycles, all piloted by men in ski masks. The driver was pulled from the car, stripped, gagged, and tied to a tree. The frightened couple were then forced out and ordered by the leader of the gang—"in perfect, unaccented English," they were quoted as saying—to hand over the undisclosed quantity of cash and jewelry they were carrying. They were then similarly stripped, gagged, and tied up. They were discovered some hours later, frightened but unharmed, by a group of bemused schoolgirls.

When Jane had finished reading, she handed me the paper, gave a dismissive wave, and said, "They always were flashy. Remember their house, remember that ridiculous pink taffeta dress she wore to the Governor's Ball? Just like a blob of taffy! A woman half her age—and weight—couldn't have gotten away with that! And look at this, look here," she said, pointing to a line in the article. ". . . *an undisclosed quantity of cash and jewelry?* Christ! Who would drive around with a carload of cash and jewels? Only stupid ostentatious yokels like them, that's who. Serves them right."

"But what abou—"

"Oh, I know what you're thinking," she said, cutting me off. "But it wasn't him. You know as well as I do that he probably never even made it there." She then picked up her pen and went back to her invoices.

I was leery of her calm exterior. I had seen the sparkle in her eyes as they scanned the article and knew it had been caused by more than her gleeful distaste for the Boatwright-Starks.

"Oh come on! France! The Boatwright-Starks! Robbery!" I cried, naming three of Max's passions. "Who else could it be?"

Jane looked up from her invoices. She stared through the crowded shop at the small strip of sunlight admitted through the door. She had taken off her glasses and her face looked softer, less severe. I knew that she was thinking of Max, but what she was thinking I could only imagine. My own thoughts of my uncle went from one extreme to another, with very little in between that was neutral, and I was sure that she felt the same. Whatever she was thinking, I thought it best not to intrude for a while so I stretched out on the large Empire sofa and took one of the small madeleines from the paper bag I'd bought at the coffee shop. I chewed absently and stared up at the ceiling, the newspaper resting on my chest.

Maybe she's right, I thought. Maybe it's not him.

I remembered the picture of the Jaguar as it was pulled from the ocean. It had fallen two hundred feet into shallow water. The hood had been accordioned to one-eighth its original length and both doors had been torn off on impact. His body had never been found. It was assumed that it had been ejected through the windshield and that what was left of it had floated out to sea. . . . Fish food. But I didn't believe it. It was him in France. Somehow I knew it. I shut my eyes and tried to remember the last time I'd seen him; he'd been walking away, into the garage. I could see the outline of his lean body, his black hair; but try as I might, I could not make out his face. I remembered that his nose was crooked where it had been broken, that his eyebrows were enviably thick, and that his jawline was square and pronounced, but I could not see the whole picture. It was all in shadow. I tried hard to imagine him winding rope around the rotund, naked bodies of the Boatwright-Starks, as the paper had described, but I could see his features no better than they had through the mask.

"Dillon." It was Jane's voice. I looked up from the sofa. She had put her glasses back on and she was smiling. "Give me some of those," she said, motioning toward the bag of madeleines. "We don't open for another twenty minutes, why don't you go lock the door and tell me about your date last night."

I groaned and made my way to the door. Lately, I'd been trying my luck with personal ads in one of the weekly papers as a new way to meet guys who were hopefully a little less shallow and a little more intriguing than the ones I met in bars or at the gym. The results had been disastrous so far, but I have to admit, I did relish giving an account of the trauma to my friends the next morning. Bad dates, like disastrous vacations and injuries requiring stitches, always make for interesting stories.

I swung myself up from the sofa and handed her the bag. Then I wove my way through the maze of desks and sideboards and tables to the front door, turned the key in the lock, and went back to the sofa, dropping the newspaper in an elephant's foot trash can on the way.

"Let's hear it," Jane said, leaning her tiny body forward on the huge desk and rubbing her hands together in anticipation.

"What can I say?" I sighed. "He was very nice to look at: broad shoulders, slender waist, beautiful hands. He had a nicely shaped head in which, unfortunately, there was absolutely nothing."

"And you already refer to him in the past tense," Jane chuckled. I went on.

"Yes. When my life is made into a stage play, the actor given his minor role will be disappointed with his brief moment in the spotlight, but at least his lines will be easy to memorize since they'll consist mostly of one-word exclamations like Whoa! Cool! and Righteous!"

"That bad?"

"Oh, much worse. I had to drink just to get through it, but even that wasn't easy," I said, sitting up on the sofa, warming to the tale. "I was just a little bit late getting to the restaurant and when I arrived I saw that he had already been seated and had taken the liberty of ordering us a bottle of wine. It was an unnaturally pink wine that tasted awfully close to spiked Kool-aid, with a picture of some kittens on the label."

I knew this last remark would offend Jane, the wine snob, more than anything.

"No!" she cried, leaning back in her chair.

"Oh yes," I said. "And I couldn't drink it fast enough. But let me get to the meal. Every time I paused he'd look over at my plate and say, in his booming voice, 'Dude, you gonna finish that?' If I said no (and I did quite often. Imagine the food in a restaurant that sells wine with kittens on the label), he'd reach one of his hamhock arms across the table and scoop it up with his fork."

"At least he knew how to use one," Jane laughed.

"Oh God, I'm not even sure he had thumbs! It's too bad, really,"

I said, shaking my head, "because, of course, the sex afterward was quite good."

"So you slept with him."

"Of course. I didn't want the night to be a total loss."

"Will you see him again?"

"I don't think so," I said wistfully.

"What if he calls?"

"Ahh," I said, raising a finger, "then the phone will ring at the pay phone down the street from my house."

Later that afternoon, as I sat polishing a long neglected silver tray that Jane was preparing to photograph for eBay, I asked her when was the last time she'd gone out on a date. Her head remained focused on the camera she was mounting on the tripod.

"A long time ago," she said, curtly. "Aren't you finished yet?"

I knew I had hit a nerve, but I continued.

"Do you think you ever will?" I asked.

Her head remained down, as if she were looking at the camera, but her eyes were looking up and off to the side. "Maybe not," she said, and then went back to the camera.

"Is that because of him?" I asked.

"Because of whom?"

I didn't answer but let the question hang in the air. She paused, shook her head slightly, and returned her attention to the camera. I went back to rubbing the tray.

"Do you think he's ruined it for us?" I asked. "I mean, you not dating anyone and me writing off every new guy five minutes into our first date."

"You're still young," she said. "Don't be silly."

"I'm not *that* young," I countered, "and you're not *that* old. Do you think we'll ever find anyone like Max?"

"Not if we're lucky," she quipped, and got up and left the room. I knew then, despite her flip response, or perhaps because of it, that

I was right. He had ruined us. And the fact that now he was probably still alive made it even worse. In many ways a ghost of the living is much worse than a ghost of the dead, for there is always the possibility that he will come back, or that someday, walking in London or Prague or Paris, I'll meet him again or even catch a glimpse of him or someone that looks like him. Max will always haunt us, I thought, just like Rebecca, or Lara, or Ilsa, or any of the other ghostly movie heroines. But instead of a monogrammed hanky, or the balalaika, or a few bars of *As Time Goes By*, I'll think of him every time I have a date.

I went back to polishing the tray and tried again to imagine Max's face, but I couldn't. I could see it no better than my own murky reflection in the tarnished silver. And maybe that was what really scared me—not that I would always be haunted by him, but that I would forget him. That I *was* forgetting him. That slowly he was fading from my memory. Soon, I knew, it would be difficult to picture him at all; and the thought of that was like a hollow space in my life, a cartoon gunshot right through my torso leaving a perfectly round hole, an empty, hungry feeling.

Maybe he hasn't ruined me, I thought, maybe I just don't want to let go.

I finished with the tray, positioned it on the wooden stand in front of the black velvet curtain, and went to find Jane. As I walked through the shop toward the back room, past the elephant's foot trash can. I looked down. It was empty. A few feet ahead sat Jane, looking dwarfish in an enormous wing-back chair, newspaper in her lap, again staring out the window at the street.

But I'm getting ahead of myself. I've started raining from the clear blue sky, as Max used to say, meaning that I haven't let the clouds build up. I've cheated you out of all the thunder and lightning. I've started near the end of the story, and I've skipped the beginning and the middle entirely. I've left out the Balzac and the climbing and the egg, and everything, really.

But when did it all start? It's hard to say. I suppose I could start with the night Max arrived, but it really began earlier, when my stepfather left us and when Lana found God. The summer I was supposed to go to camp, but then at the last minute, thanks to Max, didn't . . .

Chapter Two

To say that Lana was vindictive would be saying too little. Add to that spiteful, jealous, bitter, selfish, neglectful, cruel, manipulative, vain, and hypocritical, and you get a much more accurate portrait. Granted those are not the nicest things to call your mother, but when you consider that *Mother* was the name she least liked to be called, the others really aren't so bad.

For those, and many other reasons, men have always left Lana. When I was five years old, my father left. When I was twelve, my stepfather left. Six years seemed to be about the limit that any man could stand to be with her. Somehow, I made it through eighteen, although certainly not by choice and not without scars.

She met my father when they were both very young and working as lift operators at a ski resort. At first, they were just casual friends, but that all changed one drunken night when they ended up together in a sleeping bag on the shore of Lake Dillon and I was accidentally conceived. That was their first mistake. Shortly thereafter, they made their second; they got married.

Jake, my father, was (and still is) a ski bum, which means that he has never wanted anything more from life than to search for untracked snow during the day and to drink beer with his buddies at night. Although that was sufficient for him, it was not nearly enough for Lana, who had read far too many Judith Krantz novels by then and expected her life to be full of champagne flutes, designer clothes, and yacht trips around the Mediterranean. Some of my earliest memories are of Lana giving very shrill vent to her material frustrations (reading Ms. Krantz had also given her an outline for dramatic tantrum throwing). My father would listen and nod his head, sometimes try to appease her, but usually he'd just grab his keys and coat and leave, not returning until the bars had closed.

One night, and unfortunately I was only about four years old at the time so I don't remember the specifics, Lana must have pushed him too far. They argued, and my father, as usual, headed out to the bar, but this time he did not return at closing time, or even the next morning. He did not return at all. She called the police and filed a missing persons' report, and the next day a massive search was begun.

Lana loved all the attention and gave several tearful accounts of his disappearance to eager television and newspaper reporters. About a week later the search was called off when we got a letter from Canada, which was, I suppose, as far away from her as my dad could imagine getting. He sent her all the money he had, said he would send more when he could, and that was it. He was gone. Out of our lives. I don't really hold it against him; I'm sure I'd have left, too, if I'd been married to her, but I've never stopped begrudging him for leaving me behind.

Years later I learned that he did try to call and did send me letters, but Lana was vindictive and mean, so I never knew. She hung up whenever he called and must have thrown away anything that he ever sent. Consequently, I did not see my father again until I was in college, and then it was an awkward meeting, in an airport bar, between two strangers who each felt as though they should have known more about the other. For the most part the conversation was slow and stilted, but on one topic it flowed like water down a hill; that topic was our mutual dislike of Lana.

Alone after my father left, Lana bundled up all of her things from our trailer and moved back into her parents' tiny house in Littleton. Since I was too big to leave on the doorstep of a fire station or push down the river in a reed basket, she packed me up and dragged me along, too. My grandparents, recently retired and happy to have the house to themselves, were not thrilled to be our hosts. Nevertheless, my grandmother, ever eager to play the martyr, did open her door to us—although I think she did it just so she could practice her bothered sigh. She helped get Lana a job as a receptionist in the office of a plastic surgeon. And since Lana did not yet have enough money for daycare, my grandmother sighed and reluctantly agreed to watch me during the day.

What I remember most from this time are two things. First, I watched an awful lot of TV. Second, it was the first time I ever heard of Max.

From the moment I got up in the morning, I was plopped down in front of the television.

"Dillon," my grandmother would say, "why don't you take your cereal and go watch some TV. That Captain Kangaroo's on. Hurry now; you don't want to miss it."

My grandmother seemed to do nothing but sit at the kitchen table with her ever-present can of Tab, smoking cigarettes, doing her nails, and flipping through travel brochures for cruises of the Caribbean. My grandfather stuck to the small greenhouse he'd built behind the house, in which he was forever potting and repotting his orchids, and listening to talk radio on his Walkman. In fact, the Walkman was pretty much always on. From sunup to sundown, even during meals, he wore his headphones, which was fine because he never had much to say other than to shake his head every now and then and yell something on the order of "THIS COUNTRY'S GOING TO HELL IN A HAND BASKET" or "NUKE 'EM BACK TO THE STONE AGE!"

To which, my grandmother would nod, take a sip of her Tab, and reply, "Yes, dear."

After we'd eaten, he'd return to the greenhouse or retrieve his metal detector from the garage and wander the neighborhood, digging up stray dimes and bottle caps as he went, yelling salutations at the neighbors. On rare occasions, like my birthday or on one of his good-humored days when he'd been nipping from the bottle of rum he kept hidden in his workbench, I was allowed to help with the repotting or go with him on his treasure hunts. But usually when I asked, he'd just pat me on the head and yell, "WHY DON'T YOU GO WATCH SOME TV!"

So I watched TV. Hours and days and weeks of TV. Cartoons, talk shows, soap operas, reruns, local news, on and on, over and over again. On top of the TV were several framed family photos, to which my attention would sometimes drift when the morning cartoons gave way to the afternoon soap operas. There was my grandparents' wedding picture, pictures of Lana as a baby, and Lana on her first day of school, and Lana artfully posed and airbrushed for her senior class picture. Far to the left of these was a small hinged metal frame that opened like a book. On one side was a photo of Lana when she was about ten. On the other was a boy, about my age, with very black hair and a menacing smile on his face. I asked about him one day while I was helping my grandfather with the repotting. His brow furrowed and he stopped what he was doing. Then he shook his head and yelled, "THE DEVIL'S CHILD, THAT BOY."

I waited for him to elaborate but he just went back to his potting, shaking his head angrily.

My childish curiosity was piqued by this response, which I took quite literally, having recently watched a matinee of *Rosemary's Baby;* so later that afternoon when I was having my snack, I asked my grandmother about it.

"Nana, who's that dark-haired boy in the picture frame on the TV?"

She paused midstroke in her nail painting and gave me an angry look, like the one she gave me when I set my glass on one of the end tables without a coaster. She took a long drag on her cigarette and arched one of her penciled-in eyebrows.

"That," she said, her voice revealing her distaste, "was your mother's little brother, your uncle, but he's with the angels in heaven now."

"He's dead?" I asked, more than a little confused about how the devil's child could be with the angels in heaven.

"Mmm," she replied, and nodded vaguely. "Oh look, it's almost three o'clock already," she said, lifting me up from my chair and directing me toward the living room. "Isn't your show on? That one with all the little puppets in the colored neighborhood? Take your snack with you; that's a good boy. And be sure and use a coaster."

I went back to my spot in front of the TV but as soon as she left I took the frame down from its spot once more. It was odd to look at that picture—a picture of someone roughly my own age—and know that he was dead.

Later that night, during my bath, while Lana was perched on the toilet lid filing her nails, I asked her about him.

"How did your brother die?" I ventured, as gently and gravely as I could, afraid she might erupt in a flood of tears and wailing. Instead, her brow wrinkled and she looked confused.

"Die? He's not dead," she said, indignantly, "Well, probably not yet, anyway. Which one of them told you that?"

"Nana."

"Well, that figures," she sneered.

"But what happened to him?" I asked.

She stopped filing her nails and smiled devilishly. "Oh, he was trouble, that boy. He had some trouble—" she said and seemed just about to tell me about it, but then caught herself and thought better of it. "He, uh, didn't get along with Nana and Grandpa so he ran away, or they kicked him out, I don't remember which one it was that last time. I was away then, up at Keystone."

This was hardly a satisfactory response.

"But why did they say he was dead?" I asked. Again Lana started, but then stopped herself and her expression darkened.

"Look, kiddo," she said, stabbing at the air in front of me with the nail file, her tone suddenly serious and impatient. "You just zip your lips on the subject for now. We can talk about it all you want someday when we're out of here, but don't bring it up anymore. They're sick of us as it is so don't you go and make it worse. Got it?"

I nodded, and sunk down among the bubbles. We did not speak of it again, and the next day I noticed that the picture-book frame had disappeared from its place on the TV. I thought about it a lot after that, trying to imagine what he'd done that everyone was so afraid to talk about, but soon all thoughts of him were replaced by another man who appeared in our lives.

As I said, Lana was young then, blonde, blue-eyed, pretty, and prone to wearing tight sweaters, short skirts, patterned stockings, and lots of lip gloss. Indeed, that was why she had been hired at the plastic surgeon's office. The doctor she worked for was well into middle age and it didn't take long for him to take more than a professional interest in her. His midlife crisis had begun the year before and he'd treated the symptoms with the purchase of a vintage Jaguar. Although this undoubtedly made him feel young and free for a while, I'm sure, as with most accessories, the novelty eventually wore off. Lana, with her firm skin and youthful breasts, was surely closer to what he was looking for, so she soon became his next accessory. That she had an accessory of her own—namely, me—he didn't seem to mind. He had two college-age daughters and a wife himself, so I was hardly the biggest nuisance in his life. In due time, he shed his wife and replaced her with Lana. She became his new model, his upgrade, his trophy wife. I was the trophy wife's baggage, but as I said, he really didn't mind my existence.

Lana, on the other hand, came to mind it a great deal. To her I suppose I was a symbol of her youthful folly, of poor decisions she had made, of failures in her early life, of her advancing age. For those reasons, shortly after she met James, my future stepfather, she developed an aversion, an allergy almost, to the word *mother,* or any synonyms thereof. From then on, I was instructed to call her "Lana" and to keep quiet and stay out of the way as much as possible. She had always been neglectful and indifferent toward me, but when she met James that indifference transformed into an active dislike.

Like many people who were spoiled as children, I suppose Lana was incapable of loving a child, even one of her own. Sensing this coldness and hostility from an early age (if I'd been brain-dead, I could have sensed it) I naturally gravitated toward my stepfather, James. Over time, I like to think that James grew fond of me, too. He often took me swimming or horseback riding or to baseball games. And yet, instead of being happy that her son and husband were getting along, Lana was jealous of our friendship and never tired of cautioning James about spoiling me.

"I really mean it," she'd say. "You're making a brat out of him."

To which he'd just laugh and then haul me up onto his shoulders and ride me around the living room while Lana seethed, her eyes narrowing into angry slits.

In spite of that, for a few years after their marriage, we all lived more or less happily in a large condominium near downtown. James would have been perfectly content to stay there, but Lana had other ideas. She had a rich husband and thought that she should, of course, have a home reflective of that wealth. Over the years she'd made friends—women she'd met while volunteering for the Junior League and the Junior Symphony Guild—who were all leaving the city en masse and moving to the suburban communities of large custom homes that were then sprouting up to the south. It all sounded so attractive and new and clean and ritzy that Lana decided she just had to join them.

Initially, James was reluctant. He liked living in town and being close to everything—his office, the country club, the restaurants and sports stadiums—but over time Lana manipulated him into submission. She had an almost feline, little girlish way of whining and pouting that was, together with her tight sweaters and glossed lips, attractive to him. Usually, she got what she wanted. This time was no exception. She found a new development of massive houses and had James sign on with the developer to build a custom home. She then hired an architect, a general contractor, and an interior designer. Although initially, James had reservations, he came to share her enthusiasm for the early planning phase of the project. Night after night I'd find them sitting on the sofa sharing a bottle of wine and going over blueprints and floor plans and swatches of fabric.

No one could ever accuse Lana of being temperate, which became readily apparent in her plans for her new palace. At first, the design for the house and the surrounding property was grand, but with Lana in charge it quickly became grandiose, verging on gaudy. Armed with back issues of *Architectural Digest*, and with her nelly, bald decorator by her side, she envisioned marble entryways and elaborate iron railing. She laid out intricate tile patterns for each of the bathrooms and planned to fill them with tiny sinks and bidets and toilets and with huge tubs that would whirl and shoot jets of water from several different angles. Her kitchen was to be a vision of heart maple, polished black granite, and industrial-size brushed-metal appliances. It would have been more than adequate for even the most discriminating chef. For the rest of the house, she chose elaborate wood floors, Persian carpets, and window treatments all complemented by a lighting system that could be controlled with a clap of the hands.

Only later, when James began to get the bills for her plans, did he protest, but by then it was too late. Lana had tasted domestic luxury and it was ambrosia. She knew just the setting in which she wanted to live, and she would do anything to get it. Never would she return to a trailer, not even to a condo in the city. This was it. She had not "arrived," but she was well on her way; and like any addict, her needs only increased over time and her demands became more insistent and shrewish. It was then that she and James began to argue.

Being older then, I remember these fights much more clearly than those between Jake and Lana. They were always about money—money she needed to pay the architect, money for the developer, money for the interior designer. She needed deposits for the window coverings, for the upgrade to the nickle-plated plumbing fixtures, and to tear out and reinstall the kitchen cabinets because the initial plan, according to the designer, "just would not do."

Each morning before he left for work, Lana would corner James in the foyer of the condo and block the door with her body. She'd then present him with a list of people's names and the amounts they needed, and she would not move until she had several signed checks in hand. James grumbled and questioned, and Lana whined and whimpered and blubbered about how much work she was putting in, driving back and forth to the house, and how he wasn't helping at all, and how it would all be worth it in the end. Eventually, usually because he was sick of arguing and didn't want to be late, he would give in, take out his checkbook, and start writing.

One year, several hundred tantrums, and God knows how many tens of thousands of dollars later, the house remained unfinished. Nevertheless, Lana decided that we would move in as scheduled so she could keep a better eye on the day-to-day progress. This was another of her big mistakes. A very costly mistake that she paid for with her marriage.

The house, at that point, was nothing more than a cavernous, dusty, incomplete shell, in which noisy workers came and went all day long. It was filled with ladders and lumber and tools, and the air buzzed with the sounds of sanders and compressors. At night, Lana took over from the machinery and whined and pleaded and yelled at James. It was a miserable time for all of us but especially for James. He not only had to bankroll all of the misery, he also had to spend hours each day commuting to and from his office in gridlock traffic.

At first, I rode with him, since I was to finish out the year at my old school and then start junior high in our new neighborhood. On our mornings together I noticed how his mood would brighten (despite his invariable bout with Lana and the checkbook) as we drove toward downtown. He'd hum and whistle and talk to me about school and cars and golf. Conversely, in the evening, as we headed back home, he was always silent; if he did speak, it was only to give curt responses to any of the questions I might ask him.

About two months after we moved in, shortly after school ended and I began my summer vacation, a frustrated James informed us that he would be attending a two-week-long conference in Argentina. He went (with his secretary, we later found out). After the first week, he called to inform Lana that when he returned, it would not be to the house or to her. She could keep the house, he said, she could keep her car, she could even keep some of his money, but she could not keep him.

To vain Lana, this made absolutely no sense. That James had left his first wife for her was understandable. That he would leave her—for any reason—was incomprehensible.

"He must have been playing golf all day without a hat on," she said, chuckling confidently as she drove me to the orthodontist one morning. "You watch, he'll come crawling back. And when he does I'll be ready. He'll have to pay for this one! I'll get that Bisaza tile in the bathroom, just you watch me!"

But weeks passed and James did not come back. Lana was a little uneasy, but his Jaguar was still in the garage and if it was not entirely unthinkable that he would leave her, it would be folly to think that he would leave both her *and* his precious car. As a precautionary measure, she had the lock on the garage door changed and kept the only key on a chain around her wrist.

Meanwhile, the workmen, as insistent and as vocal for their money as a nest full of starving baby birds, feared a connection between James's long absence and their sudden lack of checks. Lana, clad in a skirt that was shorter than usual and a gauzy shirt with no bra, addressed their concerns one morning. She pooh-poohed their suspicions and told them, in honeyed tones, that James was just off doing some work in Argentina and had forgotten to sign any checks before he left.

"Those Argentines! They just love that reconstructive surgery! He's very busy," she cooed, shaking her own augmented mammaries.

On witnessing this pathetic display, the interior decorator immediately packed up all his samples and left. The contractor threatened to pull all of his men off the job, but like all the rest of the straight male workers, he was bewitched by Lana's feminine charms and said he reckoned it wouldn't hurt to wait a little longer.

A month passed and still no word. Then one day a perky young paralegal appeared on the scene and served Lana with divorce papers. This shook her composure a little, but still she held on, figuring that if he did actually intend to divorce her (which she still didn't believe), she could bleed him white in the process. She took the papers to her closet, stashed them far from the eyes of the workmen and emerged again in the gauzy shirt she planned to wear that evening for her meeting with the contractor. The same contractor who had telephoned more than once that day demanding, "A check! In my hands! Today, lady!"

Then something happened that Lana could not have foreseen and that all of her tricks were powerless against. The aforementioned contractor had come to our house, been unswayed by her tits, and collected the check (on which she had, in a panic, forged James's signature). He then disappeared. Forever.

Over the next few days, it came to the attention of the developer's accountant that massive amounts of money were missing from several different jobs, and that all of the accounts overseen by our contractor were empty. On closer inspection, it was revealed that the contractor's energy and enthusiasm (on which Lana had often commented) were largely drug induced, and for a long time he had been embezzling money in order to finance his little habit. Rather than face death or dismemberment at the hands of his dealer or prosecution at the hands of the bank, he had fled, taking Lana's hot check with him. The news of his departure spread among the workmen like the news of a coming tornado, and they wasted no time packing up their tools and materials and driving back down the hill.

And that was it. The end of the work and the beginning of our isolation. The next day our cul-de-sac was like a ghost town. All construction on our house and the houses around it came to an absolute halt and did not begin again for more than a year. Our house, due to Lana's impatience, was the only standing structure. The others were nothing more than driveways leading up to big holes in the ground. Some had concrete foundations; some had the skeletal beginnings of wood framing; but most were just eerie, lonely, muddy holes. There was no traffic on our street, other than the mailman, who came once a day. There were no streetlights. In fact, there was nothing but sidewalks and mud and empty prairie stretching off for miles in all directions.

Chapter Three

Of course, there were eventually phone conversations between James and Lana, as much as I'm sure James would have liked to avoid them. One in particular stands out in my mind. I remember it mainly because, for a while, it was the end of the phone and because it was the beginning of Lana's drinking.

"So greeaaat!" Lana said. She has a flat sarcastic way of saying "great" that makes the word sound anything but.

"Greeaaat. You're saying I can have the house but I can't have the money to finish the fucking thing! Greeaaat. No paint, no carpeting, no landscaping. Fucking fantastic! . . . Uh huh . . . uh huh . . . Well, here's what I think of you and your fucking pre-nup!" She yanked the cord from the wall and threw it and the receiver off the balcony and into the muddy field behind the house. At this point I crept off my barstool at the kitchen counter and moved to the relative safety of the living room. I watched her through the window as she paced angrily back and forth on the deck, puffing furiously on her cigarette. Then suddenly she stopped. She clenched her jaw and looked back into the house. She pitched the remainder of her cigarette the same direction she had pitched the phone, blew out a huge plume of smoke, and marched back through the kitchen to the hall closet. She opened it, selected one of James's titanium drivers from his golf bag and then marched off into the garage. A moment later I heard several dull thuds followed by the sound of breaking glass. A few moments after that Lana reappeared, her hair a mess, her face streaked with mascara tears, and the club (now bent in the middle) still in her hand. She dropped it absently on the floor and then walked slowly up the stairs to her bedroom. I waited a few minutes after I heard her door shut and then crawled out from my hiding space behind the sofa. Quietly, I made my way toward the garage. I opened the door slowly, so the hinge wouldn't creak and peeked in. The overhead light was on and I saw just what I'd expected but could still hardly believe. James's treasured Jaguar—the one Lana had always hated because she suspected (and probably rightly so) that he loved it more than her—now had a shattered windshield and several pronounced dents in its hood. I'm sure she could easily have done more damage, but I've always suspected that she was probably stricken by remorse in the middle of her deed, by the thought that maybe this was taking things a little too far, by the realization that if the marriage wasn't completely lost, this would ensure it. I shuddered as I looked at it: the cracked green paint and the exposed metal underneath, the tiny shards of glass, almost like thousands of tiny ice cubes, now covering the seats and the floorboards. I had rarely seen James angry, but I knew he would be livid when he saw this.

That's when Lana took to the bottle. It was an easy thing for her to do because instead of a basement, her custom home had been outfitted with an elaborate wine cellar, stocked with wines that someone (someone to whom James had written a big fat check, no doubt) thought were worthy of having in a suburban wine cellar. For months after the Jaguar clubbing, I never saw Lana sober. I would get up in the mornings, dress and feed myself, and then wander down the muddy street to the main road where the school bus would collect me. When I returned, she would already have started drinking. At least one bottle of wine would be open and she would be slumped on the couch, in the middle of her dusty palace, either watching TV or flipping through the pages of a magazine. I would kiss her on the cheek, ask her if there was anything she wanted, to which she'd usually respond by grunting and shaking her head, and then I'd go and fix myself a snack in the kitchen. When I finished eating, I'd go upstairs to my room and do my homework or my finger exercises on my clarinet, never daring to actually play it for fear of sparking her rage or annoyance. Later, when I was fairly sure she had passed out, I'd tiptoe back down and collect all the bottles and glasses and empty the ashtray. I'd gently cover her with a blanket and then, as quietly as I could, tiptoe back upstairs and read until I fell asleep.

I was so quiet and careful because to wake her, or to disturb her in any way was to risk unleashing a beast whose words were sharper than any teeth or claws.

"You know why he left, don't you," she seethed at me one drunken afternoon when she'd cornered me in the kitchen. I said nothing.

"Well, I'm 'onna tell you." She stood before me, swaying, wine bottle in one hand, cigarette in the other.

"He left a'cause a you!" she spat. "He was sick of having a brat around! Same reason your shitheaded dad left. Sick of you cryin' all the time in that fuckin shithole trailer, sick of the smell of diapers! Sick of it all! Sick of you! Nobody wants fuckin' kids around. Nobody!"

Shocking words, but it was not the first time I'd heard them and I knew better than to give any response. I had learned that responding at all only made things worse. Protest was useless. Indignation was useless. Crying was useless. I just stood there and took it, which is not to say it didn't hurt. Each blow struck me, destroyed little pieces of me, but I could never show it.

In elementary school I'd learned a game called Stone Face, in which two players square off and just stare at one another, each trying to maintain an expression that is completely impassive. This would go on until one of the two cracked, until someone twitched or broke into a fit of giggles. I never lost at that game. Life with Lana had made me a pro at Stone Face. Each time she went into one of her angry tirades, I immediately started the game and erected the blank facade, behind which my soul would quietly implode and collapse in on itself.

"It's a'cause you that we have to live in . . . this!" she shouted, gesturing at the huge, unfinished house.

"God! To think what I could've been if it weren't for fuckin' kids!"

Although my home life was miserable, it was, believe it or not, preferable to the wretchedness I was then enduring at my new school.

Junior high. That warehouse of raging hormones, angst, and acne in which society places it's twelve- to fourteen-year-olds. The place where differences are delineated and a caste system based on physical beauty, sports prowess, and popularity is established. Sadly, I found myself on the bottom rung of this new social ladder.

To make matters worse, my own hormones chose that point to release themselves in my body and wreak havoc. Seemingly overnight I was six feet tall, weighed a whopping 102 pounds, and wore a size eleven shoe. Acne bloomed on my chin, nose, and forehead, and my voice creaked when I spoke like an out-of-tune bagpipe. Add to that a new mouthful of braces and unwieldy headgear, and you've got a good snapshot of my adolescence.

But the worst part—the most torturous thing about it for me—was the fact that my newfound hobby, masturbation, did not at all involve thoughts of the opposite sex. The guilt of having thoughts about sex at all was bad enough, but the guilt of having thoughts about members of my own sex increased it tenfold.

Lonely, ugly, and afraid, I kept to myself as much as I possibly could in my new school. It was not all that hard to do except in gym class when I was forced to interact. This was torture. I was horribly uncoordinated, and it seemed that every activity involved some sort of a ball—hitting a ball, catching a ball, throwing a ball. I couldn't do any of it very well. I'd never had a dad or an older brother to do these things with. James had taken me swimming sometimes, but we had never played any games with a ball! In this gym class it was nothing but ball sports—football, baseball, basketball, dodge ball, medicine ball—and each day I was assaulted with the comments: "You throw like a girl!" "You dribble like a pussy!" "You couldn't catch that ball with a glove the size of the Grand Canyon!" Or, when they were feeling especially eloquent and succinct they'd just yell, "Fag!"

The class itself was agony, but what came after was a lower circle of hell.

"Okay, men!" the big-gutted gym teacher would bark. "Hit the showers!" and we were all prodded into the locker room and ordered to strip. It was torture. My body was not pretty. I was tall, alarmingly thin, and just beginning to sprout pubic hair, of which I was terribly embarrassed because there were only a few other guys in class who had any. I was also terrified because I really wanted to look at all the other bodies, but whenever even the vaguest thought of it crossed my mind, I could feel something stirring in my loins and, in the words of Lana's decorator, "that just would not do." That could not be. I could not be the "Fag!" they had branded me. So, every day when I stripped down, I kept my eyes on the floor. Then, lifting my head, I'd stare over the heads of all the nubile male flesh and march resolutely to the huge open shower room. I went quickly because from the time I got my underwear off to the time I reached the shower—a space of probably five seconds—I could already feel my dick stirring and I knew that I had to get to the shower fast, or else! Once there, I turned facing the wall and twisted the tap labeled *C* as far to the right as it would go. Only when the icy needles of water hit me, and I felt my balls retreat and my scrotum tighten up, did I relax and release the shuddering breath I'd been holding since dropping my underwear. I would thoroughly chill myself before returning to my locker, so that hopefully the cold would last at least until my dick was safely back inside my underwear. This procedure was effective, but it was also responsible for the charming little nickname that I was given and that stuck with me all through school.

Goose—on account of the fact that when I returned to my locker after my arctic shower, my skin was covered with goose pimples.

My principle torturer at this time was a boy named Aaron Lewis. Aaron was Italian-looking, with black hair and brown eyes, a square jaw and a Roman nose. I wish he had not been so good-looking because, if he had been ugly, it would have been even easier to hate him. In many ways he was everything I was not: he was good at sports; he was good-looking and well developed; and he had nice clothes that always seemed to fit him. By contrast, I was clumsy, ugly, skinny, and stuck with last year's fashions since Lana had been too drunk to take me shopping.

That my clothes were out of style was bad enough, but I'd also grown so much over the past few months that my pants never reached past midcalf and my shirtsleeves never covered my skinny wrists. Aaron had clear skin and straight teeth that didn't need braces let alone headgear with a hideous, robin's-egg blue, satin strap, which was the only color the orthodontist had besides pink.

Of course Aaron was popular and always had a group of boys or girls hanging around him. He was always talking, in his loud and cocky way, or laughing, or playing some sort of game, usually at my expense. At lunch, he held court at his table in the center of the cafeteria, surrounded by his gang and all the pom-pom girls. I sat alone or, if the tables were full and that wasn't an option, with the "special needs" kids, who were even more outcast than I, but within whose ranks I was easily camouflaged with my too-small clothes and my headgear. Most often, though, I would grab whatever food

I could carry in my pockets and go to the library or the band room. These two places were preferable to the playground, since I knew sand wouldn't be poured down my pants and my shoes wouldn't be taken and tossed around the playground while I made vain attempts to catch them as they flew back and forth above my head.

Looking back I see that I was like the chicken with the blood spot that all the others peck at. I don't know why I was singled out—perhaps because I was new, perhaps because I was ugly, perhaps because I never gave any reaction to being tormented. I just sat there, stoically, while Aaron wrung out a wet sponge on my head in art class or stuffed me into a hall locker. I never fought; I never cried out. I just let my body go where they pushed it and then waited patiently in the dark for the janitor to pry the door open. Aaron and his friends would trip me in the hallway so that I'd fall and send books scattering in front of me or sit behind me in history class and pepper the back of my head and neck with spitwads shot through a straw they'd saved from lunch. They'd grab my backpack in the morning and throw it on top of the school building or push my face down into the fountain when I leaned over to get a drink. But I never fought back and I never told.

I know I'm painting a pathetic picture here, I feel it myself. I'm putting things down as accurately as I can remember, and yet even I am thinking "How pathetic!" Even I am wondering why I didn't fight back, why I didn't tell anyone. But then I remember the fear: the fear of reprisals, both physical and mental; the fear of Lana hearing from someone else how pathetic and weak her son was; the fear of making things worse both at school and at home, which is all I could imagine would happen if I protested.

As awful as my life sounds then, it was not without moments of joy. In fact, two things made it bearable. The first was playing my clarinet, and the second—well, it will be apparent all too soon.

I had started playing the clarinet a few years before in elementary school, when I'd joined the band and was allowed to pick out an instrument. I'd wanted to play the flute, but Lana had squashed that idea, telling me I would just have to pick something else because the flute was "a girl's instrument." I tried the violin next, but after listening to a torturous five minutes of my practicing that first night she nixed that choice, too. I came to the clarinet by default, I guess, but I grew to love it so much I might have switched to it anyway. The band teacher at my new junior high, Mr. Sullivan, was a clarinet player himself so he favored our section and favored me because I was a good player. I wasn't especially talented but I did practice when I could, which was more than most of the other kids would do.

The first day, we were given several songs to take home and practice. One was "Rainy Days and Mondays." Later that night, as I sat in my room, silently doing the finger exercises so as not to wake up Lana, I noticed that underneath the bars and notes on the page, the words to the song were also printed out. Like most adolescents I was attracted to the dark, romantic, almost-doomed-but-ultimately-hopeful lyrics, but it went beyond that. I felt that someone had taken all the chaotic, jumbled feelings I'd had over the past few months and somehow made sense of them, given substance to the airy nothing. For the first time since we'd moved to the house, I didn't feel completely alone.

In class, the band was having immense trouble translating the notes on the page into anything resembling the song. After a week of listening to us wheeze and snort and squeak through it, a frustrated Mr. Sullivan brought in a record so we could hear what the song was supposed to sound like. I think I'll always remember that day; the sight of him lowering the needle onto the record, the faint sound of the scratches as it eased into the groove, the soft piano and mournful harmonica at the beginning, and then that voice! That deep, rich, impossibly low alto. It sent chills all through me and I had the feeling that all of my hair was standing straight up. By the end of the song I was swallowing hard and my eyes were watering.

Immediately I felt a kinship with that voice, not just the sound and how its low tones were so similar to those of the clarinet, but with the person singing those sad lyrics.

After class, after all the other students had filed out, I went up to Mr. Sullivan and asked who it was.

"Ahh, you liked that, did you? That was Karen Carpenter. Great voice, huh." I nodded. "Did it help you get an idea how the song is supposed to sound?"

"Yes . . ." I said, hesitating.

"You seem to play pretty well, though. I can tell you practice, and I appreciate it. Keep it up."

He started gathering up his papers and was getting ready to leave.

"Um, sir?" I asked, timidly. He looked up at me. I fingered my headgear nervously.

"Do you think maybe, if I was really careful with it, I could borrow that record some time, maybe make a tape of it?"

He chuckled.

"Here," he said, going over to the stack of records next to the small portable player. "You can have it. I got it for fifty cents at a used vinyl place. Not many people want Carpenters' records nowadays."

And he was right. The year was 1985 and I don't think the Carpenters were ever less in vogue. They had been relegated to the music world's Hall of Shame, right next to ABBA and the soundtrack to *Saturday Night Fever*. Of course, in later years, they were dusted off and made fashionable again; but in the eighties, they were not something spoken of with anything other than derision.

He gave me the record in its tan jacket, with the horribly dated photo of Richard and Karen on the liner, and I thanked him.

"It's too bad about her," he said. "They made such a good team."

I looked up at him, questioningly. "Too bad?"

"Oh she's dead," he said. "Anorexia. Starved herself to death. Never happy with her appearance, I guess, when her appearance was the last thing anyone cared about."

"Was that her husband?" I asked, pointing to the picture on the liner. He laughed.

"Oh God, no, that's her brother, Richard. They look pretty geeky, eh?" I nodded.

"Was she ever . . . married?" I asked, timidly.

"Who, Karen? You know, I don't know. Why? You carrying a little torch for our Karen?" he asked, teasingly.

I turned crimson. Me: nerdy band fag, standing there in my too-small clothes and my headgear with the robin's-egg-blue satin strap, clutching my clarinet case and a Carpenters' album. Since I couldn't disappear into the carpet, I switched the subject.

"I, uh, I can't really practice at home," I said. "It kinda bothers La-, er, my mom. Is there any way I could maybe practice here. Like, during lunch, I mean."

He looked at me, trying to read my face. He saw something there—fear, most likely—and his expression softened. He turned his attention to his teacher's book, resting on the podium, and flipped through the pages.

"Let's see, well, we have staff meetings here during your lunchtime on Mondays, and the choir rehearses here on Thursday, but you're welcome to come the other days. Are you sure you want to?" he asked.

I gave an eager nod.

"Okay then, it's all yours."

And so I was able to escape the cafeteria and the playground every Tuesday, Wednesday, and Friday, which was nice but still left me vulnerable to attack on Mondays and Thursdays.

One of Aaron's cleverest stunts happened one day as I was coming out of the band room. I was headed to the bathroom before my next class, but at the entrance, Aaron stepped in front of me. This was bad. I said nothing, did not try to go around him, but just looked down at the carpet and waited.

"Hey, Goose," he said. "Do you know what time it is?"

Nervously, I consulted my watch and mumbled that it was twelve forty-five.

"Are you sure, Goose," Aaron said, shaking his head from side to side, a savage grin on his face. "Cos I don't think so. It's not twelve forty-five. Check again."

My head down, I looked at my watch again.

"What time is it?" I said, my voice barely audible.

"What's that, Goose? You say something?" I kept my eyes down at my feet. My face hot with embarrassment and anger. He waited in silence.

"What time is it?" I asked again, hoping that if I cooperated it would be over soon.

"You hear that, guys?" Aaron said, looking around to his friends who were now circled around me. "Goose wants to know what time it is."

The friends laughed and moved in closer.

"It's time, Goose. It's time . . . to get wet!"

And suddenly, four of his gang took hold of me—two had my legs; two had my arms—and together they lifted me off the ground and hauled me into the bathroom. There, I was turned upside down and my head held inside the toilet bowl, which they flushed repeatedly. I emerged, gasping for air, my hair swirled on top of my head, while they all laughed. I stood dripping, as stoic and agonized as St. Sebastian, wishing I could just die and get it over with.

For a while after that, I made it a point to never drink anything during the course of the day so that I'd never need to go within fifty feet of the bathroom. If I had to go, I just held it until I got home. Then I ran up the muddy street to the house, as fast as I could, to finally relieve my poor bladder.

On one such day, I ran up the hill, whipped open the front door, eager to get to the bathroom, and was greeted by Lana's scowling head, peeking over the back of the sofa, which she was in the process of vacuuming.

"Hey!" she yelled. "Take off those muddy shoes before you come in here!"

I was shocked, not because she seemed concerned about me tracking mud onto a plywood floor, but by the fact that she was up, and appeared sober, and was using the vacuum—a machine I was not even aware she knew the location of. It was odd, but the next day was even more so: I came home, as usual, full-to-bursting, and as I reached the house I noticed a strange car in the driveway. It was not the Jaguar, or Lana's little white BMW, but a large boxy Oldsmobile. I approached it and peeked inside. From the rearview mirror hung a cardboard air freshener, but instead of being shaped like a leaf, or a flower, or a piece of fruit, this one was in the shape of a crucifix. I remember looking at it and wondering what smell they could possibly have assigned to that. I wondered also who the car belonged to and in what condition they had found Lana. I didn't want to go in, but my bladder bade me do otherwise. I opened the door and took off my muddy shoes as quietly as I could. Low voices were coming from the living room, but I had to pee so badly that I knew I'd have to wait to see who they belonged to. I ducked into the tiny bathroom under the staircase, the one in which the ceiling was so low I could barely stand. I did my business, zipped up my still-too-tight pants, and was about to flush when I heard voices just outside the door. I hesitated. The Oldsmobile owner must be leaving. I turned off the light and opened the door just a crack. There was Lana, and I was relieved to see that she was dressed and had combed her hair, although she still had not put on any makeup and looked pinched and tired. She was talking to a man, probably in his forties, not fat, but large and in clothes that fit him as tightly as my own. His hair was stiffly styled, like a newscaster's, and parted severely to one side, exposing a white valley of scalp. He was not unattractive, but there was an excessive neatness about him, and something synthetic in his tight-lipped smile and soft expression.

"Think about what I've told you," he said, taking Lana's hands in his. "Will you do that?" She nodded.

"And look over some of the literature? If you have any questions, we can talk about it next time, okay? Or you could call me." Again, she nodded.

"Thank you," she said, and for a moment they held eye contact. He gave her hands a final squeeze and left.

Although I didn't know it then, as I stood hiding in the little bathroom, Lana had found herself a new man. One who would always love her and never leave her, no matter how big of a bitch she became. No, it was not the Oldsmobile owner, but, rather, his boss. None other than Our Lord Jesus Christ.

The Oldsmobile owner was Wayne Blandings, and he was the assistant pastor at The Church of the Divine Redeemer. It was the church our cleaning lady attended, and she had sent him over after she had come by one day and found Lana so sauced she couldn't even speak. After that first meeting, Wayne came by frequently and often brought other "spiritual counselors" with him. Many days I'd return home from school and (after I'd peed, of course) would go into the living room and find them all huddled around the coffee table holding hands with their eyes closed.

I suppose in some ways Lana's rebirth was a good thing. She did quit drinking and even decided that she ought to go back to school and try to get a job. This she had been encouraged to do by her attorney months ago, since there was some loophole in her prenuptial agreement with James that could be twisted to make him pay for the majority of her education. Until then, she had not been sober enough to even consider it, let alone actually do it, but then, with Jesus behind her she applied, and was accepted to, a nursing program at the city college downtown.

With her faith, a shiny goal, and a new church to attend, Lana was much happier, which made life somewhat easier for me. Unable to share her happiness (I was not a "believer"), I tried at least to be happy for her, and several nights a week I would accompany her to "the Gatherings," as they were called, which took place in an old abandoned K mart that had been transformed into a church.

I was wary of the church and of Lana's conversion, for much the same reason I am wary of parties where everyone has done hits of Ecstasy. In each situation the participants are all so unrelentingly friendly, they hug you and pat you and smile at you as though you're an intimate friend, but it's a false intimacy that has left out the entire gritty step of getting to know someone. I wasn't buying it. Especially since I saw how easily Lana could put it on. The second we walked through the big glass doors of the church, she'd switch on her smile and happy demeanor and be nice to everyone, including me. You'd have thought there were cameras rolling. And yet, it seemed that somewhere along the line Lana had missed the part about God being all-seeing and all-knowing, because as soon as we left she switched it off and became her demanding, impatient, bitchy self. At least with me.

After my first few gatherings, I was, without my consent, enrolled in the YFC group. Youth for Christ was a group composed of kids, roughly my age, who sat around in a circle, singing alarmingly right-wing folk songs, and talking about the hellfire and eternal torment that surely awaited those foolish heathens who had not accepted Jesus Christ as their personal savior. And I was duly afraid, although more of the other kids in the group than of what might happen to my poor filthy soul on Judgment Day.

At the end of the five weeks in the group, I was to be baptized and receive my first communion. Not having been baptized, I was a big novelty.

"Aren't you afraid?" one pop-eyed girl asked me. "What if you get hit by a bus before the five weeks? Why you'll go to Purgatory then."

"I never met anyone one wasn't baptized," one of the boys added. "Well, no one but Jews, anyway, but then that's a different bird altogether."

The gatherings grew weirder and weirder the more we attended.

35

There were fire-and-brimstone sermons, of course, but occasionally, when the pastor had really whipped his flock into a frenzy, the service would climax with "the laying on of hands." This little piece of theater involved some of the parishioners lining up before the altar and waiting for the pastor to touch their foreheads. When he did this, it was like a spiritual jump-start, and the person would fall backward, apparently unconscious, into the arms of waiting ushers. At other times, the people in the pews would move to the aisles and fall convulsing to the ground, or they would look blankly ahead and start speaking in tongues, which I found more reminiscent of the possessed girl in *The Exorcist*, than of the presence of the Lord. I found it frightening, yes, but more than that I was afraid that I might be called on to participate, which for someone as painfully shy and self-concious as I was would have been unimaginable. The amount of audience participation required at the church—the singing, the hand holding, the hugging and swaying back and forth, the shouting, "Halleluia" and "Praise the Lord!" and "Thank You, Jesus!"—was about more than my nerves could stand. I would often look with sympathy up at the agonized Jesus on the cross and think, *I know just how you feel!*

My first communion, however, did mark a turning point for me, although not in the way you might think. I did not have a spiritual awakening; I was not born again, but I did, quite by accident, discover a way to make it all a bit more bearable.

Chapter Four

On the day of communion, the pastor made his way down the line dropping the host on our awaiting tongues repeating, "The body of Christ?" as he went and marking our foreheads with the sign of the cross. After I'd swallowed the host, I waited patiently as Wayne, carrying the large silver chalice, made his way down the line. When he got to me, he brought the cup to my lips and said, gravely, "The cup of salvation."

I leaned forward obediently and took a sip, but then I realized I was in trouble. I had forgotten about my headgear. The metal frame had slid easily into the metal cup, but when I tried to pull back, the frame expanded and the whole chalice came with it. Wayne, looking perturbed, shook the cup slightly, but this only sloshed wine up my nose and onto my shirt. I was terribly embarrassed and looked up at him over the rim with pleading eyes. He jiggled some more, but that just spilled more wine. Finally, I opened my mouth and took several huge gulps. It was cheap, chalky tasting stuff, and like all children, I had a natural distaste for alcohol. But there was no alternative, so I kept sucking it in until the cup was nearly empty. Eventually, it occurred to me to squeeze the sides of the headgear and when I did the cup slid right off. It fell to the ground with a thud, followed by silence. I coughed several times, picked up the chalice, and handed it back to a bewildered Wayne. With all eyes on me, I returned to my seat in the pew next to Lana. She wouldn't even look at me. She just closed her eyes in prayer and shook her head, but I knew I'd catch hell for it later. I slumped as far down in the pew as I could. The initial embarrassment passed, but in a few moments I noticed how warm I still felt. My ears were hot and I feared they must be bright red, but I felt relaxed, too. For the first time in so many months I felt less . . . self-concious, I guess. The tension drained out of my shoulders, and I even felt as though I might be able to sing the next song instead of just mouthing the words as I usually did. It was a wonderful sensation and I found myself thinking that maybe there was something to all this Jesus hooha after all. Of course, the spell eventually wore off. I realized it had been the wine and not the Lord that had invigorated me, and it was then that I really went to the devil. I discovered the second thing that could make me really happy.

You'll recall that I mentioned Lana's having built a wine cellar underneath the house. Well, after my first communion I skipped the middle man and took to administering the sacrament myself. Late at night, after Lana was asleep, I'd venture down to the cellar from time to time and sneak bottles back up to my room. I loved how easy it was to recapture that warm relaxed feeling with just a few glasses and, having lived with Lana, I was so good at being quiet and making myself inconspicuous, that most people never even noticed a change in me. Few ever came close enough to smell my breath, and I was usually so clumsy and awkward anyway that any effect liquor had on the way I carried myself could be easily explained by my inordinately large feet.

Yes, I became a teenage alcoholic, as trite as that sounds. My drinking started out slowly, just a few swigs in the morning to give me the courage to face Aaron's tormenting, and then a few swigs when I got home to help me face Lana and Wayne (who were by this time seeing a lot of each other) and to help get me through that evening's inevitable tedious gathering.

Since my twelve-year-old's palate was fairly unsophisticated, I gravitated more toward the sweeter wines, and under my bed there was a growing collection of stubby port bottles. I developed a particular fondness for port; it was syrupy and sweet and seemed to go into my system much faster than other wines. I favored a brand called Sandeman, although more for the name and the label than the taste. The name reminded me of the Sandman, which I thought appropriate since the wine itself was a very effective sleep aid. I liked the label because I found it strangely erotic.

The logo consists of a male silhouette—a mysterious, sinister-looking figure—wearing a cape and a wide brimmed caballero's hat, holding up a tiny glass of the port. The figure seemed enigmatic and sexy to me then and I invested it with all sorts of meaning and significance. As I drank I would stare drunkenly at the dark man, imagining him as several different people: sometimes it was Aaron, ready to jump out at me and attack, and sometimes it was the mysterious faceless male I imagined when I masturbated, the one who would take me away from the miserable life in which I was trapped. Other times it was the devil, who was surely in possession of my wicked, drunken, perverted soul, and sometimes it was my father, whose face I could no longer remember. Sometimes it was my step-father, James, and sometimes I even imagined it as the dark-haired boy I had seen in the picture-book frame so many years before in my grandparents' house.

When I had drunk enough and had recorked the bottle and rolled it back under my bed, I'd close my eyes and abandon myself to these spinning images. All of the men in my life, cloaked and masked, and menacingly silent, would whirl and dance in my head like a mobile; each part moving independently but still somehow attached to all the others.

Of course my drinking was discovered. Despite my best attempts to maintain my public poise, I got sloppy. My schoolwork was late, if I turned it in at all, and I started cutting gym class. Some days I didn't even bother to go to school but just wandered out past the bus stop into the prairie until I found a sunny grassy patch out of the wind where I'd read, and nap, and play my clarinet, my thermos full of port beside me.

My truancy eventually would have been detected, but it was an instrument check in band class that exposed me. It was nearing the end of the spring semester and we were to have a final concert that coming Friday. Mr. Sullivan and his assistant decided they should take a look at everyone's instruments before then, just to make sure there weren't any missing pads or bent keys. They did this section by section, and as fate would have it they got to the woodwinds on a morning when I'd had a few morning shots of cognac. I'd recently made the discovery that the warm feeling from cognac lasted a little longer through the day than a few swigs from the port bottle, so I'd started experimenting with it. That morning I'm afraid I overdid it. I'd miscalculated the dosage. My head was spinning and it was hard to keep my eyes focused. When they got to me, I removed my pickled reed from the mouthpiece so that Mr. Sullivan could replace it with his own fresh one and give it a few toots. I handed the clarinet over to him and as he was attaching his reed he got an odd look on his face, as if he'd discovered something really wrong with my instrument. He sniffed at the mouthpiece and then abruptly pulled back his head. He looked directly at me, his eyes wide, and stood up.

"Miss Johnson," he said, his eyes still on me, "could you take over for a minute? Dillon, please come with me."

I knew I was in trouble, but at that point I really didn't care. I got up, with difficulty, and stumbled my way through the class to where

Mr. Sullivan was waiting just outside the door, my clarinet still in his hand. He shut the door, pulled me by the arm into the middle of the deserted hallway, and sniffed at the air around my face.

"You've been drinking!"

I wobbled for a moment but before I could respond, I threw up.

What followed was a trip to the nurse's office, my arms over the shoulders of Mr. Sullivan and Miss Johnson. There, it was debated at length between the nurse, the principal, the assistant principal, the principal's secretary, the band teacher, and the guidance counselor whether they should call an ambulance, a social worker, or my mother. An hour later Lana arrived, dressed completely in white, looking saintly and fresh and cooly concerned. Like a snow-covered volcano, she hid her simmering fury and managed to sound as bewildered and worried as her acting talents would allow.

She said nothing to me in the nurse's office and nothing as we walked out to the car. She got in, put on her large white-framed sunglasses, and started the engine. She drove until we were a safe distance from the school and then she pulled over to the side of the road, reached over and slapped me as hard as she could. But I was numb. It was like part of me was dead. At school with them or at home with her, which hell did I prefer? I was proud of the fact that I had almost never cried in front of Lana, but then I could not help it and a single large tear rolled down my cheek. That was evidently a sufficient reaction; when she saw it, she repositioned herself in her seat, put the car in gear, and continued driving.

Church took up a lot of my time after that, although it was hardly by choice. I'd been suspended from school, which wasn't all that bad since there were only two weeks left until summer vacation. For a week or so after that, I was literally the center of attention at the gatherings. I stood in the middle of prayer circles while all the parishioners formed a chain around me. With their eyes closed, first one, then another, and then another, would spontaneously ask God to help me or command the devil to stop tempting me.

Another time I was called to the front of the congregation and the pastor led his flock in a round of "We renounce him!" This started slowly; the pastor, with his eyes closed, kept one hand on my forehead while holding the microphone in the other.

"Lord? Can you hear me, Lord?" he'd ask, as if the connection was a bit fuzzy. "Lord, we ask your help tonight for one of your children, young Dillon, who's been tempted away by Satan. Tempted away by a weakness of the flesh. He's been drinking, Lord, and having impure thoughts, and falling down that slippery slope of sin! We're all gathered here tonight in your name, Lord, to praise you and ask for your help for brother Dillon. Hear our prayer, Lord."

"Hear our prayer!" the congregation boomed.

"Give him strength, Lord!"

"Give him strength!"

"To resist the forces of Lucifer!

"Give him strength!"

"To resist his impure mind!"

"Give him strength!"

"To resist what he knows is an abomination in your eyes!"

"Give him strength!"

"To cleanse his thoughts and get back on the path of righteousness!"

"Give him strength!"

Give me a break!

You see, it wasn't just the drinking they were worried about. In fact, that became almost a footnote. When Lana drove me home from school that afternoon after the failed instrument check, she immediately searched my bedroom. Of course, she found the stash of bottles under the bed and my collection of Sandeman's labels, all of which I had painstakingly removed from the bottles and arranged into a sort of spooky satanic-looking collage. But, worse than either of those things, her search revealed the catalogue pages! The ones I'd carefully cut from the hefty tomes of JC Penny, Sears, and Montgomery Ward and kept pressed between the mattress and the box springs. The pages and pages of headless male torsos, all scantily clad in briefs or boxers or pajamas, with whom I'd indulged in the most shameless of fantasies.

The slap in the car was only a preview of the blows Lana gave me when she found these pages. She was furious, and I still wonder how far she would have gone if the doorbell had not rung. It was Wayne. He was told all the details by a shrieking, hysterical Lana, but instead of shock or anger or disgust, he seemed strangely happy, almost glad to have another crisis for the Lord to fix. In minutes we had all joined hands and were on our knees in the living room while Wayne prayed and asked for guidance. My face stung from my beating, but it didn't hurt half as much as my hand, into which Lana dug her clawlike nails as we prayed. It was just her lit-tle way of telling me that although she was a Christian now, she was not above doing some things she might have to ask forgiveness for later.

After that as I said, the church-going became annoyingly regular. At night I'd go to gatherings, of course, but during the day, while Lana was at school, I was to go to the church with Wayne, and he would put me to work. In three weeks' time, I was to be shipped off to Bible Camp in North Carolina, where it was hoped, I would mend my ways. If, by the end of summer, I had not seen the light, Wayne knew of a wonderful military school in East Texas that he felt sure he could get me into.

Wayne came to pick me up each morning before Lana left, and together we'd ride to the strip mall where the church was housed. Once there, we'd pray with the aged pastor, attend the morning services if it was a Monday, Wednesday, or Friday, and then I'd work cleaning God's own Kmart. I straightened out the prayer books and the hymnals and made sure there were two of each for every pew. I sprayed and sponged off the vinyl kneelers, and swept, and dusted, and vacuumed all around the pulpit and the altar. I scrubbed the toilets and the bathroom floors, and even spent an entire day scooting around on my back scraping gum off the undersides of the pews. All of this was to keep me busy until it was time to go to camp, but then, thank God, something happened. Something really deserving of thanks, at least from me.

Chapter Five

Being a weatherman in Denver during the summer is quite possibly the least complicated job on Earth. Almost invariably each day begins with blue skies and sunshine. About noon, big, fluffy white clouds roll in off the mountains, and by three o'clock they have usually built up into a thunderstorm. It rains for half an hour at most. In the evening, the clouds move on and there is a clear sunset. A numbingly regular pattern that begins in May and repeats itself well into the middle of September.

The storm that began late that May afternoon was anything but regular. Oh, the morning arrived, clear and sunny, as usual, but when the afternoon clouds appeared from behind the mountains they were not cottony and white, but dark and low and accompanied by a cool wind. It was Monday. A week after my suspension and two weeks before I was to be carted off to summer camp. I had just finished my all-day-under-the-pew-gum-scraping and was getting into Wayne's car when the first drops of rain began to fall. He was taking me home briefly, only long enough to get cleaned up and eat some dinner, before Lana and I drove to the gathering later that night.

I remember thinking, as we rode silently through the suburbs, that my mood was as black as the sky overhead. I felt hollow and empty and lonely. I wanted a drink, but that was considerably harder to get since my suspension. My bottle under the bed had been confiscated; the wine cellar was off limits; and even during communion, the goblet passed by me and I received a blessing instead.

When Wayne pulled into the driveway, the rain was falling steadily. I flipped the door handle, but he had set the child-safety lock so I couldn't open it.

"Dillon," Wayne said, looking over at me with that sickly sweet smile he had perfected. I didn't respond, but I knew he was going to give me some long-winded homily before we parted or he would not have locked the door.

"Dillon," he said again, and took my hand, sandwiching it between his soft fat fingers. "I'm going to leave you now. On your own. Lana won't be home for another hour." He gave my hand a squeeze.

"Now, son, you're not going to do anything that will make me sorry I trusted you, right?"

"No," I said, shaking my head as confidently as I could and returning his squeeze. "No need to worry. That's all behind me now."

But what I thought was more like: *I have just spent eight hours scraping chewed gum and crusty boogers off of the underside of church pews, and in a little while I'm going to have to spend several more hours sitting on top of one of those very same pews watching people I don't even like as they sing and writhe and moan and make fools of themselves. If you think I am going through all that without the one thing that can make it tolerable, you are wrong!*

I knew that the very second I was safe inside and saw him drive down the hill, I'd head straight for the cellar. Maybe he made his comments because he knew it, too, but nevertheless he let me go. Probably because he felt confident that I could come to no real harm. The week before, he and Lana had mounted a cheap padlock on the cellar door and in their minds that made it as secure as the drug closet at the Betty Ford Clinic. What they didn't know was how easily I had outsmarted them, simply by removing the screws from the hinge of the lock and effortlessly flipping the whole mechanism, lock, hinge, and all, to the side. I had done this the first time just a few nights before and had almost succeeded in getting a bottle when I heard Lana coming and had to abandon my quest. I barely had time to replace the screws and stash the screwdriver in my back pocket.

"Shall we pray for some strength?" Wayne asked, raising an eyebrow. I nodded.

And so we prayed. Right there in the middle of the driveway with the rain tapping hard on the roof of the Oldsmobile. Wayne prayed out loud, and asked God to fortify me against the easy temptations of the flesh, against the seductive lure of liquor. I prayed silently, although no less fervently. *Please, God, please make him unlock the door. Please make him let me out of the car before I kill him.*

Eventually he released the lock, and I ran quickly up the walk to the house, not bothering to wave as he backed out of the driveway. The wind was stronger now and the rain blew almost horizontally. By the time I got inside and ran up the stairs to look out the small octagonal window on the landing, the rain was coming down so hard that all I could see were the Oldsmobile's red taillights as it crept slowly down the muddy river that was burying the street.

It was to be the storm of a lifetime—at least that's what the weatherman said—the kind that happens only once every hundred years, and sometimes not even that often. The rain turned roads into rivers and real rivers soon came up over their banks. Shingles were ripped off roofs and fences were carried away by the wind, smashing into the houses they once surrounded. Trees were uprooted and power lines snapped. Nature had suddenly and inexplicably chosen that day to show off.

Lana made it home, but just barely, as the street leading up to our house was so choked with water and mud and debris that her car had almost not made it up the hill.

"I don't think we'll go to the gathering tonight," she said, removing her dripping clothes and hanging them in the bathtub. "But, maybe it's a blessing in disguise," she continued, "because I've got a huge test tomorrow and I haven't even opened the book yet."

Since there was no power in the house, we ate a cold dinner together by candlelight. When we'd finished, Lana retired to her room taking the two remaining candles and the only flashlight with her, leaving me in the dark. But I didn't mind. Sitting alone in the dark was ten times better than having to go to another gathering. I felt my way up to my room, lay down on my bed, and did some silent scales on my clarinet. I finished off the bottle of Sandeman's that I'd stolen from the cellar and, at some point, passed into a boozy sleep.

Much later I was awakened by what I perceived as loud hoofbeats. With effort, I opened my eyes but saw only darkness and felt sure I must be dreaming. The hoofbeats continued, very loud, but never coming any closer and never moving farther away, like a herd of animals running in circles overhead. I sat up and tried to orient myself, but I could feel the thick heaviness of drink still affecting my brain. The noise, coming from outside, grew almost deafening, like handfuls of rocks were being hurled at the house. Unsteadily, I crept over to the window and lifted up the blind. The sky was still dark but the ground was covered with white pebbles that appeared to be popping like popcorn. I stared for a while, bewildered, but then I realized that it must be hail, since that often came with spring storms. But hail at night? I had never heard of that. I watched it for a while, as it popped and piled up on the lawn but soon, the steady rhythmic drumming became almost tranquilizing, and I returned to my bed.

The next time I woke up the room was white with morning light. I sat up, and a moment later my brain followed, clanging on the sides of my skull like a bell. I squinted at the clock, but it was flashing a meaningless neon red 12:00. My head hurt, and the brightness only made it worse. I was thirsty, too, so I decided to get one of the cold bottles of water Lana kept in the refrigerator.

On my way down I stopped again at the little octagonal window and peered out. The ground was still covered in white, but it looked less brilliant now than it had the night before, more soggy and transparent. I saw two narrow tire tracks leading in a graceful arc out from the garage and then off down the hill.

Lana must be gone, I thought, and felt relieved, but at the same time I wondered why she hadn't awakened me. It was surely past the time for Wayne to arrive. I looked outside again and figured from the angle of the sun that it was well into the morning, at least nine o'clock. Maybe he hadn't been able to make it, maybe a bridge was out, or something. I went down the stairs and into the kitchen. No note from Lana but, oddly enough, there was a guitar case propped up against one of the kitchen walls.

It's probably Wayne's, I thought to myself and shuddered as I imagined us all in a group at church singing an endless version of "Michael Row Your Boat Ashore."

I went to the refrigerator, got the water, and drank it eagerly. My head throbbed and the thought of the chores Wayne had planned for me that day made it even worse.

I've got to have at least a swig, I thought, so I went over to the kitchen drawer and took out the Phillips-head screwdriver. *I'll just take one good drink from the cognac bottle, just to get rid of the headache, and then I'll get dressed.*

I shuffled over to the entrance of the cellar but stopped suddenly and stared at the door. The padlock was undone! The lock was sitting on one of the steps and the hinge was open. I panicked for a moment and felt sweat break out all over my body.

Had I forgotten to put it back?! No, no, it was *unlocked* now. I had never unlocked it. I didn't have a key. Maybe Lana had gone down to inventory the bottles, or worse, maybe Wayne! But, no, no, there had been only one set of tracks and they were leading away from the house. Lana had probably just gone down for something, to trip the breaker, maybe, and had just forgotten to lock it back up. It was a good thing! A blessing in disguise, as Lana would say.

I crept quietly down the stairs, as if in danger of being seen or heard. There was a light switch, but I didn't turn it on. There was no need. I knew the exact location of the bottle I wanted, so I made my way confidently over the cold concrete to the tall rack at the far end. The cognac was up fairly high, but I was tall and could reach it if I stood on the tips of my toes. I had just grasped the neck of the bottle with my thumb and forefinger and was inching it out when I heard something scratch behind me. I spun around and the bottle fell. It hit the floor and exploded, sending glass and cognac all over my feet and legs.

It was dark. Silent. Had I imagined it? I could see no one, hear nothing. I held my breath and did not move. As my eyes adjusted to the darkness, I saw, from on top of one of the racks, the burning ember of a cigarette end. I shuddered but dared not speak. Silence. Nothing but the glowing ember and the mingling smells of smoke and cognac.

Although I liked to think I was above all the Christian nonsense to which I had so recently been overexposed, I could not help trembling and feeling I was in the presence of something not of this world.

"Can you keep a secret?" a voice asked and then a cloud of smoke drifted down toward me. It was a voice I had never heard before. A man's voice, gravelly and rough, but not entirely unfamiliar. I was still shaking. I tried to step back but stopped when I felt a sharp pain from the broken glass under my heel. I said nothing.

"I think you can," the voice said. I heard a click and a bare bulb illuminated. A shirtless man was reclining sideways on top of the wine rack, propped up on one elbow. In his left hand he held the burning cigarette, oddly between his third and fourth fingers. His hair was dark and long and quite curly, which contrasted with his pale skin and blue eyes. Smiling down, he assessed me and my predicament.

"Yes," he said, clearly amused by what he saw. "From this situation I think one could infer that maybe you are quite talented when it comes to keeping secrets. I am, too, and that's good. People talk too much. Less talk and more action; that's my motto. I'll need you to talk very little today, if you know what I mean."

I nodded, although I certainly did not know what he meant. He saw my confusion and added, "No one can know I'm here, and I'm afraid that very soon there are going to be lots of people looking for me."

"But who are you?" I asked.

He looked back at me, faintly surprised and confused, almost offended.

"Your mother didn't tell you?" he asked.

"No," I said, and shook my head.

"Strange. I thought she would have. No wonder you're scared." He took another drag on the cigarette but offered no explanation. He smoked luxuriously, like people in the movies, inhaling deeply and then pulling the cigarette away from his mouth so that a small white cloud appeared and then just as quickly disappeared up his nose.

"Is . . . Lana home?" I asked, tentatively, afraid of the trouble I'd be in if she found me down here.

"Your mother? No, she's gone to school, but what's—Why do you call her Lana?"

I thought about how to respond to this, as I did every time someone asked about it. I had been calling her Lana for years then so I really should have had a better response prepared, but I did not.

"She, uh, doesn't like to be called mother," I said and shuffled my feet in the sticky wetness beneath me. I had most definitely cut my heel, and as my fear ebbed away, I could feel pain take its place. He did not respond to what I said but just kept looking down at me, assessing me, and smoking. Again I asked, "Who are you?"

He put the cigarette in his mouth, sat up, and stretched his arms high above his head. He had made a sort of bed on top of the wine rack, with a flat board and several pillows and blankets. He whipped one of these blankets up into the air, like a bullfighter, and then, leaning over the rack, he let it fall on the ground so that it covered the broken glass, making a sort of path for me to walk on. That done, he grabbed on to one of the overhead pipes with both hands and swung his body in a circle, depositing himself as gracefully as a dancer on the floor some feet in front of me, lit cigarette still between his lips. He made an elaborate bow and extended one hand to help me across the blanket.

"Max is the name," he said, with an emphasis placed on the word *is*, as if Max was the only name any sane person would consider being called. I took his hand, very rough and calloused, and he helped me across the blanket. His grip was firm, which was surprising because he did not look at all strong. He was thin and wiry, with long lithe arms and legs, and a flat chest.

Once I'd made it to the dry concrete he released my hand, and only then did he take his cigarette from his mouth, again holding it between his third and fourth fingers. He noticed the bloody prints I'd left on the blanket.

"It looks like you'll need a bandage," he said, and in one movement he had swooped me up and was carrying me up the stairs. It was then that I realized who he was; he was my uncle, the boy in the picture about whom I had heard so annoyingly little over the years.

Emerging into the upstairs after being in the cellar was painful. The brightness and the ache in my head quickly eclipsed the pain in my heel. I had not gotten the cognac and realized, with a little pang of sorrow, that I probably would not.

Max set me gently in one of the kitchen chairs and propped my wounded foot up on the table. As he made his way around the kitchen, grabbing a roll of paper towels and filling a bowl with water, I examined him more closely. He wore a pair of red-plaid pajama pants with a drawstring at the waist, but his feet and upper body were bare. Again, I noticed how pale he was, so pale that blue veins were visible beneath the surface of his skin.

I directed him to the bathroom, where I told him he'd probably find a first aid kit, but he ignored me and proceeded to combine several odd ingredients from the kitchen in a tall glass. From what I could see these included olive oil, a raw egg, sugar, the juice of one lemon, half and half, several grinds from the pepper mill, a teaspoon of instant coffee, Tabasco, and vinegar. The glass was then three-quarters full, and he stirred it noisily as he carried it back down to the cellar. When he emerged a few moments later, he was still stirring but now the glass was full. He removed the spoon, cleaned it off in his mouth, and threw it in the sink. He set the glass on the table in front of me and then disappeared into the bathroom to get the first aid kit. I looked at the milky maroon liquid and the stench of it wafted up to me. It was a sour smell but underneath that odor was the spiky scent of alcohol. I picked it up and took a sip. Ghastly. Like rotten barbecue sauce. I stopped breathing through my nose and took another drink. I managed to get about half of it down but then had to stop as the feel of the grainy texture in my mouth made me afraid I might throw up. It burned as it made its way down, but I could not tell if that was the familiar burn of the alcohol or only the pepper. Max returned and began cleaning and bandaging my heel.

"What is this?" I asked, stifling a cough. He looked up and smiled, a cigarette in his mouth and one eye closed to keep out the smoke.

"Part penance," he said, "and part cure. I just invented it. Do you like it?"

I said nothing. I thought it was a mean thing to do, but I defiantly drank the rest of it and then set the glass on the table. He had dried the wound and was dabbing at it with a cotton ball soaked in hydrogen peroxide. I winced, but he held my foot firmly. I remembered Wayne and wondered if maybe he had already come that morning.

"I'm supposed to be in church," I said. "This guy from the church, the assistant pastor, Wayne, he usually comes to get me about eight."

"Not today," he replied, but then offered nothing further.

"Why . . . not?" I ventured, somewhat timidly, afraid that maybe I was in more trouble.

Without looking up he replied, "Let's just say there was some divine intervention on your behalf last night."

I looked at him, confused, and in my hungover state I must have looked sufficiently pitiable because he added, "The wind tore the roof off of the church. You're free for today."

I relaxed a bit in my chair. I was relieved, yes, but more than that I was glad that I would get to spend more time with such an intriguing stranger.

"You remember me asking if you were good at keeping secrets?" Max asked, his attention still focused on my wound. I nodded and watched as the smoke from the end of his cigarette rose up in a narrow stream and then ballooned out like a mushroom a foot above his head.

"And how are you at lying?" he asked, looking straight into my eyes. I hesitated for a moment. Was this a test? Had Wayne and Lana put him up to this? I decided that silence was the best response. He was now wrapping my foot with a long strip of gauze bandage.

"Well, let's hope, for my sake, that you *can* do more than just keep quiet because today I'm going to have to ask you to go a bit further."

As if on cue, the doorbell rang. We both looked up, first at the door and then at each other. He quickly taped off my bandage, pitched his cigarette into the sink, and wordlessly leaped over to the cellar door. He looked back at me for a moment. His face was grave but amused. He put his index finger to his lips, then turned and descended, pulling the door shut behind him.

I did not know what to do. Everything was happening so fast and my head was less than clear. I stood up. The doorbell rang again. In spite of what Max had said, I thought it might be Wayne, so before going to the front door I limped down the steps to the cellar and replaced the padlock on the hinge.

When I opened the front door, it wasn't Wayne but rather a man and a woman I had never seen before. The woman was short and plump, with an enormous blond hairdo. Her face was heavily made up and she was dressed in a pink skirt and jacket, with ropes of gaudy, gold jewelry dangling from her wrists and neck. The man, who was missing several front teeth, was absurdly large and his body, clad in a dark suit, filled the doorway.

"Good morning, young man," the woman said. Her mouth moved when she spoke but all of the sound seemed to be coming from her nostrils. I said nothing, but just looked up at them with my best stone face.

"Maybe you can help me," she said. "I'm looking for a man, could be he's your uncle or your cousin maybe, goes by the name of Max. He here?" she asked peering around me into the house.

I stared back blankly and then silently shook my head. The two exchanged tired glances and then focused once again on me.

"Has he been here?" the woman asked, her voice impatient. "You do know who I'm talking about?" I wrinkled my brow, feigning confusion and cocked my head to one side, like a dog when it hears an unfamiliar sound. She gave the man a nod and without a word he pushed me aside with one of his enormous hands and marched into the house. She followed.

"You don't mind if we check for ourselves, sweetie, do you?" she asked, not really caring how I responded. I followed behind her, leaving the door open in case I needed to flee. The man, who seemed to be missing a neck in addition to his teeth, headed directly upstairs while the woman walked casually into the kitchen.

"You home alone, today?" she asked. "No school?"

"I've been suspended," I said, feeling suddenly proud of the fact.

"Suspended, eh? Then you must be related to Max. What for?"

she asked, pacing the kitchen, her hands behind her clutching the handle of her purse and her large bust pushed out. She looked like an angry hen.

"For drinking," I said.

"For drinking," she said, but there was no surprise in her voice. Instead, I thought I detected a tone of disappointment. "For drinking," she repeated. I nodded. "Well then maybe you're not related because Max never drinks. That's part of the reason I trusted the little shit." She paused and chewed her gum angrily.

"Drink makes you sloppy. Remember that, er, what's your name?"

"Dillon, ma'am."

"Remember that, little Dillon. Drink makes you sloppy. You heard it from Doris."

The large man came back down and into the kitchen.

"Anything?" she asked. He shook his head. Together, they searched the study and then the living room, looking under all the furniture and opening all the closet doors. Finding nothing, they disappeared briefly into the garage. When they returned, they paused in front of the lower stairwell.

"What's down there?" the big man asked, pointing with one of his meaty fingers to the cellar door.

"Wine cellar," I said.

"Why's it locked?" the woman asked.

"Because of me," I said, trying to look ashamed. "Remember?"

They exchanged glances once again and she gave a nod to the door. Without a word the man charged down the stairs and threw his body against it. It didn't give the first time, so he backed up and positioned himself to charge it again.

"Wait!" I cried, imagining the trouble I'd be in if Lana and Wayne returned to find the door busted off its hinges. He hesitated.

"Wait," I said again. "I can get it open. Just a minute." And again

I got the Phillips-head screwdriver and began unscrewing the hinge of the lock. I did it slowly, hoping it might give Max time to find an adequate hiding place. When I'd finished, I went back up the stairs and let the man go down and open it. He did so and the pungent vapor from the evaporating cognac quickly wafted up the stairs. I thought for sure the game was over, and Max was caught. But a minute later the big man emerged alone, trudging slowly up the stairs and shaking his head.

"No?" she asked.

"No," he replied. They both looked dejected and stood for a moment trying to think what to do next.

She turned and walked toward the door.

"If he has been here," she mused, more to herself than to me, "he probably won't be back. And if he hasn't been here, he'll probably show up sooner or later. Hmmm. I'm gonna bet he has been here. Hell, he probably is here now, watching us." She looked up and around the ceiling, as if Max might be clinging to the chandelier.

"But, whichever it is," she said, turning to me and wagging a heavily jeweled finger, "if you see him, you tell him that I was here looking for him, okay? You hear that, Max!" she yelled back into the kitchen. "Doris is on to you!"

As soon as they left, I ran once again up to the top of the stairs and peered out the window. They were in a large blue Lincoln, Doris behind the wheel and her large friend in the passenger seat, his massive arm hanging out the open window. Almost all of the hail had melted now and most of the water had gone, so the tracks they left as they drove down the hill were in the thin brown mud that remained. I watched until I was certain they wouldn't come back and then I limped down the stairs, yelling, "They're gone! They're gone! You can come out now!"

But Max did not come out. There was not a sound in the house. Soon I found myself looking up and around the ceiling, just as Doris had done. I went down into the cellar and pulled the light string. There was the blanket on the floor, still covering the broken glass, but the pillows were gone from the top of the rack and Max was not there.

"It's okay," I called out. "They're gone."

But Max had vanished. I searched every corner of the cellar, climbed up on every rack, but he wasn't there. I went back upstairs, still calling out. Nothing. I stood in the middle of the kitchen feeling very self-conscious, as if someone was watching me, but I could see no one. Then the doorbell rang. I froze, not knowing what to do, like an actor on stage who was missing a page of the script. Was it the couple again? Was it Wayne? I ran quickly and replaced the lock on the door to the cellar. The bell rang again and then twice more before I'd finished replacing the final screw. I pocketed the screwdriver, ran to the door, and looked through the peephole. It appeared to be a woman with a large purse over her shoulder. She was kicking her boots on the step trying to get the mud off the soles. I opened the door a crack.

"Hello," she said, and smiled at me. She was a short chubby woman, maybe forty, with her hair cut in a pixie that only accentuated the roundness of her face. Her makeup was both inexpertly chosen and applied, with the end result that she looked a bit like a clown, albeit a somewhat soggy clown who had been through a rainstorm or who had just emerged from a swimming pool.

"Hello, I'm Meredith Brown, I'm here to see Max Naylor."

"He's not here." I said quickly and closed the door. The doorbell rang again, insistently, three times. Again, I opened it.

"Ex-*cuse* me," she said impatiently, "he had *better* be here. I spoke to him in my office just yesterday and he assured me that he *would* be here."

I shrugged and was about to shut the door again when Max suddenly swung into view. He had been on the roof just above the front door, and once he'd discerned who it was, he grabbed onto the gutter and swung down, swooping just over the head of

Meredith Brown. He landed in a somersault on the floor of the foyer.

"Here I am!" he said jovially, as he got up from the floor and bounced back to where Meredith and I were standing, open-mouthed. "Just as promised! Meredith, I'd like you to meet my nephew, Dillon. Dillon, my parole officer, Meredith."

We shook hands and she stepped inside, setting down her purse to remove her muddy boots.

"I'm so glad you *are* here," she said, unsnapping her coat, "It's been a real nutty morning, with this crazy Colorado weather and all. The first client I went to see was living in some grody crack house and I had to talk to, like, ten different people before I found one who'd even heard of him."

"Well, you'll find none of that here, Meredith," Max said reassuringly. "Here, let me take your coat. Dillon, could you get Miss Brown a beverage? What will you have, Meredith? We've got, well, I don't really know what we've got. I'm sure we must have water and coffee, maybe tea or soda . . ."

"Oh, why thank you, water's fine."

"A glass of water for Meredith," he said, giving me a smile and a wink. "And I'll have coffee. Black."

Still shiftless and shoeless, he took Meredith by the hand and gently escorted her into the living room. He sat her down on the sofa and then, instead of seating himself in the chair opposite, or even at the other end of the sofa, as might have been expected, he sat right next to her. I observed them from the kitchen, as I opened her bottle of water and waited for the coffee to brew; each time I looked up, Max seemed to have inched even closer to her.

"So this is your sister's house?" she asked.

"Yes, her husband left her a few months back. It's been hard on her, you know. I'm hoping I can help her finish the house, since she's going to school full-time and all, maybe help take care of the boy."

"That is *so* nice!" she said, beaming at him. "I wish I'd 'a had a brother like you when I got my divorce."

"Surely you're not divorced, Meredith," he said, his arm now creeping up the back of the sofa.

"Oh, yeah," she said. "Six years now."

"He must have been crazy!"

"No kidding!" she giggled, both flattered and nervous. Suddenly, she noticed how close he'd come to her on the sofa. She leaned forward and shook her head, as if to dispel some intoxication, then cleared her throat. Remembering the purpose of her visit, she bent down and dug a clipboard and what looked like a small radio attached to a Velcro strap out of her purse. Again she cleared her throat.

"Now, um, as a condition of your parole you'll have to have a full-time job within two weeks and you'll have to wear this," she said, holding up the radio. For a moment they both stared at the thing wordlessly.

"And what exactly . . . is that?" Max asked, looking concerned and leaning forward on the sofa.

"Oh, it's a new thing we're using called an in-house detention monitor. I strap it on your leg, like so," she said, leaning down and looping it around Max's ankle, "and every time it beeps you call in from a particular location and punch in your password and the phone number. It's real simple."

From Max's initial reaction to the thing, which I observed from my post in the kitchen, one would have thought she'd just wrapped a spitting cobra around his leg. But only for a moment. In an instant he had regained control. He took a deep breath and relaxed the muscles in his face. If I hadn't been watching so closely, I would have missed it. Meredith never noticed. She was too busy looking through his file trying to figure out how to activate the thing.

"This really won't be necessary," Max said, loosening the Velcro and removing the band.

"But it's in your file," Meredith cried, "you have to wear it!"

"Meredith, really!" he scolded playfully. "You should know better. This is me, remember? Max. I'm not going anywhere. I'll be right here helping my sister and her kid. I don't want to feel like an animal, all tagged and tracked."

He had taken both of her hands in his and was staring intently in her eyes. I entered bearing their beverages. Meredith looked up and nodded her thanks, but Max did not even acknowledge me. I sensed that my presence was neither required nor desired, so I retreated back to the kitchen and pretended to busy myself, all the while eavesdropping and glancing up now and then to see what was happening. Max stared at Meredith and she stared back, nervously. He raised one of his hands and gently brushed a lock of hair from her forehead.

"Trust me," he told her, his voice low and sweet. "Helping my sister will really be a full-time job. The boy's got troubles and he needs a father. Surely I don't need to tell you about that. *You* know. You've been through it. I thought that maybe I could be that father to him—the one he never had. I hoped that he and I could work on the house together, over the summer."

These last words were spoken in almost a whisper and when he said them his hand, which had been hovering near her forehead, drifted lightly down her cheek and rested on her shoulder. She blushed, and when she spoke, her voice was quiet and hoarse and flustered.

"I, uh, it's in your file," she said, and turned again, somewhat primly, toward the coffee table. Again, she picked up the Velcro anklet.

"Meredith," he sighed, grabbing her hand and bringing it and the anklet to his chest. He pressed them to his heart.

"Feel that," he said, staring once again into her eyes. "Just feel how frightened that makes me. Please, Meredith, let me be a human. Prison was so hard. Let me move on. Don't shackle me down again."

There was silence for several seconds after this, but then Meredith again released herself.

"I can't," she said, swiveling to face the coffee table again. "I really can't."

Max gasped and fell back on the sofa. "I understand," he said and lifted his ankle so that she could attach the monitor. She did so; but when she looked up, there were tears streaming down Max's face.

"Ohh, don't do that," she pleaded. "Please don't cry. I have to do this. It's in your file."

Max nodded, as if to say he understood, that he knew she was just doing her job. But the tears continued to roll and it appeared he could not speak. His crying was silent—the way babies sometimes do right before they let loose with a wail.

"Ohh," Meredith moaned, frantically waving her hands, "Please don't. It won't be that bad. You'll get used to it and if you wear longer pants you can pretty much cover it up."

This did not appear to appease him and his body began to heave with his sobs.

"Ohh, darn it all!" Meredith cried. "I'm not supposed to do this, oohhh, I'll tell you what I'll do. How 'bout this. I'll waive your employment requirement if you'll wear it, how's that sound? You can work here instead of going out and looking for a job. Is that fair? That's fair, isn't it?" The tears continued to roll, but Max looked interested.

"That way you can stay here and work on the house," she said brightly. He leaned forward on the sofa and Meredith patted him on the back. Max smiled.

"There. You see, I'm not such a meanie."

"No," Max said, and then grabbed her head in both his hands and kissed her firmly on the lips. "You're wonderful. Thank you."

Initially, she was too surprised to say anything. He released her head but kept one hand on her shoulder. She stood up suddenly, smoothing her shirt and trying to appear professional, not quite sure if she should be offended or not. She cleared her throat.

"But the next time I visit," she warned, "you have to show that some progress is being made on the house."

"Of course," he nodded, rising and once again placing his hand on her shoulder. "Yes. That makes perfect sense. Thank you. Would you like to see my quarters, here. Just so you'll know where to picture me when this, this . . . this leash electrifies me and I telephone you? Yes? You would? It's just right down these stairs . . ."

From the kitchen I watched as Max took her by the hand and led her downstairs, clicking the door shut behind them. I found this curious, and when they still hadn't emerged, several minutes later, I strolled over to the stairs and stared down at the closed door. I was just about to tiptoe down and press my ear against it when again the doorbell rang again. I jumped. My eyes darted back and forth from the cellar door to the front door. I was excited by who it could possibly be next, since the first three visitors had been so interesting, but then my excitement deflated as I realized it was probably just Wayne. He'd been busy all morning but now he was finally coming to pick me up to come help with the church roof. "Better late than never!" he'd cluck, or something equally stupid and cliché. It rang again. I decided not to answer it. I'd go up to my room, close the door and pretend I hadn't heard it. Oh, he'd figure some way in, but at least it would delay him. I ran up the stairs and looked out the window, but it wasn't Wayne's car in the driveway. Meredith's red compact was there, but next to it was an old black Volvo station wagon.

I ran back down the stairs and flung open the door. A woman was descending the front steps back toward the driveway, but she turned when she heard the door open. Unlike the other two, this woman was tall and elegantly dressed all in black, with long straight black hair pulled back from her face. She wore a matching skirt and jacket, the jacket accented with an ermine collar and cuffs, and on her left forearm, which she kept elevated by her side, a shiny black purse was suspended. Her groomed perfection was totally incongruous with the muddy, windblown landscape behind her, and it was only when I glanced down at her tiny shoes and noticed the mud that I realized she had not just materialized there. I could not see her eyes, as they were hidden behind a pair of large sunglasses, but on seeing me, her mouth widened into a smile and she approached.

"Good morning," she said, extending her hand, encased in a white glove. From the small amount of her face that was not hidden by the sunglasses I could tell that she was quite young, maybe in her early twenties, but her rich voice and calm deliberate manners made her seem much older.

I shook her hand, bowed my head slightly, but I did not say anything.

"I'm here to see Max. Is he in?" she asked, and peered over my shoulder into the house. Again, I said nothing. Something about her made me not want to lie as I had to the previous visitors so instead I said nothing. She regarded me calmly and waited for my answer, aware that I had both heard and understood her question. We both stood expressionless for several seconds, but then her lips widened into a smile and her head tilted slightly to one side.

"He's instructed you well," she said, both hands in front of her now, clutching the curved ivory handle of her purse. "You've done an admiral job. If I didn't know better I'd almost think you were autistic, or that I'd stumbled on the wrong address . . ." Her voice trailed off but her eyes were locked on me. She elevated the pointy toe of one of her shoes and rotated her foot back and forth slowly on the spiky heel. It was a feline gesture, the annoyed flit of a cat's tail when you block the sun in which it is lying.

"However," she said, leaning forward and peering at me over the frames of her glasses, "I'm afraid I do know better."

I noticed, when I saw her eyes behind the glasses, that she was Asian, and that surprised me. I suppose at that age I expected all Asians to speak with an accent, but her English was, if anything, far more clipped and precise than any I had heard outside of British movies. She reached in her purse and produced a white business card, which she handed to me with the following instructions:

"Be a friend, won't you, and give this card to Max. Tell him I'll be waiting tomorrow, ten o'clock, Paris on the Platte. He knows where it is."

I took the card and she snapped her purse shut. She was just turning to go but then paused and looked back at me. "You come, too," she said. "If you *are* able to open your mouth, they have lots of sweets and things that you might like."

My expression cracked and I smiled. That seemed to satisfy her and she turned and walked down the steps to her car, heels clicking on the concrete.

A half hour later, Meredith crept up from the cellar, her hair mussed and her cheeks like two rosy apples. Around her neck I saw what appeared to be a necklace of purple hickeys. In a fluster, she collected her coat and bag from the floor in front of the sofa and, without a word, went straight for the front door, pulling it gently closed behind her. A few moments later Max emerged, smiling and yawning and stretching, as if he'd just woken up. He wore only a pair of boxer shorts, and as he reached the top of the stairs, I noticed that both his ankles were bare.

Chapter Six

The next visitor arrived while Max was in the shower. It was after noon and my hangover, thanks to Max's cure, was gradually ebbing away. The doorbell rang and again my heart rose and then fell, fearing that it must be Wayne. I hopped to the door and peered through the peephole. It was not Wayne, so I opened it. A large man, well over six feet, stood on the porch. He was wearing a red fleece jacket, the arm of which had been patched with duct tape, and held in his hand a pale blue carton of cigarettes.

"Ah, hello," he said, in a voice that was heavily accented. "Max, is he here?"

I shook my head, no, and his shoulders fell.

"Has he left already? I mean, was he here?"

His face was weathered and tan, with white crow's feet around his eyes where the sun had not reached, and his windblown hair, once very blond, was now beginning to turn gray. He was wearing shorts, with lots of strange metal pieces hanging from a loop on the side and a well-worn pair of leather hiking boots. Something about him, his desperation or disorder maybe, made him seem harmless, so I did not lie. But I remembered what Max had told me and said nothing. The man waited expectantly for my answer and his brow furrowed. Then his face relaxed into a smile.

"Oh, but of course!" he said, and tapped his forehead with his palm. "To you, I'm stranger. I am Serge, a very old friend of Max's."

He extended his hand and I shook it, noticing that it was even rougher and more calloused than Max's had been and that most of the knuckles were covered in scabs.

"Can I come in?" he asked, his voice lilting up at the end of his question. "Maybe I could leave him a note, and I've brought him some cigarettes, *Gitanes*, his favorite kind."

Before I could protest he had marched past me and on into the kitchen, looking up and all around, just as the previous visitors had done. Not seeing Max, he fell into one of the chairs, as if the walk to the kitchen had exhausted him. He fished in his shirt pocket and removed a rumpled box of cigarettes, and then fished in his coat pocket for something to light it with. He found nothing, and then began to search all his pockets, patting himself down and removing bits of paper, more odd pieces of metal similar to those attached to his shorts, his car keys, a few pennies, but no matches. He looked up at me, a somewhat pleading expression on his face, his cigarette dangling lifeless from the corner of his mouth.

"Just a minute," I said, and went over to the kitchen drawer. I poked around but found no matches. Then I remembered that Lana had taken them up to her room the night before when the power went out.

"They're upstairs," I said, limping over to the staircase, "I'll be right back."

Up in Lana's room, I quietly shut the door behind me. The shower was still running. I gently knocked on the bathroom door.

"That you, Dil?" Max asked.

"Yes," I whispered, opening the door a crack. I was blinded by a cloud of fragrant steam.

"There's a man downstairs," I hissed. Immediately, the water stopped.

"Downstairs?"

"Yes."

"Why did you let him in?"

"I *didn't*," I protested. "He just sort of came in."

I could hear him frantically toweling off and I felt bad, as though I hadn't been able to keep up my part of that morning's pact.

"He sounds foreign," I added. "Says his name is Serge."

"Ohhh," Max sighed, and I could hear the relief in his voice. "I should have known. Tell him . . . Well, tell him I'll be down in a minute."

I retrieved the book of matches from Lana's dresser and made my way back down to the kitchen.

"Max will be down in a minute," I said, handing him the matches. "He's in the shower."

Serge smiled so broadly the white creases in his crow's feet nearly disappeared.

"Ha ho!" he cried, slapping his thigh. "I knew he would be here!" He lit one of the matches but as he brought it up to the cigarette, his hand shook so badly that the match went out. He lit another but this time he dropped both the match and the matchbook. I picked them up and struck one myself. He leaned forward, touched the end of his cigarette to the flame, and inhaled deeply. He nodded his thanks and then brushed away a few bits of tobacco that clung to his lips.

"I knew he was here!" he said, jovially. "I knew it! I had hoped he would come to me, I suspected that if he didn't, he would come to his sister."

He smoked quickly, but his hand was still trembling and he caught me looking at it.

"It's the morning," he said. "It usually passes by this time of day but today . . . maybe was the storm, it affects one, you know?" I nodded.

68

"You are the *neveu?* The . . . nephew?" he asked. Again, I nodded.

"I could tell. You look like him, the face is the same, and the same body." He looked around the kitchen, as if he were looking for something in particular. Then he looked at me. He started to say something, stopped himself, and then started again.

"You wouldn't have, eh, something to drink?" I knew what he meant. I nodded and went down to the cellar door, which had been left open when Max and Meredith emerged. Although the smell of cognac was still strong, when I turned on the light I noticed that the broken glass had been swept up and disposed of and that the pillows and a fresh blanket had reappeared on top of the wine rack. My adolescent mind was curious about what had transpired there so I quietly crawled up on the rack and examined the bed, wondering what tale the scene would tell, but all I saw was a rumpled blanket and a pillow smeared with some of Meredith's makeup. I stared at the makeshift bed for a few moments, not quite able to believe that two people had actually had sex there, and as I crawled back down, I had to reposition my erection in my still-too-tight pants. I went over to the rack that held the cognac, carefully slid a bottle out, and went back upstairs. Max had still not come down so I handed Serge the bottle and then got him a glass from the cupboard.

"Thank you," he said, pouring about two inches of liquid in the glass and downing it in one gulp. He then poured another inch and replaced the stopper in the bottle. He sipped from this and smoked and asked me questions about Max: When did he get here, and how did he look? Had I ever met him before? Did other people know he was here? I answered what questions I could with my limited knowledge and as I was talking I noticed Max tiptoeing down the stairs. He motioned for me to be quiet and not give him away so I kept talking.

"No," I said, "I hadn't met him until this morning actually, but I had heard a few stories about him from Lana and my grand-parents."

"Oh yes," he said. "There are always stories to tell about Max! I remember one time, this was some years ago . . ."

At that point, Max was only a foot away from Serge's back. He leaned forward and whispered in his ear, *"Dans une bouche ferme, n'entrons pas les mouches."*

Serge rose up and spun around. Cigarette still clenched between his teeth, he grabbed Max in a bear hug and effortlessly lifted him up and around. He then set him down, pushed him an arm's length away, and exclaimed, *"Eh, mon petit, que tu es pale!"*

"Prison has that effect," Max replied. Serge then pulled him close and kissed him on the cheek.

"But why didn't you come to *me?*" Serge asked. "You know I would love to have you back, and there is plenty of room above the shop. You could teach and climb everyday!"

"How about I make us all something to eat," Max said, avoiding the subject. "I see it's already cocktail hour for you, but Dillon and I haven't even had breakfast yet."

For the next half hour, while Max made us an elaborate break-fast, I sat entranced and dizzy as the two of them talked. They spoke about the storm the night before and about Max's arrival, about Serge's business and about rock climbing, all in a language that seemed almost of their own invention.

"Did you bring any gear with you?" Max asked.

"Yes, of course," Serge said. "You know I always keep a few ropes in the truck. Why? You want to climb today?"

"Mmm," said Max, in between bites of food. "Harnesses?"

"Yes, yes," Serge said, becoming more and more excited. "I hoped you would want to; I even brought your old shoes! Where shall we go?"

"I was thinking," Max said, chewing meditatively. "Maybe we could try the house."

Serge and I exchanged confused glances.

"The house?" Serge asked. "This house?"

"Yes, there's a facade of sandstone blocks on the front," Max said. "It goes from the ground all the way up to the roof and seems to me it would be a good start for Dillon."

"Ahh, yes, yes, okay," Serge said, getting up and heading to the front door, "I'll go and see what I have. What size foot is yours, Dillon?"

"Uh, eleven," I said, somewhat timidly.

"*C'est vrai?* Fine, then you can wear a pair of my shoes."

Max poured himself another cup of coffee and lit a cigarette from the carton Serge had brought him. I began clearing the dishes and putting them in the dishwasher.

"Do you have any other pants?" Max asked me, turning around and looking me up and down. "Maybe some that aren't so tight."

I blushed again and shook my head.

"I only ask because it's easier to climb in loose clothing. You can borrow a pair of my shorts for today and tomorrow we'll get you some. Also, any chance you can survive without that contraption on your head?"

I fingered my headgear self-conciously.

"I'm supposed to wear it all day, at least for another six months," I mumbled.

"Oh yes," he sighed, exhaling a huge plume of smoke. "I'd forgotten about the suburban obsession with straight, white teeth. Give me a gap-toothed grin any day rather than another one of these bridled adolescents. Every time I see you with that thing on I keep expecting you to rear up and whinny."

I said nothing but could feel my face grow even more flushed. He got up and came over to me.

"Don't take it personally," he said, clenching his cigarette between his lips and lifting up my chin. The scent of coffee, shampoo, and cigarette smoke mingled around him. I looked into his eyes and saw a kindness there that I was not used to seeing.

"It's a sign of weakness to take offense. I didn't mean anything by it, really; it's just that I think you'd be happier if you were free of it during waking hours, don't you?" I nodded. Max sat down again.

"Think of it like a mud mask, or like hair curlers—Oh, they might make you look better, but do you really want anyone to see you while you have them on?" he asked with a wink.

I shook my head, no, and slowly removed the headgear.

"There now, much better! You look human!" Max downed the rest of his coffee, got up, and motioned for me to follow him downstairs.

"Come on, let's get you some more comfortable clothes."

A few minutes later, after I'd been outfitted in Max's shorts, we met up with Serge, who was busy winding up a brightly colored climbing rope in the sun on the front porch. Since there was no lawn, the yard consisted of thick sticky mud. For that reason we dared not venture off the porch, but there was enough of the rock wall going up from the concrete to give us a good start. Serge tossed me a pair of elfin-looking climbing shoes with smooth rubber soles and when I'd squeezed my feet into them, he laced them up tightly. So tightly that I could feel my foot throbbing where it had been cut earlier that morning, but I said nothing, afraid that maybe he wouldn't let me climb if he knew I was injured. He and Max showed me how to put on the harness and then both carefully demonstrated how to attach myself to the rope with a figure-eight knot.

"It may look difficult from down here," Max said, looking up at the wall, "but there are plenty of handholds and footholds between the stones, you see?" And he showed me how to take advantage of the tiny spaces of recessed mortar between the rocks. "You just work your fingers and the tips of your toes in there and keep looking up for the next place."

Then, as effortlessly as a spider, Max crawled several feet up the wall. He stopped, turned, and grinned down at me.

"You see?" he asked.

He made it look so easy, so possible. He then jumped down and explained the basics of climbing with a rope: Serge would stand at the bottom with the rope around his waist and release just as much as Max needed to climb, a technique called belaying; Max would then climb up to the roof, untie himself, loop the rope around the chimney, and then toss his end back down to me. I would then tie it to my harness and Serge would belay me to roof, pulling in the rope as I went up.

Max started climbing and Serge and I stood below watching him, Serge releasing the rope as he went.

"Just look at him!" Serge whispered, his voice full of admiration. "He looks like a dancer!" And indeed he did, a little, as he went up, and from side to side, with a steady, almost fluid rhythm.

"Your uncle, he is one of the best," Serge said, proudly. Max reached the roof in less than a minute. He anchored the rope and then tossed an end back down to me.

"Come on up, Dil!" he yelled. Serge helped me tie my harness to the rope and gave me a hearty pat on the back. I swallowed hard. My throat felt dry and my hands and feet were cold. I stepped up next to the wall and looked up at Max.

"Don't worry, I've got you anchored in up here and Serge is right under you." I looked over my shoulder at Serge. He was busy lighting a cigarette and kicking at a bug on the concrete. I made a coughing noise to get his attention. He looked up and smiled.

"Oh, sorry, I'm watching now. Climb when you are ready."

I looked back up at the wall. It seemed so steep and so far to the roof, when in fact it was probably only about thirty feet. I reached up and grabbed onto one of the stones. I placed first one and then the other foot into a little niche and stepped up. The rubber soles of the shoes were surprisingly adhesive and that gave me a little surge of confidence. I took another step and then another reach with my hand, pulling myself up even farther. Then again and again, hand, foot, hand, foot. The stones were irregularly spaced, but they were all rectangular and there were tiny ledges on the top of most of them, which made progress easy.

"Good job, Dil!" Max called down. "Keep coming!"

"Beautiful!" I heard Serge say and I looked back down to smile at him. It was then that it happened. I freaked. I realized how high up I was and just panicked. I pulled my body in closer to the rock and felt gravity take over. Both feet slid from their holds and my hands soon followed. I did not fall even two feet before Max clamped down on the rope from above. I dangled for a moment and then clung frantically to the wall. As far as I could tell there was no physical damage to me other than a small scrape on my knee, but psychologically I was almost ruined. I could hear and feel my heart beating in my head, and my stomach muscles were so tight I could breath only in short gasps. My hands and feet were frantic, each trying to find some stable surface to cling to.

"Ho la!" I heard Serge cry, and was disconcerted to look down and see that although he was watching me, he was too far off to the to side to catch me if I fell. Worse than that, he was still grinning and puffing calmly on his cigarette. I remembered, too, his shaking hands and the three inches of cognac he had consumed and that did nothing to help my state of mind.

"Dillon!" It was Max's voice. "Dillon! Look up at me!" I did so briefly and saw the shadow of his face, the sun shining brightly behind him. I squinted up, but then felt one of my feet slipping and looked down again to try and find somewhere to place it. I gave up trying to find handholds then and grabbed the rope itself.

"I don't . . . I don't think . . . I . . . can do it!" I cried, hardly able to speak.

"Sure you can!" Max said. "You were doing great, just got blender-headed, that's all."

I tried to breathe and avoided looking down.

"I want you to let go of the rope," Max said. His voice was stern but patient. "Do you hear me? Let go of the rope and lean back.

Don't worry, I've got you, Serge is right below, we're not going to let you fall. Trust me." I squinted up at him. His words took a moment to register, but there was something reassuring in his tone, not encouragement really, but an absence of worry or concern.

"Let go of the rope," he said again. "Let your arms relax a minute. Your legs'll hold you."

Slowly, tentatively, I did as he said and tried to put my arms at my sides, but it was like they suddenly had a will of their own and wanted to keep going back to the rope. I leaned forward.

"No, don't do that," Max said. "Lean back," he said slowly, "leeaan baacck. I know it feels wrong, but sometimes when something feels wrong, it's right anyway. You'll have to trust me on this one. Lean back. Put your weight over your feet and use your hands for balance."

Gingerly, against every message that my panicked brain was sending to my body, I did as he said. I leaned back a bit and tried to reach out to the wall. Again, I panicked and my hands went back to the rope.

"Good. Now stay back and let go of the rope. Just let go with one hand. Find a handhold."

I did so with one, and then quickly with the other, finding holds and clamping on to them with trembling fingers. I could still feel the harness held taut by the rope.

"Good. Now breathe and relax a minute," Max said. "Keep back and keep your weight angled in on your feet. Good. Now start again. You can do it. I've got you. Serge has got you. You're not going to fall. Good. Start climbing."

I looked up at the wall and saw that there were several possible places to go. *Lean back*, I said to myself. *You can. Weight over the feet, balance with the hands.* I moved one hand up, then one foot. My weight was on just one foot then, and as I went to switch it to the other, I felt the muscle in my leg spasm. I paused, took a deep breath, and told myself again to lean back. I did so and the weight on my leg stopped the tremors. I quickly lifted it up to the next foothold and stepped up. I looked up and saw that I was now only a few feet from Max.

"Come on, buddy, almost here. You're doing great!"

Step, reach, step, reach. I looked down and realized the rope was now slack and I was climbing under my own power. I reached the gutter and as I lifted myself up and over it I felt the sun on my face. Max took my hand and pulled me up.

"Welcome," he said, giving me a pat on the back. I did not reply. I felt sweat break out all over my body, as if it had been waiting until I was safe to release. I was exhilarated and relieved at the same time. My muscles and my breathing relaxed and went back to normal, but I felt recharged and excited—as if my blood had been electrified. Max put his arm around my shoulder and led me over to the other side of the roof. We looked across the plains to the foothills and then at the mountains beyond. I looked down. The tire tracks in the muddy street below seemed patterned and graceful, and even the dug-out basement holes, now nearly full of rainwater from the storm, sparkled and shimmered in the sunlight.

"It's beautiful," I said. Max's face relaxed into a smile.

"Yes," he said. "The world isn't nearly so ugly *à la distance.*"

Just then Serge crested the roof and pulled himself up. He was not connected to any rope, and he still had a cigarette clenched between his teeth.

"How do you feel, Dillon?" he asked, clapping me on the shoulder with one of his enormous hands.

"Better," I said, and smiled.

"Keep at it and you'll be a beautiful climber, just like your uncle." Then he came up behind Max and encircled him in his arms. They stood like that for some moments, just staring out at the mountains, both seeming to forget I was even there. I was so shocked that I nearly fell off the roof. It was such an intimate, familiar gesture, in which I instinctively sensed something sexual. My head, however, kept trying to dismiss it. It was probably just some French thing, like how they kissed both cheeks when they greeted someone. My head could try and dismiss it, but my heart, again beating like a drum, knew that it was something more. Max turned to look at me and I quickly looked away, embarrassed. Like I'd been caught looking at something I shouldn't. They separated and Max unlooped the rope from the chimney.

"Come over here, Dillon, and I'll show you how we set this up to rappel down."

When the rope was ready, first Serge, and then I, rappelled off the roof. Then Max tossed the rope down and followed after us, down-climbing with as much grace and agility as he'd gone up. At the bottom, they showed me how to wind up the ropes and how to organize the equipment in the back of Serge's truck, explaining the various functions of different metal clamps and carabiners. After that, the three of us sat in the sun on the driveway, and they showed me several knots to practice. I got so engrossed in the challenge of making the rabbit come out of the hole and go around the tree, and then back down the hole, and so on, that it was probably twenty minutes before I noticed their absence.

I looked around. It was late afternoon, and the sun was just moving behind the foothills. I got up, placed my bits of rope back in Serge's rusty red truck and stared back at the house. I went up the walkway and back in the front door. All was quiet. I closed the door and went into the kitchen. The cognac bottle was on the counter where I'd left it that morning, and next to it was a jar lid holding several of the filterless cigarette butts. Again, all was quiet.

I walked over to the basement stairs and looked down. The door was closed. My heart was pounding again and my throat felt dry. I had my suspicions about what was going on behind that door, considering what I'd witnessed on the roof, and yet somehow I could not believe it. It seemed too fantastic. I had taken about three steps down, just to see if I could hear anything, when the doorbell rang again. I froze. Then I scrambled up the stairs as fast as I could, afraid Max might suddenly open the door. I stood at the top of the cellar stairs and felt guilty, even though I had really not done anything wrong.

I cleared my throat and walked slowly over to the door. This time it was Wayne. His familiar round fleshy face appeared through the peephole, and he looked as big and pink and as tightly groomed as ever. I opened the door, but I did not protest or even question where he'd been. I did not speak to him at all. I stepped out on to the porch, closed the door behind me, and made my way down to the waiting Oldsmobile, smiling and nodding as he explained about the church and the delay.

"We've been scrambling like the dickens to get the roof patched in time for the gathering tonight," he said, backing out of the driveway, a smug grin on his face, "and it looks like Mother Nature was no match for the good Lord and his followers, because I'll be doggone if we didn't get her done!"

"Greeaaat," I said, adopting Lana's deadpan tone. The car backed out of the driveway and we drove away. Sadly, I watched the red truck recede and then disappear from view.

Chapter Seven

The gathering that night was brief. Many in the congregation had spent the day working to repair the damage to the church and were weary from their efforts. The "alleluias" were less numerous and more subdued; no one danced in the spirit or spoke in tongues; and even the singing sounded heartless and tired.

I sat on a pew in the front row in between two of the older ladies in the congregation. Ordinarily, I sat with Lana, but when the service started she still had not arrived. I kept craning around to see if she had arrived late and was somewhere in the back, but she hadn't come. Wayne, being the assistant pastor, was of course up by the altar and from the way he scanned the crowd I could tell that he was looking for her, too.

"I hope your mother's all right," he said when we met by the front door after the service. He wrinkled his brow and scratched his helmet of hair. "Not like her to miss a gathering, especially on a night like this when it's so important that we stick together."

I nodded and shrugged my shoulders.

"She probably didn't think we'd be up and running again so soon, but you'd think she'd wonder where you had gotten to," he said, patting me on the back. "Let me go get changed and I'll take you home."

When we arrived at the house, I was sad to see that Serge's truck was gone, and I hoped that Max had not gone with him. Wayne pulled gently into the driveway, shifted into park, and then, as was his habit, methodically shut off the lights, the radio, and the ventilation system. Only then did he release the door lock. We both got out of the car and walked up the path to the front door. As I opened it, I heard laughter. We went in, and Wayne shut the door behind us.

When we entered the kitchen, I saw Lana and Max sitting at the table, both talking and laughing, each adding parts to a story that it was clear they both already knew but were relishing retelling. I scanned the room, searching for the many wine bottles I felt sure must be fueling their mirth, but I saw none—only two water glasses on the table amid the remains of what looked like Chinese takeout. Lana was laughing and talking as happily as a parrot, but, more surprising than that, she was smoking! A habit she had given up after her conversion. They were both oblivious to our entrance and we stood watching them for some moments before Lana caught sight of us.

"Wayne!" she cried, popping up from her seat and quickly stubbing out her cigarette. He said nothing, but stared disapprovingly at the ashtray.

"I didn't hear you come in," she said, and scowled at me, as if I should have warned her that we'd arrived. "Have you eaten?" she asked, turning to Wayne.

"Yes," he said, and again patted my back. "All fed and taken care of. We grabbed a couple of corn dogs before the gathering, didn't we, Sport?"

I nodded. I looked over at Max and he gave me a wink.

"We thought we'd see you there . . ." Wayne trailed off, looking at Lana.

"Well, yes, uh yes, yes," she fumbled, "and I would have been there if I hadn't gotten out of class so late, and if, well, my brother here just got into town and I thought I should stay home and make sure he got all settled tonight."

Wayne eyed Max suspiciously. I could tell he was seeing Max's long hair and the cigarettes, the silver bracelet, and the pirate shirt, unlaced at the collar, and that he wholeheartedly disapproved of it all.

"I don't believe I've had the pleasure," Wayne said, advancing and extending his hand. Max put his cigarette in his mouth, got up, and shook Wayne's hand in both of his, much the way he'd done with Meredith earlier that day, holding on a bit longer than could be called acceptable.

"I hope we'll be seeing you at some of our gatherings," Wayne said. "The door is open to everyone. Your sister is usually so good about attending."

"Oh, Wayne," Lana purred, getting up and encircling Wayne's neck with her arms, "Now don't be that way. I tried to call you, I really did, but the phone lines are still out . . ."

This was a lie.

". . . and I knew you'd be bringing Dillon back tonight. How was he today?" she asked, trying to change the subject.

"Oh, he was great! He's a great kid, aren't you, Sport?" I gave an outward shrug and an inward groan. "I was pretty busy all morning repairing the roof, but I made it over and collected him a little past four. He was a big help raking the trash and getting it all bagged up. He's earned a good night's sleep, I'll say that much." And yet again he patted me on the back.

"Thank you, Wayne," Lana said, and again gave him a hug, pressing her breasts into his stomach. There was an awkward silence. I thought Lana would ask Wayne to pull up a chair, but she did not. Instead, she continued thanking him and slowly ushered him to the door.

"Hope to see you again soon," he called out to Max, as he was being led to the hallway. When they'd gone, Max came up to me and rubbed my head. He gave me a playful sock in the arm and said, "Sport!" I rolled my eyes.

"I wondered where you'd gone to," he said. "Serge was sorry he didn't get a chance to say good-bye, but he left a present for you on your bed and he wants to take us climbing next week—someplace real this time. Whaddya say . . . Sport!" and he fell back in his chair in a fit of giggles. I smiled, in spite of myself.

Lana returned and soon, believe it or not, we were all laughing, each of us taking turns telling stories about my grandparents while Max did riotous imitations of them both. I was happy about it all, but at the same time a little scared. I was so used to Lana's artificial public laughs that the hearty, genuine way she was laughing then made me ill at ease. It was as if, for once, she was not scripting it.

Of course, like all good evenings, my part in it ended too soon and I was sent to bed. When I got to my room I saw on my bed the climbing shoes I'd borrowed that morning. Next to them were several sheets of paper on which were drawn the diagrams of some knots to practice. "You can do these with the laces from the shoes," it said, at the bottom of the page. It was signed with a rather shaky *S*.

Again I heard the sound of Lana's laughter, echoing up the stairs. I knew I couldn't go back down, so I crept out into the hallway, lay flat on the floor, and peered through the spindles of the banister.

They were doing the dishes, standing side by side at the sink.

"Think about it," Max was saying. "I could help you with some of the work on the house and help keep track of Dillon."

"Oh, don't worry about him," she said. "He'll be going off to camp next week so he won't be in your way."

"I'm sure he wouldn't be in the way," he said. "I was thinking . . . maybe he could help me. I mean, I'm sure that camp you want to send him to costs money, and it's money that could be much better spent on finishing up this house, don't you think?"

"Mmm, but it's all arranged," she said. "Besides, he's gotten into some trouble. It's probably best if he goes. We're already looking into military school for him in the fall."

"We?" Max asked.

"Wayne and I, the guy that was just here, the assistant pastor from the church. He's been a great help with Dillon since James, that fucking prick, walked out!"

She paused here to let her venom dissipate before continuing.

"Wayne takes him to the church in the mornings. I don't really know what they do there, but he hasn't been in any trouble for the past two weeks, so whatever it is it must be good."

"When did you start going to church?" Max asked.

"Oh, after James left," she said.

I wondered if she was going to mention her own misadventures with the bottle, but she did not.

"I was feeling a little bit blue so some friends got me to go with them one night, and, uh, I've been going ever since."

I noticed that she said this nervously, as if she was suddenly a bit embarrassed by it all, and that she left out all the details of her conversion, which she usually loved to recount: how she had seen the light and stopped drinking, how she knew that light was the power of Christ driving Satan out of her heart, how she had accepted Jesus as her personal savior, etc.

"Oh," he said, and then let the silence hang between them. This made Lana uncomfortable and I could see her trying to think up something to say, some way to justify it to him, but she couldn't. Max knew her too well. He knew, like I did, that her faith was just something she had pulled out of the closet like a new outfit and was now realizing that it no longer really suited her.

"It's good for Dillon," she said. "It keeps him out of trouble."

"How long did you say you've been going?" Max asked.

"About six months, I guess, maybe longer."

"And when did Dillon get suspended?"

"That's different!" she cried.

"Of course, it is," Max said and started to laugh.

The next morning I was awakened suddenly. Max slipped into my room and whipped open the blinds, flooding the room with sunlight.

"Rise and shine, young man! We've got places to go, things to do, people to see! Up, up, up!" he yelled and whipped the sheet off the bed. Never a morning person, I lay there squinting like a newborn kitten while he danced around the room singing "Frère Jacques."

"Did you know," he said, coming round and perching on the edge of the bed, coffee cup in hand, "that there is a very exotic looking automobile in the garage? I've just come from there, and that, in addition to my consumption of several caffeinated beverages, accounts for my morning's exuberance!"

I rolled over and faced the wall.

"Don't you realize what that means?" he asked. "Freedom! *La liberté*, my boy! I was thinking we were going to have to thumb it downtown today, but now we can get there in style."

"Did you notice the hood?" I grumbled.

"Details," he said with a dismissive wave.

"There's no windshield," I added.

"As I was saying, young Dillon, details. Details that I have already dealt with over the telephone this morning, while you were up here sawing logs. However, I've reached the point in my plan where I require your assistance. Up, up, up!" he yelled and gave my ass a pinch.

"Ow! All right!" I cried, jumping out of the bed. He then strode out of the room and I followed him out into the hall.

"Now, we'll need a pair of nylon stockings and some golf balls," he said, checking the two items off on his fingers. "And I'll need some clothes. Some of your stepdad's clothes. He did leave some behind, didn't he?"

For the next half hour, we rummaged through James's closet, trying to find something that would fit Max. This was not easy. My stepfather was stout and short and Max was tall and thin, and Max was keeping me in the dark about what he needed the outfit to be appropriate for. In the end we found a pair of blue slacks (which fit only because they were new and had not yet been hemmed), and a blue-and-white-striped shirt. He tried on a tweed sport coat but his forearms stuck out a good six inches, so he opted for a tweed vest instead, and a smart little bow tie. The result was something like a young, long-haired Orville Redenbacher, and Max frowned when he saw himself in the mirror.

"This won't work," he sighed, so we returned to the closet. He tossed the vest and bow tie on the floor and selected a more conservative looking red necktie. In James's dresser he found a matching tie tack and cufflinks and to complete the picture he put on a pair of James's glasses. As he was brushing his hair and pulling it back into a ponytail, he told me again to round up a pair of nylons and some golf balls. I found the nylons in Lana's dresser drawer and then went down to the hall closet where James kept his clubs. In his bag I found a box of six golf balls. As I emerged with these Max was stumbling down the stairs, unable to see clearly through James's glasses but unwilling to take them off.

"Scissors," he said, and I led him to the junk drawer in the kitchen. He took the stockings, cut the legs off, and discarded the top half. He then opened the box of golf balls and dropped three of them in the leg of each stocking. He lifted the glasses and looked at his watch. His eyes widened.

"Yikes! We don't have much time, so we're going to have to hurry."

That said, he handed me one of the pendulous stockings and pushed me in the direction of the garage.

"But what are we doing?" I asked. "What do I do with this?"

"Ahh, be innocent of the knowledge, dearest Sport, till thou applaud the deed."

He switched on the light in the garage and walked up to the Jaguar. Despite the dents and the broken windshield, it still looked stylish, with its long hood stretching almost three times the distance of the cab. James had loved that car—worshipped it. It was his golden calf, his most prized possession, the thing most contentious in his pending divorce settlement with Lana.

He would cry if he could see it now, I thought to myself.

Imagine my horror then, when Max swung his golf ball–filled stocking and smacked the roof of the car, not once, not twice, but three times. He then paused and looked over at me impatiently.

"Jump in any time, Sport, we're on a tight schedule," and he gave it another smack.

"But . . . what? Stop!" I cried, grabbing the stocking from his hand. "What are you doing?" He looked at me, shocked for a moment, but then he smiled and whacked it again.

"Insurance, Dil. Insurance."

More whacks.

"What? Stop!"

"In-sur-ance," he said, prying my fingers off of his wrist. "Oh God," he sighed. "Remember the hailstorm?"

I nodded.

"Well that storm, to borrow one of your mother's platitudes, was a *real* blessing in disguise. She told me last night, rather offhandedly, about the car, and I must say, Dil, I was a little disappointed that you hadn't told me about it earlier, I mean, really! To neglect to mention something as vital as transportation! Anyway, I was reading the paper this morning while having my coffee and there, of course, were several articles about the storm and the damage it caused. Well, one of the businesses hardest hit, pun very much intended, were car dealerships! It only makes sense if you think about it. Almost all of their cars are parked outside, exposed to the elements. Well, that got me thinking . . . Are you following me yet?"

"I think so," I groaned, and rubbed my forehead.

"Good. Well, then, I thought to myself, I bet I could make that car look hail damaged. And then I thought, I bet old James has got a good insurance policy, and sure enough I was right. A platinum policy! With the premiums paid up through the end of the year. Not only will they come out and assess the damage, but they'll bring us a loaner until this one is fixed. So come on!" he said, tossing me one of the stockings and tapping at the face of his watch impatiently, "He's supposed to be here at nine-thirty."

And so, for the next five minutes we smacked the hood and roof and trunk of the car with the stockinged golf balls. When the damage looked natural enough we stopped, and Max hit the garage door opener. He put the car in neutral, and we pushed it out into the driveway.

"Okay, now go get dressed," Max said, pushing me back into the garage. "And make it look like you're going to school. Have your little book bag and whatever other accessories you school kids have. Go on. *Go!*"

When I returned, some minutes later, my clarinet case in one hand and my book bag thrown over my shoulder, Max and another man were talking in the driveway. The man, I gathered by his clipboard, was the insurance adjuster. Silently, he made his way around the car, carefully noting the damage, while Max examined his fingernails and tapped his foot impatiently.

"Certainly was quite a storm!" Max commented.

"Mmm," the man grumbled, running his fingers over some of the dents on the hood. "It's kept me busy. Say, some of these dents here look deeper than the others, like maybe they didn't come from the hail."

Max approached, lifted up his glasses, and examined the three gashes Lana had inflicted with the golf club. They were much deeper than the subtle impressions we'd made moments before with the golf balls.

"Well, yes, of course," Max said, without a moment's hesitation. "That's because they were not caused by the hailstones."

"Pre-existing damage?" the man asked.

"Ha ha ha, hard-ly!" Max bellowed. "As you can see we live in an area that is, how shall we say, a work in progress. The contractor skipped out, and, well, it's all tied up in the courts now, a big legal mess. Anyway, as you can see when the workmen pulled out, they left all their scrap lumber and crap lying around, so when the wind kicked up, of course, Murphy's Law, it all flew onto my property. Really did some damage," he said, shaking his head and fingering one of the gashes.

"Young Dillon here," he said, pointing to me, "certainly earned his allowance yesterday bagging it all up, didn't you, boy?"

I nodded, amazed at how quickly he was able to come up with a plausible explanation.

"Ready for school, I see, Sport," Max said, and then turned to the insurance man. "Listen, we're in quite a hurry. Any chance we could wrap this up? I'd hate for him to be late, it's the start of finals this week, and I was expected at the office over an hour ago. You do understand." The man nodded and made some more notes.

"Yes, yes," he said, handing Max a set of keys and looking at his watch. "Here are the keys to the rental," and he pointed down the driveway to a late model Ford parked next to the sidewalk. "I just need your signature here." Max signed. The man looked at his watch once again.

"The tow truck should be here soon." he said. "I'll catch a ride back into town with him. Here's my card. Give me a call this afternoon and I should have a time estimate for you on the repairs."

"Thank you so much," Max said, and ushered me down the driveway to the car.

"Oh, Mr. Sawyer?" the man called out. We were almost to the car. Max did not respond, so I elbowed him in the ribs. "I'm sorry sir, just one more thing." Max turned and gave a questioning smile. I got into the car, shut the door, and immediately rolled down the window.

"I'm sorry, I don't mean to sound suspicious, but it is my job and I have to ask. Uh, why is it that the car wasn't garaged?"

"Ahh," Max said, not missing a beat. "For that you can thank my wife. Terribly lazy, absentminded woman. Which is why, among other reasons," he whispered, cupping one hand around his mouth, "she's soon to be my ex-wife. But that's another story entirely. Any other questions?"

The man nodded, knowingly. "No, I don't think so," he said.

"Good. Well, I'll be off then," and Max got in the driver side and started the car. I was sweating as we drove off down the hill, and too awed to speak. Max was smiling and humming, still very much in character, swerving from side to side of the road, unable to see through James's glasses. When we had driven a few blocks away he took them off. He pulled the rubber band from his hair and shook it out, lit a cigarette and inhaled.

"You were very good, Dil," he said and gave me a pat on the thigh. "Do you think he suspected anything?"

I smiled and shook my head.

"You seemed pretty confident," I said. Max smiled at the compliment and exhaled a cloud of blue smoke.

"That's what it's all about, Dil, ninety-nine percent of the time. If you can appear confident people usually won't fuck with you, although I have to admit that was a little easier than even I had hoped. Poor guy!" Max said, looking in the rearview mirror. "He needs to rent a copy of *Double Indemnity*."

We were about half a mile from the house when I saw Wayne's car headed in the opposite direction. He didn't recognize us because of the strange car we were driving.

"Oh no," I groaned. "I forgot about Wayne. He just drove past us!"

"You can thank me later," Max said, patting my leg. "But while you were snoozing this morning I was busy composing a note, which Wayne will find tacked to the front door, telling him about your early orthodontist appointment." He looked again in the rearview mirror and scrunched his brow. "I only hope he doesn't spoil things with our gullible friend back there."

Chapter Eight

After our performance with the insurance adjuster, Max drove us into Denver. I had not been downtown at all since I started at my new junior high, but I still knew my way around fairly well, having lived there with Lana and James for several years, and could orient myself by several different landmarks. The area of town that Max took us to that morning, however, was completely foreign to me: a run-down, forgotten strip of land between the highway and the Platte River. It was a single street, with old, mostly abandoned buildings on either side. There was a grizzly looking bar, crowded with patrons even though it was not yet noon; a fenced-in warehouse with two vicious looking German shepherds on patrol; an abandoned factory of some sort; and last, but certainly not least, a small coffee shop called Paris on the Platte.

Paris was a small low storefront, sandwiched between two much taller buildings, each of which were unoccupied and had their windows boarded up. In contrast, the small café looked inviting and alive, with its pink neon sign and tables and chairs spread out on the sidewalk. Inside, it was dark and cluttered. There were more tables and chairs, chaotically placed around the room, and nearly all the walls were lined with shelves of used books. To one side, there was a glass case from which they sold a variety of exotic cigarettes, and in the back, resting on another display case containing cakes and pastries, was an enormous antique espresso machine.

Paris catered more to the late night crowd so when we arrived, at ten o'clock in the morning, it had just opened and was nearly deserted. Its sole patron, Jane, was seated in a sunny spot by the front window, casually flipping through a magazine. She was dressed smartly, in a pale blue skirt and suit jacket with a simple strand of pearls around her neck. Her long hair had been twisted back tightly into a bun and was capped off with a pill box hat of the same hue as her skirt and jacket. As before, her eyes were concealed behind enormous sunglasses. She had not seen us come in. We wove through the labyrinth of tables and chairs and stopped in front of her.

"Good morning, Miss Nguyen," Max said, bowing deeply. She looked up and her mouth widened into a smile. She closed her magazine, got up and offered her cheek to be kissed. Max obliged. She then took both his hands in hers and gave them a squeeze.

"Oh, it's good to see you!" she said, and leaned back to take a look at him. Her brow wrinkled then and the smile disappeared from her face.

"What *are* you wearing?" she exclaimed, lifting her glasses and casting a disapproving glance at Max's borrowed outfit. "You're not actually thinking of going out and getting a job, are you?"

"God, no," he replied, "but you know me, always working! The clothes are borrowed, just until I can get something else."

She nodded and then turned her gaze to me and extended her hand. It was an extremely small hand, all the nails a uniform length and painted with a clear polish. On her ring finger she wore a large sapphire, encircled by small diamonds.

"Hello again," she said, smiling at me. "I don't believe I introduced myself last time. I'm Jane."

"Dillon," I mumbled, shyly taking her hand and looking at the floor.

"Well, Dillon," she said, leaning back and picking up her purse. "I'm starving! Shall we get something to eat?"

I nodded, and she took me by the hand and led me to the counter.

"The usual for you?" she called back to Max.

"Please," he said.

When we returned, with more pastries than we could possibly consume, Max was gone. He emerged from the shelves a few moments later carrying several books and a fresh pack of cigarettes.

"So," Jane said, addressing me, "has your uncle here been getting you into trouble?"

I looked at Max and smiled, but said nothing.

"Only potentially," Max said. "We haven't been caught yet."

Max and Jane then lapsed into a conversation I found hard to follow, speaking of things I knew nothing about. They had been friends a long time, that much was clear, since they were both at ease in each other's presence and spoke with a vocabulary full of their own slang and internal references. The conversation went on, lively and animated, and it was only when the tone changed that my attention returned to it.

"You don't look so good," Jane commented, reaching across the table and running a finger along Max's pale cheek. He pulled away and an impatient expression crossed his face.

"Yes, well, it wasn't a fucking picnic," he said.

"Bad?" Jane asked gravely. Max thought about this. He cocked his head to one side and gazed up at the ceiling.

"More like a long exercise in patience."

"I don't know how you got through it," Jane said, a pitying look on her face. "It must have been awful!"

"Oh, it wasn't so bad, really. It had a definite beginning and a definite end. That helped. You can get through anything as long as you know it will end someday. I knew I would get out, so I just put it on autopilot until then. Focused on what I'd do when I was released."

"And what might that be?" Jane asked.

"In due time, *chérie*, all will be revealed. But I'll tell you this much: it doesn't involve sticking around in this cow town much longer. But enough about me, let's talk about you. How's the family?"

Jane's expression clouded over at the mention of the word *family* and it was obvious that she didn't welcome the change of subject to this particular topic.

"The same," she groaned, and her shoulders fell, "only larger. New ones step off the boat every day and my father tries to get me to marry every one of them."

"And how's the shop coming?" Max asked.

"Still nonexistent," Jane sighed, and her shoulders fell even further. She pushed up her glasses and rubbed her eyes. "At least for the moment, anyway. I've got a booth in one of the antique malls. Me, and all the bored housewives and retirees in the city, arranging and rearranging the petty stock we amass from thrift stores and garage sales. Small potatoes, really, and it's just a wee bit degrading. Percy helps as much as he can."

"Percy?" Max asked.

"Oh, yes, I guess you wouldn't know about him, would you? He's one of my Tottering Ogres."

"Your *what?*"

"Tottering Ogres. At least that's what I call them, in private, anyway. They're all old and ugly and very rich, and I'm young and pretty and, how shall I say? hungry for a life I can't afford. There's a nice symmetry there, don't you think? A sort of yin and yang? Oh, now don't act all shocked!" she cried, shaking her head at Max, whose eyes had widened as she spoke. "You of all people."

"I didn't say a thing," Max protested.

"You didn't have to, I can tell by the way your brow went up. I should be used to it by now. Anyway, Percy is very nice, the nicest of all of the Tottering Ogres, and it gives me an excuse to get out of the restaurant and the nail salon. Of course my dad's livid and doesn't like Percy at all, so at first I told him Percy was just a business friend. When that wasn't enough, I'm afraid I told him he was gay. 'Like Maxey?' he said. 'Yes, just like Max' I said. 'Only older.' That quieted him down a bit, but I don't think he believes it."

When I heard this, I choked on the scone I was eating.

"Oh, my goodness," Jane said.

"You all right, Dil?" Max asked.

I coughed and smiled, took a sip of my water. What Jane said had jolted me as much as if I'd stuck my finger in an electrical outlet. Suddenly I knew my suspicions about Max and Serge had been right and my heart raced.

"Dil didn't really know about that yet," he said to Jane.

"About what? Your being gay? Please!" she scoffed, and then looked at me. "I guess I've known for so long it just seems obvious to me now. Well, Dillon, your Uncle Max likes boys," she said, matter-of-factly. "But don't worry, I think you're a little young for his taste."

They both laughed and then went back to the subject of Percy as if nothing out of the ordinary had been said. But I was shaken. I could hardly believe what I'd heard. My mind was spinning. I sat watching Max with a newfound sense of awe and respect and I couldn't wait to tell him that I was gay, too.

"And how is your dad's restaurant?" Max went on, taking another sip of his coffee.

"Booming," Jane said. "It has to be, really, to support our ever-expanding family of boat people. I've managed to weasel out of my shifts a few nights during the week, but he's still adamant about me putting in time on the weekends, and to tell you the truth, I need the money. I can usually get away with doing lunch on Saturday and dinner on Sunday, so that leaves my Saturday nights free. Which reminds me," she said, changing the subject and lowering her voice. "Doris came in last weekend. She wasn't happy. Asked a lot of questions about you."

"What did you tell her?" Max asked, leaning forward on the table, trying to appear unfazed. His lip twitched.

"Relax, darling. There was nothing I could tell her. You haven't been very communicative these past two years, never calling or answering letters. In fact, I probably learned more from her than she did from me. I mean, I knew nothing about your release."

In these last words there was a tone of angry sarcasm, and she paused after she said them, for effect.

"She's not pleased with you," she continued. "That much was clear. I *thought* you were done with her . . ."

"Yes," Max replied, but his tone was vague, and he casually lit another cigarette. She reached over and placed one of her hands on his.

"She's not one to toy around with," Jane said, looking straight at him, her tone level. "You do know that."

Max nodded.

"What is it she wants?" she whispered, looking around to make sure no one was listening. I continued eating my scone, trying to appear preoccupied, but aware that the conversation was moving into deeper waters.

"Oh, I have something of hers," Max said airily. Jane waited for him to elaborate, offered nothing.

"You're not going to tell me, are you?"

"No," he said, crushing out his cigarette in the ashtray. "I'm not."

"It's not drugs, is it?"

"No. I will tell you that. I'm not going there again."

"Then it must be money."

"What makes you say that?" he asked.

"Because Doris doesn't value anything else. Money for money's sake. That's Doris. It's money. Or drugs, which she'd just sell to get more money."

It took a moment but soon the significance of what she'd deduced sunk in.

"You stole money from Doris!" she whispered, her voice urgent.

"Not stole, really," Max replied. "It's more like I took what I feel I'm entitled to. A little something to compensate me for two fucking years of my life!"

"How much?" Jane whispered.

"Not enough," Max said bitterly. "But it's a start."

"But you can't stay here. She'll find you."

"She already has," Max said. "Dil met her. Didn't you Dil?"

I looked up, my mouth full, and nodded.

"She came to the house," I whispered, thrilled to be included in the conversation. "Just before you did."

Jane looked at me, her face troubled, then returned her attention to Max. "So she knows where you're living?"

"I suppose."

"What are you going to do? You can't stay. Where will you go?"

Max shrugged. He took a chunk of brownie and tossed it up in the air catching it on the way down in his mouth.

"What are you going to *do?*" Jane asked again, more insistently this time.

"I'll stall her," Max said. "At least until the end of the summer. Then I'll have enough money to get where I want to go."

"And do I even need to ask where that might be?" she asked, her voice tinged with sarcasm, but returning to normal volume.

"Probably not," Max replied, grinning.

Jane shook her head and rolled her eyes. She fell back in her chair, both hands clinging to the handle of the dainty purse on her lap. She gave an exasperated sigh and looked across the table at me.

"Your uncle," she said, shaking her head. "For as long as I've known him—and what has it been, my dear, ten years now?—has had an unnatural obsession with the country and people of France."

I looked at Max and then back at Jane.

"Confused?" Jane asked. "Well, you're not alone there, young Dillon. France is his brass ring, his promised land, his El Dorado. French fries, French toast, French movies, French perfume, anything having to do with the place, or even the idea of it, sends him into a swoon."

She leaned forward, picking up items from the table.

"Look here, Dillon, just look at these cigarettes, *Gitanes!* Look at the novels he's picked up." She reached over and plucked them off the table. "Maupassant, Balzac, Molière!" she said, reading the names off the spines and tossing them over to me. "Good Christ! I could have guessed without looking."

"What's there to guess about?" Max countered. "French writers are some of the best, most sophisticated, and most innovative in the world. France is the world capital of style and fashion, a notorious center for visual artists, a country that produces the most coveted food and wines in the world. I could go on and on—"

"And he will," she said, rolling her eyes, *"ad nauseum."*

"It's a dignified, civilized country, full of educated and enlightened people," Max replied.

"Tell that to my father," Jane said. "They did wonders for his native land."

"I'm sure other countries were just as bad in their colonial practices, *chère* Jane. It was the U.S. and not the French that made a mess of it all. Why do you always have to be so cynical about it? Why is it so strange that I'd want to live there?"

"Oh, it's not," Jane said, and her voice took on a softer, almost sympathetic tone. "I know it means a lot to you; it's just that I think you may be unpleasantly surprised when you arrive, that's all. You want what you see in the travel brochures, when what you'll get is a lot of cheap souvenirs and crumbling architecture. Men who don't bathe often enough and women who don't shave their pits. Now don't get me wrong, I've never been there so I don't know for sure but I have a gut feeling that it's not all April walks through the grounds of Versailles. I doubt that every window in the city has a view of the Eiffel tower, and I'd be willing to bet that there are one or two women in Paris who aren't quite as beautiful as Catherine Deneuve."

"Of course I know all that," Max replied. "I'm not expecting a cultural Disneyland for Christ's sake, but I'm pretty sure it'll be better than this," he said, gesturing out at the city. "France will be less ordinary," he said confidently. "More exceptional and rare."

Jane gave an exasperated sigh and fell back into her chair.

"Rare!" she exclaimed. "Rare! You know what's really rare these days?" she asked, not really wanting an answer. "Well, I'll tell you. Being happy where you are. That's rare. Everybody wants to be somewhere else, thinks that if they pull up and go somewhere else, everything will be different, better, 'more exceptional and rare.' Well, it won't be. The dream is what you want, not the reality. The craving is always much better than the having."

"And you're an authority on this?" Max asked smiling at her.

"Yes," she said. "As a matter of fact I am. I see it all the time, especially with my relatives. They spend years and years dreaming of coming to America only to arrive and pine away for their homeland. They make their own little Vietnam right here and then rarely, if ever, venture out of it."

"Well, I won't be like that," Max assured her.

"Of course you won't," Jane sneered.

"When I arrive I intend to wallow in it! I'll set my feet deep down in the French mud and let them take root."

Jane looked over at me and rolled her eyes. Then she looked back at Max.

"And just how do you propose to finance your relocation?" she asked. "Or do I even want to know?"

Max grinned when she said this. He leaned forward on the table and rubbed his hands together eagerly.

"I'm glad you asked, Miss Nguyen," he said. "Because I have a plan. A plan that could be very profitable both for me and for you, if—"

"Oh, no!" Jane said, waving her gloves in front of his face. "I don't want any part of it. Your schemes tend to go awry and I can't afford any screw-ups right now. I've got my own means of financial salvation, thank you very much."

"But this is different!"

At that moment a large black Mercedes rolled into view outside. Behind the wheel an elderly gentleman was leaning over, peering through the passenger window, trying to see inside the coffee shop. Jane gave him a little wave and stood up.

"That's *my* plan!" she said, collecting her gloves and nodding to the man in the car.

"The Ogre?" Max asked, his voice filled with distaste.

"You bet! He's got more money than he knows what to do with and he thinks I'm the cat's pajamas. I've got to go," she said, adjusting her sunglasses and kissing Max on the head. "We're having lunch at the family place with his mother."

"His *mother?*" Max cried.

"Yes, she's ninety-three today, the dear," Jane said. "This is the first time I'll meet her so I'm hoping to make a good impression. If all goes well, a walk down the aisle may be in my future, and you know what that would mean, don't you?"

"Years of sex with the lights out and a hope for a vivid imagination?"

She scowled and slapped him playfully with her gloves.

"No, silly. It means I'd be on my way to getting away from restaurant hell, away from the nail salon, away from all of the eligible Vietnamese bachelors that my father wants to hook me up with, and far, far, far away from my little booth in the bourgeois antique mall. A walk down the aisle would help get me comfortably installed in my own posh little boutique! And that's why it is so important to impress Mrs. Geritol this afternoon. If she likes me, I'm a shoe-in with Percy. He told me she likes blue," she said, smoothing her skirt and assessing her reflection in the window. "And I certainly hope so because I spent a mint I don't have on this little Easter egg ensemble and it's making me nauseous to even see myself in it. Blue really doesn't suit me, does it? Anyway, wish me luck!"

She kissed us both on the head and clicked toward the door. She paused when she reached it, turned, and called back.

"Hey, I'm working at the restaurant Sunday nights. It slows down after eight. Why don't you two come by? We'll feed you, and I know my father would be thrilled to see you again, Max. Think about it."

Max nodded and blew her a kiss. She waved at me and went out to the waiting car.

When she'd left we sat in silence while Max smoked and finished his coffee. Now that we were alone I wanted to ask him about what Jane had said earlier about him being gay, and about what had happened the day before with both Meredith and Serge and how I couldn't really make sense of it. I was on the verge of speaking several times but was unsure how to start. Max sensed my frustration.

"What's on your mind, Dil?" he asked. I looked up at him and swallowed.

"You know what you guys were saying earlier . . ." I said my voice timid and low. The question was vague and he looked at me, waiting for me to continue.

"*You* know," I said, my face reddening. "About your being . . . gay."

This last word was whispered and I had to look down when I said it. Max laughed.

"Yes, why?" he asked. "Does it bother you?"

"No! No," I whispered, wishing he wouldn't speak so loudly. "No, it doesn't bother me at all. I mean, I, um . . ."

Max grinned, again waiting for me to continue and offering no assistance.

"I mean, I . . . I think I might be, too. Be that way, I mean. Do you know what I mean?"

I'm sure my face was the color of a brick.

"Yes," he said, and gave a little wink. "I know."

"And it's . . . okay?" I asked.

"Yes, of course!" he laughed. "Why wouldn't it be? In fact, in some ways you'll find it can be a real advantage. You'll see. But in the end it's not really a big deal, remember that. You're young now, but by the time you're my age, you'll be able to fill a book with the names of all the people who will tell you it's bad and that you're bad. Well, take it from me, it's not, and you're not. You heard it here first. You like boys. That's it. No good or bad about it. It just is."

I heard what he said and yet I almost couldn't believe it. For years, my whole life, really, I had kept my desires a secret. I'd kept them hidden for so long that when they were brought out into the open that day, in such a matter-of-fact way, and with no shame, I could not really believe it. It had the unreal quality of a dream from which I felt sure I would soon wake up.

I thought back to the church, and the hours of "We renounce him" that they'd subjected me to after Lana had found my catalogue stash, and I realized that the whole point of that exercise had not been to save me, but to shame me, to show me that what I was doing was bad and wicked and evil. And yet, in my heart, in the core of myself, I'd known they were wrong. I'd resisted. And that was why they were so persistent. Enough drops of water on a stone will dissolve it to nothing, and they poured buckets on me everyday. But Max had arrived, and suddenly I had the reinforcements I needed for my side of the battle. In him I found the one person who confirmed what I already knew: my desires were not wrong; the way I felt was not wrong; I was not wrong.

"When did you . . . know?" I asked, my voice, again, barely above a whisper.

"When did I know what?"

"That you were . . . gay?" I said.

He thought for a moment, raising one eyebrow and gazing off into the distance.

"Oh, I guess I thought about it the first time when I was six or seven," he said. "I was over at a friend's house and we were down in the basement playing one of those kid's games: Truth or Dare, or Spin the Bottle, something like that. There were girls and boys, and I remember wanting to kiss all of them and see them all take off their clothes." He paused and laughed at the memory. "I guess I knew I was different then because although the girls didn't really seem to mind kissing each other; none of the boys wanted to let me kiss them."

He lit another cigarette and puffed on it a while.

"But I guess I really knew when I was about your age. There was a neighbor kid, and, well, another guy I used to play around with. It was fun, but we should have been more careful. My parents found out and, well," he said, shaking his head and crushing out his cigarette, "they weren't happy."

"They found out!" I cried, remembering my own dismal stay with my grandparents.

"Yes," he said. I waited but he offered no more.

"What'd they do?" I asked, imagining that their reaction must have been even worse than Lana's.

Again, he looked off into the distance, but this time his eyes narrowed.

"What did they do . . ." he repeated. "Some things that were not very nice. I guess their names were the first I entered in the book of people who tried to tell me it was wrong."

He smiled, reached across the table and gave my hand a squeeze.

"But don't worry, Dil. You'll be fine. I can tell you already know what's true and what's not. You already know when to trust yourself. And that's a lot. That's a lot . . ." he said in a wistful tone, gazing down at the table. Then he looked up and his tone became serious.

"Just be careful when you do experiment, and I don't mean just about getting caught. I mean about AIDS."

AIDS. That was another word I could barely say above a whisper. It was a threat as frightening to me as any Lana could dish up, all the more so because I knew so little about it. So little, that is, except that it killed gay men.

"Do you know what to do so you don't get it?" Max asked.

"I think so, yes."

I really had no idea, but the frankness of the conversation was becoming almost too much for me to take.

"Hmm, that's not a very good answer," he said. "Do you or don't you?"

I looked down and shook my head.

In an unashamed and unhurried way, Max then went on to explain, in graphic detail, all that was involved in man-to-man sex. He told me what men did with their mouths, and what they did with their cocks, and what they did with their asses; how to use condoms and common sense to protect myself. In short, he gave me a primer on all the techniques and tools that were needed to have sex safely.

I wish I could say I sat and listened attentively while he spoke, asking pertinent questions in all the right places, and making mental notes, but I did not. I squirmed and writhed in embarrassed agony. My palms were sweaty: my face was red; and I was terribly afraid that the other people in the coffee shop might overhear him. Nevertheless, I took in much of what he said and am, to this day, grateful to him for making the effort and taking the time. It might be a bit much to credit him with my still being alive today, but, when you think about it, who else in my unenlightened world would have done even half as much?

"But enough of the free clinic for today, do you have any other questions about all things homosexual?" he asked.

I had thousands but I was so embarrassed I shook my head, no.

"Really?" he asked. "Nothing?"

I looked around the coffee shop. The other patrons seemed intent on their newspapers or their books. I leaned in closer to the table.

"What's it like?" I asked. He looked at me, confused. I tried to clarify what I meant: "When you're with a guy, and you're safe, and all that, what's it like?"

He laughed, leaned back in his chair, and grinned at me. "That's a hard one to answer." He took another cigarette from the box and tapped the end of it on the table to compact the tobacco. He lit it, inhaled, and puzzled over the question.

"What's it like?" he repeated, exhaling and gazing up at the ceiling. "What's it like? I guess it's like anything, really; like food, or an empty canvas, or what you see when you look out the window. It's what you make of it. It can be good; sometimes it's bad; sometimes it just is. A lot of it depends on how much enthusiasm, and style, and imagination you put into it. But most of all, it depends on who you've got to work with. That's important. I don't mean you have to be in love with them, or anything, but there does have to be a spark, a fire. If that's not there, then the love never really will be. Does that make sense?"

I gave a halfhearted nod. What I'd really wanted to know was what it felt like to kiss another man, what it felt like to do all of the things he'd so graphically described earlier in the conversation. Max sensed my disappointment.

"No? Well, that's about the most I can tell you," he said. "If I say any more it'll be like telling you what happens at the end of a book or a movie. Finding out is most of the fun."

"So you like being . . . gay?" I asked. "I mean, you wouldn't change it, if there was like a pill or something you could take?"

"You know," he laughed, "in spite of all the shit I've taken about it, I don't think I would. Being different has its advantages, I'm sure you can see that."

But I could not see it, and my thoughts immediately returned to Aaron and the other kids at school, and how they sought, seemingly above all else, to stamp out anyone who was different. In my experience being different had a distinct disadvantage. I tried to explain that to Max, giving a synopsis of my junior high agony, but before I could finish he interrupted me.

"That's different. It was the same for me when I was your age. It's the same for kids the world over. As you get older, though, you'll see what I mean. Being different gives you a clearer view of things and you don't buy into as much bullshit. I'm sure, knowing that you're gay, you don't buy into all the stuff they feed you at church. You're smarter than that, I can tell. Well, maybe not smarter, really, but being different has made you able to see. You see that a lot of what they say just isn't true. You see that the message they preach isn't the same as what Jesus said."

I nodded eagerly.

"So being gay is a good thing," I said.

"Like I said in the beginning, it's not good and it's not bad, it just is."

I shook my head. I couldn't believe all that had happened that morning, even in just the past half-hour. I felt so relieved to know that I wasn't alone. There were others out there. Others who had gone through the same trouble and had lived to tell about it. Max was one of them, and I felt grateful that he had appeared in my life.

"But remember," he added, "being gay is just a part of who you are. Do remember that. There's no need to make a career out of it."

I didn't understand this and looked at him questioningly.

"Hmm, how to explain?" He took another long puff on his cigarette. "It's like this, Dil: there are some people in the world who love to see themselves as victims. They get off on being martyrs. Does that make sense?"

I nodded, but could not see where he was going with it.

"Your mother is a bit that way, and your grandmother! Oh, how that woman *loved* to drag the cross around. Well, don't you be that way, Dil, because a lot of gay people are. They wrap themselves in the rainbow flag and cry and whine about how tortured and oppressed they are. It's a bit much. Don't be that way," he said. "That's the best advice I can give you. Life might toss you some turds but self-pity, no matter how justified it may be, is never very productive, or, for that matter, very attractive."

I nodded, not really understanding all of what he'd said, but feeling glad he'd said it.

"No, self-pity is not very attractive," he repeated, and then stood and looked at himself in the mirror. "And neither are these clothes. What do you say we get out there and fix what we can, Dil?"

Chapter Nine

Stealing, for those of you not familiar with the practice, can be highly intoxicating. The rush you get from theft is almost narcotic, and I can see how someone could become as obsessed with stealing as, say, skydiving, or snorting cocaine, or wrestling crocodiles. It is the risk, really, that is so attractive, the very real possibility of arrest and imprisonment, the possibility of profound embarrassment. As Jane said, the getting is often much more satisfying than the having. The risk of being caught is often far more exciting than acquiring the object you are after.

Maybe none of this is really news to anyone. It may seem obvious and fundamental, but to me at the time it was a novel discovery.

In addition to being novel, stealing was also empowering. It gave me a sense of superiority, a feeling of vindication, a means to redress wrongs, a way to obtain compensation from society for the slaps it had inflicted on me. A successfully executed theft gave me an almost smug feeling, and more confidence in my abilities than a library full of self-help books. After I'd done it a few times it became a sport, like any other, at which I wanted to improve, to perfect my stroke, or serve, or shot. I practiced whenever I could and was always trying out different tools and equipment to help me improve. Best of all I had a terrific coach.

"Have you ever stolen anything, Dil?" Max asked, as we walked away from the coffee shop that morning, headed under the railroad tracks toward downtown. I thought about it for a moment. I had stolen Certs and small change from my grandmother's purse, some pens and promotional items from James's desk, but other than that, nothing really.

"What about the wine cellar?" Max asked, looking ahead and continuing to walk. I reddened. I did not know how to respond or where this was leading, so I said nothing and we walked in silence. He seemed to want me to think it over. I stopped walking. He turned and looked back.

"Oh, don't worry," he said, returning and taking me by the hand. "It's our secret. Just like my being at your house is our secret. We can trust each other, right?" I nodded and resumed walking alongside him. We went on in silence and Max started to speak several times but then stopped himself. It was clear that he wanted to say something but was troubled by the best way to go about it.

"I don't know how much you've heard about me," he said, his pace quickening. I struggled to keep up. "But I am what the French call *un voleur.* A thief. A cat burglar. A larcenist. I pilfer and purloin for a living. I am, as they say, fond of taking the five-fingered discount. Are you following me?"

"I think so."

"Good. So here's the way things are today," Max continued. "We are both desperately in need of clothes, are we not?"

I nodded and looked down at my clownish pants.

"But neither of us has any money, right? Well, we're going to get some new clothes but we aren't going to pay for them, are you with me?"

"Yes," I replied, without any hesitation. He stopped walking and there was a somewhat surprised expression on his face. I think he expected me to be shocked, expected that maybe all the church-going had rubbed off on me and that I would start proselytizing and warn him of the dire punishment that awaited those who disobeyed the seventh commandment. But there was certainly no danger of that. I did not think stealing was all that bad. In fact, my time at church had, if anything, the opposite of its intended effect. Instead of giving me a moral framework to govern my life, going to church only made me feel that I was absolutely beyond redemption. I was damned, I figured, so what I did really didn't matter.

Let me try to explain: there was no question that I was a sinner. I drank and got in trouble and had impure thoughts about boys, and I knew that all of those were damnable offenses. Nevertheless, Wayne and the pastor and all the parishioners assured me that no matter how grave the sin, God was always willing to forgive, and they never tired of encouraging me to repent. The problem was, although God may have been ready to forgive, I was hardly willing, or, more significantly, *able* to repent. I knew that even if my sexual desires were wrong, they were so strong that they completely overwhelmed any concerns for what might happen to my soul. I knew that the way my dick reacted when I was in the showers at school had absolutely nothing to do with being an upright God-fearing Christian. I had tried everything in my power (ice-cold water, averting my eyes to the heavens, even pinching myself) to control it, but my body instinctively rebelled and the mast went up. When that happened, and it happened with an annoying regularity, it almost made me want to curse God for what seemed to me his wicked sense of humor. God was playing a game with me. A game with rules he had made that were impossible for me to follow. For that reason, my moral sensibility was not shocked by what Max was saying. I knew it was wrong in God's eyes, but then so was I.

That stealing was wrong in the eyes of society bothered me even less. In a way I actually felt good about it. I felt that society owed me something, much the way Max thought that Doris owed him something for his taking the rap and spending time in prison. Life was not fair, that much was clear, and if that was the case then what was the point in playing fairly.

Add to this the fact that Max was stealing to help me and you'll see I had even less resistance. He was doing it to get me some less ridiculous-looking clothes, to get me some acne medicine, to get me some shoes that fit. He was doing it to do all of the things that Lana had neglected to do and I was so grateful that I felt I ought to help him. It was the least I could do.

"Now today," Max went on, "you just watch and learn. I'll need you to play along with my lead, okay? The most important part of stealing is confidence. Remember that. Be confident. If you can't *be* confident, *act* confident, and if you can't act confident, then you nonchalantly make your way toward the exit and wait outside, you follow?"

"Yes."

"Excellent. You play the clarinet, right?"

I nodded.

"Jazz?"

"Sometimes."

"Good, because stealing has a lot in common with jazz; you've got your basic tune every time but you vary the melody, improvise. Like I said, follow my lead at first, play along, but then, as you see fit, jump in and add your own notes."

We started out quickly that day, with a trip to a cluttered army surplus store on Larimer Street, where I watched, awestruck, as Max deftly pocketed several items: a retractable razor knife, some sunglasses, a small tool set. The first time I saw one of these things drop into his pocket I nearly gasped. I thought if *I'd* seen him take it, surely someone else had too, but the fat man behind the counter was too busy chuckling at the comics he had spread out before him to notice, and the lanky stock boy was busy trying to look busy with a broom, so neither one paid any attention to us. When Max had all that he needed, we headed toward the exit. Then, to my dismay, Max turned to the right and approached the counter.

"Do you have airplane glue?" he asked the man.

Why is he doing this? I wondered.

"It's for my son here, he's building a model."

"Nope!" the man replied, not looking up from his paper. "Used to. Drunks were always coming in and stealing it. To sniff. Bunch a crazy coots. Whatcha building?" he asked, looking down at me. I gulped and looked at Max. He was gazing at me like a proud father.

"Don't be shy, Sport, tell him what it is."

I knew nothing about airplanes or models, but I did know that most of the models other boys in my class had built were cars.

"It's, a, uh, Oldsmobile," I sputtered.

"An Olds, eh? What kind? An SS? A Cutlass?"

"Um, neither," I said, trying to picture Wayne's car in my mind. "It's, uh, a, Delta Eighty-eight!"

"A Delta!" he exclaimed, raising an eyebrow above the frame of his glasses "That's not very sporty."

"No. No, but it's an easy model," I said, "and, and, and I thought it would be good to start with an easy one. It's the first time I've done one. A model I mean."

"Ah," he said nodding. "Start out easy till you get it figured out. Smart boy," and he reached over and gave me a pat on the shoulder. "Try the Ace Hardware. There's one up on Corona or over off of Thirty-eighth. They should carry that kind of stuff."

"Thanks," Max said. He smiled at the man and gave me a gentle nudge out the front door.

When we had walked a safe distance away, Max spoke. "Not bad, Dil. Not bad. You still with me?"

"Yes," I said, and wiped the sweat from my forehead on my sleeve. "But why did you stop to talk to him?" I asked. "We could have just left."

"Ahhh, it was a little test," he said, "and I'm glad to say you passed. Oh, your performance can definitely use some polishing, that stuttering was a bit out of control, but overall you did well."

From the surplus store we walked over to Sixteenth Street, and without a word of direction I followed Max into Fashion Bar. The store was crowded with people on their lunch break, and all of the clerks appeared to be busy helping customers or ringing up purchases. Max wandered slowly around the men's section, selecting clothes for us both and now and then asking my opinion. When he had amassed six or seven things, he walked by one of the vacant counters; as he did, I noticed that he dropped one of the shirts he was carrying.

"Hey," I whispered, bending down to pick it up, "you dropped one." He turned, a somewhat flustered look on his face, and knelt down to pick it up. In a flash I saw the razor knife come out from under the pile of clothes and slash through a metal cord. It was the cord tethering the device for removing theft protectors to the counter. When it was cut, Max quickly concealed the device and the knife under the clothes, got up, and continued walking. We went on browsing for about ten more minutes, and when we had a large pile of clothes, we headed toward the dressing rooms.

Fashion Bar was never very strict about their dressing rooms. There was no attendant watching to give you numbers or direct you to a particular booth, so we wandered in together and Max handed me several pants and shirts to try on.

"Pick the ones you like best and put them on," he whispered, his voice firm and clear. "Remove the clamps and any tags, and then put your own clothes on over them." He then pushed me into one booth and took the one next to it for himself.

I was sweating from every pore and my breath was coming in short gasps. I bit my lip and tried to relax. I took off my clothes and put on a pair of new khaki pants and a blue-and-white nautical sweater. I had barely pulled it over my head when I saw Max waving the remover under the partition separating the two booths. I bent down and took it. I tried to remove the clamp from the sleeve of the sweater, but my hand was shaking so much that I couldn't get a grip on it. I took the sweater off and set it down, to use the floor for leverage. I attached the remover to the clamp, gave it a squeeze, and it popped open like the mouth of an alligator. Sweat dripped down the bridge of my nose. I put the sweater back on, popped the clamp on the pants and then passed the remover back under the partition. I pulled my sweatshirt on over the sweater easily, but when I tried to pull my pants on I discovered they were far too small and tight to fit over the khakis. I thought my heart would beat right through my chest. I wanted to ask Max what to do, but there were other people in the dressing room now so I knew I couldn't. I took off my old pants, wadded them up in a ball and shoved them under the small bench in the corner. I hoped I could get out wearing the khakis, but they were deeply creased where they had been folded and looked new.

Confidence, Dillon, I told myself. *Act confident.* I looked at myself in the mirror. I was still sweating, but the air-conditioning had kicked on and as my sweat evaporated I felt myself cooling down. I focused on breathing normally. Max's door opened and he knocked on mine.

"Any of those gonna work for you?" he asked. I opened the door. Max was dressed in the same conservative clothes that he'd borrowed from James's closet that morning, and, if anything, the layers he had put on underneath filled out the clothes and made them look more natural. He assessed me and did not look displeased. I pointed to my pants in the corner. He nodded and then motioned for me to kick the clamps I'd removed under there, too. I did so and together we walked out of the dressing rooms. Thankfully, the store was still crowded and it appeared that no one had noticed us. Max hung several garments on the rod outside the dressing room, and we browsed around the store for a few more minutes, idly commenting on the cut of this jacket or the color of that shirt. He then looked at his watch with an expression of surprise.

"We'd better go," he said, and we did just that, walking through the front doors and out onto the street without setting off any alarms.

When we'd made it about a block, I could not help but grin. I was so elated that I wanted to break into a run. I felt like all the anxiety I had dammed up inside of me had suddenly burst out and was coursing through my veins.

"We did it!" I said, unable to conceal my excitement. I looked up at Max, wanting to take him by the hand and skip up the street. He brought his index finger up to his lips and shook his head. We turned off of the crowded shopping street and walked down the comparatively deserted Seventeenth Street. Only then did he speak.

"Not bad, Dil. Not bad at all. You nearly choked in the dressing room but you got it under control. I could see you were nervous, but you did all right." He lit a cigarette and inhaled it deeply, shaking out his shoulders.

"You had it all figured out!" I gushed, jumping in front of him and walking backward so I could see him as we were talking. "I never would have thought to steal that clamp remover, never in a million years, that was so great!"

He grinned and smoked, clearly relishing my admiration.

"And the razor, I never would have thought of the razor!"

"You flatter me," he said, but then his tone grew serious. "But flatter me more by remembering it. The order of things is perhaps the most important, Dil. Before you can go to the party and loot the cloakroom, you first have to steal the invitation."

I gave him a confused look.

He offered another comparison: "Get the ring before you announce the engagement. Get the clamp before you steal the clothes. It's the order of things. Understand?"

I nodded.

We walked back to the car, took off some of the clothes, and then Max drove us up to Capitol Hill where, for the first of many times that summer, we went to the movies. The theater was called the Ogden and, at the time, it was a run-down, art house cinema with movies that changed daily. Max loved it because they showed a lot of older movies that you couldn't see anywhere else and, perhaps more important, because you could smoke in the balcony.

The movie we saw that day was, appropriately enough, Hitchcock's *Marnie*, in which Tippy Hedren portrays a crafty kleptomaniac. The Ogden was in the middle of a Hitchcock marathon, mixing up the chronological order of the director's films, until they had shown them all. I know this because, with few exceptions, we saw each one that was shown over the next few weeks, although we saw very few of them in their entirety.

One of the more peculiar and annoying things about Max was that he often got up and left before the end of the movie. We'd be sitting in the dark and suddenly he'd nudge me, motion toward the exit, and out we'd go. At first I thought this was because we had someplace to go by a certain time, or because maybe he'd seen someone down below that he wanted to avoid, but then we'd make it outside and his urgency would disappear. He'd suggest getting a hamburger at the Wendy's next door, or even hanging around to get tickets to the next movie. This made no sense to me and I asked him why he always left. He just grumbled something about needing more cigarettes. After the third or fourth time I began to protest, but Max would not stay. Even when I refused to leave, usually at the point when the climactic violins started up, Max would just shrug, grind out his cigarette with his toe, and say he'd wait for me outside.

It wasn't until years later that I understood. I was watching a movie by myself. I think it was *To Catch a Thief*, and it was at the end, when the young French girl is revealed as the cat burglar, clearing Cary Grant of suspicion. Instead of feeling happy, I remember feeling almost deflated by it. I realized that I'd really wanted him to be the burglar all along, and that I had wanted the young girl, who was in love with him, to win him over. But, of course, Cary Grant could never be the bad guy, and what female, young or old, could possibly win out over Grace Kelly. I understood then why Max would often leave. Although he loved the style and the manners, the witty dialogue and the glamorous locations of old movies, he could never take the Hollywood endings. He could never take the way everything was tidied up and sanitized. The way conventional morality always triumphed.

In *Marnie*, for example, the movie we saw that first afternoon, the main character's motivation is so completely explained that the ending is completely forgettable. Instead of just having her steal and connive because she's greedy, or because her equestrian hobby is too expensive, her kleptomania is all explained away in the last five minutes of the movie by a flashback reference to a childhood trauma. She had killed a man who was attacking her hooker mother—which is not to say that childhood trauma is an entirely implausible cause. After all, I've just finished saying how I stole as a sort of compensation for my own miserable childhood. Still, psychological explanations (especially when they come in the last five minutes) are sometimes just so disappointing. Especially when you consider that through most of *Marnie*, we are manipulated by Hitchcock into rooting for her. She is strong and capable and shrewd. She dyes her hair and reinvents her identity, embezzling from one bumbling employer and then moving on to the next. She's so classy and self-assured that you actually want her to succeed.

But of course she doesn't. Her behavior is shamed in the end and blamed on a psychological disorder, and it's all just so lame.

So, any time the ending of an otherwise great film threatened to get sappy, or happy, or just too tidy (as most of the old ones do), down the balcony stairs Max would go. In *Rope*, when the killers break down and confess their crime, Max walked out. In *Spellbound*, when Gregory Peck's craziness is pinned on childhood trauma (in a scene almost identical to *Marnie*'s), Max walked out. *Rebecca? Psycho? Dial "M" For Murder?* Out, out, out. Nor was his disillusion limited to Hitchcock—he did not stay to see the end of *Gilda*, *Mildred Pierce*, or *Suddenly Last Summer.* Crime in classic cinema rarely, if ever, goes unpunished or unexplained, so Max would walk out. A hollow protest against all the easy endings, the pathetic weakness of the criminals, the lovers hurled together by a contrived fate.

Or maybe, just maybe, it was fear that made him walk out. Fear that their weakness might be contagious, and with Max sentimentality was a weakness he could never afford to have. Then again, maybe I'm falling into my own trap here, trying to explain Max and his motivations with simple psychology. I suppose this is the point in my story where he would, once again, shake his head and walk out.

Chapter Ten

After our day of shoplifting, we didn't get back to the house until nearly seven-thirty, by which time Lana had already gone to the gathering. The house was empty and quiet, which was good, because it would have been difficult to explain where all our newly acquired clothes had come from. After the movie we had again hit the shops along Sixteenth Street, stealing shoes, an antique cigarette lighter, some cheap watches, acne medication, and anything else we could get our hands on, more for the practice and confidence building than because of want or need.

As we pulled into the driveway, Max commented on the fact that the gas gauge was near empty. Gas was something he did not want to risk stealing.

"We're going to have to get some cash somehow," he said. "I'll have to think up some way to get it from your mother. Try and be especially agreeable tonight," he said. "I do have a plan."

When Lana returned, she immediately questioned Max about the missing Jaguar and about my supposed orthodontist appointment. He told her about the Jaguar first, which was a good strategy because she was so relieved to find out that James had not taken the car and so happy that Max had found a way to fix the damage she'd done that she completely forgot about the phony appointment.

"So how was the gathering?" Max asked, quickly steering the subject in a different direction.

"Oh, all right," Lana replied.

"Just all right?" he asked. "Is that boredom I hear?"

Lana frowned.

"No, it was okay, really, I just wish some of those people would put a little more effort into their appearances. I mean, this woman next to me was clearly at least a size ten and she'd somehow squeezed herself into a size six dress. It was so tight she couldn't breathe and just sat there wheezing and whistling through her nose all night."

The irony of this struck me so hard I almost screamed. I thought to myself how my own ridiculous looking outfits that were several sizes too small had never bothered her. But I remembered what Max had said about being agreeable, and I said nothing.

"That doesn't sound very Christian of you," Max scolded.

"No, I know, but don't people usually dress up for church? I mean even Wayne, who's usually so neat, was a mess. He actually wore these bright plaid golf slacks under his pastor robe. Can you imagine? It's not like we couldn't all see them poking out the bottom. He looked like a clown."

I could sense Lana's disillusionment with the church; like most everything in her life, she had grown bored with it quickly. Max saw this, too, and carefully fueled the fire.

"Yes, it seems to me people should dress up for church," he said. "Or at least try to, since it is God's house and all. But didn't you say they meet in an old Safeway or something?"

"No," Lana chuckled, "it's a Kmart."

They both laughed heartily at this, Lana trying to stop herself.

"The place shouldn't matter," she said, adopting a serious tone, but her attempt at gravity was betrayed by her smile. "We've met some really good people there, haven't we, Dillon?"

I nodded, and tried to appear serious, but soon Max was imitating the woman's wheezing and her nasal whistle, and all three of us were laughing.

Later that night, after I'd been sent to bed, I again crept quietly to the stair rail and eavesdropped on the conversation between Max and Lana.

"It's not just the drinking that was the problem . . ."

There was a long pause as Max waited for her to elaborate.

"I mean, there's a reason I've been so stubborn about him going to church." Again she paused. "How do I say this? He's, well, he's not like the other boys," she whispered.

"What makes you say that?" Max asked.

"Oh, come on! Look at him. He's not the most masculine kid in the world, always skipping around humming Carpenters' songs, and, well, just other things."

I knew that she was thinking of the catalogue ads but was too ashamed to say.

"It must be hard for him without a dad," Max went on.

"Oh, I'm sure," Lana said. "And that's where Wayne comes in. He's been great. He knows all about, uh, Dillon, and thinks we better nip it in the bud before it gets out of hand."

Nip it in the bud. It was exactly what Wayne would have said. Exactly what he would have pulled out of his never-empty bag of clichés.

"He's really taken to the kid," Lana went on, "and I think Dillon's warming up to him too."

Guess again, I thought.

"Hmmm," said Max.

"What?" Lana asked.

"Oh, I just wonder why you think Wayne is such a good role

model. I mean, I was sure picking up some strange vibes from him the other night."

"From Wayne?" Lana cried. "Like what vibes?"

"Oh, I don't know, just the way he looked at me, I guess, and the way he held onto my hand when he shook it. Doesn't it seem strange to you? I mean, how old is he and he's still not married? Is that really the type of guy you want spending time with your son? They disappear all day long. Where do they go? What happens when you're away?"

There was a pause.

"No, no, you're barking up the wrong track," Lana chuckled. "Wayne's just geeky, a little bit nerdy, he's not *that* way. And anyway, Dillon will be off to camp in another week and then he'll be in a strong, moral environment with lots of other boys his own age."

"And you think that will be better?" Max asked his voice full of derision.

"Well, yes, of course I do."

"Uh huh."

"Wait a minute, what does that mean?" she asked.

"What?"

"That uh huh."

"Oh, come on, Lana. Do I have to spell it out? A bunkhouse full of hormonally charged boys, communal showers, lots of chances to be off in the woods alone. I wouldn't be surprised if the kid came back in worse shape than when you sent him away."

"It's Bible Camp!" she cried.

"Mmm, Biiiible Camp," Max sneered. "Full of lots of namby-pamby counselors who will be cookie-cutter versions of Wayne. You know how those preachers are. You read the papers. They're just waiting for some confused boy like Dillon to come along. Prison was full of 'em, I can tell you that, and the stories they told . . . It'd curl your hair!"

There was a longer pause this time.

"Why don't you let him stay?" Max said, "I'll put him to work on the house, toughen him up a bit, give him a good, solid role model to follow. Really, it's safer to leave him here. Not to mention less expensive." He paused. "Think about it. Will you promise me you'll think about it?"

I heard no response but assume she must have nodded because Max moved on to a different topic. As for me, I went back to my room, closed the door, and beat off, imagining myself as the center of attention at the marvelous camp he had described and feeling a bit sad that I might not get to go after all.

Later that night, I got up to go to the bathroom, and as I headed back to my room I could hear music playing, softly, like someone had left a radio on with the volume turned down low. I went to the top of the stairs and listened. It was coming from below. I crept down the stairs. It sounded like a guitar and someone singing or humming. I went around to the cellar stairs and saw a light from the crack under the door. I could smell cigarette smoke, so I knew Max must be awake. But was he alone? The question lingered in my mind. I tiptoed down the stairs until I was two feet away from the door, and then stopped to listen. I heard only Max's voice and the guitar, but he was singing in French so I couldn't understand any of the lyrics. The guitar playing stopped but the singing went on, low and gravelly. Then the handle turned and the door was pulled open.

"I thought I heard something," he said. I looked up, but I could not see his face since the light was behind him.

"What are you doing out there?"

"I didn't know you played the guitar," I said. "I heard the music, and . . . I just came to see what it was."

Looking behind him I could see that the cellar had been made much more inviting since that morning. Max had brought down a few table lamps and a chair from the living room. His guitar was propped up next to the chair and a large ashtray was on the floor along with several empty coffee cups. He had evidently been smoking a great deal because the air was thick with a blue fog, and I could feel it in my eyes and in my throat.

"Got kind of rusty in prison," he said, turning and picking up the guitar. "So it's taking me awhile to get it back. Close the door. Sit down; sit down."

I took the chair and Max crawled up on the wine rack, where he had his bedroll. He propped his head against the wall and strummed a few chords, trying to recall a certain melody. He found it, and started playing the chorus of the Carpenters' "Superstar." It took me a moment to recognize it, but once I did, I looked up at him and smiled. He smiled back, cigarette clenched between his teeth, and winked at me.

"Thought you'd like that one," he said, and then closed his eyes and went back to playing. When he'd finished, he fumbled through a few other Carpenters' songs, but "Superstar" was the only one he really knew, so he played it again, much better the second time. He sang along when he knew the words and hummed the parts that he didn't. I was touched, and just like the first time I'd heard their music, back in band class, I got goose bumps. He put the guitar aside and took a sip from one of the coffee cups.

"I think I may have a way to keep you out of camp," he said, eyeing me over the rim as he drank. I didn't let on that I'd eavesdropped on his conversation with Lana. "I put the idea in your mom's head, now we'll just sit back and see what she does with it. But it looks good, Dil. The odds are definitely in your favor."

I nodded my head and leaned forward on the chair.

"I think she may be getting tired of the church thing, too, but until we're certain you just play along, okay? Just go when she tells you and maybe be extra nice to Wayne, maybe ask if you could even spend the night there sometime."

My face registered my sour reaction to this proposal.

"Trust me," Max said. "The more enthusiastic you are about spending time with Wayne, the less likely you'll be going to camp."

"Okay," I said.

Max hopped off the rack and set his coffee cup down. He squatted down in front of me and put his hands on my knees.

"Listen," he said, looking me straight in the eye, his expression serious. "If I can work it so you'll stay here, do you promise to help me? To do whatever I might ask?"

"Of course," I said, and swallowed hard. There was nothing all that peculiar in his words or in the fact of his hands on my knees, and yet I found the situation strangely erotic. I tried to dismiss the feeling, to shut it out of my mind, but my body betrayed me, just as it had in the showers at school, and I felt the mast going up under my robe. I suddenly remembered that I was in the room where Meredith and Serge had passed eventful times with Max and that made it even worse.

Oblivious to my trouble, Max went on: "Life is like a seesaw sometimes, Dillon. If I do this favor for you, it's like I'm taking all the weight off your end and letting you go up, you see?"

"Yes," I said, my voice creaking.

"Eventually I'm going to ask you to do the same for me. That sounds fair, doesn't it?"

"What do you want me to do?" I asked. Max smiled.

"Nothing worse than what we did today. Don't worry. Nothing bad, really. I just need to get some money, you know, and with my record most of the traditional routes to success are closed, do you follow?" I nodded and shivered again.

"Come up here," he said, climbing up onto the wine rack. "Either you're cold or this is making you nervous. Come up here and let's read for a while. We'll forget about this and talk about it later. Do you like to read, Dil?" I nodded and creaked out another "yes." I was so flustered and confused. I repositioned my bathrobe so it concealed my erection and then climbed up on the rack and sat at the far end, near Max's feet. He was using the empty racks below us as a sort of storage unit for his things, and he reached down and grabbed one of the books he'd purchased earlier that day at Paris on the Platte.

Max read aloud to me that night, as he did nearly every night after that. He was a great reader, which is not something many people can do well. It requires intense concentration and a quick intellect because the reader must be able to anticipate who is speaking, what tone of voice they are using and at the same time must concentrate on his own comprehension of the text. Max was a pro.

The book he read from that night, and for the next several nights, was Balzac's *Père Goriot*. As with all the movies we saw together that summer, I have in years since revisited this book, always looking for answers, for some hidden key to what made Max tick. But during those summer evenings my understanding of the story was more impressionistic. It was difficult for me to follow, as it was a bit beyond my reading and vocabulary level, and because it dealt with foreign situations in a foreign land, almost two hundred years ago. And yet, the beauty of Balzac is that his books are accessible on many levels. They may be great art, but they are, first and foremost, great stories, full of carefully fleshed-out characters in dramatic, exciting situations.

In Balzac, characters who appear in one novel often reappear in another one, so reading his books is a lot like watching an episode of *Happy Days* and suddenly seeing Laverne and Shirley in the Cunninghams' living room. It is strange to see them there, but you're not really surprised by it.

As I said, the book Max read from that night was *Père Goriot*. It is the story of Eugene, a young man from the French provinces who has come to Paris to study law. He has grandiose ambitions to launch himself into high society, but he is poor, and his poverty forces him to live in a grimy rooming house with several shady characters. One of these is an old foolish man called Goriot.

Goriot has two beautiful daughters whose material happiness has been his life's only concern. Consequently they have grown into spoiled brats with expensive tastes. They return, several times throughout the novel, only to leech money from their poor father. He lives in rags so that they can have new party gowns.

Eugene witnesses all of this greed and sacrifice, and the story is really about his own struggle between the two. A classic literary boxing match between the forces of Good and Evil.

All that was interesting enough, but what really piqued Max's interest in this story and drove him to plow on through the rest of Balzac's novels, was the appearance of a character who boxes in Evil's corner. A character called Vautrin.

Vautrin, aka Jacques Collin, aka *Trompe la Morte*, is a notorious criminal, a master of disguises, a sharp, incisive wit, and, best of all, a homosexual. When we first came across him in the pages of *Père Goriot*, he has just befriended Eugene. He pulls the boy aside one night after dinner and gives him a long talk on how to succeed in Parisian social circles, by playing false and abandoning his principles. It is an interesting conversation, but what is really interesting is that during the course of his speech, Vautrin makes some subtle attempts to seduce Eugene.

I still remember Max pausing at one point and wrinkling his brow. He glanced at me over the book and saw the same question in my face.

"Are you getting what I'm getting?" he asked.

"I think so," I replied, but thought maybe it was just my own hypersensitivity to even a hint of anything gay.

Max read on, and there were more subtle hints about Vautrin's sexuality, which we were both, at first, reluctant to believe. After all, this was the nineteenth century we were reading about. Things like that were presumably not discussed, let alone written about. Max reread the parts again and the second time the hints were less subtle. Of course Vautrin's attempts at seduction, both physical and moral, are unsuccessful with Eugene (It was, after all, the nineteenth century). But with both Max and me they were a hit!

After that, Vautrin became our mythic hero, our mascot, our idol. And we became his disciples, spending many evenings that summer searching through volume after volume of Balzac, elated whenever he would reappear.

The reading became part of the nightly ritual, but it was not the only part. On the contrary, reading was just the preface to the events that would follow, but more about that later . . .

Chapter Eleven

The next morning, at Max's suggestion, I went to the church. I knew what he was implying when he said I should appear eager to spend time with Wayne, but in spite of the lusty picture Max had painted of Bible Camp, I thought that given the choice I would rather stay home for the summer.

I got up early and had breakfast with Lana before she went off to nursing school, all the while doing my annoying best to mince and flit around the kitchen, humming an endless stream of Carpenters' tunes. When I sat down to eat I made sure to cross my legs, which she was forever telling me not to do, and to comment on how nicely her nail polish matched her lipstick.

"I wish I could paint my nails," I said, taking another spoonful of cereal and turning my attention back to the issue of *Woman's Day* I was flipping through. She gave me a hard look, grumbled, and went back to her coffee.

When Wayne arrived I made sure to appear enthusiastic, running to the door to let him in and then giving him a great big hug.

"Well, good morning, Sport!" he said, somewhat surprised. "Missed you at the gathering last night."

"And I missed *you!*" I said, getting my windbreaker from the closet.

Wayne approached Lana and touched her on the shoulder. "And how's the prettiest little lady in the city this morning?"

"Fine," she said, flatly, and took another sip of her coffee. She turned to look at him and her dismay registered on her face. Wayne was dressed in khaki pants and a pink polo shirt with the collar flipped up. He had tucked the shirt in, and this only emphasized the tube-like shape of his body. On his feet he wore penny loafers with no socks. This outfit was nothing out of the ordinary for him, but I could see that in the light of her conversation with Max, Lana saw him differently now.

"Something wrong?" he asked.

"No. Just tired, that's all. What, uh, what will you two do today?"

"Well, most of the day we'll probably spend shopping," he said.

"Shopping . . . ?"

"Yes, I've got Mother in the car and I promised to take her shopping today. We've also got to stock up on some things for the church since so much was ruined in the storm. That's about it, really. We'll run some more errands and probably break for lunch at Furrs. Mother loves Furrs."

I knew then, perhaps even before she did, that our churchgoing days were numbered.

"I'll have him back about four. Then I'll have to take Mother home and get ready for the gathering. You'll both be there, of course."

"Mmmm," Lana said, nodding her head. "If I get out of class in time. Traffic's bad sometimes. You know how it is."

"Well, let me know. Dillon could certainly come to church with me and I could bring him home afterward," Wayne said.

"Or maybe I could stay," I blurted out, almost without thinking. "I mean, at Wayne's." They both looked at me. Wayne smiled; Lana did not.

"I'm sure Wayne is busy," she said. "He is the assistant pastor, after all, and he has a lot to do."

"Oh, poppycock! If Sport here wants to stay with me," he said, putting me in a headlock and rubbing my head with his fist, "he's welcome anytime."

"Just bring him home," Lana said. "I'll try and make it on time."

"Well, okay then. You all set, Sport?" I nodded, and we left.

Out in the Olds with Wayne and his mother, I reverted to my usual surly silence, but neither one of them noticed, each intent on getting to the mall and the subsequent lunch at Furrs.

All through the morning, as we wandered the depressing Cinderella City mall, I kept contrasting this trip with Wayne and his mother to the trip the day before with Max. It was like comparing dry toast to chocolate cake. The day with Max had been so fun and new and exciting, whereas this never-ending stroll through the Muzak-filled worlds of Sears and Wards and JCPenney's on a fruitless quest for a girdle was almost unbearable. I was so bored I decided to practice stealing, which was fairly easy because no one was really paying any attention to me.

Since I was confined to the women's department, the selection of items to take was rather limited, and most of the things I took were rather stupid—a pair of stockings, a cheap necklace, a scarf, sunglasses. I didn't really want any of them but I made a game out of it, eyeing something when we first walked in and then analyzing the best way to slip it into my pocket. I was successful six out of the seven times, but then, in Montgomery Ward, as I was sliding a pair lace panties, of all things, into my pocket, my luck ran out. A huge hand gripped my shoulder and I turned to see an enormous security guard.

An hour of trouble followed. The guard hauled me into a back room where I was photographed, and scolded, and shamed, and then scolded some more by the store manager, Wayne, and Wayne's mother. But the thing I remember most, the thing I was most afraid of, was not that I would be in trouble, not that this would go on my "permanent record," as they threatened, not even that I'd probably be beaten to a bloody pulp by Lana. No, what really frightened me was how Max would react. What would he say about it? Would he ever trust me again after I'd shown myself to be so inept? The thought of his disappointment brought tears to my eyes, and that was evidently what everyone had been waiting for, because as soon as I started crying, they all stopped scolding. All they had wanted was to see a little remorse on my part, and when I realized that I really played it up.

"I'm so, so sorry!" I bawled. "I don't know why I did it, I'm just stupid! I'm a stupid, awful boy! Oh, I wish I was dead!"

The room went silent except for the sound of my choking sobs.

"We'll keep him on file here," the store manager told Wayne. "I think he's been scared enough. He won't try it again."

Wayne nodded.

"But next time," the manager said, waving a finger at me, "we'll have to press charges."

"There won't be a next time," I wailed. "I promise! I'm so sorry!"

That night was tense. Max was out when we got home and I crept quietly up to my room. I still had a bottle of Sandeman's stashed in the closet and I went for it. I uncorked it and was about to take a drink when suddenly I decided maybe I'd better not. Wayne had gone to drop off his mother, but I knew he would return and I had to be sharp to try to figure out how to handle this. A drink would only make me slow and stupid and probably get me into more trouble, and I didn't want that. I replaced the cork and put the bottle back in the closet.

When Wayne returned, he let himself in and came up to my room. It was almost six o'clock and I wondered if he'd come to take me to the gathering.

"Dillon," he said, poking his head into my room. I was lying on my bed facing the wall. "You awake?"

"Yes," I said, my voice hoarse from crying. Wayne approached the bed. He sat down and rubbed me on the back.

"Why don't we pray?" he said. "God will always listen, and I think if you'd just open your heart and let Him in, He'd forgive you. He'd help you. All you have to do is ask, son. Shall we give it a try?"

His sincerity could be touching at times. I sat up and he took my hands in his. He closed his eyes, and in his booming, assistant pastor voice, he prayed. It went on for a very long time. I opened my eyes at one point and saw Lana standing in the doorway, her book bag on her shoulder, staring at us.

"What's going on?" she asked, looking to one, then the other, for some explanation. Wayne turned and gave her a grave look. He then turned back to me, shook both of my hands and said, "Amen."

"Why don't we go downstairs?" he said, rising from the bed and walking toward Lana. "I'll tell you all about it."

Before Wayne closed the door, she shot me a burning scowl.

I waited for a few minutes after they left and then opened my door a crack. I could hear them talking below, but I couldn't hear what they were saying. I went out once again and crept over next to the banister.

"You shouldn't smoke," he said. They were in the kitchen, right below me.

"Well, my kid shouldn't drink, or fucking shoplift! Or fucking be a fucking faggot! Stealing *women's panties!*" she shrieked.

There was silence after this. Wayne was unaccustomed to profanity and so far Lana had managed to hide that aspect of her vocabulary from him.

"You're angry," he said. "That's natural in this situ—"

"You're right I'm fucking angry! He's more fucking trouble than he's worth. God damnit!" This was followed by the sound of a cabinet door slamming shut.

"Listen," Wayne said, "he'll be going to camp next week. That'll do him wonders, you watch. Just wait and see. It's been a difficult time for both of you. You need a break. Why don't I have him stay with me for a while, until you cool off, or until he goes?"

From the sound of breaking glass that followed, that option clearly did not appeal to her.

"He's not going to fucking camp!" she screamed. "And he's not going to your house. And we're not fucking going to fucking church anymore because it doesn't fucking do any fucking good!"

I gathered that while she said this she was pushing Wayne out because when she'd done so I heard the front door slam. Then all was silent. The dead bolt clicked and I heard her set the chain. I got up off the floor. The doorbell rang, again and again, and I knew it was Wayne trying to get back in. He was pounding on the door with his fist. Lana's heels clicked across the floor and I saw her charging up the stairs. I turned and ran back to my room. I tried to shut the door, but she was already behind me and blocked it with her body.

I'll spare you the description of what followed because it wasn't pretty. In a way I was glad that she did some visual damage (there was a black eye, and bloody scratches on my neck, a gash on my forehead where the clock hit me), because it was the real guarantee that I wouldn't be going to camp or back to church for a while. I think she was afraid, too, about what I might do, because she was quite civil to me for weeks afterward. Needless to say, Wayne was not allowed back. He called and called all that evening, and Lana lied and lied. She said we had talked it all out and were just going to spend some family time at home. No camp, no gatherings, and no, please, don't come by.

As for Max, I didn't see him until the next morning when he once again entered my room, buzzing like a caffeinated bee.

"Well Dil, you did it!" he said, brightly. *"Fait accompli!"* Then he saw my face and his expression darkened.

"Maybe a little too *accompli*," he said with a sigh. He came over and sat next to me on the bed, assessing my face.

"I knew something was up when I came home and the chain was on the door. I had to climb in a window and then I found *ta mère* in the kitchen, just about to tip another bottle. I knew she'd done something bad but I didn't know she'd gone this far. Are you all right?" he asked. "Is what I see the worst of it?"

I nodded. Lana had focused her blows on my head. The rest of my body she had left alone.

"Good," Max said, "that's one good thing. But this isn't the first time it's happened, is it?"

I looked away, not wanting to answer. He came over and lifted up my chin, forcing me to look him in the eye.

"Is it?" he repeated. I shook my head. He moved away and began pacing the room, cigarette in one hand, coffee cup in the other.

"Why does she hate me?" I asked. There was no self-pity in my question, just an honest desire for an answer from one who had known her longer than I. He stopped his pacing and looked at me. He took a big drag on his cigarette and then exhaled noisily.

"Oh, it's *them*," he said.

Somehow I knew he meant my grandparents.

"It's not her; it's them. I know you can't see that, but it's true. They were worse than she'll ever be. Really fucked-up people. She just repeats what she saw, and what she got. I was lucky. I got out pretty young, and for a while before that I had her to protect me, but she wasn't so lucky. They did some damage. Much worse than this," he said, approaching and running a finger over my forehead. "Much worse. She doesn't know how to react. She gets her wires crossed and sometimes the spark causes an explosion."

This made little sense to me. I knew my grandparents were not nice, but to blame them for what Lana had done, for the way she was, I couldn't accept that. If it had been done to her why would she do it to me? I had no doubt she was a little crazy. I'd seen it in her eyes the night before, and many times before that. A look of rage that was almost always in excess of whatever had provoked it.

Max finished his cigarette and his mood brightened. He seemed to realize that pity and outrage would do no good, so he smiled.

"It's a drag," he said with a shrug, "but you're getting too big. She'll realize that. It won't go on forever, and in some ways this is actually quite good. Not the beating so much, but the effects of it," he said, again gently touching the bump on my head. "You really played your hand well! Just how well, you don't even know yet. Ouch! She really did a number on that eye! Of course you haven't iced it. Come, come, let's do it now."

He pulled me up, gently draped my robe over my shoulders, and I followed him down the stairs. We went into the kitchen and I sat down on one of the bar stools. Max brought me some ice wrapped in a towel and had me hold it on my swollen eye.

"There," he said. "The swelling's bad but this will make it go down."

He lit a cigarette and smiled at me.

"I'm not going to camp, am I?" I asked, fairly certain of his response.

"Oh no, you certainly made sure of that! In fact I feel like you deserve a round of applause for how well you managed, well, everything."

And he began counting my accomplishments on his fingers.

"You got yourself out of camp. You got rid of Wayne. You've pretty much scared your mother away so she'll leave us alone, and last but not least, you convinced her—and let me say that the irony of this is not lost on me—you convinced her that I am the only hope of salvaging your heterosexual boyhood. 'I'll leave him home with his butch, prison uncle . . .'" Max said, doing a high pitched imitation of Lana's voice. "'. . . to do construction on the house, that'll make a man out of him! That'll straighten him out!' Oh, what a hoot this all is!" And he fell back on the sofa, laughing and kicking his feet in the air.

"But you know what the best part is, Dil?" he said, sitting up again and peering at me over the overstuffed back.

I shook my head.

"She gave me some money! She gave me the money she was going to use to pay for camp so that I'll look after you. I'm the baby sitter! The lunatic has been given the key to the asylum! She even gave me a credit card to buy paint and supplies for the house, and a gas card for the car! And it's all thanks to you, Dil! I don't think Vautrin could have done it better himself. I can't tell you how proud I am." He gave me a kiss on each cheek and then went about making breakfast.

As I sat holding the ice on my eye I reflected on the situation. The night before, I'd gone to bed feeling afraid and ashamed, only to be awakened the next morning with praise and congratulations on a job well done. Granted, most of my success had been accidental, and I had no desire to again travel the road that had gotten me there, but I had succeeded. Max was proud of me and I basked in the glory of that all the rest of that day, running to the mirror several times to admire my black eye and the cuts on my face. To me they had become like medals, badges given for an operation successfully completed. And yet I knew that the only thing that gave them significance at all was that Max admired them, was proud of the lengths to which I'd gone to do what needed to be done, and to me that was better than any medal.

Chapter Twelve

The morning after my beating, after we had eaten breakfast, Max and I drove to Boulder. We were to meet Serge at his shop, load up some equipment, and then do my first "real" climb at Eldorado.

Eldorado Canyon is about three miles south of Boulder. It was once a somewhat fashionable resort, drawing visitors to the mineral-rich hot springs that bubble beneath the surface. Today the resort has essentially been abandoned—an old hotel is all that remains—but the natural beauty of the place is still there, and the steep sandstone walls of the canyon have become a big attraction to climbers. Such an attraction, in fact, that on summer weekends the walls are so crowded they look more like huge slabs of wood, crawling with colorful termites. For that reason it is best to go on a weekday, when the only people you'll run into are university students cutting class.

Serge's shop was on the east end of Pearl Street, about four blocks away from any other shops. It was an old, two-story building of rough gray stone with a storefront below and residential space above. Above the door was a large rectangular sign on which was printed "Rostand's Climbing Shop," and under that, a picture of

Serge's logo: a curly-horned sheep balancing on top of a pointed peak. The yard out front was overgrown, and the mailbox, the base of which was nearly hidden by weeds, tilted slightly forward and to the left.

Inside, the place looked like anything but a sporting goods store. In fact, it was so dark and dirty that it was more akin to the army surplus store Max and I had hit earlier that week. The big difference, however, was that the army surplus had been a random, chaotic mess, whereas Serge's shop, although dirty, was almost mathematically ordered. Behind the large oak-and-glass counter hung several of the brightly colored climbing ropes, and behind those, on a pegboard wall, were climbing tools he sold, some factory made, and some, more specialized pieces he had forged in his shop out back. All were meticulously arranged and sorted according to size, use, and strength.

Serge was behind the counter when we came in, busy looking over a topo map with two scruffy-looking students. He smiled and gave a wave when he saw us, but then he noticed my eye, and the gash on my head, and his smile disappeared. He quickly finished his business with the two, folded up the map, and when he had seen them out, came over to us.

"What happened!" he cried, kneeling in front of me. He took my head in both of his giant calloused hands and examined my face. I had not thought of how to explain it, so I said nothing. We both looked to Max, but his face was blank, and his eyes were hidden behind his sunglasses.

He shrugged and said: "The family curse."

Serge looked down at the floor. It was an awkward moment and I remember sensing something in the silence; something that was being communicated without words. When Serge spoke, it was to ask me if I was okay to climb.

"He's fine," Max said before I had a chance to answer. "Aren't you, Dil?"

Serge looked at my face again, and then, questioningly, at me.

"I'm okay," I said, with as much enthusiasm as I could summon. "Really. I want to climb."

"Look," Max said, his voice flat and weary, "we've got to get him on some real rock before he forgets everything he learned last week."

Serge was wary and kept looking at one, then the other of us. Then he shook his head and stood up, his knees cracking. "Maybe we try something easier today," he said, patting my shoulder. "A shorter climb, or maybe just some bouldering."

"No!" Max cried. "No. We need to do Bastille. He'll be fine! Let's just stick to the plan, okay."

We both stared at Max but said nothing. It was a strange outburst, but not out of sync with the surly mood he'd been in all morning. "He'll be fine," Max said. "Fine."

"Did you bring your shoes?" Serge asked me.

I nodded and pulled them out of my bag.

"Okay then," he said, putting an arm around my shoulder and guiding me over to the counter. "Okay then, let's get some gear together and we go."

Wordlessly we gathered up all of the things we needed and got into the cab of Serge's old red truck. As we drove toward Eldorado, Max's mood improved, and he and Serge got into a spirited conversation about past climbs and about the different places in the world Serge had been climbing in the two years Max had been in prison.

"I wish you could have gone with me the last trip, *petit.* You would have loved it," Serge said.

"Yeah, well," Max grumbled, "it's hard to climb out of a locked cell."

We drove on in silence for a while after that, but then Serge spoke up again.

"Why did you do it?" he asked. "I still don't know why."

"Why did I do what?" Max asked.

"You know what I mean," Serge said.

"Why did I steal? Sell drugs? Get caught? What?"

"No, you know what I mean," Serge repeated. "Why did only you take the blame? She was the boss. Everyone knew it. She was more guilty than you! But she stayed free and you went to jail. Why?"

"Ahhh, you mean why didn't I snitch on Doris?"

Serge looked confused.

"I don't know, what is . . . snitch?"

"A tattletale. A rat. A stool pigeon," Max said. Then he lowered his sunglasses and looked over at Serge. "A snitch is someone who talks when it's better to remain silent."

Serge said nothing. He returned his attention to the road and the muscles in his jaw contracted.

"You, of all people," Max said with a laugh, "should know that I do not talk."

Again, Serge was silent. He was looking straight down the road and I could tell he was angry.

"Why didn't I tell on Doris? Is that what you mean? Is that what you want to know?" Max said.

"Yes" Serge said, as calmly as he could. "That is what I want to know."

Max chuckled. He lit a cigarette.

"I don't really know why," he said, exhaling and then picking stray bits of tobacco from his tongue. "I don't know. Maybe I didn't tell because it didn't seem right. I don't know. Maybe there is some honor among thieves, as stupid as that sounds. I don't feel any affection for the woman. I know she's ruthless, and a bitch, and would never do the same for me. But I was caught, and I knew I was going to jail. I didn't see any use in pulling her down, too. Besides, this way she owes me. She owes me for my little favor, and she'll pay. Don't worry. She'll pay."

This did not put Serge's mind at ease. On the contrary, he became more agitated, and when that happened his accent became much more pronounced.

"What!" he cried. "What are you doing? What do you mean by

this, 'She'll pay'? You need to stay away from her and that trouble! She's dangerous, you know that. You need to stay away!"

Realizing he was yelling, Serge stopped himself and tried to regain his composure. He exhaled, ran his fingers through his hair and started again, this time in a softer tone.

"Look, you're smart," he said. "You could maybe go to school for something. Get a degree. Or I could give you work again. You were a great guide. The people loved you. I could have three climbing classes a day for you tomorrow, if you want. I could do it. Only say the word. You'd make lots doing that. Just don't mix with her again. Don't do it! No money is worth that. No money is worth all that time in prison."

Max laughed and shook his head, as if to say that Serge had it all wrong.

"Don't worry," he said. "I can handle Doris. I worked for her for three years, remember?"

"Just be careful," Serge said, and he reached over and ran his hand along Max's cheek. "Please."

When we got to the canyon, they were both much more at ease. We got out of the car, loaded ourselves with the equipment, and I prepared myself for a long hike. From the parking lot, we walked all of about seventy-five feet and then Serge and Max dropped their bags and looked up. I followed their gaze. Above us was nothing but a solid, almost vertical slab of rock, the top of which I could not see.

"This is it?" I asked.

"This is it!" Max said. "*La Bastille!* The Bastille Crack. Get your harness on; you'll go up after me."

"Yes, it's a good day. We're lucky today," Serge said, excitedly running the rope through his hands. "Usually there is a line for this route."

I looked at the wall before me. I could not even see anywhere to start!

"Are you sure I'm ready for this?" I asked, my palms growing sweaty.

"You'll do fine, Dil," Max said, smiling and nodding.

"You're a natural climber, just like your uncle," Serge said. "Just remember to lean back this time and to use the jams we talked about. Jams, and lateral moves, and you'll do fine. Climbing *la Bastille* is easy! Beautiful! You'll see."

When we had all the rope and protection together, they explained the route. It was to be a four-pitch climb. I would belay Max, and he would climb up several feet and place some "protection" (which is the name they used to describe all of the little metal clamps) in between the rocks. The rope would run through this protection, so that if one of us fell he would fall only until the protection stopped him and not all the way to the ground.

Since there were three of us, I would go in the middle. I was to follow Max's route with the rope threading through two carabiners attached to my harness. When I got to the protection, I would open one of the two carabiners, lift it over the protection, and then clip it back onto the rope. Then I'd repeat the move with the other carabiner. The idea being that I would never be free to fall, one of the pieces would always be attached to both my harness and the rope. It was a bit like having the eyes of two needles around my waist, one of which I needed to keep threaded the whole time.

When we were ready, Max approached the rock. He jumped up about a foot, grabbed a handhold, and wedged in one of his feet. He then made several spiderlike moves upward so I had to be quick about releasing more rope for him. He went on for about five minutes and then called down that he had anchored in and I could start.

"Okay, Dillon," Serge said. "Storm the Bastille!"

I stood staring dumbly at the rock. I could see nothing. I approached, tried to grab the handhold I'd seen Max use, and made a weak attempt to place my foot. Nothing. I looked back at Serge, who was clearly amused by my predicament, but offered no advice. I turned back to the rock. I saw one place to possibly put my hand, but it was at least a foot above my head. Seeing nothing else, I decided to go for it. I jumped up, pushed my hand into the crack, and pivoted it slightly, so that it locked in place. It worked! I was then suspended, rather painfully, by my wrist wedged in the stone, with my legs dangling below me. I managed to place the balls of my feet on the rock and take a few steps up until my chest was parallel with my wrist. I was barely breathing, and again I could feel the muscles in my calves spasming. I paused, and tried to gather confidence, tried to breathe normally and remembered to lean back.

"If it feels wrong, sometimes it's right," I mouthed. "If it feels wrong, sometimes it's right." I saw another hold up above, placed my free hand in it, and then released my wrist from the jam. Again, I found places to put my feet and again, I moved up.

I could hear Serge below, whispering encouragement, saying, "Go Dillon. Beautiful. That's it."

As I moved up, the crack in the rock became more evident. It was a fracture in the face of the stone, one side of which had been pushed slightly over the other. Once I realized how to climb it—using a sideways grasp with my hands and swinging laterally upwards—I moved quickly, stopping only when I arrived at a piece of protection. In a few minutes' time, I reached Max. He gave me a hand up and we both perched on a small ledge.

"Excellent, Dil! Excellent! I knew you'd do well." And he put an arm around me. He pulled me close and kissed the top of my head. I smiled and looked down at my bloody chalk-covered fingers. I felt like I'd just passed another round of some initiation, and my fingers were, like my black eye, the badges to prove it.

We belayed Serge up and he arrived a few minutes later, having stopped along the way to remove all the protection Max had placed. He handed the pieces back to Max, who reattached them to a strap on his harness and then began climbing up the second pitch.

"You watch your uncle," Serge said after Max had gone, "but don't be so crazy. He is sometimes not so safe, you know? Use your own judgment. Push yourself, but know your limit. You under-stand?"

"I think so."

"Good, you're doing very well; you have your own style. That's good."

The rest of the climb went smoothly, and I arrived at the top in about half an hour.

Reaching the top was an incredible experience. I looked down the three hundred feet I'd climbed and couldn't believe I'd actually done it! It gave me the same feeling of triumph and accomplish-ment I got from stealing: an adrenaline rush that made me feel alive and free and extremely capable. A feeling that somehow anything was possible.

Max set me up so I could belay Serge and then took a few steps back.

"I'm going to hike on up a little way," he said. "You'll be okay, right?"

I looked at him anxiously, but was so surprised I didn't know what to say. Nor could I really protest since Serge was on his way up and I had to pull in all the slack as he climbed. Max emptied out his backpack and put it over his shoulders.

"If I'm not back soon," he said, "don't wait around up here. I'll meet you at the bottom, okay?"

I nodded, started to protest, but before I could, he was gone. I kept my eyes on the rope, kept pulling it in, but my mind was off wondering what Max was up to.

When Serge reached the top, he immediately asked about Max and I told him just what Max had told me. He got angry. He said some words in French, spat, and then shook his head from side to side in disbelief. Wordlessly we reracked the protection and wound up the ropes.

Descending from the top of Bastille was much less interesting than going up, since there was no climbing or rappelling involved. Instead, we put on our packs and hiked down a long, winding trail. Serge could never stay angry for long, and before we were even a third of the way down the trail, he was whistling again.

As we walked, I decided to take the opportunity of being alone with Serge to grill him about Max.

"Did you meet Max through climbing?" I asked.

Serge was walking behind me and did not respond immediately. When he did, it was in an uncharacteristically quiet tone.

"No, I met him when I was a teacher. I was a teacher and he was my student."

"What did you teach?" I asked. I knew from Lana that Max had never been to college so thought they must have met at a climbing school.

"Gym," Serge said. "I was a gym teacher."

"Where?"

He did not respond. I thought maybe he hadn't heard me so I turned around to look at him. His head was hanging down.

"I taught at a school called Emerson. Max and his friend Jane. You have met her? They were both my students."

That was odd. I had heard the name Emerson, but I knew that it was a junior high school.

"Your uncle," Serge continued. "He was always in trouble, even back then, always sent to the principal and always having the detention after school."

"So that's where he met Jane?" I asked.

"Ah yes, she was a new student—very new. I think her family had just come from Vietnam maybe a month before she started. Her English wasn't very good and her clothes were different, and, well, you know how kids are, they pick on her. But your uncle Max, he wouldn't allow that! No, no! He was her protector. Like a big brother. Always getting in fights with the other kids over Jane. His eyes were more often black than normal then, you know what I mean?"

I laughed and ran my fingers over my own black eye, feeling even more proud of it.

"So I became a friend to both of them."

Once we reached the bottom of the trail, Serge directed me up the road a bit farther to where there were some large boulders. We set down our bags and the ropes, and for the next hour or so we practiced bouldering. Around noon, Max finally returned.

"Where did you run off?" Serge asked, eyeing him suspiciously.

"Oh, I just hiked up a ways," he said, climbing effortlessly up the boulder that I had been falling off for the past twenty minutes. "It's been so long since I've been free to roam outdoors," he said, his voice lighter than it had been all day. "I just couldn't pass it up."

I noticed that when he joined us he didn't take off the backpack he was wearing. He had emptied it at the top but from the way it hung on his back it was clear to me that it now contained something bulky and heavy.

We were all getting hungry, so we headed back to the truck and returned to Serge's house. We took a back stairway up from the shop, entered Serge's living room, and were greeted by a graying golden retriever, gently whining and wagging its tail.

"Stella!" Max cried, embracing the dog and pulling her down on the floor. She licked his face and whimpered. "I'm so glad you're still here," he said, "but look how old now!"

Serge beamed down at the two of them.

"She's missed you," he said, and then joined Max and Stella on the floor. "We've both missed Max, eh, Stella?"

Serge's place was comfortable, but it was clear that he lived alone and took little interest in his surroundings. The room we'd come into was large and sunny, and like the downstairs, terribly dusty. It appeared spacious, but that was probably because it was so sparsely furnished: an old sofa and a chair, a coffee table made out of bricks and a piece of lumber, and a TV.

Off of that room was the kitchen, which, it was clear, had last been remodeled sometime in the fifties. The handles and the pulls on all the cabinets were shaped like small silver boomerangs, a motif that was repeated in the pattern on the formica countertops and in the worn linoleum on the floor. There was a kitchen table and chairs of chrome and vinyl at which Max and I took a seat while Serge prepared us a lunch of truly ghastly bologna and ketchup sandwiches, most of which Max fed to Stella when Serge wasn't looking.

All through lunch we talked about the climb that day. Again and again they told me how well I'd done, and how proud of me they both were. It made me so happy I never wanted it to end, and especially not the way it did.

After we finished lunch, the conversation dropped off and we all got quiet. Max lit a cigarette, Serge poured himself another glass of whatever liquor he was drinking, and I sat on the floor in the sun, petting the dog.

"Dillon," Max said, "why don't you take Stella for a walk."

I was content where I was, and was just about to say so when Serge added: "Yes. There's a place up the street for you to get ice cream, would you like that? Here, I'll get you some money." And before I could say anything Serge returned with the dog's leash and a five dollar bill.

I did not go get ice cream. It seemed like such a childish thing to do. Instead, I walked the dog around the block, getting angrier and angrier. I wasn't stupid. I knew why I'd been pushed out and it bothered me. I was being treated like the annoying little sidekick, the pesky kid brother, the third wheel, and that was quite an abrupt switch from the camaraderie I'd felt all morning. I knew what was going to happen between them, and I knew that it was natural that I would be excluded from it but I still felt jealous and angry and couldn't quite figure out why. Whatever was going to happen during my absence was mysterious to me, and, instinctively, I wanted to find out about it. Again, I wanted to know what it was like: what it was like to lust after someone, the way that Serge lusted after Max, and what it felt like to have someone want you that much. I wondered who that someone else would be for me. Who that shadowy first person would be, and where he was. I remembered the way Max had described it in the coffee shop. The clinical mechanics of sex had been clear enough and of course I wanted to do them, but what I was really curious about was the more abstract part. The part Max had described as being like food, or an empty canvas. I wanted to know what people said during sex, how their faces looked, and what they felt. It was like a carnival ride I'd never be old enough or tall enough to ride so I just stood at the gate stamping my feet in frustration.

About forty-five minutes later, sensing movement in the kitchen, I crossed the street and went back inside. I tromped slowly and noisily up the back stairs to give them ample warning, and then emerged into the apartment. Except for the fact that Serge had bed-head, one would have thought that they had not moved from the kitchen table. Max sat smoking and Serge sat drinking, just as before, both talking and laughing.

Max smiled when he saw me. Then he looked down at his watch.

"We should go," he said, and got up and retrieved the backpack from the couch. "We can still make the four o'clock movie if we hurry."

We all walked downstairs together, said our good-byes to Serge and Stella on the street, and then Max and I drove away. We had gone about a block when Max realized he'd forgotten his cigarettes. He went up to the next block and made a U-turn.

"I'll be right back," he said. He shifted into park, left the car idling, and ran back inside.

The backpack was right next to me. Initially I only meant to look inside to see if maybe he had left his cigarettes in there, but then I remembered his disappearance up the hill and how the backpack was suddenly full when he returned. I probably shouldn't have, but I opened it and looked inside. It was full of money. Stacks and stacks of hundred-dollar bills, some of which appeared to have gotten wet at some point because they were stained and muddy. As soon as I realized what it was, I quickly zipped up the bag. I knew this must be the money he had mentioned to Jane and to Serge; the money he had stolen from Doris. I looked down at the bag and felt uneasy, like it wasn't safe to be near it. A moment later Max came bounding out to the car, a new carton of *Gitanes* in hand, and we drove back to Denver. We went straight to the Ogden, as planned, and saw another Hitchcock film. *Strangers on a Train.* I remember that Max stayed through to the end this time. The ending is sappy and neatly sewn up, and one he certainly should have walked out on in principle, but the out-of-control-carousel-climax that gets you there kept us both rooted to our seats until the credits started rolling. We were still talking about it as we walked outside and around the block to the car. We got in and Max was about to turn the key when there was a knock at the window. We looked over and saw the gun, pointed at Max's head. He rolled down the window and a man bent down and looked in. It was the same gap-toothed man that had been with Doris the morning of Max's arrival.

"You're to come with me," he said, his voice low and level. "Get out of the car and come with me."

Max had set the backpack on the seat between us, and as he got out I carefully pulled it on to the floor and covered it with my sweater.

"You too," he said, waving the pistol at me. "Out of the car"

I did as he said and walked over to where they were standing. He waved the gun, motioning us over to a van parked on the other side of the street. He opened the back doors and motioned for us to get in. Once inside, he slammed the doors and made sure they were locked.

It was a cargo van so there were no windows or seats in the back, just metal walls and a rubber mat on the floor. We were separated from the cab by a perforated metal screen, through which I saw the unmistakable outline of Doris's large, blond hairdo. She did not look back when we got in but continued smoking and examining her long fingernails. The man got in the driver's seat and we drove away.

"Why hello, Doris," Max said, moving up close to the screen. "I was wondering when you'd call again."

"Maxxx," she said, her voice was high and nasal. "How've you been?"

"Not bad, baby, not bad. Two years in the tank does wonders for your skin. No sun, damp climate, it's great. Maybe you should try it sometime. Does wonders for your soul, too. Provided you've got one"

"Uh huh. Look," Doris said, her voice impatient, "you know what this is about. Let's resolve it and we can both go on with our lives and never see each other again, how's that sound?"

"Okay, I guess."

There was silence as she waited for him to say more. He did not.

"Honey," she said, "I'll be blunt. Doris wants her drugs or her money. I've waited two years. That's a lot of interest I could have been making. Don't make me wait any longer. If you've spent some of it, that's okay. Understandable. Everybody has expenses, but the bulk of it I just can't let get away, now can I?"

"You can and you will," Max said. "Write it off, Doris. You're not getting the money." His voice was hard and angry, and I was alarmed by how much it resembled Lana's. "I took the rap for you, remember? Remember that day in court when I just couldn't re-member anything? Well, that case of amnesia cost me a fuck of a lot, and now it's gonna cost you! Don't think of it as a payoff, think of it as still having me on your payroll for the past two years."

That said, Max leaned his back against the side of the van and crossed his arms over his chest.

"Look, I appreciate what you've done," Doris said, her voice that of a parent dealing a petulant child, "but no one's time is worth that much! We can definitely come to some compromise, but you're not keeping the bulk of it. Un-huh, sweetie. Doris needs her money back."

There was a long silence. We could not have gone out of the city but wherever we were, there were few streetlights and almost no traffic. I looked at Max but he was up next to the screen, his face close to Doris's.

"I'll ask once more," she said, her voice full of warning, but at the same time almost weary. "Are you going to give it back?"

"No, I'm not," Max replied, shaking his head.

Doris touched the driver's arm and then pointed to the right. He slowed the van, made a turn, and then drove on. A moment later he stopped and turned off the ignition and lights. He got out and shut his door. I heard his footsteps as he walked around and opened the back doors. He crawled in and tried to grab Max. There was a brief scuffle, but the man got hold of Max's ankles and dragged him out. Then he shut the door and locked it again. The sounds of the beating followed. I could tell that the man had Max up against the side of the van and was punching him. From the sound of it, he started with his face and then moved down to his stomach, each punch punctuated by the sound of Max's body slamming into the side of the van.

"Still drinkin', sweetie?" Doris asked me, and then gave a little chuckle. I didn't answer. I could hear that Max was on the ground and that the man was kicking him.

"You ever watch *Sesame Street?*" Doris asked. Again I did not answer.

"Used to watch it with my kids when they were growin' up. You can learn a lot from *Sesame Street.*"

She paused and I could hear the sound of her gum popping in her mouth.

"Cooperation," she said. "They're always goin' on and on about cooperation. Mister Hooper, Maria, Gordon, and Susan. Cooperation, cooperation, cooperation. Makes sense."

Again, she paused and popped her gum. Max's body hit the van so hard it shook.

"Now myself," Doris went on, "I don't like to get rough. Most people don't. This whole scene could have been avoided with a little cooperation from your uncle out there."

The doors opened suddenly and Max was hurled back in. He was covered in dirt and his face was a bloody mess. He lay down on his back, held his stomach, and tried to catch his breath. I crawled over to see if I could help him, but he held up a hand and shook his head. The man got back in the cab, started the van, and resumed driving.

"Feel like talkin' yet, Max?" Doris asked, after we'd driven a way. She lowered the sun visor and checked her makeup in the vanity mirror. Slowly, meticulously, she applied her lipstick. When she was satisfied, she looked back at Max.

"Ooooh, ouch!" she said, and then blew a bubble with her gum. "Looks like that might leave a mark."

We turned the corner and Max rolled into me. I grabbed him and tried to prop him up. His face was in bad shape and his breathing sounded soggy. His nose, which had first been broken years before, had been broken again.

"Any time you're ready," Doris said, flipping the mirror back up. "Any time."

"Fuck you, Doris!" Max spat, and then fell back, groaning from the effort. I tried to smooth his hair out of his face and clear away some of the blood, but there was nothing to mop it up with. I had left my sweater in the car and had on only a short-sleeve shirt. It was hot in the back of the van and I was sweating, but I was so afraid that my whole body was shaking. I looked to Max for some direction, but he had his eyes closed.

We drove around for about ten more minutes. We seemed to be going in a circle and eventually I saw enough out the windshield to realize that we were driving around City Park. This made sense because it was nearly always deserted, especially at night, and was never well lit.

"Max," Doris said, "don't be silly. Just give me back the money and we'll send you on your way."

"No!" he growled, and then turned to the side coughing. The

van halted abruptly and again the driver got out. Again, I heard his steps coming around to open the doors, and again he reached in and grabbed Max by the ankles. I held him under the arms and tried to keep him from being pulled out, but the man was strong and pulled us both out and onto the pavement. I skidded on my shoulder, tearing the sleeve off my shirt, and it took me a moment to realize what had happened. The night air felt cool after being in the stuffy van. I looked around, dazed. We were definitely in City Park and, from the smell of it, were on the north side by the zoo. That was all I had time to see before the man scooped me up and threw me back into the van, slamming the doors behind me. The sounds of beating resumed, although slower this time. He was having to pick Max up after each punch. I started crying. I panicked. I had to do something and I think if the same thing happened today I would do just what I did. I crept up next to the screen and looked at Doris. She was smoking now, calmly, seemingly oblivious to the sounds outside.

"Make him stop!" I cried. She ignored me and looked out the side window.

"Please! I'll get you the money," I whispered. "I know where it is."

She flipped down the visor and glared back at me in the mirror.

"Don't play games with me," she said, shaking her head. "I don't like to play games."

"I'm not," I sobbed. "I know where it is."

"Where?"

I hesitated. I knew Max would kill me, but at the time I thought that preferable to listening to him get killed.

"*Where?*" she yelled and turned around. I'm sure she saw the fear in my face. "He'll kill him out there if you don't tell me!"

I had no reason not to believe her.

"Take me back to the car," I sobbed. "Make him stop and take me back to the car. Let me out and keep Max here. I'll get the money, I promise."

"You *better* not be playing with me." she said, pointing the long nail of her index finger at me. "No fucking games, hear me!"

"Yes, no games, I promise. I'll get it, just don't let Max know."

She stared at me for a good ten seconds, trying to read my face, while outside the noise of the beating continued.

"You're a good kid," she said. "Smart."

She opened her door, stood up on the runner, and pounded on the roof of the van with her fist.

"Okay, that's enough," she said. "Put him back."

The doors opened and Max's limp body was tossed in. He looked worse and was barely conscious, mumbling things I couldn't understand and spitting out teeth. I held on to him, my body still shaking, as the driver got back in and drove us back to the Ogden. The car was parked behind the theater on a residential sidestreet. They parked the van a few spaces behind it and the man came around and opened the door. I hopped out. Max made a weak protest, but I assured him it was okay and that I'd be right back. Doris was waiting outside. The man, who had me by the arm, led me to her. She had her purse on her shoulder and I saw that it was shielding the small pistol she held in her hand.

"It's all right," she said to the man. "Get back in. I've got him."

He released my arm and Doris motioned me to the car. I opened the passenger door, reached down and got the bag from under my sweater.

"Lemme see," she said, waving the gun. I opened it. She peered inside and then snatched it away. She motioned for the van to pull up. The man drove alongside the car and got out. He came around back, opened the van doors, and then opened the back door of the car. Once again, he pulled Max out, more gently this time, and set him on the backseat. Then he closed the car door, closed the van doors, and returned to his seat behind the wheel. Doris climbed in the passenger side of the van. She was about to shut the door but then paused and beckoned me over. I approached, trembling. She reached in the bag and took out one of the stacks of money.

"I'm not going soft," she said, holding it out to me, "but you've been good and I don't think that oughta go without something. Here. Take it." I did so and she quickly shut her door and they drove off.

I stood there, holding the money and shaking, staring after them as they drove down the street and turned the corner onto Colfax. I went back to the car, not knowing what to do. Max was sitting up in the back, looking like some horror film monster, blinking his eyes, and trying to orient himself.

"You okay?" I asked. He looked over and it seemed to take him a minute to recognize me.

"Can you . . . drive?" he asked, and then laboriously reached in his pocket for the keys. I had never driven before, other than sitting on James's lap and steering, but I nodded, accepted the keys, and got in the driver's seat.

Given my mental state and my lack of ability, it was not a smooth ride. It took me a good five minutes to extricate us from the parking space we were wedged into and it was not without damage to the vehicles in front and in back of us. Once out, we had several jerky moments as I experimented with the gas and brake pedals, while Max lolled and moaned on the backseat. The steering wheel was much more responsive than I anticipated and the first turn onto Colfax took us up on the sidewalk and nearly into the lobby of the Ogden. Somehow, I got us straightened out, and in about fifteen minutes we had made it down Broadway to the on-ramp for the highway, at which point Max said he would take over. He mopped away the blood on his face with my cotton sweater and then managed to get us home, one hand on the wheel and the other clutching his stomach. I was nervous enough about our safety as we drove, but added to this was my dread of what Max would say once he realized I'd given up the money.

When we got home it was about ten o'clock. Lana's bedroom light was on. I knew there was probably no way we could avoid her seeing Max, and I was right. As soon as we entered the front door, she appeared at the top of the stairs.

"What happened!" she cried, and ran down to us, getting under one of Max's shoulders to support him.

"I had a little . . . climbing accident," Max said. "It's nothing."

We got him to the bathroom and then Lana took over. She pushed me outside, poking her head out from time to time with impatient commands for bandages, or antiseptic, or more towels, clearly relishing the chance to actually put into practice some of what she'd learned at nursing school. I brought everything she asked for, but for the second time that day I was nearly overwhelmed by feelings of jealousy and anger. I was the one who had saved Max! I had stopped the beating! I had gotten him home! Now Florence Nightingale was moving in to take all the credit! But worse than that I was angry that she had not even asked if I was okay. I was covered in blood, my own or Max's she could not have known, and yet she immediately rushed to comfort him, excluding me from any part of it, even going so far as to lock the bathroom door after I'd given her what she'd asked for!

I felt hot tears rolling down my cheeks and had to fight the urge to beat the door with my fists. I had been terrified that night, more scared than I think I'd ever been before, or have ever been since, but there was to be no comfort for me. I paced around. I tried to get control of myself, tried to remember what Max had told me about Lana growing up, about her having damage inside, but it was not much help. It did not explain why she doted on him and hated me. I thought she must really hate me to exclude me from the one small room of the house that had any comfort in it! I leaned my back against the wall and slid down to the floor, staring at the bathroom door. Lana's commands for more supplies had ceased and I knew they would probably emerge soon.

I didn't want her to see me crying, so I got up again and went upstairs to another bathroom. I took off my clothes, washed the blood off of myself, and then went to my own room and closed the door. I got the half-empty Sandeman's bottle from the closet, took several large swigs, and sat down on the edge of the bed. I stared at the wall, nervously picking at the label, waiting for the alcohol to take effect. I wanted the night to end, but I was dreading the next day, when I would have to tell Max that the money was gone. I drank more. I drank until the bottle was empty and I fell asleep.

The next morning it was Lana who woke me up. "I'm off to school," she said, poking her head into my room. "Max is still in pretty bad shape so I'll need you to take care of him, all right?"

I could tell Lana was nervous talking to me about injuries, having recently made my own face such a mess, and was eager to get away.

"Sure," I said, sitting up and hoping I'd remembered to roll the bottle under the bed. "I'll take care of him."

"Okay then," she said, backing out of the room, "I'll see you tonight."

After she'd closed the door, I lay back down and stared at the ceiling. I did not think any more about Lana. She was, after all, just being herself. No, my thoughts were on the missing money and what I would tell Max. I knew there had been no real choice. Doris would have killed him, and probably me, too—but that money was all Max had. It had been the foundation for all his future plans and in an instant it was gone. I had given it away. Of course he didn't know that. He didn't even know that I knew there had been money in the bag. I was off the hook, so to speak, but that didn't make me feel any better. I got up and went down to the cellar. Max wasn't there. I went back upstairs, thinking that maybe Lana had put him in one of the bedrooms, but he was not there either. I stood on the landing, trying to think where he could be when I heard his voice coming from the living room.

"Dil?" he called weakly. "That you?"

I went back downstairs and there he was, on the couch. He was propped up and he looked bad. Lana had wound an excessive amount of bandages around his head, making him look almost car-toonish. His face was bruised and swollen and he, too, had a black eye.

"Dil, come quick!" he said, and his head bobbed, like it was too heavy to hold up. "Lana gave me some pills . . . I didn't know it till after . . . Quick tell me," he said, fighting to keep his eyes open, "did Doris get it? Did she get the bag?"

I looked down, ashamed, and nodded.

"Shit," he sighed, and his voice was sad, almost defeated. "It had money in it. All that . . . money . . . gone." And he fell back and closed his eyes.

Lana had given him Rohypnol, the ridiculously powerful sleep-ing aid that James had prescribed for her, known today as "the Date Rape Drug." Even if she had given him just one, which wasn't likely given his condition, I knew that he would be out for several hours.

I looked down at him sleeping and realized I'd been right: he thought I didn't know anything about the money. He thought I'd just innocently given up the backpack. I wouldn't have to explain it at all. I would be lying, but it would not be such a bad lie; and being gay, I was naturally used to lying.

Lying, prevaricating, hiding the truth, whatever you want to call it, gay people do it better than any other segment of society, ex-cluding politicians, of course. It is a Darwinian survival mechanism designed to protect us from persecution. The need to lie becomes obvious at a very early age. From the moment we realize that we are attracted to members of our own sex, and how reviled that at-traction is, the lying starts. From the moment we hear our first snide queer joke, or a slur against fags or dykes, the lying starts. We realize then that we are, without choosing to be, in a society that is hostile to our very existence. We learn to lie, are encouraged to conceal our identities and deny our feelings. Lying is sanctioned. Expected almost.

And for me, lying was *very* easy. I lied at home; I lied at school; and I lied at church. It was what everybody wanted and what I had to do to protect myself. And once I had done that, once I was false on such a grand scale, the smaller lies seemed trivial by comparison. They came easily, naturally. What's more, I became an expert at hiding the evidence. No twitches or stutters to give me away. For years I had practiced making my stone face, and rarely, if ever, could anyone make it crack.

It would have been so easy to lie to Max about the money. It was a lie of omission, really. The easiest kind. And yet, for some reason, as I sat there watching him sleep, I knew I wouldn't. Not because the truth would hurt him less, because it certainly wouldn't do that. The money was gone either way, if I had given it away or if it had been taken without me knowing about it. No, I decided to tell the truth because I respected him. He was the only person who had shown any interest in me since, well, since Mr. Sullivan had given me the Carpenters' album back in band class.

Later that afternoon, when the drugs wore off and Max began to wake up, I brewed him a cup of strong, hot coffee and I told him the truth. I told him I had looked in the bag when he ran back into Serge's house and had seen the money; that I had told Doris where it was when he was outside being pummeled, and had then led her back and given it to her.

If he was mad he didn't show it, but I could tell he was sad, and that made me sad. He retreated back down to the basement, like a turtle returning to its shell, and sulked. All his dreams of escape to *La Belle France* had disappeared with the backpack, and he spent the subsequent days idly thumbing through back issues of *National Geographic*, sighing over the glossy, aerial shots of Paris and Marseilles and Nice. He played his guitar and sang, but only sad, slow songs, in French, of course, and wondered aloud if he was ever going to get out of the suburban hell he'd fallen into.

Since we couldn't go to the movies and since it was hard for Max to read aloud with his broken nose, I took over the nightly reading of Balzac. I thought for sure this would cheer him up, but I was wrong. My reading was rough and stilted, and when we finished *Père Goriot*, it was only to discover that Vautrin gets captured and sent back to jail.

During those days in the basement, I'll admit that in a perverse way I was glad the money was gone. Glad, because I saw how close Max had come to leaving and I realized how much I would have missed him if he'd gone. Still, I hated to see him sad, so I kept looking for anything that would pull him out of his funk. At the end of the week, when something did happen to lift his spirits, I was genuinely happy and relieved.

The phone rang one morning at about eleven and the man on the other end asked to speak to Mr. Sawyer.

"He's, uh, just stepped out. Can I take a message?"

This was the standard response I had been ordered to give by Lana, who was still hoping to find out more information before the divorce.

"Yeah," the man replied. "This is Steve, over at McConnel Imports, I was just calling to let him know we've got his Jaguar finished up and he can come pick it up anytime. We're open till seven."

"I'll be sure and tell him," I said. "Thanks."

It turned out that this was just the kick that Max needed. As soon as I told him, he smiled and there was a sparkle in his eye. He emerged from the cellar, removed the elaborate bandage, and took a shower. Half an hour later we were out the door.

Max seemed to want a new image to go with the car so before we picked it up we took the thousand dollars from Doris and spent most of it on ourselves. We went to a barber and both got very short haircuts. From there, we went to a department store and actually *bought* some clothes and, more important, some sunglasses to conceal our black eyes. After that, we finally drove to the body shop, where they drove the gleaming car out of the garage and parked it at an angle in front of us. It looked more sleek, and shiny, and powerful than ever. Without a moment's hesitation, Max forged the necessary paperwork, and when he had finished, the man gave him the keys. Five minutes later we were gunning down the freeway toward downtown.

Chapter Thirteen

When Sunday evening arrived, Max and I drove to the restaurant owned by Jane's father. Denver was, and still is to a certain extent, a segregated city, with each ethnic group occupying its own section of turf and not mixing much with the others. As we drove north on Federal Boulevard that evening, through several different neighborhoods, I remember being amazed as the signs on all the businesses changed from English, to Spanish, to Chinese, and eventually, to the odd Roman letters used by the Vietnamese.

The Vietnamese section was poor, a fact made obvious by the ubiquitous graffiti and the badly maintained road, and Nguyen's restaurant was located in the center of the squalor. It was housed in a building that had clearly once been something else: a Tastee Freeze or a Kentucky Fried Chicken perhaps, with a peaked roof of wooden shingles, long ago painted red. The paint was peeling, and the brick facade below had been repeatedly patched with a brick-colored paint, to hide the graffiti. From the outside, it looked dismal, but the parking lot was, nevertheless, full of rather expensive cars, alongside which the Jaguar fit quite nicely.

Inside, the restaurant was dark, fragrant, and noisy. Next to the hostess station, there was a large fish tank, in which two enormous eels circled slowly. Through this I saw the spacious dining room crammed with as many people as it could hold. I thought it a good omen that as we waited, we were serenaded by a nasally Vietnamese version of "Close to You" being piped in through a hidden sound system.

You made it!" a voice called out, and I looked up expecting to be greeted by the enchanting, elegant Jane I had seen on the two previous occasions. What I saw instead was a harried girl in a black polyester waiter's pantsuit, her hair spilling out of the weak bun she had twisted it into. On one arm she carried an impossible amount of dishes, while in the other she held menus and an order book.

She paused when she saw our battered faces.

"What happened?" she cried.

"Car accident," we both replied, having agreed that we would adopt that as the party line to explain our injuries. She gave us a dubious look. Max shrugged.

"Well, come on," she said, motioning us to come with her. "We'll talk about it later. There's a place for you over by the kitchen."

We followed as she wove through the tightly spaced tables to a small table near the back of the restaurant. We sat down and Jane disappeared through the kitchen door. When she emerged, both arms were loaded with steaming plates of food that she quickly delivered to a table by the aquarium. She then took another table's order, refilled some water glasses, and wove her way back toward us.

"It's busy tonight, but believe it or not the whole place will be deserted in an hour. Stick around."

She kissed us both on the head, gave a concerned look at the gash on my forehead, and then disappeared again through the kitchen door. At various times over the next hour she brought several plates of food to our table: softshell crabs that had been dipped in a spicy batter and fried; tightly wrapped spring rolls stuffed with white noodles, shrimp, and basil; steaming bowls of peppery soup with floating tentacles of octopus and squid; and finally, a strawberry chicken dish unlike anything I had ever tasted.

Jane had been right about the crowd, and over the next hour we watched it thin to no more than a few groups of people spaced far apart. By nine-thirty, the place was nearly empty, save for the waiters clearing and cleaning and chattering away. Jane approached, carrying a tray with three Vietnamese coffees. She set them on our table, pulled up a chair, and collapsed into it.

"God, what a night!" she sighed. We thanked her for the food.

"I wanted to bring you steaks for those eyes!" she said, sitting up and leaning forward to get a closer look. "What *really* happened?"

I looked over at Max.

"We have no comment at this time," he said, and lifted his sunglasses to reveal his own shiner.

"You better tell me," she said, "or I'm going to charge you for all that food."

"Doris happened," Max sighed. Jane shook her head and then wagged a scolding finger at Max.

"I warned you not to mess with her."

Just then the kitchen door swung open and a short, squat, powerfully built Asian man emerged. He was dressed in badly stained chef's pants, and a blue and orange Broncos T-shirt. On his enormous round head he wore an absurdly small triangular paper hat. He saw Max and his face broke into a grin.

"Maxey!" he cried, extending one chubby hand to Max and giving him a hearty pat on the back with the other. "She tell me you here," he said, gesturing at Jane. "So I make special food, just for you!"

"It was great, Jimmy, best food I've had in a long time!"

Jimmy pulled up another chair, set it down with the back facing us, and straddled it.

"You been to France, she tell me . . ."

Max looked questioningly across the table at Jane. She grinned and nodded.

"Uh, yes," Max replied. "I, uh, just got back last week."

"Food pretty good there?"

"Doesn't even come close to yours, Jimmy."

Jimmy smiled and turned to me. "He a smooth talker. How you say, bullshitter! Professional bullshitter, that one!"

I laughed nervously.

"You look like Vietnamese," he said, pointing at my swollen eye. "You . . . boxer?"

I blushed and shook my head. I made a mental note that the next thing I stole would be an eye patch.

"Oh, he shy, that one," Jimmy said, and extended his hand to me. "Jimmy my name."

I shook his hand and introduced myself.

"He's Max's nephew," Jane said.

"I thought he look too young to be the boyfriend!" Jimmy said, laughing heartily. "You have little boyfriend in France?" Jimmy asked. Max laughed.

"No, still single."

"Then why you not marry her?" he asked, gesturing at Jane. She rolled her eyes.

"She only want rich man," Jimmy continued. "She go out with old man, more older than me." He scrunched his face into a sour expression and thumped his chest. "More older than her own father. You believe that? I don't like it," he said, folding his arms across his chest and shaking his head.

"Dad—" Jane started to protest.

"She want her own work, her own business," he continued, ignoring her, looking only at Max and me. "'That okay,' I say, 'Don't have to work in restaurant all the time, but have to work. Have to work hard!' She work hard, but she work harder to find more old husband with big money! That wrong."

"Daddy, stop," Jane pleaded, but he did not.

"I wish she the faggot, like you." he said, giving Max another slap on the back. "Much, much easier! I rather have daughter with wife than daughter with grandfather!"

Mercifully for Jane, there was at this point the sound of breaking dishes in the kitchen followed by several loud exchanges of Vietnamese invective. Jimmy grumbled, excused himself, and returned to the kitchen to see what it was all about.

"He's going to drive me to drink!" Jane said, pulling at her hair with both hands. "Thank God he didn't get started on grandchildren. There's no stopping him then."

"So?" Max asked. Jane looked confused.

"So . . . What?" she asked.

"So how did it go with Percy's mother?"

To this Jane did not respond. Instead, she pounded the table repeatedly with her forehead.

"That bad, eh?"

"Oh it couldn't have been any worse," she mumbled. She sat up, removed the small stick from her hair, and let her black mane fall around her shoulders, which made her look very small and tired.

"Do tell," Max said, leaning forward and stirring the layer of black coffee into the layer of condensed milk beneath it. She looked at both of us and rolled her eyes again. She stirred her own coffee, poured it into the glass of ice, and took a drink before starting. She began slowly, almost reluctantly, to recount her tale, but as she went on she became more and more animated.

"Well," she said, "he picked me up, you saw that, right?"

We nodded.

"I got in the car and he assessed me. He approved of my outfit and my hair, so we drove straight over to his mother's house."

"Where is it?" Max asked.

"Oh, it's one of those big stucco houses over by the Country Club, you know, right off of Speer?"

"Big?"

"Enormous! Anyway, I was nervous enough, but as we're walking up to the front door Percy tells me that he didn't tell his mother I was Asian. Odd, I think, so I ask him why not. 'Well,' he tells me (and here Jane began to mimic Percy's deep, elderly voice), 'Mommy's kind of old-fashioned, you know how old people are, I wouldn't worry about it.'"

"He calls her Mommy?" Max asked.

"Yes, but believe me, that's not the worst of it. So, he tells me she's old-fashioned. And that would have been fine if 'old-fashioned' weren't a euphemism for 'fucking crazy bigot bitch on wheels'! Anyway, I'm getting ahead of the story. So we go in, and I keep thinking, should I leave my sunglasses on, maybe she won't notice, but then I think, no that's pretentious, so I take them off. I go in, and oh my God, if there wasn't the most gorgeous Empire console I have ever seen right there in the foyer! I went right over to it and examined it top to bottom. Just beautiful! and with the original finish and gilt work. Percy said it was a gift to Napoleon from some rich Jew or something, which I highly doubt, but there was no doubting it was from that period."

"What about the mother?" Max asked, leading her back to the original subject.

"Okay, yeah, sorry, but they had some fantastic stuff in that house! Anyway, so the first thing I notice is that everyone working there—the maid who answered the door, the cook, the gardener out back—all black. Not a good sign. I knew it was really bad when I ducked into the little powder room off the foyer to check my makeup and I saw that Mommy has one of those metal lawn jockeys in there as a toilet paper dispenser. You know, the kind with the big white eyes and the huge red lips that you don't see anywhere except in front of a few trailer homes in Alabama. So anyway, I come out of the bathroom just in time to see the black maid wheeling Mommy out in her wheelchair, which was silver plated and had a blue button-tufted cushion on it. Silk velvet, if I'm not wrong, and the tassels alone must have set her back a couple hundred. Did I mention that everything was blue? No? Well it was. Blue walls, lapis lazuli floors (I can only imagine what *that* cost), blue moiré drapes, everything! And Mommy was dressed in some hideous, blue lace getup, with a matching hankie and a high Edwardian collar fastened at the top with (what else?) a Wedgwood broach. Christ, even her hair had been given one of those ridiculous blue rinses!"

Jane paused to take a sip of her coffee, but then resumed her tale with even more vim and vigor.

"Well, at that point, in my little blue Jackie O outfit, with my Princess Diana–knockoff sapphire ring, (which, incidentally, went right back to the pawn shop after this disastrous outing), I'm feeling pret-ty darn sure of myself, in spite of the racial red flags. Percy introduces us, I extend my hand, remove my sunglasses, and I'll be damned if the old bag of bones didn't have a stroke right then and there! Oh, she didn't, of course, but she pulled back like she'd seen a ghost and one whole side of her face just fell. Her hand went limp as a dead fish, and she glared over at Percy with those ice-blue eyes of hers (which is probably how she got started on the whole blue theme in the first place. Stupid.) He looked down and I could tell he was going to catch hell for it later.

"Well, for a while she managed to be civil, if nothing else, but then she had her maid bring out a bottle of anisette and some dainty little cobalt glasses. Percy and I had a glass, and she had about twenty glasses, one right after the other. She actually snapped her fingers when she wanted her glass refilled, and I thought the poor maid was going to get carpal tunnel she was tipping the bottle so often to refill the old cow's glass.

"As you can imagine, the more she drank, the looser her tongue got, and somehow she got it into her head that I was Japanese (you know how we all look alike), and she went on and on about how 'Old MacArthur really gave you Japs a whipping!' and 'I never trusted the gooks myself. Shifty people, if you ask me.' At one point she actually sent the maid to fetch her shawl because, as she put it, 'there's a little nip in the room.'"

Max and I were laughing in spite of ourselves. Jane went on, trying not to smile.

"Lunch only got worse," she said. "She couldn't remember my name, so she kept calling me Suki. 'You been stateside long, Suki? You need some chopsticks, Suki, my dear.' It was awful. And Percy did nothing to defend me! Just sat there smiling, pushing the food around on his plate.

"Then she started telling me all about his charming ex-wife, and then all about his other charming ex-wife, and the children, and the grandchildren. Which, I have to admit, is something I hadn't really given much thought to, but I sure did then! The thought of a whole family of these bigots was more than I could bear. This was definitely not the klan I wanted to join. I also started doing the math: Mommy's old, and still going strong, if I do marry Percy, which hardly seems likely while she's around, I could conceivably be with him for thirty more years! Although the family has money, when I thought of it divided up among children and grandchildren and great grandchildren, I saw nothing more than a few pennies being tossed my way. Oh, it might be enough to get established in my little shop, but only just. Percy isn't wild about the idea in the first place and now I know why—he's still paying heaps of alimony to his two ex's and God knows how much in child support. I'm sure that if I do get an engagement ring it won't be before I sign a lengthy prenuptial agreement.

"I was almost in tears as I sat there in the dining room thinking about how stupid I'd been. I figured the possibility of getting my shop was even more remote, and I was mad that I'd wasted so much time and money on my fucking blue outfit! I had to get out of there and try to compose myself so I got up and went to the loo again. I sat on the pot, getting angrier and angrier, and actually thought of just getting up and leaving, but eventually I calmed down and resolved to just get through it. I resolved that when lunch was over, that would be the end of it. No more putting out for Percy. I headed back to the dining room, but on the way something caught my eye. A bauble. On one of the end tables in the sitting room, I saw a tiny little clock. It was a small bronze, a Venus standing on a blue enamel base surrounded by four whirling balls that ticked off the seconds. I knew it was a Breguet even before I picked it up and saw the name stamped on the bottom, but nevertheless, my heart skipped a beat when I saw that it was genuine and quite obviously nineteenth century. It was so small and delicate, and—"

"You took it!" Max cried, slapping his thigh with his hand.

"Yes, how did you know? It fit so easily into my purse," Jane said. "I looked around to see that no one was watching and made sure to slip a tissue under the chime so that if it went off during lunch no one would hear it. Then I returned to the dining room, just in time to catch the punch line of yet another one of Mommy's jokes about the Jew and the Chinaman."

"So what will you do with the clock?" Max asked.

"It's already sold," she said. "I would have loved to keep it, but I'm not in a position to start my own collection just yet."

"Aren't you worried it will be traced?"

"No."

"Well, why not?"

"The person who bought it doesn't care where it came from. He specializes in, how shall I say, creating a paper trail. He makes up invoices and sales receipts, and in the end makes it appear that the last owner has just died and that's why it's for sale. He then ships it elsewhere to be sold and gives me a chunk of money once it has. He's very clever."

"Who is it?" Max asked, leaning forward, suddenly very interested.

"My secret."

"A collector?"

"No."

"Oh come on, tell me!"

"No."

Max leaned back and scowled.

"I won't tell you because there's no reason that you *should* know. It's not that I don't trust you but this person trusts me and he's really all I've got right now."

"Ahhh," Max said, "the little clock isn't the first thing he's sold for you . . ."

"You always were perceptive," Jane said. She leaned in close and looked around to see that no one else was listening.

"It's like this: my dates with the Ogres have gotten me into a lot of the swank little palaces of Denver. At first, I was just in awe of all the things I saw, the odd pieces of porcelain, the Chinese snuff bottles, the eighteenth-century miniatures . . . I always knew more about them than the owner, and there were several occasions when I thought to myself, 'Jane, it would be so easy to just stick that in your purse. No one would be the wiser.' Well it was only a matter of time until thought became deed. The first time, I'll admit it, I was drunk. I doubt I'd have had the courage if I'd been sober. I found myself alone in a fantastic room at the Boatwright-Starks' house. There was a corner cabinet where they displayed some of their treasures and I sauntered over to it and looked in. There was huge collection of micro-mosaics, so tiny and delicate, but they were so small I couldn't really see them so I opened the case. I only wanted to get a better look. I know I shouldn't have, but I picked one up. A little scene of Venice, only about two inches wide, done in the tiniest pieces of granite and marble you've ever seen. Some no bigger than a hair! Then I heard someone coming so I quickly closed the cabinet, but I'd forgotten to replace the mosaic. I held it tightly, my hand sweating, and then eventually slipped it in my purse, telling myself that when the coast was clear I'd put it back. Well, of course that didn't happen."

I looked across the table at Max and he was beaming, proudly. I was smiling, too, because as Jane spoke it was as if something was connecting the three of us, as if we had secretly joined hands under the table.

"I'm afraid . . ." Jane said, and then trailed off. Her brow was furrowed.

"Of what?" Max asked.

"Of getting caught, of what I'm doing. I mean, I shouldn't really be doing it. I do feel bad."

"Remorse at this point—at any point—is foolish," Max said firmly. "You can't be afraid of what's already been done."

Jane looked up and directly over at Max.

"I'm more afraid . . ." she continued, "of what I'm thinking of doing."

"Don't be," Max said, shaking his head, very matter-of-factly. "There's no reason you should be. Look, you're trying to establish yourself, to get out of this greasy kitchen, and you're running up against a brick wall doing it the conventional way. You want your own business; then do what you have to do in order to get it. It's the means to an end. Keep your eyes on the end—not on the road that gets you there. You have to focus on getting to the end any way you can, and the means be damned!

"But!—"

"But nothing! Look, you don't want to spend your whole life as a tadpole stuck in the pond, do you? At some point you've got to evolve into a frog and hop out of the mire."

This sounded vaguely familiar to me but it wasn't until later that I realized Max had been paraphrasing Vautrin's advice to Eugene in *Père Goriot*.

Jane nodded, but it was clear from the brittle expression on her face that she still had some reservations.

"Listen," Max continued, "you said yourself that your Ogres and their friends don't appreciate half the stuff they've got, right? That they have more money than they can possibly ever use. Well, then stealing from them will not make any more difference than scooping a bucket of water from the ocean!"

Again this sounded more like Vautrin than Max.

"Despite what Grandpa Reagan tells us," Max went on, "trickle-down economics is a sham. It sounds good in theory, but it doesn't take into account the fact that the rich are usually reluctant to let any of the water flow out. For that reason you've got to reach up and twist open the tap yourself. Tell me what you're thinking."

Jane's head seemed to be swimming in these soggy comparisons, but it appeared that she was giving them real consideration. We sat in silence for what seemed like a long time, the clink of dishes being washed in the kitchen the only sound.

"I'd need some help," Jane said, leaning in close, gripping her glass with both hands.

"That's what we're here for," Max said, elbowing me and grinning broadly.

And so it began, the plot that would dominate the next three months of our lives. The plot that would affect each of us, for better and for worse, for a long time to come.

Chapter Fourteen

To commit a crime successfully, three elements must be present: desire, ability, and opportunity.

Desire: the reason, urging, or yen to do something.

Ability: the tools and the know-how to get the job done.

Opportunity: the window that has been carelessly left open (or, in some cases, been propped open), the door that is left unlocked.

All three of us had the desire. All three of us had some ability. Jane alone supplied the opportunity.

On the surface the plan was deceptively simple: Jane, on the social arm of one her Tottering Ogres, would, via parties, friendship, and so on, gain access to some of the wealthier homes in the area. While there, she would scope them out, using her knowledge of jewels and antiques to note the things of value and their location. If possible, she would duck into a bathroom and sketch diagrams of the layout, and record her impressions into a small tape recorder. She would also investigate the security system and possible ways to outsmart it. Through observation and subtle conversation she would discover if they had servants or a cleaning lady, and if so, on which day they usually came. The next morning she would present all of her information to us and with it Max and I would then plan our attack.

How to outsmart the alarm system took up most of this time, but Max was familiar with most systems and he had a special technique for rewiring them to a dummy box so that they appeared to remain armed after they'd been disabled. Usually, though, Jane had made our job much easier by disconnecting one of the windows from the alarm and unlatching the screen. Once inside, we would follow Jane's directions and steal the pieces she had deemed most valuable.

Later, usually the next day, we would rendezvous with Jane, either at Paris on the Platte or in the wine cellar at Lana's, and she would pick up the loot from the night before. She sold what she could to her mystery man and then, usually a week or so later, would return bearing cash.

The first job was almost too easy. It was a house that belonged to an elderly couple, the Stanovers, who, like most people their age, sometimes had difficulty remembering. For that reason, they rarely kept the alarm on, and when they did, they kept a cheat sheet tacked to the wall next to the box, on which the four-digit code was plainly written.

One evening, when they were out dining with Jane and one of her Ogres, Max and I went over and jimmied open the back door. Once inside, we had a full sixty seconds to find the box and enter the code before the alarm started whooping. When that was done, we made our way up to the bedroom and stole what jewelry they had (which was, unfortunately, not all that much since they, like most people, kept the really valuable pieces in a safe deposit box at the bank). From there, we went back downstairs, took their silver candlesticks and their entire collection of Meissen porcelain figurines, which were in the exact spot Jane had said they would be, and then snuck back out the same way we'd come in.

There were only two little snags in an otherwise seamless job: schnauzers and Vautrin.

Snag number one: Jane had neglected to mention (and continued to neglect to mention over the entire summer) the fact that the couple had dogs, an aged pair of schnauzers that came charging and snarling out of the bedroom as soon as we opened the door. We both panicked. I ran as fast as I could down the stairs and jumped up on the dining-room table. Max veered off into the kitchen and, luckily, the dogs followed him, barking all the way. A moment later all was quiet and Max emerged wiping his hands on his pants. I looked up at him, wide-eyed, afraid to hear what he'd done.

"Schnauzers like ham," he said.

Snag number two was, as I said, Vautrin, although it would probably be more accurate to say it was Max's ego. We were finished with the job, our little velvet bags loaded with jewelry, and porcelain, but Max was lingering. The schnauzers had finished the ham and were clawing at the kitchen door. I was over by the back door, ready to go but Max was looking in the desk for a piece of paper and a pen.

"What are you doing?" I whispered, exasperated by the delay. "Come on!"

"Just adding a little style," he said, and started writing. I came up behind him and looked over his shoulder. In elegant cursive he had written, "This house has been burglarized this evening as a courtesy of the disciples of J. C." He then folded the paper in thirds, put it in an envelope, and propped it neatly next to the lamp. "J. C." was of course, Jacques Collin, the real name of Vautrin, but no one other than Max and myself would ever have made the connection from those initials. In fact, when the burglary was reported in the paper a few days later, it was hinted that it may have been carried out by members of some bizarre religious cult.

The following Monday, Jane came to the house and we had a rendezvous in the cellar.

"Oh, this is lovely!" she exclaimed, examining the Meissen figures. "Just absolutely lovely. I hate to have to part with them. I can't believe you got the whole collection, and without a single chip."

"We are professionals," Max said. "How long until you get the money?"

"My my, but you're greedy. Relax, my man knows what's coming so he should be able to pay me C.O.D. I don't see why I shouldn't have the money by the end of the week."

"What's next?" Max asked. Jane grinned devilishly and wrapped up the figure she'd been holding.

"Well," she said, digging excitedly in her purse and removing some crumpled sheets of paper on which she had written her information.

"It looks like Ned and Jocelyn Wilson will be next. Percy and I went to a cocktail party at their house the other night and there were a few things that caught my eye."

"Do tell," Max said

"Well, over the years they've amassed an incredible collection of Southwest pottery and baskets. Unfortunately, Mrs. Wilson has taken that theme and run with it. Their whole house is really a hideous mistake. I mean, when did the colors teal and pink, and the image of little howling coyotes with bandanas around their necks come to represent the Southwest? Never, that's when! Anyway, the baskets are great. Truly great! Museum-quality stuff. In fact, some of it I've never seen outside of museums and I'd be willing to bet they were bought on the black market. If we could get those pieces, I think they'd have a hard time reporting them stolen."

"Where are they?" Max asked, examining the floor plan she'd sketched out.

"They're all in two pine display cases in the living room. They look like they'd open from the front but that's the trick, they don't, they open from the top. No lock, no latch, just lift up. But they look quite rustic and heavy so be careful. One of you will have to hold up the lid while the other reaches inside.

"The one on the right contains the baskets, but don't take any that look too fragile or any that are fragments! These things have a way of turning to dust if they're handled incorrectly so take only the ones that look fairly solid. What you'll really want to concentrate on is the pottery in the case on the left: the black and white pots and the brown and white pots. Again, be very careful. If you can get them, they'll be worth a lot of money—but they must remain intact. Take some of that egg-crate foam and line the bags with it. Take extra pieces for padding in between."

"When could we do it?" I asked.

"Soon. Very soon. Like, this weekend. They'll be going to their son's wedding in Arizona. They leave on Friday afternoon at three and from then on the house will be empty until Monday. No servants, no cleaning lady, no—"

"Dogs?" I asked.

"Oh, as a matter of fact, yes," Jane said, smiling as she remembered them. "Three cute little Chihuahuas, but I'm pretty sure they'll be going to a kennel."

Max and I exchanged weary looks.

"Now, listen up," Jane said, "because here is the downside. There's a doorman on duty twenty-four/seven, who buzzes everyone in. A real ex-military, Soldier of Fortune weirdo. There's no way to get around him and I noticed that he keeps a loaded thirty-eight behind the desk. I thought maybe you could go in the back, through the delivery dock, but there's a camera and it's just too risky. The upside of the downside is that since there's so much security downstairs, they don't have an alarm system in the residence; so once you're in, you're safe. Getting in, however, may be the difficult part."

"How so?" Max asked.

"Well if you're going to do it, you'll have to go in the sliding glass door off the balcony, which is locked, and has a broom handle stuck in the track as an extra precaution."

"No problem," Max said, confidently.

"But . . ." Jane paused here and looked at both of us.

"But what?" Max asked.

"It's a high-rise. The balcony door you need to enter is eight floors up."

"Jane, Jane, Jane," Max scolded. "Not to worry. Not to worry."

"We like a challenge!" I added.

The rest of that week fell into a steady routine. Each morning as soon as Lana left for school, Max and I got in the Jaguar and drove to Boulder. We'd have breakfast with Serge, and then go climbing in Eldorado, where Max introduced me to the practice of free climbing (climbing without a rope) in order to prepare me for the upcoming heist. It was scary at first, but as the week went on and I got more experience, that fear turned into excitement. Soon, I was scrambling up rock faces right behind Max, almost without a thought.

Around noon, we returned to Denver. We'd buy sandwiches at a deli and take them to Cheesman Park to eat, staring up at the building we were soon to attack, discussing different angles and strategies. After that we usually went shoplifting, or to a matinee at the Ogden, and returned home in the evening to eat dinner with Lana. When she was asleep, I'd come down to the cellar and Max would again read from the Balzac. He had gotten over his depression about Vautrin's imprisonment in *Père Goriot*, ever since the little pipe-smoking bookseller at Paris, a fellow Balzac fanatic, had given Max three new books from his own collection, in which Vautrin was alleged to reappear.

But it wasn't just Vautrin that Max became fascinated with. He grew to relish Balzac's detailed and realistic depiction of French so-ciety—into which he, Max, felt sure he would soon be venturing himself. He read the novels as a sort of primer for his upcoming voyage, almost like a Michelin guide. Never mind that it was nineteenth-century society Balzac was describing. In Max's mind, I think he truly imagined he'd be running into all these well-dressed

Mesdames and Messieurs, trotting along cobblestone streets in horse-drawn carriages emblazoned with their coat of arms. I suppose it was the equivalent of some French person sitting in a Paris tenement reading the *Little House on the Prairie* books and imagining life in the United States as some pastoral, uncharted paradise.

As Max read on, night after night, filling a notebook with sights to see, and places to eat (most of which, I'm sure, no longer exist, if indeed they ever did), I remembered back to that first morning we met Jane at Paris on the Platte, and how her face had suddenly taken on a look of sad compassion when Max started spouting off about France. For an instant I wondered if maybe he might be a little bit crazy. The look Jane had given him was the same look you give a bride-to-be on the eve of her disastrous marriage. You know the groom's a loser and her life with him will not be what she imagines, but she's so upbeat and excited about it you really don't have the heart to tell her she's making a mistake, and even if you did she wouldn't listen. No, Max had his own vision of France and it was of such density that truth could not penetrate it.

When Friday arrived, we met with Jane at Paris and finalized our plans for the next "opportunity."

"As far as I know," she said, "they're gone for the whole weekend. I called once about three o'clock, and there was no answer. Here's their number," and she handed Max a piece of paper. "Call again right before you go in."

We reviewed the plans one last time, and then Max and I returned home and ate dinner with Lana. When she went upstairs to study, we went downstairs and got ready. Earlier in the week we had each bought a pair of black running tights, two black cotton sweaters, and some black knit hats. We put them on and then waited for Lana to go to bed. After her light went out, we waited another half hour just to make sure she was asleep. Then we snuck out of the house to the driveway where the Jaguar was parked. I got in the driver's seat and shifted it into neutral. Max stood in front and pushed the car as hard as he could down the driveway and back into the street. I then jumped over to the passenger side, Max ran and jumped in the driver's seat, and gravity pulled us down the hill. Once at the bottom, out of earshot of Lana, he turned the key, started the throaty engine, and we were on our way.

Twenty minutes later we were parked on Race Street about a block away from the building. It was after midnight and all was quiet. Before we got out, we reviewed strategy.

"Okay Dil," Max said, "once we're out of here, no talking, so if you've got anything to say, any questions to ask, you do it now."

"I think I'm ready," I said, trying to exude a confidence I didn't really feel.

"Good. Good, then let's go."

We got out and walked quickly along the sidewalk. We were both wearing the pointy toed climbing shoes with smooth rubber soles and had our velvet bags, stuffed with the foam egg crates, on our backs. Max had a rope draped over his shoulder, which we would use to rappel down once the job was done.

We went around the front of the building and saw the doorman sitting at his desk, smoking. Behind him was a wall of TV monitors, showing various shots around the building, but the set that held his attention was a small portable on the desk in front of him. We watched him a moment and from the way he was chuckling, I gathered he was not watching a picture of the loading dock. We moved on around to the west side, the side facing Cheesman Park, and looked up. The first balcony was at least fifteen feet above us. We would have to climb along the side of it, resting only when we reached each railing.

Max went first, moving steadily up the aggregate blocks. He made about five moves before he reached the first balcony. He then grabbed on to the railing, turned, and looked back down, nodding for me to start. I rubbed my hands together and approached. We had been planning this for days so I knew I was ready, but my heart was pounding nevertheless. I got my fingers in between the blocks, pulled myself up, and set my feet. The shoes stuck nicely and made it fairly easy to move. Once I started, Max moved up to the second balcony, stopping when he'd reached it to check on me. We continued this way until Max reached the eighth floor, at which point he disappeared over the railing. I looked down and could see only a few streetlights in the park, and the orange koi swimming slowly in the illuminated ponds in the Botanic Gardens. I turned back to the wall, climbed the last stretch to the eighth balcony, and Max grabbed my arm and pulled me over.

Without a word, we removed our bags and set to work. Max had a glass cutter that was attached to an engineering compass. He put it up against the glass door, about three inches away from the handle, and etched a perfect circle. It made a slight grating noise the first time around but once it had etched a groove, it was almost silent. When that circle was complete, Max moved down to the lower corner of the door and etched a similar circle. That done, he gave me the compass and I handed him a large suction cup—the kind designed to hold a ski rack onto the roof of a car. He spit on it, rubbed the saliva around to moisten the rubber, and then gently placed it over the fist etched circle. He pushed it into place and pulled back on the small lever on the side. Doing this made the rubber concave and created suction, thus enabling Max to pull out a perfectly cut glass disk. He removed the disk from the suction cup, handed it to me, and went to work on the lower circle. While he did that, I slid my hand in the new hole and unlocked the door. Once he had the second disk removed, I moved down, slid my hand through that hole, and plucked the broom handle from the door track. Then I pulled my hand back out and we both stood up. Max had replaced all of the tools in his bag and the two disks were moved far off to the side so we wouldn't step on them when we left. Max looked at me, took a deep breath, and slid the door open.

It was always hard, that first step into a dark house or apartment. Almost like stepping out onto the moon. We had called beforehand from a pay phone down the street, so we were sure the house was empty; and yet, the first minute was always the most frightening. If anything really bad was going to happen, it invariably occurred in the first minute. If the alarm was going to go off, or if the dogs were to come charging, it would happen in the first minute. If someone was home, or if we were in the wrong house, we would discover it within the first minute. But once that minute passed, the rest of the time was incredibly satisfying. Like the feeling you get when you painstakingly put something together, plug it in, and find that it actually works. A sense of pride and amazement bordering on disbelief. It is incredibly satisfying to be given directions and have them lead you to your goal; pleasing to have something described to you and then find it exactly as it is supposed to be. Of course the places were never quite as I'd imagined from Jane's description, but they were close enough to give me an odd sense of déjà vu. And whenever I got that feeling, I knew it would go well. It was comforting, a feeling like someone was watching out for me.

Once inside, we turned on our flashlights and moved through the house. Max had said we should try and get any jewelry first, so I followed him down the hall to the master bedroom.

He always took the women's dressers and left me to go through the men's, which I hated. The men's dressers were never very exciting, always much more utilitarian and sparse than the women's and that is probably why Max never let me near the women's. He saw the sentimental streak in me and knew that I'd be less likely to take something that I thought might mean something to the homeowner. The men's dressers were safer. There were rarely any baubles, or sentimental remembrances. I never found anything more than small change, cufflinks, perhaps a watch, but that was about it.

Max finished about the same time I did, and we moved back to the living room. There was probably silver we could take in the dining room, and there were certainly other valuables throughout the house but we were limited by the space in our bags so we moved on to what Jane had deemed most valuable.

We found the pine display cases and shone our lights inside. The pots and baskets were there but difficult to see with the light. Max felt around the front and sides of the case and found a switch. When they were lit up, it was evident that much thought and planning had gone into their arrangement, and it was clear that the most valuable pieces, those they were most proud of, were in the front.

I lifted the lid of the case and held it while Max carefully removed the pots, setting them carefully on the floor behind us. When he finished, I lowered the lid and we began wrapping the loot in the egg crates. Once that was done, we put our bags back on and went to the door. I stepped on to the balcony and then turned to get direction from Max, but he was not there. I shone my light back in the living room and saw him walking back down the hall to the bedroom. In a moment he returned and stood before the cases. He had a small lipstick in his hand, one he had evidently taken from the master bath. He twisted it up and then wrote something on the glass. Curious, I returned inside and saw that he had written, again in rather ornate cursive, "This burglary brought to you by the disciples of J. C." And then, just as a further hint, he drew a little Eiffel Tower beneath. He then took a step back and assessed his work, cocking his head from side to side. When he was satisfied, he recapped the lipstick, put it into his pants pocket and went out to the balcony.

I rappelled first, and Max followed. We could only make it to the fourth floor before the rope ran out so we paused there and rerigged the pulley. Then we rappelled down the remaining distance to the ground, gathered up our belongings, and quickly coiled up the rope. When that was done, we walked slowly back around the building to the car and drove home. We usually arrived home from these outings at about four or five—always at least an hour before Lana woke up.

I suppose I should elaborate here on "Max's calling cards," which is how Jane and I referred to the messages Max left for the home-owners. Jane laughed at the cult reference in the newspaper after the first burglary, clearly thinking it had something to do with the ham we had fed to the schnauzers. It was only later, when she was at an opera fundraiser with both the Stanovers and the Wilsons, and heard them each talk about the mysterious messages from the disciples of J. C., that she got angry.

"What are you doing?" she demanded when she came by the next day to retrieve the haul from the night before. "What does that mean?"

"Relax," Max soothed. "It's just to add a little spice to the recipe."

"It's going to add our little asses to the prison dock if you don't cut it out," she said, grabbing him by the shoulders and giving him a shake. "We're doing something illegal, remember? This is one time in our lives (maybe the only time, so far) when we don't want to draw attention to ourselves. The police never would have known the two jobs were connected if it weren't for your dumb little egotistical messages!"

"Don't worry," Max said, petting her arm. "We're not going to get caught."

"No, I bet *you* won't, but *I* might!" she screeched. "You've made a little link between these two jobs, well great. Fine. But you know what else they have in common? *Me!*

"Dillon," she said, turning and pleading with me. "Can't you do something about him?"

"I'll try," I said, but I think we both knew it was useless.

Chapter Fifteen

All through the month of July we worked hard. The rationale behind this was not, as you might assume, to speed things along for Max's departure or Jane's acquiring her shop. No, the reason for our frantic pace was the fear that there was only a limited amount of time before the publicity surrounding the heists became too big and the police really started taking an active role in the investigation. Very rarely is stolen property recovered from a burglary, so the police don't put much effort into it, preferring to focus instead on prevention. But when a group like ours pops up, one that systematically and successfully knocks off house after house after house in an organized and efficient manner, it is only a matter of time before they zero in on it.

The fact that Max's calling cards had indicated a connection between all of the robberies didn't help. Once the jobs were connected, we should, arguably, have laid low for a while, but we did not. Despite what Jane had said about not wanting to draw attention to ourselves, both she and Max were narcissistic and loved that their deeds had been noticed. They loved to see their work referred to in the paper, especially when it was accompanied by phrases like "well planned" and "flawlessly executed." If anything, it just made them more cocky.

Toward the middle of July, Jane's tactics became bold, bordering on reckless, and more often than not she was blinded by her desire and greed, placing all three of us in difficult situations. Usually, she was meticulous about planning our jobs, making detailed notes and floor plans, discreetly discovering when would be the safest time for us to strike. Usually, she would discover when the homeowners would be out of town, or out for the evening, when the servants were off, and so on—usually. But as June turned to July, Jane got impatient, and it was then—when she saw something she lusted after and just had to have; some silver bowl made by Paul Revere, or a piece of export porcelain with a *doré* mount—that she got reckless and would do whatever it took to get them out. Usually, she would hurry and call us from the house itself, give us hasty, improvised directions over the phone on how to get in and what to steal, and then assure us that it was "perfectly safe. A sure thing." Any time I heard her say that, I knew to be wary.

These hurried jobs, which Max and I came to call the "haphazard night raids" went beyond exciting to frightening, for the obvious reason that the victims were usually still in the house. But what really bothered me was how Jane's obsession with antiques could smother her usual practicality! She was sometimes so blinded by her desire for baubles that she was less than thorough when it came to getting information on the alarm system or the layout of the house, or the comings and goings of the help. Things were always sloppy on these jobs, and we never quite got all of what we were after, never quite got away without leaving any clues for the police. There was always some dropped glove or something that we tipped over and shattered.

Max was no better. The more notoriety we got in the paper, the more outrageous his calling cards became. They went from being vague literary allusions scribbled on paper and left propped on a desk to grand murals, executed in spray paint and glitter, proclaiming that "Vautrin was here," or that "Father Carlos Herrera has given you his blessing," leaving the police to puzzle over just what the hell it was all about. Finally a professor of French literature made the connection, and from then on we were dubbed the Balzac Bunch.

I remember sitting at Paris one day with Jane and Max going over the plans for the next heist when the little beret-wearing bookseller came rushing over to show Max the paper detailing one of our crimes.

"Isn't it funny?" he said, puffing excitedly on his pipe. "I mean, we were just talking about Vautrin, when? Last month, was it?"

Jane and I froze, our eyes wide.

"Yes," Max said, calmly tapping the ashes from the end of his cigarette. "I've been meaning to get those books back to you. I've been so busy I never did get a chance to read them. Are all of these names here in the paper, this . . . Carlos Herrera, and J. C.," he said, pointing to the article, "are they all referring to that character, Vootrim, was it?"

"Vautrin," he corrected. "Yes, yes! The very same. It's so exciting! I can't believe this is happening right here!"

"Imagine that," Max said, cocking his head and grinning at Jane. "Right here in Denver. Of all places!"

"Who'd have thought," Jane said, tentatively entering the deception, "that such, uh, literate criminals existed, hee, hee."

On the home front the situation was not much easier on my nerves since Lana began to wonder what, if anything, was happening to the house. It had been over a month since she gave Max money to get started on the exterior painting, and she still had not seen any progress.

"It's the prep," Max said one night, in answer to her question about it. We were all seated at the kitchen table eating dinner. "Of course you can't actually see it," he went on, "but it's all the important work that has to be done before you can paint. Isn't that right Dil?"

"Uh, yes. Why yes, all the prep work like . . ."

"Like caulking the gaps in the siding and, uh, priming."

"Ohh," Lana said, nodding. Max was very good with Lana. Rarely did she question him.

"Yes," he said, warming to the story, his voice becoming more authoritative. "The painting itself is a breeze. It goes on in no time. It's the priming that takes a long time since it's the foundation of any good paint job. And you know, you never want to skimp on the foundation."

"Hey, wait a minute," Lana said, her voice full of suspicion again. "Isn't primer usually white?"

Max was not prepared for this, and I saw him struggling to think up a response.

"There's no primer on this house!" Lana exclaimed, placing both hands on her hips.

"This is clear primer," I said, jumping in with my own quick lie. My tone was knowing and a little condescending. "It's much better than the white. That contractor started using it before—well, you know, before he left town. We found a few cans of it in the basement, so we've been using that."

Max gave me a visual high five.

"Oh," Lana said, somewhat appeased. "Well. But when do I get to see some colors? This is taking forever!"

"Sometime next week," Max said. "Or the week after. They left a lot unfinished, those damn contractors. As soon as we fix their mistakes, we'll sit down together and pick out colors."

The conversation then veered off onto safer subjects and Max and I were free—at least for another two weeks. At least from Lana.

Unfortunately, at about this same time Max's parole officer, Meredith, resurfaced. She appeared one morning at 9 A.M. looking less bright and spunky, and more businesslike and serious. Gone was the colorful dress and the clownish makeup replaced by a black pantsuit and a light application of mascara. When I opened the door, she was several feet down the walkway, looking up at the house and making notes on her clipboard.

"Oh hello," she said when I opened the door. "Remember me?"

Yes, I thought, picturing her necklace of hickeys. You made quite an impression the last time.

"I'm here to see Max," she said. "Is he around?" I stood back and made way for her to enter, closing the door behind her.

"Did I wake you up?" she asked, looking at my robe and my messy hair. I nodded.

"I don't know if Max is up yet," I said, rubbing the sleep out of my eyes. "Come in and sit down. I'll go check."

I led her into the living room, and she perched rigidly on edge of the couch. I went down to the cellar and knocked on the door. Max grumbled a reply, so I went in.

Waking Max was never pleasant, and it was rare that I had to do it. Usually he was the one who arose first; by the time I got up, he had consumed enough coffee to reanimate a corpse. Before coffee was another story, and I dreaded having to wake him before I had a cup of the stuff to hand to him. We had been out late the night before and had not made it back until almost five that morning. It had been a stressful, difficult job, another one of Jane's hastily thrown together plans, and when we were safely back home, we had each retired to our beds without even saying good night or brushing our teeth. Being awakened after less than four short hours of repose did not put either one of us in the best humor.

I entered the dark cellar and shook the sleeping lump on top of the rack.

"Meredith's here," I said. "She's waiting upstairs."

This took a moment to register, but when it did he rolled over on his back and groaned.

"What time is it?" he asked.

"Early. A little after eight."

"Is Lana gone?"

"Yes. I'll go make some coffee."

When I emerged once again into the morning sun, Meredith was up and walking around the living room, looking with disapproval at the unpainted walls and plywood floor of the living room.

"He'll be right up," I said, and made my way over towards the kitchen. "Coffee?"

"No, thanks," she replied, still looking around and shaking her head. A few minutes later Max came up from the cellar, dressed only in boxer shorts and dragging his blanket behind him. Meredith looked at his eye and his nose, which still bore traces of the beating.

"Meredith," Max said, his voice froggy. "How nice of you to call . . . and so early."

He shuffled over to the couch, wrapped himself in the blanket and sat down. He stared straight ahead, a glazed expression on his face.

"Yes, well," Meredith said, bubbling and cheerful. "I've got a really big caseload today, and you were at the top of my list!"

"Lucky me," Max said, and then made a series of loud, snorting noises as he cleared his sinuses.

"What happened to your face?" Meredith asked, "and, uh, his face?" she said gesturing at me in the kitchen. Max said nothing for a moment, clearly annoyed with a question requiring a pat response this early in the day.

"On-the-job accident," he said wearily. "Yeah, an accident that happened on the job."

"Golly, what happened?"

Max's head wobbled as he looked her direction, one eye more open than the other. I reentered the living room and handed Max his coffee. His hands came out of the blanket and he took the cup without even looking at me. "Why don't *you* tell her, Dil. About the accident."

I was not much more alive than Max, but I turned, faced

Meredith, and said: "Um, it was pretty bad, you know. Like, we got really hurt."

Meredith's face registered her confusion, "Did you fall?" she asked.

"Yeah," I continued, "a pretty bad fall, like, on my face. And, um, there was this rock down there where I fell and it, like, hit me in the eye. And, well, Max tried to catch me, but then, you know, like, he fell, too."

"On his face?" she asked. Her tone and expression skeptical.

"Uh-huh."

"On the same rock?"

"Uh-huh. I mean, no, a different one."

Max groaned into his coffee and rolled his eyes.

"What on earth were you doing?" Meredith asked.

"Um, we were, like, putting up this ladder. You know, outside. For the painting.

"Yes."

"And it was really muddy. Yeah, really, really muddy," I said, push-starting my brain. "And the ladder sunk way down and sort of tilted to the side and I fell off. Max was on the roof and he reached over to try and grab me—before I fell, you know?—and then, like, he fell too. It was pretty bad," I concluded, fingering my eye and the scab on my forehead.

"Well," Meredith said, again placing her hands on her hips. "Sounds terrible. Now, about the house . . ."

Max looked up at her.

"Now I'm no expert," she chuckled, "but it doesn't look to me like all that much has been done since the last time I was here. What exactly have you been working on?" she asked, pen poised above clipboard, ready to take notes.

"The prep," Max and I said in unison.

"The prep?"

"Yes, Meredith," Max said, his voice tinged with impatience.

"The prep. The preparation. All the unseen work that has to be done before the actual visual work can begin." He held out his empty cup, dangling it from his pinky by the handle, which was my cue to refill it. I took it and returned to the kitchen, glad that Max was finally taking over. "Maybe you better have some, too, Sport," he called after me. "Your wits are, like, a bit slow this morning."

Meredith began tapping the clipboard impatiently with her pen. "You need to show me *something*," she said. "Because to me, it doesn't look like anything at all has been done in here and I did tell you last time that I would have to see some progress, remember?"

"Oh, now of course I do," Max purred, rising and taking one of Meredith's hands in his. The blanket fell away and he stood before her in his boxers. "And there has been progress, plenty of it, hasn't there, Dil?"

I set his coffee on the table and scowled. I did not particularly like being pulled into this lie again, but I nodded and gave a non-committal, "Sure."

Meredith made a noise like *tshk* and rolled her eyes. She shook Max's hand away and crossed her arms on her chest.

"Yeah, right. Like what? I'm not blind and I'm not stupid. You haven't done *anything*."

Max's own eyes narrowed and again I was alarmed at how much he could resemble Lana when he was angry. His stab was quick and efficient.

"Meredith," he said, his tone low and precise. "Progress has been made. Trust me. Perhaps you were a little . . . preoccupied on your last visit so you didn't notice what a shambles the house was. Maybe you weren't seeing things as a professional. You certainly weren't acting like one."

He paused here for effect. "Progress has been made, Meredith. You'll just have to take my word for it."

She said nothing but swayed slowly back and forth, enraged at what he was doing and that she was powerless to do anything about it.

"Look," she said. "I'm only saying all this for your own good. Next time it might not be me who comes to check on you, so—"

"It had *better* be you who comes the next time," Max said sternly. "You make sure of that, Meredith. For both our sakes. Neither one of us wants trouble, do we now? Let's work together to make sure there won't be any."

She was too angry and bewildered to speak so she just took her clipboard and marched out of the house.

"She got the message this time," Max said, after she'd left, "but next time, if there is a next time, we might have to play hardball. We might have to tell it to her straight, that she'd lose her job if they find out she's slept with one of her clients. Especially when I have you to back up the story, Dil."

I said nothing in response, but my thoughts about it were uneasy. Lying to Meredith was one thing, but blackmailing her into silence was something new, and I wasn't quite sure what to make of it. On the surface it didn't seem all that bad: just something that needed to be done. But underneath, it seemed an awful lot like bullying to me, and was the kind of cruel manipulation I would have associated with Aaron, or Lana, or my grandmother, but never, until then, with Max.

Another problem that arose that month involved the car. James's lawyer, going over the financial paperwork for the upcoming divorce, had red-flagged the insurance bill on the Jaguar, noting that a two-hundred-dollar deductible was due for repairs on a car that was not even in his client's possession. When that was brought to James's attention, he immediately called Lana, and the call came while she and Max and I were eating dinner.

"It's James!" she hissed, covering the receiver with her hand. "He got the bill for the car and he wants to know what happened. What should I tell him?"

Max lit a cigarette and puzzled over this for a moment.

"Tell him the truth, so to speak, that the car was in the driveway during the hailstorm and it got pummeled."

She nodded, took a minute to formulate her speech and then put the phone back to her ear.

"Yeah, James? You still there? Yeah. The car. Well, you remember the storm we had a couple weeks ago? Uh-huh. Well the car was in the driveway during that stor—"

Lana abruptly stopped speaking and held the phone away from her ear, wincing. We could hear James screaming on the other end.

"James, listen," she said. "LISTEN! If you're going to yell, I'm not going to talk to you." She hung up.

"He's mad," she said, looking dumbly at the two of us. "He loves that car."

I knew the repair job was great, but the fact that the car had been damaged at all is what made James crazy. It was bad enough that Lana was holding it hostage.

"He'll call right back," she said, the terror evident on her face. She could stand up to James on any topic except the car. "What should I tell him?"

The phone rang. We all looked at it and then Lana and I turned our attention to Max.

"Tell him . . ." Max said, and paused to take a drag from his cigarette. He closed his eyes and drummed his fingers on the side of his head. "Tell him . . . that it was out of the garage because you were, uh, uh, you were having some lumber delivered, for . . . for the . . . crown molding. Some lumber for the crown molding that you're having put all through the house and you had to make space for it in the garage so that it wouldn't get wet and warp."

Lana made a brief mental review of all this information. She then answered the phone and quickly regurgitated what Max had said, almost verbatim.

"So that's what happened," she said, pausing to take a breath at the end. "But it's fixed now, so don't worry. It's nothing really, it looks brand-new . . . What? . . . No . . . No, no, no, no, no! Possession is nine-tenths of the law! I'll keep it until my lawyer says I should give it back, thank you very much! . . . Look you prick, you're the one who walked out on me, remember?" And again, she slammed down the phone.

So we got to keep the car a while longer. The court date for the divorce was not until October, and it appeared that as long as we were careful Max and I would have transportation at least until then. The issue seemed to be settled; but of course, it was not. James's lawyer communicated with the insurance people who said that Mr. Sawyer himself had requested and signed the approval for the repairs and had picked up the car himself when they were completed. The lawyer asked James about this and James asked Lana and Lana asked Max who had no good answer. Soon, men began to call and appear on the doorstep. Strange men dressed in suits wanting to speak to Lana or Max. For that reason, Max again went into hiding. If he were to get caught for forgery, on top of violating his parole, he would be sent straight back to jail. He retreated to the cellar, but this time around both Lana and I had to screen the people at the door and never let on to anyone that Max was even living there.

Oddly enough, it was in our concern for Max that Lana and I found some common ground. We were both afraid of him getting caught and having to go away so we cooperated, without question, when it came to keeping him safe.

My own reasons for wanting to protect Max were clear: he was a friend to me when I had none, and I didn't want to lose that. Lana's reasons for doing so were more enigmatic to me. I knew that she and Max had endured a difficult childhood together, but, as an only child, I don't think I was capable of understanding that bond between them. At the time, it hardly seemed reason enough for her to endanger herself by protecting him, but I suppose it probably was. Looking back, I think she must have felt guilty for leaving the house when he was still young, leaving him alone with my grandparents, and that maybe she saw protecting him from the police, from the insurance investigators, from Doris, and Meredith, and whomever else was after him, as a way to make up for that.

As if things were not chaotic enough right then, Wayne also resurfaced. I had contacted him on my own, the day after my beating, since I knew he would be worried and, well, I guess because I wanted to reassure him that I was all right. Even though he was hokey and annoying, there was something honest about him that I always sort of respected. He was so earnest in his desire to help, to make situations better. I didn't necessarily agree with the way he went about it, but I guess I did respect him. Little did I know then, but Lana had also been in contact with him. They had been actively conferring behind my back on the subject of my future. A fact I discovered one day when he showed up on our doorstep with a thick envelope for Lana.

"Hello, Sport," he said, smiling his thick smile. "Got some paperwork for your mother. Will you be a good kid and make sure she gets it?"

"Sure," I said, and as soon as he left I went straight over to the stove and steamed it open. Thank God I did because inside there were several different brochures and information packets on various military academies! I was stunned. The summer was going along so well, and I was so happy that the thought of returning to school at all, let alone a military academy, seemed just awful. I'd felt sure that idea of military school had been tossed out with the idea of Bible Camp, but as I thumbed through the brochures with their pictures of neat, orderly youth, all uniformed and marching around, I realized I had been mistaken. I was worried, yes, but at the same time I really thought that Max would devise some way to keep me at home. I had faith in him. He would not allow me to be sent off when I was now such a vital, integral part of the thieving organization. He would run interference for me the same way I was doing for him with Meredith and the insurance companies, I felt sure. No way he would let me be sent off to one of these jarhead schools, no way.

I replaced the brochures in their envelope, threw them in the trash, and hardly gave it another thought.

Chapter Sixteen

It is probably appropriate that the book we were reading when I began to doubt Max's infallibility was titled *Lost Illusions*. It was, of course, another Balzac book, and one in which Vautrin reappears, although not until the very end.

Like the previous book we'd read, the main character in *Lost Illusions*, Lucien, is yet another ambitious young man who leaves the dull and dreary provinces for the bright lights of Paris, with dreams of entering high society. Throughout the book his success goes up and down, but in the end he is a failure, his progress hampered by society's prejudice and his own lazy decadence. He has soured his friendships, plunged himself and his relations into poverty, and is just about to drown himself in a deep lake on a lonely country road when who should come along but old Vautrin.

Vautrin, older now, more cynical and less jovial, is disguised as a Spanish priest, Father Carlos Herrera. Of course he takes a fancy to the youthful, handsome Lucien and, after hearing his troubles and his plan to solve them all through suicide, Vautrin offers him a deal. He will pay the money Lucien owes and in exchange Lucien will return to Paris with him and Vautrin will employ him as a front for his dirty work and keep him as a sort of sexual concubine.

Max loved it all and eagerly thumbed through page after page of the book. I enjoyed it too, but less so than before, due in part to my sentimental nature. I had grown fond of Lucien. There was something about his bumbled attempts at legitimacy, and the way he was savagely teased and taken advantage of by the snobs, who made fun of his clothes and his manners, that struck a sympathetic chord with me. Oh I knew that he was foolish and had squandered his opportunities, but beneath all that I saw that Lucien was not a bad person. He had been seduced by the flash and glamour of the big city into pretending he was something he was not. In short, he was all too human, and when he made up his mind to commit suicide in the end, I felt terribly sad.

Max, on the other hand, was so sick of him that I could easily imagine the two on the country road, Max filling the pockets of Lucien's waistcoat with stones and giving him a firm shove into the water.

When Vautrin reappeared at the end of the book, I suppose I should have been thrilled, like Max was, that the scamp had returned, but I was not. Don't get me wrong, I liked Vautrin. I respected him as a fellow thief and homosexual, and I was glad that he was able to prevent Lucien's suicide, but I couldn't help feeling uneasy about it.

As for my illusions about Max and Jane, they were not quite lost. I still idolized them both, but lately some of their gilt had begun to chip off and I was beginning to suspect that underneath it all I might find they were made of nothing more than common plaster. Their selfish motives were becoming more and more obvious and that was disappointing. Oh, it was admirable that they were so intent and focused on their goals, but that focus often had the added effect of making the jobs we did almost joyless.

I had never minded the fact that I did not really get any material things or any money out of the racket. When you are fourteen years old, there is only so much you need that is not already provided for, and any material thing I wanted (usually nothing more than books or records or clothes) was so trivially inexpensive that Max or Jane would not hesitate to buy it for me. No, what I really wanted, more than anything else, was for the stealing to be fun again—to be as exciting and thrilling and taboo as it had been in the beginning, in the days before Jane and Max had become so greedy. As the summer progressed, our outings were less fun and more like work. Work in which it was assumed I would participate whether I wanted to or not.

Another thing that bothered me was the day Max bought us both guns. We were down at one of the pawnshops on Larimer Street, trying to unload some of the lesser items we had stolen that Jane couldn't use, when Max's attention was drawn to a display case containing several antique guns. There were pearl-handled pistols, Saturday Night Specials, .22s, and .38s. He asked to see one of the pearl-handled pistols and listened as the salesman explained all about it.

"Used to belong to Merle the Pearl," he said, handing the gun to Max. "He was called 'the Pearl' on account of his shiny bald head. In fact that's what did him in."

"How so?" Max asked.

"Well, he was running away, after doing a safecracking job over at the Wells Fargo, and the police were on his tail. He tried hiding, but there was a full moon out and it reflected offa that bald head like a mirror. They got him in one shot."

Of course Max bought the gun on the basis of that story, which was as good a reason as any to buy a gun, I guess.

So he's got a gun, I thought at the time. *No big deal.* But a few days later it became quite a big deal when he came into my room one morning and gave me a gun of my own. A small black pistol that he twirled around on his finger. Initially, I was excited by the whole thing; we went out into the field behind the house and practiced shooting at cans. I loved the way Max used to stand behind me and encircle me with his arms, his head close to mine, our hands both clasping the gun as he showed me how to aim and fire. It was only later, when he insisted I carry the gun on all of our jobs, that I began to get nervous. It seemed like an unnecessary precaution, something that could make a simple situation suddenly very complex. It just didn't feel right somehow, in my gut, but then I remembered how at first the climbing had not felt right either. How the idea of leaning back had felt so absolutely wrong. Max's words echoed in my ears: "If it feels wrong, sometimes it's right. Trust me." So I did.

At that point it was easy to do since I was in love with him and would have done just about anything he asked, even if I had misgivings. It might sound strange to say I was in love with him, since he was my uncle; but when you think about it, it makes perfect sense. Max was sexy and witty and smart—the most exciting adult, and the only other gay man I'd ever met. How could I help but fall in love? I knew he was my uncle and I knew that was wrong. But I couldn't deny the way I felt, and Max did little to discourage my crush. On the contrary, at times he even seemed to encourage it, subtly fanning the flames of my teenage lust, always with just enough subtlety to make me wonder if maybe I wasn't imagining it. He did this in the mornings when he emerged from the cellar, his morning wood tenting his boxers, and in the evenings, when he sat behind me teaching me chords to a Bachrach song on the guitar, his chest pressed against my back and his hands on mine. He did it at the Ogden, when he casually draped his arm over the back of my seat and repeatedly brushed my arm with his fingers. It was maddening! It was frustrating! It was confusing! But above all, it was terribly, terribly wonderful.

And yet, why, I wondered, was he doing it? If I was right, and he *was* sending out signals, why didn't he act on them? At the time I thought it was because he knew it was wrong, knew it was taboo, but that wasn't it at all. No, the reason was far more calculated. He didn't take action because that was his ace in the hole, the card he would pull out and use if and when he needed it. It was the same thing he had done with Meredith but instead of veiled threats, he offered me veiled promises. Promises in the form of back rubs, or views of his body as he changed clothes, or meaningful winks over the top of the book as he read to me, until he had whipped me up into such a frenzy that I got a hard-on every time he brushed against me, or if I even caught a whiff of his cigarette smoke. Of course I didn't realize any of that then. Lust makes you blind, and teenage lust makes you blind, deaf, and dumb; so I went on, eagerly doing whatever he told me, pausing every now and then to reposition my hard-on in my pants.

Chapter Seventeen

The card game.

Like all the other jobs, it started out simply. And, like all the other jobs, it did not stay that way. Max, Jane, and I were sitting at Paris one Sunday morning, each reading a section of the paper, when an article caught Max's attention.

"Listen to this," he said. "'Society mavens Lloyd and Beverly Boatwright-Stark were the hosts Friday evening for the wedding reception of their eldest daughter, Donna Anne, as she became the new Mrs. Jarvis Q. Pittredge III.

"'The seven hundred plus guests were treated to a never-empty fountain of Veuve Cliquot and a five-course meal prepared by Chef David Yzek of Raquin's Bistro, who was also responsible for the twelve-tiered, spun-sugar cake, the frosting on which echoed the lace pattern on the bride's Vera Wang dress. Music for the evening was provided by a string quartet that kept the crowd dancing well past midnight, long after the bride and groom had jetted off for their honeymoon on the private Caribbean island belonging to the bride's parents.'"

"Their own private island!" I cried. "Could you imagine having that kind of money?"

"Oh, I could imagine," Jane said wistfully, "but that's about as close as I'll come, I'm afraid. Percy was there. At the wedding. But of course whenever there's a really important function, I take a backseat to Mommy."

"Have you ever been to their house?" Max asked.

"The Boatwright-Starks'? Once, yes, no twice actually, both times this past spring. They had a silly polo party last May. That was the first time, although I never really met either of them then because there were so many people."

"What was silly about it?" I asked.

"Oh God, what *wasn't* silly about it! They'd converted their whole front lawn into a polo ground, which was a bit of a waste since none of the people attending knew how to play polo. The whole day degenerated into a sort of equine petting zoo/croquet game. If nothing else, it gave everyone a chance to wear their best Ralph Lauren outfits and practice acting blue bloodier than thou. Stupid, really. I got drunk and puked in the bushes.

"But their house!" she continued. "Oh my God! Or perhaps I should say, oh my gaudy! It is absolutely nouveau riche, overdone trash, but it is huge! And they are huge collectors. I'd be thrilled to have even a few of their things to call my own. In fact . . ." she said, leaning in close to the table and lowering her voice, "it was from their house that I pinched the little micro-mosaic I told you about. You remember, the one with the tiny scene of Venice. They probably haven't even noticed it's gone. They have a whole collection of them—all the different cities in Italy. Can you imagine what that would be worth? It's even been rumored, although I don't know that I believe it, that they have a Fabergé egg!"

"You stole the mosaic at the polo party?" Max asked.

"Oh, God no. I didn't even get to go inside then. I stole it on bridge night."

"Bridge night?" I asked.

"Yes, they are card-playing fanatics. Percy and I were on our way to dinner one night and made the mistake of dropping by for cocktails on their bridge night. They were short one person, so he joined in."

"Did you play?" Max asked.

"Me? Please! I don't even know how to . . . oh, what's it called when they mix the cards up."

"Shuffling?" Max asked.

"Yes, that's it. I don't even know how to shuffling the cards, let alone play bridge, or canasta, or euchre, or whatever! I sat in the corner, drank several martinis, and then got up and wandered around. Percy swore he'd only play a few hands and then we'd go to dinner. Well, of course Percy's 'few hands' were more like twenty, and they take it all so seriously. No one even knew I was there."

"Could we hit that house?" I asked eagerly, images of polo parties and Fabergé eggs whirling in my head.

Jane shook her head.

"Why not?" Max asked.

"Well, because it's guarded like, well, like, *really* well guarded!" she said, unable to find a suitable comparison. "It's in a gated community with a guardhouse at the entrance. Once you're through that then there's another gate and another guard house at the entrance to their driveway. From there you have to go up the drive a quarter mile to get to the actual house, which is always full of servants. It would be impossible."

"It would be a challenge!" Max said, rubbing his hands together, a demonic look in his eyes.

"Oh, no," Jane said, shaking her head and waving her finger. "No, no, no. These people live in a higher strata of wealth. Nothing like the people we've been picking off. They have some big league security. "

"Big league, shmig league," Max said, waving his hand from side to side. "That's all the more reason. When do we do it?"

And so it began. The card game plan. Again, it sounds simple enough on paper, but lift the veil . . . Well, you know. Here, then, is a synopsis:

Jane and Percy would get themselves invited to play cards. Once there, Jane would carefully case the house, making sure to find out how many servants were on duty, what type of alarm system, the what and where of the valuables, and so on. With any luck, she and Percy would be invited back the following Wednesday to play again. She would volunteer to mix the first round of cocktails and would spike them with Rohypnol. That done, she would excuse herself to go to the ladies' room and on her way would make a detour along the gallery and unlock the large French doors leading out to the back lawn. Max and I, dressed in our black outfits and black ski masks, would enter through these doors and overpower whatever servants happened to be on duty that night. Once they were secured, and once all of the guests had passed out, Max and I would rendezvous with Jane in the game room and the three of us would go on a looting tour of the giant house, loading our velvet sacks with as much jewelry and as many collectibles as we could carry. When that was done, we would return downstairs. Max and I would exit once again through the French doors and Jane would consume her own Rohypnol martini, so that when the police arrived, she could claim to be as bewildered and clueless as the rest of the party.

As for the difficult task of getting in and getting out, Max and I had, of course, thought of a way to do that without going through the many guard stations leading up to the house. Instead of coming through the front, we would come in across the back lawn. This we would be able to do because the back lawn of the Boatwright-Starks' house butts up against the country club golf course. The same country club, conveniently enough, to which James, my ex-step father, belongs, and the entrance pass for which was still in the glove compartment of the Jaguar. We would show up, Max and I, golf clubs in tow, and play the course, as usual, until we got to the sixteenth hole. At that point we would cache our clubs in the pines, change into our black outfits, and scale the brick wall separating the golf course from the booty-stuffed Boatwright-Stark mansion.

Sounds simple enough, right? But lift the veil . . .

The first problem to arise was the rather glaring fact that Jane had no idea how many cards were in a deck, yet she needed to become a competent bridge player in less than two weeks. Fortunately, we found someone who knew all the ins-and-outs of bridge and who was willing to teach her. Unfortunately (for Jane, anyway), that person was none other than her own father, who had perfected his game over many tedious months in a Lao refugee camp. Of course this meant Jane would have to spend hours of time with her father, which was probably the thing she least wanted to do, made worse by the fact that every time she lost a hand he made her pay for her losses with promises to go out with a cousin or to work additional nights in the restaurant. They played at night, after the restaurant had closed, and several times Max and I stopped by to see them on our way to a job.

"I don't know why she no open nail salon like her sister," Jimmy said one night, as he examined and sorted his cards.

He and Jane were alone, sitting at a small table in the middle of the darkened restaurant, drinking strong Vietnamese coffee and playing hand after hand of bridge.

"Good money in nails!" he continued. "She alway want more money, but she alway try tricky. Now she learn bridge to impress more older man. That not right," he grumbled, shaking his head. "But I make her pay to learn. She have to pay!" he chuckled and threw down his trump.

In the meantime Max and I kept up on our evening work. Before Jane went into her bridge hibernation, she had managed to give us the plans for three more jobs, which we executed on the nights she had prearranged. They all went off without a hitch. No problems whatsoever. The problem came when we had finished and had time on our hands. Max began to get antsy. He feared not having enough money, and he couldn't bear the fact that there were all of those houses out there, just ripe for the picking, and there we were sitting on our hands. Instead of simply biding our time, waiting patiently until after the card game heist when Jane could again supply us with more prescreened houses, Max started us doing something really scary—even scarier than Jane's "haphazard night raids." We started hitting houses with no advance planning whatsoever.

On these "shot-in-the-dark-suicidal-night-raids," as I called them, we would drive around late at night in rich neighborhoods scoping out houses (which is easy to do without arousing suspicions when you do it as we did, in an expensive car) until we saw a house that looked empty. We would watch it for a few minutes, take a few minutes to develop a plan, and then attack.

I realize this is the random way that many burglars execute every job they do, but I did not like it. It seemed unnecessarily dangerous to me, and worst of all, somewhat amateurish. Max thought otherwise and was, as usual, very persuasive.

Anytime I was reluctant to do something, he would pull out his ace. "Look, Dil," he'd whisper, as we sat in the car, looking up at some dark ivy-covered mansion. "I've done a lot for you this summer, remember?" And he would then proceed to list it all: how he'd kept me out of camp and got me new clothes, how he'd taught me to climb and play guitar, how he'd bought me some sheet music and essentially gave me money for anything I really wanted; and if I wanted his benevolent largesse to continue then I'd better help! And why wouldn't I? Was I that selfish?

It was the seesaw of favors again. I had been riding high because of what he'd done and now, he told me, it was his turn. Usually that rationale was enough, and I would give in. If not, he'd push things a little further and take my hands in his, or gently massage my thigh and look into my eyes, his own eyes full of suggestion and possibility. That always did it. Yes, I was grateful for all he'd done, of course, but I would have moved mountains to sleep with him, and even the hint that there was a possibility of that was the only kick I needed.

Nevertheless, I was naturally afraid of going into these jobs without any prior information. I was afraid of the alarm system we weren't familiar with and that often went off the second we opened a window, or of the dogs that came running as soon as we entered. But most of all, I was afraid of getting shot. Afraid of some homeowner coming round the corner and surprising us with a gun. Thankfully, this never happened, but it was always in the back of my mind, especially since, on these random jobs, Max insisted that I carry my gun.

It felt like the devil in my pocket. It was such fun to shoot when we were out on the prairie behind the house harmlessly toppling cans, but I could not even imagine using it to shoot a sparrow, let alone another human being! For that reason I always made sure to trail a few steps behind Max as we crept across the lawn toward the unknown house, emptying the chamber of bullets as I went. I could use the gun as a threatening prop, I thought, but never for anything more than that.

Finally, after a week of card practice with her father, Jane was ready to put her playing skills to the test. She convinced Percy to get them invited to the Wednesday night bridge match, and as it turned out, Lloyd and Beverly were thrilled to have some new blood injected into their tired old game since they'd been playing with the same couple for the last eight years. They were charmed that a young person like Jane was taking an interest in the game since their own children made it plain that they had absolutely no interest in it.

We met up with Jane the Thursday after her first big game, when she came to the house to pick up the paltry goods we'd gotten the night before and to get us started devising the plan for the following Wednesday.

"How did it go?" I asked eagerly. For my own sake I hoped it went well as it would mean an end to the unplanned jobs.

She sighed, dropped her purse on the floor and collapsed into the sofa.

"It was really hard," she said, rubbing her temples. "I don't know if I can do it."

"Of course you can," Max said, bringing her a cup of coffee and some toast. "Tell us all about it."

Max and I sat down opposite her and listened eagerly. Jane did not sit up, but remained slumped into the cushions.

"Oh, they were all patient with me," she said, taking a sip of her coffee, "but there is just so much to remember! Beverly and her friend, Mrs. Gouldstein, they get so competitive sometimes, almost as if their husbands' fortunes were at stake. I don't think either one of them is very fond of me and I sensed the green-eyed monster as the motivation for their glee whenever I folded my hand."

"How did the house look?" I asked, rubbing my hands together. "Is there lots of treasure?"

"Oh, Dillon," she said nervously, "I wish I knew! I was concentrating so hard on my game that I barely had a chance to look around."

That was not what I wanted to hear. After a week of shot-in-the-dark-suicidal-night-raids I dreaded another job for which we were not prepared.

"Can we still do it?" I asked.

"Of course, we can!" Max snapped.

"Yes," Jane sighed. "I suppose we can, but it won't be easy. I got enough information to get us in, and I did find out about the servants, but I don't really know what we're going after. I mean, I didn't get a chance to see the upstairs at all! I only really saw the foyer, the dining room, and the game room, so we'll have to do a room-by-room search once everyone is knocked out. It would be better if I knew what they had first, because then I could ask my man what he'd take and we could avoid taking a bunch of stuff we can't unload."

"We'll just have to make the best of it," Max said. "Now let's go over the layout."

* * *

When Wednesday rolled around again, the three of us met once more at Paris to go over the final plans. Max gave Jane another packet of Rohypnol and told her to make sure and grind it up well.

"I'm a little worried about one thing," she said. Max and I looked at her, questioningly.

"Well, Mrs. Gouldstein doesn't drink, and she's got a bladder condition so she doesn't even drink water or anything! How am I going to get her drugged!"

Max didn't conceal his annoyance at such a large oversight on Jane's part. He scowled at her and shook his head, but then looked away and puzzled over the the problem.

"What if . . ." he said, still formulating the plan as he spoke. "What if you brought a box of chocolates? Something fancy. Truffles maybe, with a coating of powdered sugar. Do you think she'd go for that?"

Jane nodded eagerly.

"Good. Excellent. Here's what to do: grind up the pills very fine, like powdered sugar, and roll the truffles in the dust. Mix some sugar in with them, of course, to hide the bitterness."

"Yes, yes!" Jane cried, clapping her hands. Then something else occurred to her and her expression fell.

"What about the truffles when it's all over?" she asked. "I mean, we can't just leave them for the police to analyze if everyone knows I'm the one who brought them with me."

"Good point," Max said, gesturing with his cigarette. "Excellent point. I'm glad you're thinking. Get two boxes and dose only one of them. When Dil and I leave, we'll take the dosed box with us. No one will be the wiser."

The rest of the day, Max and I prepared our end of the plan. We got all of James's golf accessories together and outfitted ourselves in what Max imagined was typical golf clothing: Kelly green, plaid slacks, white polo shirts, and two ridiculous tweed caps. I tried to tell him that was not really the way people at the country club dressed, but he wouldn't hear it.

"Nonsense," he said. "We look perfect! Just like the golfers on TV!"

"Maybe so," I groaned, "but matching outfits?"

He gave me a dismissive wave and went back to admiring himself in the mirror as he practiced miming his golf swing. I knew it was useless to protest once his mind was made up, so I put on the ridiculous outfit and loaded the clubs in the back of the car.

Around four o'clock, we left and drove to the country club. It had rained earlier that afternoon, but the sky had cleared by the time we arrived. I took that as a good omen. Our plan involved hiding out in the bushes for several hours until the bridge game started, so I was glad we would not have to wait in the rain.

As we arrived at the country club, we encountered the first hurdle. We drove up to the guard station and I handed Max the entrance pass. He flashed it at the guard, the guard glanced at it, and then waved us by. We were just through the gate when we heard him call out.

"Wait! Stop!"

Max stopped and looked back impatiently. He leaned out the window.

"Yes, what is it?"

"I'm sorry, sir, could I see your pass once more?"

Max handed it to the guard who took it and returned to the booth. I felt sweat break out on my forehead. Max sensed my anxiety and gave my thigh a reassuring pat. A moment later the guard returned.

"Mr. Sawyer?" he asked.

"Yes," Max replied.

"I'm sorry to hold you up, sir, but I'm showing that this pass has been replaced. You don't happen to have the replacement pass with you?"

There was a momentary pause.

"Oh, that woman!" Max cried, slapping the steering wheel with his fist. "Listen," he said, turning to the guard, "my goddamned wife lost *her* pass. I never lost mine. 1 told her to replace *hers*, not mine!" His tone was so impatient and angry that the guard became a bit intimidated.

"Oh," he said. "Your *wife's* was lost."

"Yes," Max said. "That's what I told you. Listen, we've got a four o'clock tee time and I have some very important clients waiting for me inside. I really don't have the time right now to argue with you."

"Yes, Mr. Sawyer, let me just call up to the clubhouse and have them check it out."

"Oh, give me that!" Max said, grabbing the pass out of the guard's hand. "I told you I'm late!"

Max's face was red and veins were popping out of his neck. It was a convincing performance.

"I'll give them an earful at the clubhouse myself! *After* my game! I pay a shitload of money to come to this place; now open the god-damned gate!"

The guard peered in at us for a few seconds more and then looked again at the car. I think it was the car that did it, because without another word he went back to his station and opened the gate.

"The insolence of these people!" Max said as we drove away, his face still red. It always took him awhile to get out of character when he'd just pulled off such a big lie so I knew better than to offer any commentary. In fact, I hoped he could keep up the charade at least until we were safely out on the course. I gave him a few directions on where to park, which he followed wordlessly until we found a space. Then we got out of the car, set up our golf bags, checked in with the starter and walked toward the first hole, quietly reviewing the plan.

Out on the course we ran into yet another obstacle. Something neither of us had foreseen. While Jane had spent hours and hours perfecting her bridge game, Max and I had not played even one round of golf and neither one of us had the slightest idea what we were doing. We stood at the first hole wondering which club to use and even which direction to hit the ball. Once that was determined, there followed another ten minutes of useless swinging before we actually made contact with the ball, having dug a large, brown trench in the grass with all of our initial efforts. This did not amuse the group that was set to tee off behind us. Needless to say, before we finished the first hole (having taken about fifty strokes each), we allowed that group to play through rather than wait on us. By the seventh hole, we had allowed two more groups of people to play through, and I was exhausted! My shoulders ached and I'd twisted my back. Max was swinging away in a sand trap, cursing loudly, while I stood watching, trying not to laugh. By the eleventh hole, we were out of balls, having lost all twenty-four that we'd brought with us. This was disappointing in a way. In desperation, we had resorted to using the bent club Lana had used to whack the Jaguar and found that it worked quite well, meaning that we could actually hit the ball with it as opposed to the swing, miss, swing, miss pattern we had both fallen into. It's probably good that we did run out of balls since we were losing daylight and were in danger of running behind schedule. Bridge was scheduled for nine o'clock and it was already eight-thirty! Realizing this, we decided to mime our way to the sixteenth hole, and our game improved markedly after that.

The sixteenth hole was deep in a grove of tall pines. We waited for the group ahead of us to finish up and then ducked to the right under the boughs and over toward the tall brick wall. We took all the clubs out of the golf bag and removed the black outfits. Once dressed, we looked a little frightening, our faces concealed with the ski masks, but then I guess that was the idea. We double-checked that we had everything we'd need and then Max started climbing. The wall was covered in ivy and looked like it would be an easy climb, but the thick vegetation was home to several small birds that darted out suddenly, flapping their wings and squawking the second we got too close to their nest, causing me to fall several times from the surprise.

When we reached the top we saw the Boatwright-Stark mansion about a hundred yards off. It was a mammoth house, with French windows stretching up three floors on the main part of the house and two lower wings shooting off to the sides. It was just getting dark and we could see lights in the room to the left, which we knew, from Jane's directions, was the game room. We were to enter from a door on the right wing and then go to the kitchen and overpower the cook and the butler. By then, with any luck, the Rohypnol would have taken effect and most of the card players would be falling asleep.

Max gave me a nod and we climbed down the wall into the Boatwright-Starks' property. It was nine o'clock. By about nine-fifteen, it was dark enough that we could make our way across the lawn and up on to the stone porch without being seen. We did so, as quickly and quietly as possible, and then peered in the large French window of the right wing. The game room was enormous, with a high ceiling and massive plaster columns in each corner. On the wall opposite us there was a cavernous fireplace in which, although it was July, a fire raged, and above which were mounted the trophy heads of several dead animals. In the middle of the room was the large rectangular game table. It had legs of dark carved wood, and a green felt top like you'd find on a pool table. The decks of cards sat ready and waiting. Two women, both with tight leathery faces and overly bleached and back-combed hair, sat talking to Percy on the sofa and eating from the truffle box. Over by the bar, Jane was mixing drinks and telling jokes to the two older men, who laughed and smiled at her, much to the chagrin of their jealous wives. We were so busy watching the scene that we almost didn't notice when one of the men broke away from the bar and stepped out on the porch to smoke a cigar. Luckily, we were able to conceal ourselves behind one of the decorative urns and, by pinching each other, kept from laughing as we listened to him fart.

Eventually, the man went back inside, and we crept back up to the window. All were enjoying their cocktails, and Jane had slipped away from the crowd to go to the ladies room. That was our cue, so we crept across the porch, along the gallery, to the other set of French doors off the dining room, just in time to hear Jane disengage the lock. She didn't see us, which I hoped meant that we were, indeed, well camouflaged. We put on our black cotton gloves, and Max slowly turned the handle. He pushed the door open, and we both crept in. Once inside, we set down our bags and removed the supplies we'd need. Max put a large roll of duct tape on his wrist, like a bracelet, and put the small packet of ground-up Rohypnol in the pocket of his pants. He then took out his gun and stuck it in the leather holster running across his chest and motioned for me to do the same. When he wasn't looking, I again made sure to empty out all of the bullets and slip them in my pocket. That done, we stashed our bags behind the drapes and crept quietly in the direction of the kitchen. Or, at least, in the direction Jane had assumed the kitchen to be, since she hadn't really discovered its location the week before.

The cook and the butler were supposed to be the only two on duty, so we did not anticipate any difficulties in overpowering them, especially since we had the guns. After several wrong turns, we found the kitchen and there, watching a small TV and smoking a cigarette, was the cook. She was a short woman, with her hair pulled back in a large bun. Her back was to us, so Max slowly removed his gun from the holster and stepped up behind her. He placed the barrel of the gun against her temple, and she jumped and gave a startled cry. Max covered her mouth with his hand. He moved around in front of her and put his index finger to his lips. He nodded for me to come over and then handed me his gun. I held it against her head and she stared up at me, wide-eyed with terror. I was just as terrified, knowing that there were actual bullets in this gun, and my hand trembled. Max ripped off a piece of duct tape and placed it over her mouth. He then bent down and taped her ankles together, going around them several times with the roll of tape. He stood her up, turned her around, and similarly bound her hands behind her back. She would probably not be able to escape, but, just to be sure, Max wrapped more tape around her whole body several times and then led her, hopping pathetically, to a pantry closet. He pushed her inside, closed the door, and then put a chair up under the handle.

I gave him his gun back. I didn't even like to touch the thing, and it made my heart pound like a kettle drum in my head. I was getting nervous again, just as I'd done in the dressing room at Fashion Bar on my first day of shoplifting. My breathing was erratic and my clothes were drenched in sweat. We had done so many jobs that summer, but this was the first time we'd had to catch and contain people. I didn't like it and we still had one more to go.

Finding Hamilton, the butler, was not difficult. We figured he would probably be somewhere near the game room in order to respond promptly to any calls from his employers. We made our way across the foyer, where, as luck would have it, Hamilton found us. We were slinking around the stairway, guns drawn, trying to find him, when suddenly I heard a voice behind me.

"Dear me," he said, his reedy voice almost deadpan. "Thieves."

I spun around and saw a man in a dark suit carrying a tray full of empty drink glasses. He did not try to run, did not even appear very alarmed. He was an old man, hunched over from osteoporosis. His nose was a large hook, like the beak of a toucan, and he squinted at me from tiny eyes.

"Madam will not be pleased," he said, shaking his head, as if he'd just discovered that one of the parlour maids had broken a vase.

"Come on," Max hissed. "Let's get him in the kitchen!"

219

I got behind the old man and prodded him along with my gun.

"Young man," he said, halting and turning his turtle-like body around, to face me. "I'm afraid the kitchen is *this* way."

In the kitchen he set down his tray and called out to the cook.

"Miss Brooks, I'm afraid these men have come to burgle the house. Miss Brooks," he called. *"Miss Brooks!"*

"Miss Brooks is busy," Max said, and opened the pantry door to reveal the bound and wide-eyed cook. Max tried to bind the man's hands behind his back, but because of his advanced age and his poor posture the hands would not come together. Nor could we imagine him standing for hours until the police arrived. We puzzled for a moment but then decided to seat him in a chair and duct-tape his hands in his lap and his legs to the legs of the chair. When that was done, Max wound the tape all around him and covered his mouth. We then hurried off to see how things were going in the game room.

The game room was, as I've said, enormous, with one side facing out on the back lawn, and the opposing side containing the large fireplace. The two other sides had tall pocket doorways leading to other rooms. The doors to the foyer were open a crack, so we crept up next to them and peered in.

All the guests were seated at the table studying the cards they held in their hands. Jane was trying to focus on her hand, but was obviously distracted and kept glancing around the room.

"It's your turn, dear," Mrs. Gouldstein said, patting Jane on the wrist.

"Oh, I am sorry," Jane said, again turning her focus to her cards. Mrs. Gouldstein took another truffle from the box and popped the whole thing in her mouth. The others sipped at their drinks and exchanged weary glances, wondering if maybe it had not been such a good idea to invite this newcomer. Percy was embarrassed by Jane's delay, and he drank nervously as he waited for her to make her move. When she finally did so, they all gave an audible sigh of relief. The play went on quickly after that, and as the round finished out, the yawning began. It started with Mrs. Gouldstein and Percy, of course, since they had each consumed the largest quantity of the drug, but soon everyone around the table was doing it.

"Maybe I should ring for Hamilton," Mrs. Boatwright-Stark said, "and have him bring us some coffee."

"No!" Jane cried, and then quickly realized her mistake. "No, I mean, none for me, thanks, hee hee. Coffee at this hour? Hee hee, why, you'd be up all night. Have a truffle," she said, snatching the box from the greedy Mrs. Gouldstein and thrusting it toward the other players. "There's plenty of caffeine in these! At least enough to keep you all awake through another one of my turns!" she joked.

They did not laugh.

"No, Percy," Jane said, smacking Percy's hand as he reached for another truffle. "You've had enough! Remember your glucose levels. Please, the rest of you, eat as many as you'd like, I sampled no less than ten of them in the shop this morning, and if I eat even one more I'm surely not going to fit in the car on the way home."

The men laughed politely at this little joke, but Percy and Mrs. Gouldstein were quickly fading, much faster than the others. Mrs. Gouldstein's eyes were getting droopy and her head lolled about. She pushed herself up from the table and wearily exclaimed that she would sit this hand out. She sidled over to the sofa in front of the fire and collapsed onto it, her heavy head wobbling onto one of the pillows. Percy said he thought he might keep her company, and stumbled over to a chair next to her. He similarly collapsed and that left four players: the Boatwright-Starks, Mr. Gouldstein, and Jane.

"What shall we play next?" Beverly asked, deftly shuffling the cards. "Canasta? Euchre? Whist?"

"Oh I don't care, sweet pea," Lloyd said, "Dealer's choice."

"Yes," Mr. Gouldstein chimed in. "But let's make it something easy, for our new guest." He smiled over at Jane and slid his leg up next to hers under the table. She was used to such treatment from men and so didn't even flinch. She smiled over at him and carefully refilled his glass from the shaker.

"A toast," Jane said, raising her glass. They all raised theirs and looked at her expectantly. In her eagerness to get them all guzzling, she hadn't really thought of anything and stared ahead blankly.

"To what, my dear?" Beverly asked, wearily.

"To . . . Uh, many more nights like this!" Jane said.

"Here, here," said Mr. Gouldstein. "I'll drink to that."

"I'll *need* to drink for that," Beverly muttered, taking a large sip of her drink and lighting a cigarette.

"You've all been so kind and patient." Jane gushed, still holding her glass aloft. "It means so much to me. More than you can ever know."

The men, of course were enchanted, and Mr. Gouldstein was so bold as to move one of his meaty hands up onto Jane's thigh. Again, she replenished his drink.

Beverly was shuffling furiously now, a burning cigarette dangling from the corner of her mouth. She looked disgustedly at her husband and Mr. Gouldstein, each smiling like giddy schoolboys at Jane, and then rapped the deck on the table.

"Jane, dear," she said, passing the cards across the table. "Why don't *you* teach us a game. Something from Vietnam, maybe. Something you learned as a child, although for heaven's sake, that was just yesterday!"

The two women exchanged frosty glances and artificial chuckles. Jane seized the deck and scooted her chair closer to the table. She tapped the cards, cut them, and gave them a clumsy shuffle.

"Okay," she said. "We'll play a game I know, one I learned in college, but everyone fill up your glasses because it's a drinking game."

Mr. Gouldstein and Lloyd both nodded their assent and refilled their glasses from the shaker. Beverly shrugged, rolled her eyes, and pushed hers forward to be filled.

"Here's how it works," Jane said, holding the deck. "I flip the cards down, one by one, and anytime a Jack appears you slap it with your hand. The one who hits the Jack first gets the pile of cards and the three who miss it have to take sips of their drinks. Whoever has the smallest pile of cards at the end has to chug the whole thing. Get it?"

"Oh good Lord!" Beverly sighed, raising her heavily bejeweled hand so it was ready to slap the Jack.

Jane dealt quickly and the men lost quickly. After three rounds, Lloyd slumped forward and rested his head on the table. Soon after that, Mr. Gouldstein gave up and went out to smoke a cigar. He did not return. Then it was just Jane and Beverly, facing each other and angrily slapping at cards, each drinking more and more.

Max and I were worried. Jane was not supposed to be drinking at all. At least not yet. Not until after she had taken us through the house and pointed out what we should steal. We sat watching help-lessly as the two women went on, hand after hand, until suddenly, Jane stopped the game.

"Hey, Bev," she said, her head swaying. "You gotta quarter?"

"Eh?" the woman asked. "I don' carry money, dear."

"Wait, wait, I think I got one," Jane said, reaching over and dig-ging in Lloyd's pants pocket.

She obtained a coin and held it up to the light.

"A dime? Guess it'll work. Even though the game's called quar-ters ye' jus' need any coin, or somethin' round, like zish."

Beverly began laughing and lit the wrong end of her cigarette. She scowled when she tasted it and both of them laughed. When the hilarity subsided, Jane tried to explain the fundamentals of quarters. She pushed a martini glass to the middle of the table and filled it to the brim. She then filled each of their glasses.

"Okay, Bev, lishen up, heres's a rules. I bounce a quarter off a the table and try an' get it in the middle glass. If I miss, I take a li'l sip of my drink. Wait. No. Yeah, tha's right. Okay, tha's right, an' if I miss, I take a sip of my drink. Yeah. If I make it—in the glass, I mean—you have to drink your glass *and* thish glass in the middle. Unnerstan?"

Beverly gave a whooping laugh that turned into a fit of coughing.

Jane bounced the quarter once and then we saw it rolling on the floor. She took a sip and then leaned over and dug in Lloyd's pocket for another coin which she tossed over to Beverly.

"Go for it, sishter."

Beverly held the coin in her hand, shook it, blew on it, pretended to spit on it and then bounced it off the table. It landed with a plop in the middle glass.

"Goddamnit!" Max whispered. "What the fuck is she doing?"

Beverly gave an excited shriek and then got up and did a little victory dance around her chair. Jane eyed the glass in disbelief.

"No, wait," she tried to protest. "Wait. I wasn' ready. Wait."

"Wasn' ready!" Beverly cried. "Wasn' ready! Whassat mean? There's no *ready* or *not ready!* Bottoms up, Janey dear!"

Jane lifted her glass with both hands and sipped, making mournful faces as she did so, looking almost as if she might cry. She glanced around, clearly wishing we'd pop out and save her. Finally, a frustrated Beverly reached across and picked up the glass from the middle. She raised it, sloshing some onto the green felt.

"Oh come on, you big baby," she chided Jane. "Drink it like you got a pair! You girls! You haven't won out over us broads yet!" And with that she tilted her head back and downed the cocktail in one gulp. She looked at Jane, her eyes spinning, gave out an enormous belch, and then her knees gave out and she toppled to the floor.

Max burst into the room and Jane stood, unsteadily.

"You're drunk!" he cried, grabbing her by the arm and giving her rubbery body a shake.

"I couldn' help it!" she whined. "I kept feeding her truffeses and drinks but she jes wouldn' go down!"

"Oh, come on," Max said, exasperated. "We better hurry before *you* pass out, too. Dil, go get the bags!"

I ran to the dining room and retrieved the velvet bags from behind the drapes. When I returned, Max was holding Jane up with one hand and lightly slapping her cheeks with the other.

"Where do we start?" Max asked, his tone almost pleading. Jane's head was getting too heavy for her to support.

"Uhsstairs," she said. "Jew'ry's uhsstairs."

I came over, took hold of her other arm, and together Max and I managed to drag her across the floor, out into the foyer and to the foot of the staircase. Then she started giggling and her knees buckled.

"Shit!" Max cried. "Shit, shit, shit!" He tried slapping her, harder this time, but she was almost gone. Even if we did manage to get her up the thirty or so steps, we realized, she would hardly be able to see, let alone determine what was worth stealing.

"Oh, let's just take her back," Max said, his voice full of disgust.

We made a loop and dragged Jane, head drooping forward, back to the game room. We sat her back in her chair, leaned her forward, and rested her head on the game table.

I remembered the truffles and took the new box out of my bag. I picked up the old box, collected the few uneaten pieces that were lying around, and emptied about half of the new box into the old, and placed the new one back on the table. When I'd finished, I looked up and saw Max prying the rings off of Beverly's bony knuckles. I went over to the sofa and did the same to Mrs. Gouldstein, and then to Jane, figuring that it would look suspicious if she remained untouched. We stole the watches from both of the men, and the cash from their wallets, and then quickly went to the next room.

"Stick close," Max whispered. "There's probably not anyone else here, but we can't be too careful."

We were in a formal living room then. Another huge marble fireplace dominated one wall and facing it were two long sofas. In the corner, Max found the cabinet housing the micro-mosaics and quickly began emptying it. There were about twenty of them altogether and they were just as Jane had described them: tiny stone portraits of Italian cities. He removed them one by one from the case and handed them to me to put in my bag.

We went from room to room on the lower level and looted similar cabinets, taking Murrano glass animals, Russian icons, ivory figurines, and whatever else we could find during our frantic search. Then we went upstairs.

The staircase was wide, with a stone balustrade on either side. It went straight up about twenty steps to a landing and then divided in two. The two sides turned at right angles and continued up to the second floor. We made our way up to the next level where we saw more display cases packed with silver trinkets. These were quickly bagged by me while Max ran off in search of the master bedroom. Our bags were nearly full at that point so we figured we had better find the valuable jewelry and avoid any more potentially worthless baubles.

The upstairs hallway was almost surreal: a long corridor punctuated every twenty feet or so by a doorway. We stood for a moment while Max debated whether we should go to the right or to the left. He went right, and I followed, trying the doors on one side while Max took the other. We opened every door along the way, finding guest room after guest room, until finally we reached a set of double doors. I turned the handle, pushed them both open, and gasped. Inside, the whole room was pink—pink walls, pink fireplace, pink carpeting, even elaborately painted pink furniture. Max came up behind me and we both stared for a minute at the odd beauty of it all. It was not an inviting room, and it didn't suit my taste, but I couldn't help but admire the incredible singularity of purpose that must have gone into orchestrating so many different pink things in a single room.

As usual, Max took the woman's dresser and I went through the man's. We rooted through them thoroughly but it didn't take long for us to realize that they contained nothing of real value. If the Boatwright-Starks had jewelry in the house, it certainly wasn't kept in the dressers.

It was as we were turning to leave, giving up on the bedroom, that we saw it. We had been so focused on the dressers that we'd not noticed it. It was lit from above by a spotlight and it shone in its gilt and glass cabinet, like a tiny, shimmering, pink sun.

It was, of course, the rumored Fabergé egg.

We both stopped and stared, unable to speak, unable to believe what we were seeing. It was a large egg, probably about the size of a grapefruit, resting on an elaborately carved base of onyx, platinum, and diamonds. The egg itself was a translucent pink enamel, encircled by three bands of intertwined silver and black garland. It was cracked in half, so to speak, and the top half was tilted back on tiny hinges revealing small black silhouettes of Nicholas and Alexandra, and all of their doomed offspring, each dark face set in its own pearl-and-diamond-encrusted frame.

It was the kind of thing words like "exquisite," "meticulous," and "extraordinary" were designed to describe. It was a hyperbole of beauty and excess, and for that reason any exaggerated descriptions could hardly do it justice. How could we even touch it, I thought, let alone take such a thing?

Max approached the case. He bent down and gazed in, wide-eyed, at the egg. Then he leaned back and examined the display case. The front panel was hinged on the left side and was held shut on the right by a simple gold clasp—the kind you might see on the diary of a teenage girl—useless to keep anyone from invading the space, but there all the same as a reminder that you shouldn't. I held my breath as I watched Max's hand undo the clasp. He slowly pulled open the front panel and as he did so I had the feeling an archaeologist must have when he opens a tomb that has been sealed for centuries: a feeling of rare air escaping.

Max's hand moved toward the egg. When he was inches away, he hesitated a moment, his hand hovering, but then moved forward and touched it, lowering the top portion of the egg and concealing the silhouettes. The two halves came together with an audible click. Max reached his other hand in the case and grasped the egg carefully in both hands. As he lifted it, the alarm went off.

Suddenly sirens blared throughout the house. In the hallway, lights were flashing on and off. It startled Max so much that he jumped back and dropped the egg. I picked it up and handed it back to him quickly like a hot potato. He gazed at it a moment and then took off running. I grabbed both bags and followed after him, running out of the bedroom and down the hall. We reached the stairs and took them three at a time. As I turned on the landing, I missed a step and tumbled down the remaining steps. I landed on my back at the bottom, still clutching both bags. I barely had time to sit up and orient myself before Max had me by the arm and was dragging me back through the foyer. The noise had been loud upstairs, but it was ear-splitting on the lower level. We ran back through the living room and through the game room, in which all the players were still snoozing soundly, and headed out along the gallery. Max was ahead of me. As we reached the dining room, he pulled back the curtain, whipped open the French door and went out. I paused for a moment. I heard pounding on the front door. My heart leapt and I jumped out onto the porch and closed the door behind me.

Outside, the house and lawn were illuminated like a prison. Mr. Gouldstein was passed out in one of the lawn chairs, his cigar dangling from his mouth. Max grabbed my shoulder and pulled me close.

"Run, Dil!" he yelled. "As hard and as fast as you can! Don't stop until you're back over that wall!"

He vaulted off the steps and took off sprinting across the lawn. I followed, the heavy bag on my shoulder bouncing with each step. The distance between the wall and the house seemed much longer this time, and the only way I could tell I was making any progress was by the slowly receding sound of the alarm and the dimming light. Max was several yards ahead of me, and I saw him disappear into the trees. A moment later I was in the trees too, branches slapping me in the face as I went. The vegetation was thick and the ground was uneven with exposed roots and rocks but I went on, resolved not to stop until I got to the wall.

Well, I got to it all right. It was so dark I didn't even see it until I slammed into it head-on. I bounced back and fell on my ass. I sat dazed for a minute, but quickly shook it off and got back up. I could hear Max rustling in the vines above me, so I grabbed on and tried to go up.

Trying to climb in a panic is like trying to swim against an undertow: dangerous, exhausting, and useless. I couldn't find any place to put my feet and tried instead to pull myself up the vines. They would support my weight for about two steps, maybe three, but then they too, would lose their grasp on the wall and I'd come tumbling to the ground. After the third fall, I stopped. I was almost hyperventilating. I was afraid, but I knew that if I was ever going to get out I had to calm down. I took several deep breaths, shook out my hands and feet and approached the wall again. My eyes were beginning to adjust to the darkness. I started climbing. I got up several feet, panicked, pulled my body in close to the wall, and fell. Again, I got up. Again, I tried the deep breaths, but they turned into hysterical sobs. I fell back down on the ground, exhausted from my efforts, my mind going in all different directions. I was losing it. I was going to get caught because I could not get up this stupid, fucking, vine-covered wall—the easiest thing I'd climbed all summer!

Then I heard something hit the ground a few feet away. A moment later I was lifted up.

"Come on, buddy. Come on. It's all right. You're all right. We're almost out. Get on my back."

I climbed on Max's back, wrapping my legs tightly around his waist. I got one arm under his arm and the other around his neck. I could feel the sweat on his head and feel his chest heaving from exertion. He placed his hands and feet and slowly started moving up. Sirens now joined the wailing of the alarm in the distance. I tried to make myself as light as possible, tried not to cling too tightly to him, but I could tell he was straining under the added weight. He would make a few moves and then stop, leaning back on his feet, giving his arms a rest. After several of these starts and stops, we made it to the top. I got off and we rested for a moment. He grabbed me by the shoulders and looked me in the face.

"Be careful on the way down!" he said sternly. "Do not jump until you're sure you're near the bottom. Got it? The last thing we need is for you to break your ankle."

I repositioned my bag and slowly lowered my feet. I clung to the top of the wall with my hands, reluctant to let go, but remembered to lean back and then felt my feet lock in.

Down, step, down, step, slowly, methodically. I got a rhythm going and was soon close enough to see the ground. I let go and dropped down. The sirens were muffled on this side of the wall and that made me feel much safer. I'd stopped crying, but I was drenched in sweat and my breathing was still erratic. Max emerged from the bushes with the golf bags and was quickly stripping out of his black clothing. I did the same, but I was sweating so much that my clothes clung to me like a skin. Eventually, I got them off and Max tossed me my ridiculous plaid slacks and polo shirt. I put them on, stuffed the bag of loot in the bottom of the golf bag, put the black clothes on top of it, and then wedged the clubs in as best I could. Max was already waiting at the edge of the trees when I'd finished. I grabbed the handle of the bag and pulled it over the uneven ground, the wheels squeaking as I went.

The course was dark and empty. We could see the lights of the clubhouse off in the distance and made our way silently across the grass toward it. Just as we were leaving the course, we heard the sprinklers come on behind us. I turned and watched as the streams of water rose and pulsed in the air, and wondered if they were supposed to come on just then, or if someone had been watching us, waiting until we'd left the course. It was another thing to worry about, but I was too tired.

We were silent as we loaded the bags back into the Jaguar and drove out of the country club. Usually, when we finished a job, we both had an adrenaline rush and would talk a mile a minute as we recounted the highlights and discussed what we'd got. This time, however, even though we had something much more valuable than anything else we'd stolen that summer, there was no exuberance,

230

no adrenaline. We were exhausted. Spent. Worn out. The stress level, from the time we entered the country club that afternoon, until we drove back out the gate late that night, had been so consistently high that once it finally lowered, we could do nothing but exist until such time as we could collapse, which we did as soon as we got back home. We parked the car in the driveway, took the bags inside, and without a word retired to our respective rooms, not waking until late the next morning.

Chapter Eighteen

The next morning Max and I slept late, which was easy to do as the sky was overcast and a steady, rhythmic rain was falling. When I got up, I found Max already seated at the kitchen table drinking coffee, the newspaper spread out before him.

"Anything about last night?" I asked. He looked up and smiled at me.

"No, I expect it all happened too late to make it into today's paper."

"Any word from Jane?" I asked, pouring myself some coffee (a habit I had recently acquired).

"No," he said, lifting up his own cup to be refilled, but still staring down at the paper, "and I'm a little worried. They'll hit her with lots of questions and I keep imagining her waking up and saying things she shouldn't. She's a smart girl though, knows when to keep quiet, even in a pinch like that, so she'll probably do all right."

I took a section of the paper and began to thumb through it.

"What would you like for breakfast today, Dil?" Max asked, getting up and moving toward the refrigerator.

"I don't care," I shrugged. "Cereal, maybe. Whatever."

"Cereal? Cereal!" he cried, in mock outrage, his back to me. "Why on earth would you want cereal?" he turned around and in his hand he held something concealed by a napkin. "Why on earth would you want cereal," he repeated, a sour expression on his face. "Or toast, or even waffles . . . when you can have . . . an egg!" And like a magician, he whipped off the napkin to reveal the jewel-encrusted wonder, setting it gently on the table before me. I had not seen it since the night before and in the grim light of morning, and in a suburban setting it looked even more spectacular. I picked it up, surprised by its weight and solidity, and gazed at it.

"The czar once held that," Max said, as proudly as if he'd laid the egg himself.

I undid the clasp and pushed back the top half. As I did so, the framed silhouettes, which were each mounted on tiny gold accordion brackets, blossomed into view.

"What do you think it's worth?" I asked, awestruck.

"I really don't know," Max said, bending down to examine it more closely. "Jane will have to say for sure, but I think this will push us over the top of the fund-raising goal. It should be more than enough to finance *ma vie française*, and enable Jane to stock the shelves of the little space she found last week."

Since the weather was so bad, we decided to stay at the house that morning. Usually we would have gone climbing, or shoplifting downtown, but that day, I remember, we were content to sit on the sofa and read, and glance proudly every now and then at the egg.

Again, Max read and I listened, and again, he read from Balzac, pausing now and then to have me enter something in the notebook he was assembling on France.

"Write down *Flicoteaux's*," he'd say, and then slowly spell it out for me. "From the description here it sounds like an inexpensive place to eat, and a place where I could meet some of the more roguish people of Paris. *Flicoteaux's* and the *Rocher de Cancale*; write that down, too."

Dutifully, I wrote, and Max resumed reading until something else caught his fancy and he'd look up from the book and muse out loud.

"I wonder how much a box at the *Italiens* will cost me?" or, "Do you think it will be difficult to find suitable apartments in the *Faubourg Saint Germain?* I suppose I'll have to start out humbly in the Latin Quarter. Probably wouldn't do to draw attention to myself as soon as I arrive."

We were reading from *Splendors and Miseries of a Courtesan*, the plot of which picks up where the last book, *Lost Illusions*, left off. In this new book, Lucien, now rescued from suicide, and Vautrin (still disguised as a Spanish priest) have arrived in Paris and started their scheme to elevate Lucien to a position of wealth and power. Soon after their arrival, Lucien meets and falls in love with a beautiful young prostitute named Esther. Their love is mutual and Esther decides to abandon her trade, mend her ways and try to become a woman worthy of Lucien. This love affair was not in Vautrin's original plan, but he manages to use it to his advantage, dangling the prospect of their future happiness before them as an enticement to get them to do whatever he wants. Having little choice but to put their trust in him, Lucien and Esther allow him to pull all of the strings, and they dance and strut as he directs. They become nothing more than pawns in his nasty game to acquire wealth and power.

Of course, Max relished the tale. He loved all the disguises that Vautrin could assume and the way he could manipulate others, like an evil puppeteer, coercing them into whichever position he desired. But while Max's admiration of the master criminal rose with each new revelation of treachery, my own regard for Vautrin sank. I was secretly rooting for the star-crossed couple, and I hated the cruel way Vautrin was using them. Worse than that, as the story went on, I began to catch glimpses of my own situation. Although Max was not forcing me to sleep with an ugly Alsatian banker, like Vautrin did to Esther, or making me woo the homely young daughter of a millionaire, as he did to Lucien, I was, nevertheless, aware that both Max and Jane were using me. They were using my efforts and abilities to help finance their own ventures, and, like Lucien and Esther, I was getting very little in return. Oh, Jane and Max gave me money, and any "thing" I desired, but that wasn't what I wanted. No, what I wanted was the same intangible thing that they wanted: freedom. Freedom from my horrible school life. Freedom from Lana. Freedom from my lonely existence. Freedom, and the chance to exist in the universe of Max and Jane, to bask in their sun, to be recognized by them as one of them. But, I was beginning to realize, those were things that not even the profit from the egg would enable me to have. So I did my best to content myself with the tangible things they gave me: a watch, an autographed photo of the Carpenters, clothing, a new clarinet, and some of the stolen trinkets that Jane could not sell, knowing all the while in the back of my mind that the days were getting shorter and that the fantasy life I was living would most likely end with the summer. With a tinge of sadness, I saw that once Jane had her shop I would rarely, if ever, see her anymore. And once Max was gone, he would not, indeed he could not, come back. Ever. And for the first time, I began to wonder what would happen to me. When they had both moved on, what would I do?

I continued staring at the egg and I realized that although for them it represented a new beginning, for me it symbolized the end. The end of summer, the end of my adventures with Max and Jane and Serge. The end of my happiness, really. When they were gone, my life would return to the way it had been, and that thought was more dismal to me than the gray sky overhead. It was the kind of thought that made me want to start drinking again, to just retire to my bed and numb myself with port. I tried to shake it, tried my best to hide the depression I felt creeping into my life that morning; but as the day went on, it just got worse.

Later that afternoon, Max and I went downtown to go shopping at the gourmet grocery store on Capitol Hill. He had found an old copy of *Larousse Gastronomique* on the bookshelf at Paris a few weeks earlier and decided that he wanted to make a huge French meal for Lana and me that night, as a sort of celebration.

At the store, I trailed morosely behind Max as he wandered the produce section, humming and gathering up all the exotic ingredients he needed. Without warning, I felt myself starting to cry. I tried to stop it, but I couldn't. My grief had been quietly inflating inside of me all morning and, quite suddenly, it popped.

Max was bagging up some shallots, turned, and caught sight of me.

"Dil, what is it?" he asked, a grave look on his face.

Again, I tried to stop myself, but I couldn't. The tears fell fast and heavy. Max looked alarmed, like he thought maybe I was physically hurt. He dropped the plastic bag he was holding, took me by the arm, and led me outside. He sat me down on one of the planters and knelt in front of me, both hands on my arms, his eyes scanning my face.

"Dil, what's happened?"

People were beginning to stare as they passed. I wiped my eyes and nose on my shoulder and looked down at my feet. My body heaved and shook. I didn't know what to say, where to look. He kept holding on to my arms, waiting for me to say something.

"I'm . . . I'm going . . . to miss you," I managed to say.

I didn't look at him, but I felt him let go of my arms. He ran his hand through his hair and then rubbed his eyes, as if he had a headache. I was aware, even before I had opened my mouth to speak, of the danger of what I was about to say. In saying it, I had opened up a landscape Max rarely, if ever, entered and beckoned him in. I knew how he hated gushing of any sort, knew it was just like the sappy climax of the movies he walked out of, knew that it was the reason he never let me go through the women's dressers. I knew, yet again, I was being sentimental, but I couldn't help it, and that disappointed us both. I wanted so much to be like him, so cool, and dispassionate, and detached, but I just couldn't. I couldn't play stone face anymore. Not then. Not with him. I knew he was going to leave and the sadness affected my body like some strange pollen, making me cry instead of sneeze.

Max stood up and looked blankly across the parking lot into the distance. I knew he didn't know what to say. I think he was honestly surprised that I was so upset. A few moments later, he looked back down at me and smiled uneasily. He rubbed my head, put his arm around my shoulder, and led me back to the car. Nothing more was said about it. Not that day, not ever. We abandoned the plans for dinner and drove silently to the Ogden where we bought tickets for the three o'clock show.

We were early, so we sat in silence in the balcony waiting for the film to start, Max smoking next to me. I sensed that he felt bad, and I suppose that was some consolation, although I still wished he would say something to me.

Like most of the movies that summer, we did not see the end of this one. I don't think we even saw half of it. But this time it wasn't Max's doing. No, this time our viewing pleasure was interrupted by Jane, who came stomping noisily up the balcony stairs.

"Max!" she whispered, peering into the darkness. "Dillon!"

She was scanning the seats trying to find us. The theater was nearly empty but there were still some "shhhs" that came out of the darkness. We got up and went to where she was standing.

"I knew I'd find you here!" she hissed and smacked Max in the arm with her purse.

"Shhh!" said the voices, more emphatically this time.

"We can't talk here," she said. "Meet me at Paris. Don't follow me out for about five or ten minutes. I'll be waiting."

She then disappeared down the balcony steps. Max and I waited, as she'd instructed, and then made our way outside.

When we arrived at Paris, we found Jane seated in a corner, away from the window, hiding behind a copy of the *Denver Post*.

"Anything about us?" Max asked, pulling back an edge of the paper. She folded it angrily and glared at us from behind her large sunglasses. With her hair pulled back and her lips tightly pursed, she looked like some angry wasp about to move in and deliver the sting. Max and I backed away.

"We'll, uh, get coffee," he said. "Anything for you?"

She scowled.

When we returned, she continued glaring at us, not saying a word. Max sipped his coffee as casually as he could and smiled.

"We thought maybe we'd hear from you sooner," he said cheerfully, "but I suppose you were tied up for a while."

Still nothing. It was obvious that she was barely containing her anger.

"So, what happened?" Max asked. "There was the hospital, I suppose, then the police, and . . ."

Silence.

Max and I glanced at each other uneasily and then back at Jane. When she spoke, her voice was low and level, almost like a robot.

"You took the egg," she said.

"Yes, we certainly did!" Max exclaimed reaching out to take one of Jane's hands in his. She snatched it back into her lap and shook her head in disbelief.

"Stupid!" she said, still shaking her head. "Stupid! How could you be so stupid?"

Max's surprise was evident on his face. We had both thought she'd be pleased we'd gotten the egg. It was, we felt sure, the most valuable thing in the entire house and we had gotten away with it.

"What's the matter?" Max asked, confused. "It's not fake, is it?"

"No, it's not fake," she said, pounding her fist on the table. "But it would probably be worth more if it was!"

Now I was really confused. She gave a tired sigh and began her explanation.

"That's a real Fabergé egg, dummy. There are only fifty-six of them in the whole world. Twelve of them are unaccounted for. That leaves forty-four that *are* accounted for. Their locations and their owners are all very well known! Are you getting it? The one you took is one of the forty-four. Our trying to sell it would be like trying to sell the Lindbergh baby or, or, or the fucking crown jewels!"

"What about your man?" Max asked. "He must be willing to take it for something. Granted, we'll have to take a deep cut in price but surely—"

She shook her head.

"He even called me when he heard about it," she said.

Max and I were a bit surprised he had already heard anything about it, since it had happened less than twenty-four hours ago. "We joked about it," Jane continued. "He said he was glad that I was not so stupid as to steal something like that!"

Max massaged his forehead with his fingers.

"How did he know about it?" I asked.

"Oh, word travels fast when something like that is stolen. Believe me! Anyone who's important in the jewelry and antique circle has heard about it. If they ever hear I'm connected to it, I'm screwed. There goes my reputation!"

"There must be someone," Max said, his mind still on selling the thing.

Jane shook her head.

"I mean it can't be . . . worthless."

Jane nodded.

Max's shoulders fell and I saw that his hands shook when he tried to light a cigarette. I knew he was upset, but he was trying to hide it. He had spent the entire time since we'd acquired the egg building paper castles in France and now he was abruptly back where he'd been two days earlier. It was almost as if all of my anxiety from that morning had suddenly transferred over to him.

"What about . . . what about this?" Max said, his voice eager and shaky. "What if we ransomed the egg back to them? The Boatwright-Starks, I mean. Like it's been kidnapped or something."

"Like the Lindbergh baby?" Jane added tartly.

"No? You don't think we cou—"

"No. In fact when I spoke to Beverly this morning at the hospital she said she was almost relieved the egg was gone as she'd always been afraid of having it stolen. She's more than a little thrilled with the insurance settlement they'll get. Face it, we've got a worthless piece of priceless art. I still can't believe you could have been so stupid!" Jane repeated, addressing us both this time. "What were you thinking? I just can't believe it."

"Oh you can't?" Max said. His tone had shifted and I could hear that he was about to vent his own anger. "Well you know what I can't believe? I can't believe you got so goddamned sloppy drunk that you couldn't even fulfill your end of the bargain! You do remember, *chère* Jane, that you were to be the one determining what we should steal? If someone hadn't lost her head and resorted to sorority girl drinking games, maybe we'd have fucking known what the fuck we were supposed to fucking take!"

This last sentence was shouted and caught the attention of the other patrons. They all stared over at us and the café went silent. Jane slumped down in her chair and put her hand on her forehead to conceal her eyes.

"Will you please lower your voice?" she said, a false smile animating her face. "We really can't draw attention to ourselves. We're taking a great risk even being seen with each other. The insurance guys are already all over this case, not to mention the police."

This quieted Max. He looked around, suddenly aware of all the other people. We were all silent for a moment.

"Tell me about it," Max said, his voice somber. "What happened after we left?"

Jane leaned forward, both elbows resting on the table. She seemed both nervous and confused.

"I wish I knew," she said. "I mean, what *did* happen after you left? The first thing I remember is waking up in the hospital. It took them a while to figure out what we'd been poisoned with, but once they did, they just let us sleep it off. By this morning, we were all fine. A little hungover, but fine. You did remember to take the box of truffles with you, didn't you?" she asked, an urgent, pleading expression on her face. "*Please* say you did!"

"We got it," I said.

"Oh bless you, Dillon. That was the one thing I was most worried about! Of course I was afraid that maybe you'd been caught, too, but oh, thank God!"

"So who do they suspect?" Max asked, his hand still trembling as he smoked.

"It's hard to say," Jane said, pensively. She then reached for the package of cigarettes and lit one for herself. This was the first time I had seen Jane smoke and even though I could not see her eyes, I knew she was as scared as Max.

"The police came into my room this morning, right after the nurse brought in my breakfast tray. I was a little nervous, but I think I did quite well, considering. I mean, it's almost better that I did pass out early, because I had even less to hide. I was almost as much in the dark about it as the others, so there wasn't very much I could tell them. They asked if I'd seen anything or anyone acting strangely at the party; and I said no, but that some of the events of the evening were all a bit sketchy. That's because of the drugs, they told me. I played dumb then, which, as you can imagine, is not easy for me. "Drugs!" I said. "I can't speak for the others, but *I* certainly hadn't been doing any drugs!" Well, they had a good chuckle over that one and explained that two men had broken in, drugged us somehow, and then burglarized the house.

"Do they suspect us?" Max asked.

"No," Jane replied. "I even asked specifically if it had been the Balzac Bunch and they said no. They said they didn't find any of the usual clues, which I'm assuming meant your little calling card, and let me just state here how proud and thankful I am that you didn't leave one this time. I don't think my poor, weak nerves could take it."

"There wasn't time," Max said. "As soon as we lifted the egg, the alarm system went whooping wild! Didn't it, Dil?"

"Well, thank God for that," Jane said. "Anyway, the detective said that the Balzac Bunch only strikes when the homeowners are out or have gone to bed. Never when they're awake and at home, like on this job. They said the cook and the butler each gave descriptions of the burglars but that they were wearing ski masks and so the descriptions can only tell so much. Then the whole thing got a little odd . . ."

"How so?" Max asked.

"Well, the cop started asking me if I noticed anyone acting strangely during the bridge game. I said no, not really. I said Mr. Gouldstein had gotten a little friendly once his wife dropped off, but that was all. They perked up when I mentioned his name and asked if I had noticed when exactly he had passed out. I said no. I said he kept getting up to go outside and smoke his cigars, but that was all. Then they asked if I had any knowledge of his business troubles. . ."

"Now that is odd," Max said, leaning forward and emphasizing the point with his cigarette. "He must be in some sort of money trouble."

"That's exactly what I thought."

"So the heat's off us."

"It would appear so, for now at least."

And it probably would have stayed off of us had not Max and I done two very stupid things. That's not entirely true. Wayne is the one who truly complicated the situation, but not until after Max and I had done our damage. Since I am the one telling the story, and you, the reader, are therefore subjected to my biased point of view, I suppose I ought to be brave and tell you my part first. But I'm afraid that would upset the chronology of the story. Besides, it was

Max's part that made me think my part might be okay to do in the first place, so I'll tell you what he did first. Confused? Buckle up and hang on.

In the days after our meeting with Jane, the "Bridge Game Burglary" was big news. It was the lead story on all the local newscasts and made the front page of both newspapers. There were tearful accounts of the things lost and colorful photos and descriptions of the egg. Mrs. Boatwright-Stark was particularly upset at the loss of her engagement ring, which was, ironically, worth nothing. A stainless steel band from a gumball machine that her husband had given her long before he'd amassed his fortune, but to which she had attached great sentimental value over the years. There were said to be no suspects, but it was not, as Jane said, believed to have been done by the Balzac Bunch, because, to quote one of the detectives, "This was a real professional job."

The implication in that was, of course, that all of the jobs done by the Balzac Bunch were petty, sloppy, unprofessional little heists. When Max read that quote, his hubris took over. He threw down the paper and immediately drove to Woolworth's where he stole a Polaroid camera and several packages of film. He bought a newspaper from one of the boxes on the street and then returned home and took all of these things down to the cellar. He positioned the egg on the floor, had me hold the newspaper behind it so that the date could be seen, and then snapped several pictures. While they were developing, he put on a pair of white cotton gloves and composed the following letter on Lana's typewriter:

> To Whom It May Concern:
> We, the Disciples of Jacques Collin (AKA The Balzac Bunch), were most gratified to hear that the recent burglary at the Boatwright-Stark mansion was executed by "professionals." We had been terribly afraid of never losing our amateur status and

are relieved that we have now, according to the Denver Police Department, entered the big leagues.

Sincerely,

The D. of J. C.

He then pulled the letter from the typewriter, placed it and the best of the photos in a plain white envelope, and addressed the envelope by hand, using his left hand to write. It was to go to the newspaper that had run the "professional" quote from the officer. Later that day, on the way to the movies, he dropped it in a mailbox near the Ogden. In the meantime, I did a little letter writing of my own.

I am, as Max had discovered, a somewhat sentimental person and the story of Beverly being grief-stricken by the loss of her cheap ring touched me for some reason. Maybe it was because my own mother had eagerly pawned both of her engagement rings even before her divorces were finalized. Maybe it was because Beverly's story reminded me of that story in which a woman cuts off all her hair to buy her husband a watch chain but her husband has sold his watch to buy her some combs for her hair. I don't know. But whatever the reason, without telling Max, I plucked the tin ring from the pile of stolen lucre in the cellar and, as Max had done, I placed it in a plain white envelope. I was careful to wear gloves, just as he had done, and to address the envelope with my left hand, so that the handwriting looked blocky and childlike. I then mailed the ring from the same box near the Ogden and felt warm and happy for the rest of the day, imagining Beverly's glee when she cut open the envelope and tapped out the contents.

When Max's letter became public, Jane was livid. She no longer came to our house, out of fear that the police might be watching her, but the ear-lashing she gave Max over the telephone was clearly audible in the next room. Max listened, recited penitent apologies to her, and grave promises not to do anything else so foolish in the future, but all the while he was smiling, and smoking, and gleefully opening and closing the egg, watching the Romanov silhouettes appear and disappear. Appear and disappear.

Some days later, when the story of the returned ring came out, Jane's outrage, like a virus, infected Max. Gone was all his puckish playful humor, replaced instead by a stern angry disbelief.

"Honestly, Dil!" he yelled, after we'd seen a news report on the ring and after I had confessed that I'd been the one who sent it. "I don't know how you could justify taking a risk like that. Stupid! Just plain, unnecessarily stupid! Never, Dil! Never give in to sentiment! How many times have I told you that?"

That he said all that with a straight face is a testament to Max's unique method of hypocrisy. His vain acts of whimsy were justifiable, whereas my sentimental gesture was just plain dangerous! Instead of yelling he really should have thanked me because returning the ring was the best PR we could ever have had. In the eyes of society the Disciples of Jacques Collin were still dangerous criminals, but I think people were glad to discover that if we were dangerous criminals at least we were dangerous criminals with a soft spot.

Max, however, did not soften. In fact, if anything, he became harder and more unyielding than ever. It was now mid-August and despite a summer of profitable thefts, he still did not have enough money to get himself out of the United States and legitimately established in France. The reality of this economic shortfall was only made worse by the fact that Jane was herself doing quite well. The last load of micro-mosaics from the Boatwright-Starks had pushed her over the top and brought her enough money to finally open her own shop. She was rapidly using her knowledge, now backed up with cash, to acquire stock from various estate sales and dealers around the world, and was selling her goods almost as fast as they came in.

Ironically, she had the most business from the people whose

houses we had burglarized. Day after day the society matrons marched into her shop, insurance checks in hand, eager to replenish what had been stolen. Max's envy was palpable, and it got even worse when Jane, still furious about our letter writing, informed us that she would no longer participate in or supply information for any more burglaries.

"Besides," she said, with a toss of her hair, "I am far too busy now."

This made both Max and me uneasy. Me because I did not wish to do anymore of Max's shot-in-the-dark-haphazard-night-raids, and Max because he knew that even if we did them, he did not have the knowledge of what to steal or where to sell it.

Despair took up residence in the house after that, and Max's spirits sunk so low that he actually considered doing some of the work he'd promised Lana we would do that summer. We even went out one morning and half-heartedly stole some painting clothes and some brushes, and bought a few gallons of paint, but that's about as far as it went. By the time we returned home, it was raining again so we parked all of the supplies in the garage where they remained, undisturbed.

The next day Max was even more depressed and listless. He lay around all afternoon smoking, and drinking coffee, and mooning, yet again, over the glossy pictures of France in the dog-eared *National Geographics*.

I knew it was bad when the *National Geographics* and the Berlitz tapes came back out. They had both come with him from prison where, I suspect, they had given hope to his caged soul like a crack of sunshine and the view of distant hills. And yet, shortly after he arrived at our house and started making real progress toward realizing his dream, they were stuffed away in one of the empty wine racks and pulled out only when he wanted to cross reference something we'd read in Balzac, or to check on pronunciation.

When I'd first heard the tapes at the beginning of the summer, it was almost as if the house had been turned into a French echo chamber. The bland nasally voice on the cassette would call out from the tape player, and Max would dutifully answer.

"*Bonjour, comment ca va?*"

"*Bonjour, comment ca va?*"

"*Très bien, merci, et vous?*"

"*Très bien, merci, et vous?*"

And yet, when Max pulled the tapes out this time, the conversations were mournfully one-sided. I sat alone in my room, practicing my clarinet, and all I could hear was the tape-recorded voice coming up from the cellar through the heating vent, followed by a heavy silence.

"*Allez-vous au marche?*"

"   "

"*A quel heur?*"

"   "

The house resonated with Max's silence. It was a testament to his misery and resignation.

When he pulled the tapes and magazines out that morning, I knew it was not to practice or plan. It was because at that point his French dream seemed further away than ever from becoming reality. The pictures and voices did not give him hope, as they had in prison, but rather, augmented his despair, making the pain of impossibility all the more bittersweet. It was as if he were slowly resigning himself to the fact that they were all he was going to get: pictures and a recorded voice, other people's impressions, other people's conversations.

At first, I'll admit, I took a perverse pleasure in his misery because I felt sure he'd stay on at the house, at least a little while longer. But later, after three days of watching the one I idolized pine away, I decided to do something about it. I put down my clarinet and went down to the cellar. The door was closed so I knocked before I went in. It was dark, but the air was thick with smoke and I saw the burning ember of Max's cigarette, so I knew he was there. I pulled on the light. Max was lying on his back on the top of the wine rack, staring up at the ceiling. I went over to the tape recorder and stopped the tape.

"I know I'm not a very good reader," I said, searching in the rack for the book we'd been reading, "but I could try and read to you if you'd like. From the Balzac."

He shrugged his shoulders, gave an indifferent grunt and turned over to face the wall.

"I'd like to know how it turns out," I lied, trying to sound as cheerful and enthusiastic as I could. In truth I hated Balzac. I was so tired of the convoluted plots and difficult names that I would almost rather have read from the hokey *Teen Bible* Wayne had given me for my disastrous confirmation. And yet I suspected that if anything would please Max it would be listening to the naughty exploits of his alter ego, Vautrin.

I found the book and opened it to where we had left off and started to read.

Lucien and Esther were both miserable in their enslaved servitude. Vautrin was pimping Esther out to the Alsatian banker and then using the money she obtained to prop up Lucien's position in society. The goal of this plan was to make Lucien appear wealthy so that the father of the rich young heiress he was pursuing would not think him a gold digger and would allow him to marry his daughter. Once Lucien had married and taken control of his wife's money, Vautrin's idea was that the three—Lucien, Esther, and Vautrin— would all take a share. If all went according to plan, Lucien would be rich and his position in society secure. He would then be able to keep Esther as his mistress. As for Vautrin, he would presumably have enough money to move to America and buy the plantation he had always dreamed of.

As I read on, it became clear that Vautrin's plan was not going smoothly. The actors were revolting against the director. Esther realized that she could not give herself, for any amount, to the despicable Alsatian and decided to commit suicide rather than sully her love for Lucien. Unaware of her plan, but himself tired of being under Vautrin's evil spell, Lucien decides to write a letter and tip off the police that Father Carlos Herrera is really none other than the master criminal Jacques Collin.

As I read we both became increasingly interested in the direction the plot was going. It was an exciting turn of events and I mentioned to Max that I was pleased to see that Lucien was finally fighting back. Max however, was unimpressed.

"It's like mice setting a trap for a tiger," he said, referring to Esther and Lucien's moves to block Vautrin's plan. "Foolish. The tiger is smarter and more powerful. He'll stop them. You watch, Dil."

He then seized the book from me and began reading on with renewed vigor. The reading had, as I thought it would, reignited his spark, given him the jump-start start he needed to pull himself out of his funk. As I practiced my clarinet in my room later that evening I was relieved to hear, once again, both sides of the Berlitz echo. By the next morning Max was back to his usual self and burst into my room again, heavily caffeinated and ready to go.

"Dil," he said, holding his index finger up in the air, "I have a plan!"

And what a plan. A miserable plan. A plan I wanted absolutely no part of. A plan more reckless and stupid than any Lucien and Esther (or Lucy and Ethel, for that matter) could have devised. A plan to get his money back from Doris.

Doris. The woman who surrounded herself with no-neck henchman and always carried a loaded pistol. The woman who would, without a second thought, have killed Max (and probably me as well). The woman who had made me afraid every time I even caught a glimpse of a back-combed hairdo.

"You're . . . kidding?" I said, and grinned tentatively. "You are kidding . . . Aren't you?"

He said nothing but went over to my closet and retrieved the pistol he had bought me. He held it up to the light and examined the chambers.

He wasn't kidding. The mouse was going to set a trap for the tiger.

"It'll be easy," he said, snapping the chamber shut and aiming the gun out the window. "You'll see."

"I won't do it," I said.

"But it'll be easy."

"No."

"Now come on, Dil, don't be difficult," he said, moving over to where I was sitting on the bed and caressing my calf. "I neeeeed your help."

"No," I said, and tried my best to look hard and unyielding, all the while conscious of his hand on my leg. We stayed like that for several moments, each staring at the other, my erection stirring under the sheets. Finally, he spoke.

"I guess it is a lot to ask," he said. He removed his hand from my thigh, stood up and walked to the door, pausing when he reached it. "Never mind. Forget I mentioned it." And he walked out.

He ignored me most of that day, sitting at the kitchen table with a pencil and a yellow legal pad making detailed notes on his plan of attack, but I would not be ignored. I could not let him do something so foolish and potentially deadly. Trying to be optimistic, I suggested various alternatives: shoplifting outings that might bring in bigger money, more shot-in-the-dark-night-raids, a jewelry store heist, but to no avail.

He rarely looked up from his legal pad while I spoke and when he did it was only to say, "Don't worry, Dil. If you're not with me, I'll do it myself. It's no big deal."

"Look," I said again and again, "I'll do anything to help you. Anything but the Doris job. I'll do the suicide-night-raids, I'll rob a bank, I'll mug old ladies at the mall, whatever you want! But not the Doris job."

"Thanks, Dil," he said, giving me a plastic smile. He was at the top of the stairs about to descend into the cellar, his coffee cup and legal pad in hand. "But they would hardly be worth it. I need money, not more stuff to unload. We're already stuck with the world's most expensive paperweight." And he descended once again to the cellar, closing the door behind him.

For the next few days, we avoided each other. I stuck to my room and pouted. Max spent most of his days plotting out his plan at the kitchen table, or target shooting out behind the house. Several times I asked if he wanted to go climbing, or to the movies, or out shoplifting, but he'd just look up at me with that same plastic smile and say, "I'd really like to, Dil, but I'm busy right now." Then he'd retreat back into the cellar and close the door behind him. When he emerged, I asked him what he was planning; but he just shook his head, gave me a condescending look, and said, "Since you're not in on it, Dil, it's probably safer if you don't know too much about it."

In the end, curiosity and loneliness got the best of me. I was tired of being left out, so I gave in. I stomped downstairs one afternoon, after having played every song in the Carpenters' songbook several times over on my clarinet and found Max, as usual, seated at the kitchen table, smoking, his mysterious legal pad on the table in front of him. I stood there, but he would not look up at me. I cleared my throat.

"Yes, Dil," he said with a sigh, "What is it?"

I said nothing, hoping that my silence would make him curious enough to look up. I wanted to see the expression on his face when I made my dramatic declaration. He would not oblige.

"All right!" I exclaimed, frustrated with his obstinance. "I'll do it."

Max did not respond, did not even look up. He just raised his hand in the air for me to give him a high five.

Chapter Nineteen

Max did not tell Jane about the Doris plan. In fact, Max and Jane did not really communicate at all for almost two weeks after the letter-writing scandal. They talked on the phone a few times, but these were mostly heated exchanges about money; and after hanging up on each other numerous times, the phone calls stopped, too. Jane did call again, but at about that time we stopped answering the phone. It was almost invariably James trying to persuade me to let him come by and get the Jaguar, or the insurance inspector wanting to know who exactly had signed the authorization for the repairs, or the police, who were now looking for Max either because of the insurance people or because of Meredith.

It was not a complete surprise then, to be sitting in my room one morning playing the clarinet and hear the front doorbell ring. I crept out into the hall and peered through the octagonal window, but there was no car in the driveway. That roused my suspicions. I stood there, not knowing what to do. I knew Max would never answer it. If he had heard it at all, he was probably busy hiding.

The doorbell became more insistent and was accompanied by loud knocking. I made my way down the stairs, set my clarinet on the floor and peered through the peephole. It was Jane. I unlocked the door, and it was immediately pushed open with such force that it made an arc on its hinges, hit the wall, and then slammed shut.

"Damnit!" she yelled, and pushed it open again. She sailed past me into the foyer.

"Where's Max?" she insisted. "And why haven't you been answering the phone? I've been calling for days!" She was out of breath.

"There are some people after Max," I said, "so we've been ignoring the phone."

She groaned and narrowed her eyes.

"People are *always* after Max. Who is it this time?"

"An insurance guy."

"What!" Jane shrieked. She staggered backward if she'd been struck.

"About the *car*," I said as reassuringly as I could. "The car. The Jaguar. My stepfather's car."

She let her shoulders relax and released her breath. Max must have heard her voice because he emerged from the cellar.

"Miss Nguyen!" he said, his voice full of sarcasm. "To what do we owe the pleasure?"

"It's hardly a pleasure, I'm sad to say."

She sidled up to Max and plucked the box of cigarettes from his shirt pocket, removed one, and Max lit it for her. She stood for a moment inhaling deeply and then sat on the arm of the sofa.

"There's trouble," she said, eyeing us both.

This was hardly news.

"Does anyone know you're here?" Max asked, seating himself in the chair opposite her and lighting a cigarette for himself.

"No, no. I took a cab and had him drop me on some street in the subdivision down below. I ran up here from there."

"Good. Fine," said Max. "Now tell us what's happened."

"It's the police."

"Yes."

"They're on to us."

"How do you know?" Max asked, still more curious than concerned.

"They came to the shop yesterday evening and brought something with them. It was a tool. A climbing tool, I think. Silver, shaped like a figure eight. They said they'd found it at the base of one of the buildings in Cheesman Park and they're sure it was used in the robbery."

I remembered the job immediately. It had been the one with the southwestern pottery. Eighth floor. We had rappelled down and used the figure-eight tool as a pulley. It must have fallen out of the bag when we were putting things away.

"Fingerprints?" Max asked coolly.

"No," Jane said. "I asked about that. One of the gardeners found it and he messed it up. 'Contaminated it,' they said."

"Wait a minute," Max said, taking a drag on his cigarette, his brow firmly set. "Why did they ask you about it? They can't connect you to that job!"

"No, no," Jane cried. "They showed it to me after they showed me the picture of Serge!"

"Serge!"

"Yes! That's what I came to tell you. They think he's behind it all!"

"But . . ."

"They said the tool was definitely his because it's stamped with his own personal logo."

I remembered the little sheep teetering on the mountaintop that he put on all the climbing tools he forged.

"But he sells some of those!" Max cried. "And he gives them away. Anyone who climbs in Boulder could have one. There's no reason for them to think he did it."

"True, but think about it in relation to the other clues," Jane said. "He's a climber; his business is not doing well; he's French."

"He's not French!" Max interrupted. "He's Canadian!"

"Oh, God! Whatever!" Jane shouted. "The point is French is his native tongue! Look, the reason they showed me the picture was to ask if I'd ever seen him before. Of course I said no, but I don't think I hid my surprise very well. It's only a matter of time before they realize I know him; and when they do, it's only a matter of time before they connect me to you, and then, oohhhh, what should we do?"

Max had no answer to this. Lots of silent smoking followed as we all considered the situation. I wanted a drink.

"Listen," Max said. "Maybe it's not such a bad thing."

Jane and I eyed him, confused. Max went on: "I mean, he obviously didn't do it, right? So the less he knows about it the better. He's got an alibi for the nights of the robberies. We better not say a thing—to him or to anyone else. If he's in the dark about it then he can't really sound guilty."

There was a certain logic to what Max was saying and yet I felt uneasy about it. I thought of Serge, alone in his sparsely furnished apartment, and how I knew he spent most nights watching TV and drinking by himself. What alibi could he possibly have other than that of his dog, Stella?

"So we don't tell him anything?" Jane asked. "We really should tell him something, don't you think?"

Max shook his head.

"We have to help him!" I cried.

"No." Max's voice was firm and his expression severe. "No. Now listen. We're not going to tell him anything! Any of us! They're on the wrong track now; let's take advantage of that."

We hashed it over for a while, but in the end Jane and I reluctantly agreed to keep quiet. At least until we could formulate a plan for Max to escape. We drove Jane back to her shop and then Max and I went on, as best we could, planning our robbery of Doris.

The next day, two days before we were to pull off the robbery, Serge was arrested. Jane had been calling to tell us about it, but, as usual, we hadn't answered. We didn't hear about it until the paper arrived the next morning with a headline proclaiming that at last a suspect in the Balzac Burglaries had been caught. I picked up the paper from the driveway that morning and quickly took it in to Max who was seated at the table, about to have his first cup of coffee and cigarette of the day. I marched over and slapped it on the table in front of him. He gave me an annoyed look and then turned his attention to the paper. He read the entire article without a single comment. When he'd finished, he pushed it away, took a sip of his coffee, and asked for an ashtray.

"Thanks. Don't let me forget we need to check your gun before we do the job. I didn't like the way it was firing yesterday, it probably just needs to be cleaned. We'll need more bullets, too, so let's go downtown. I've got to get some passport photos taken and maybe find some smart little piece of luggage. You know, one bag that will hold everything. Then there's a three o'clock showing of *Gilda* at the Ogden today. You up for it?"

For several moments I was too shocked to even speak. I stood there not believing I had heard all he'd just said. "What about Serge?" I demanded, pounding with my fist on the newspaper.

"What *about* Serge?" he shrugged.

"*What!* Don't you even care? He's your friend. We can't just leave him like that. He didn't do anything!"

"Precisely!" Max said, pointing at me with his cigarette. "That's exactly my point. And if he's smart he'll play dumb and that will keep him out of trouble. It's best if we do the same and just pretend we haven't even heard about it."

He picked up the paper and put it in the garbage.

"But he's your friend!" I protested. "We have to do something!"

"Oh, Dil," Max said, flicking his ash, a condescending tone in his voice. "Sentimental little Dil. That will be your downfall, *mon enfant*, if you're not careful. It's your Achilles' heel, the albatross around your neck. You really need to try and give it up. Serge is a big boy, perfectly able to take care of himself. He's been in scrapes before."

I turned and left the room. I stomped angrily up the stairs and slammed the door to my bedroom. It was too much, I thought falling back on my bed. Too much. All Max wanted was his money, and his France, and it didn't matter who he had to sacrifice along the way. Focus on the end and ignore the means, just like his hero Vautrin. And yet, I could not believe that even wicked Vautrin would abandon a friend the way Max was abandoning Serge. But Serge was even more than a friend! Serge was a boyfriend, a lover. How could Max just turn away? If Serge had been my boyfriend, I knew I would have ripped through stone walls, swam across oceans, done whatever I needed to do to help him. Max, however, was not going to do anything. He was genuinely unfazed by the arrest. All the rest of the day he continued along his path, parroting his Berlitz tapes, planning the Doris job, and worrying about where to find the perfect bag.

The rest of the morning we spent in testy silence. Max tried to break it by offering to read some Balzac or suggesting that we go out and do some target practice, but I resolutely refused to do anything with him. Later that morning he came into my room again, pen and legal pad in hand, wanting to review the scenario for the Doris job.

"I won't do it now," I said, crossing my arms on my chest and shaking my head.

"Won't do what?" Max asked.

"The Doris job. I won't do it. Not after this morning."

"Ahh, Dil, not again! Come on, don't be that way. I *need* your help. It's a two person job."

"Well, Serge needs your help," I countered, my voice full of righteous indignation. "And you're not doing anything about that! All you're worried about is your own self! You and Jane both! Your dumb France and her dumb shop. Well what about the rest of us? What happens to Serge? Does he just go to prison? What happens to me? At the end of the summer you just leave!" I yelled, pounding the bed with my fists. "Well, what do I do? I can't leave! I'm stuck right here. I have to stay right here!"

Hot frustrated tears ran down my cheeks, but I quickly wiped them away. I was mad, and I got even madder at my body for betraying me by producing tears.

Max said nothing. He sat next to me on my bed and put his arm around my shoulder. I could smell his musky, smoky odor.

"Serge is going to be all right," he said, stroking my hair, his voice low and calm. He reached over and placed his other hand on my chest, which was heaving as I tried to control my crying.

"We're not going to let anything bad happen to Serge. Trust me. And as for you, well, we'll work on that, too. I'm not going to forget about all that you've done for me. We make a pretty good team, don't you think?"

I nodded and began crying even harder. He pulled my head into his shoulder and kissed the top of my head.

"Don't worry, Dil. It'll all work out."

"What can we do?" I pleaded. "We have to do something, at least about Serge."

"We will," he said. "We will. Of course we'll figure something out, we'll get some plan going. Trust me . . . Just as soon as we finish the Doris job."

I jumped off the bed as if I'd been shot up by a rocket. I was so mad I wanted to hit him.

"We're not going to do the Doris job!" I screamed. "At least I'm not. And if you don't help me think of something we can do to help Serge right now, then, then . . . then I'm going to the police!"

That was an empty threat I had no intention of following through on and it was obvious from Max's calm expression that he knew it. He got up, stood very close to me, and gently rubbed his hand across my cheek. I turned away from him.

"I love Serge," he said. "I know you know that. I wouldn't let anything really bad happen to him. We'll figure something out. I love both of you."

He was standing behind me. He encircled me with his arms and pulled me back close to him.

"It's all right," he said, running his hands up and down my chest and stomach. "It's going to be okay."

We stood like that for several moments, no noise other than the sound of our breathing. I could feel Max's heart beating against my back. Max's hand lowered briefly and then came up again but this time under my shirt. I froze, my arms rigid by my sides. I felt his rough calloused hand as he slowly traced light circles on my flesh. He lifted my chin up with his free hand, turned my head back toward his and kissed me, briefly at first, light kisses, again and again, and then slowly his lips began to part. I kissed him back tentatively, clumsily, but then my adolescent lust took over and I turned around to face him. It was as if the sexual tension that I'd kept hidden all summer was suddenly released, and I reached my arms around and pulled him closer to me. The pace accelerated. He pulled my shirt over my head and then began kissing my ears and my neck and my chest. He undid the button on my shorts and lowered them and my underwear to my ankles. His hands roamed my chest, and stomach, and ass. He put both arms around me, lifted me up off the floor and dropped me on my back on the bed. When I was down, he pulled my shorts and underwear off my feet and then stood and removed his own clothes.

I had seen his lean, taut body before, but never as it was then. The funny thing was that I felt I should have been looking at his body, but I wasn't. I kept looking at his eyes, trying to make contact with them, but he wouldn't do it. He kept them downcast, and I knew he was avoiding mine. I guess that was my first indication that something was not right. A small misgiving, but one that I quickly shelved when I felt the pressure of his body on mine, felt his arms wrap around my shoulders, felt his lips on mine. I had imagined this moment hundreds of times over the summer and finally here it was. And yet, when he straddled me and put me inside of him, again I had the nagging sense that something was not right. It was the same feeling I'd had when we were first climbing and he told me to lean back. Leaning back felt wrong, but it was really the only way to keep from sliding off the mountain. It felt wrong but it was right. What he was doing to me then, as he slowly rocked above me, felt so warm, so good, but again, something was not right. This was probably because it was so different, I told myself. So new and foreign. It was bound to feel strange. He was my uncle, after all, and considerably older than me. But no, that wasn't it. That wasn't it at all. Those things didn't really bother me. Even today I do not think what we did then was wrong for that reason. No, the reason it felt wrong was much less complicated. It felt wrong because at the last moment I realized that it *was* wrong. He didn't want me. He wanted me to do something for him and this was the way he got it. He was indulging me, bribing me, appeasing me. Doing what had to be done to keep me cooperative.

Like ghosts, the images of Serge and then Meredith appeared to me and I shuddered. I pushed Max off with all the force I had and he landed hard on the floor. I sat up on the bed and looked down at him angrily. He knew he'd been found out and he did not insult me further by looking up at me with a false expression of bewildered shock. He didn't look at me at all but just sat there for a moment staring off into space. Then he calmly reached into the pile of clothes on the floor and retrieved his cigarettes. He lit one and inhaled, staring out the window. I took my clothes and went into the bathroom. When I came back, he was gone.

I didn't know what to do with everything I was feeling then, or even what I was feeling. I got the port bottle from my closet and took several large swigs, revelling in the familiar warmth as it went down my throat and into my stomach. Soon that warmth had spread all through my body. My thoughts stopped racing around in circles and my shoulders relaxed. I picked absently at the label on the bottle. The cloaked and masked caballero stared back at me. A silhouette, just like the portraits in the egg, just like the gypsy on Max's cigarette box. They all seemed emblematic to me then, half-realized ideals of people I could look up to, representatives of all the shadowy, dimly remembered men in my life—of my father, and

James, and somehow, I knew, of Max, too. I knew that he would be leaving and once he'd gone the mental picture I had of him would start to fade, his features becoming more and more indistinct as time passed. I felt I'd always be stuck with poor substitutes, like Wayne.

Then I heard gunshots. Terrified, I got up and ran to my bedroom window. Max was dressed and out behind the house, shooting at the bottles and targets we had set up earlier that summer. He was just testing my gun. No reason to fear he might do himself harm. Max would never do that. I realized that he had probably wanted to make me think that he might, and I felt stupid for even having considered it. In his scenario I would run out into the yard, crying "No, stop!" We would have an emotional struggle as I wrestled the gun away from him, and then, slowly, he would begin to weasel back into my favor. I could see it clearly. I could see what he was doing and it made me mad. But what made me even madder was that I knew if I stuck around much longer that day he would succeed. I would give in and we'd go back to preparing the Doris job.

I turned away from the window and paced the room, wondering what I should do. I was still worried about Serge and decided that if Max wasn't going to do anything to help him then I would do it myself. I got dressed quickly, went downstairs, and got the newspaper and the Yellow Pages. After making a few phone calls, I found out where Serge was being held. I threw a few things in my backpack and without a word to Max went out the front door. I walked quickly down the muddy street into the lower subdivision. As soon as I got to a busy street, I started hitchhiking. It took quite awhile to get a ride, but I was so angry and so resolved to my task that I didn't mind the wait. After about fifteen minutes, a truck driver picked me up and took me to the outskirts of downtown where I caught a bus up Lincoln to Fourteenth Avenue. A little less than an hour after my departure from home, I arrived in front of the city jail.

The woman behind the Plexiglas at the information desk informed me that visiting hours were not until afternoon, so I put my name on a list and then took off walking downtown. It was hot, the last week in August, and the sun seemed to be challenging the leaves on the trees to stay green. I walked between the art museum and the library and then across Civic Center Park over to Sixteenth Street. I had about an hour to spare so I walked slowly, up and down the streets, looking absently in shop windows, remembering all the times I'd looted them with Max. I walked all the way down the street, past the post office and the railroad station, and went under the tracks and then over the river. Eventually, I arrived at Paris. I ordered a coffee and sat out at one of the tables on the sidewalk.

Max was surely going to leave soon, I thought as I sipped the hot bitter liquid and stared down at the street. I could not entertain any more romantic notions to the contrary. I wondered if he would, as he'd said, really give any thought to what would happen to me or if he had just said that to appease me. If he said nothing to Lana, I would certainly be sent off to military school, and the thought of that made me shudder. I was pretty sure he would do nothing to stop it. He and Jane both had a list of priorities and "Dillon's Fate" was somewhere at the bottom of the page, a footnote, if it was there at all. The thought of their selfishness made me angry again. It was always Max, Max, Max and Jane, Jane, Jane. Well, what about Dillon? What about me when all the jobs were done, when all the money was counted, when Jane had her shop, and Max was off counting his francs on some beach in St. Tropez? What would happen to me then?

It hit me like a slap. The realization that I was no better. Serge was rotting away in jail and there I sat, mewling and puking about my own wants just like Max and Jane, more concerned with my own future than anything else. I stood up, took my cup and saucer back into the café, and started walking back downtown. I told myself I would not be like that, if for no other reason than to outrage them. I would not be that selfish and greedy. Serge was a good friend to me, always offering his time and his patient instruction. He was a true friend, and I owed it to him to tell him what was going on. That was the least I could do. I would tell him what we'd done and then leave it up to him to decide what he would do with the information.

As I headed back downtown, I found myself hoping that maybe Max would have had the same idea. Maybe he was going to see Serge as well. As I walked, I imagined running into him in the lobby of the jail, or being told by the woman behind the Plexiglas that Serge was busy talking to someone else. But that was just me being sentimental again. When I arrived, Max was not there. I was given a sign-in sheet and told to wait. About ten minutes later my name was called and I was led through a door to a room filled with several cubicles; each cubicle cut in half by another thick Plexiglas wall. In each cubicle, on either side of the wall, there were telephone receivers—one for the visitor and one for the prisoner. I was instructed to take a seat at cubicle number three and wait, while they went and got Serge.

When he arrived, dressed in the usual orange prison garb, he smiled when he saw it was me. Then he looked around and his smile faded. I knew he had been hoping for Max. He came over and picked up the phone on his side.

"Dillon, what are you doing here? Is Max with you?"

I shook my head. "No, I came alone. I saw the story in the paper and I . . . I wanted to tell you. I wanted, I mean, I know you didn't do it."

He silenced me with his hand and gave me a look that said I should say no more. He looked nervously over my head to the guard who was standing a few yards behind me.

I ignored him and continued. "I know you didn't do it," I whispered, "because Max and I and Jane are the ones who did it. *We* did it, not you."

Again, he tried to silence me. He shook his head quickly and held his finger to his lips.

"It's all right," he whispered. "I know."

"No, you don't," I protested. "You don't know anything, we did it all! Max and Jane and me, we were the Balzacs, we took the egg and—"

"Dillon, shhh. Stop it! I know. I knew all along. Please, don't say any more. Please!"

"How do you know?" I insisted, not believing him. "How?"

He looked at me and his expression softened. He smiled and gave a little laugh. "I knew when I first read it in the paper. I knew it was Max. Who else could it be?"

"But why—"

"Dillon, don't. Don't say anything. Shhh. I know Max very well. It's okay."

"But you're in jail! You didn't do anything! We did it! Why are you doing this? We should be the ones in jail, not you!"

"Dillon! It's okay. Max will leave soon and then everything will be clear. He hasn't left already, has he?" Serge asked, suddenly anxious.

I shook my head.

"I probably won't see him before he goes . . ." he said, and his words trailed off wistfully. For the next few moments, he seemed to forget I was there, seemed to forget where he was. Then his eyes focused on me again, and he smiled. I did not return the smile. I was angry. Here again was someone over whom Max held sway, another victim of his charms. I was angry that Serge was willing to take the fall for him and because I knew that if I'd been in Serge's shoes I would have done the same thing! Of course I was still smarting from Max's attempt to sexually manipulate me, but I was alarmed to realize that the anger was slowly being replaced by regret! Regret that I had stopped it, regret that soon Max would be gone and with him would go the opportunity for it to happen again under different circumstances.

I looked at Serge then and knew that he felt the same way. He, too, was a victim, but it was an odd victimization. It was like Max was a vampire, and we were two willing victims, offering up our necks, hoping that his bite would somehow bind us to him, make us like him. I was still angry, but worse than that I was becoming jealous. Jealous of Serge's love for Max but also jealous of Max and his ability to make everyone fall in love with him, jealous of his charisma and charm, his fearlessness and audacity, his lack of sentiment. Jealous that when I looked in the mirror it was myself that I saw and not him.

I did not know what to say then. My head was swimming. Suddenly I was not sure why I had come. Serge looked at me and I could tell by his expression that he understood my confusion. "Dillon," he said, "do you remember that day climbing when you asked how I met Max?"

I nodded.

"I told you I was his teacher, yes? But there is more to the story than that."

I waited for him to continue. He stared at me but his expression was vacant.

"You see," he said, and looked down at his hands, "Max was more than a student to me. It was maybe not so healthy to do, a thirteen-year-old and me, a much older teacher. I had never done it before. I'm not like that. And I have not done it since, but I did it then even though I knew it was not right. Maybe you won't understand . . ."

I swallowed hard and felt my pulse quicken.

"I think we both needed each other then," he continued. "We both needed to—oh, I don't know, I was still married, but not happy, and Max, well, he was alone, as most boys like that are alone."

He looked directly at me and held my gaze. "You know how it is, Dillon, you imagine you are the only one in the world." He paused then, waiting to see if I had any response. I did not, but I felt a lump in my throat and found it difficult to swallow.

"Maybe it was wrong," Serge continued. "What we did. I still wonder about that. The wrong is more society's problem, I think.

265

Not mine. Not Max's. No, it was not wrong," he said, more to himself than to me. "It was not dirty. I would do it again. We were both alone. We were different, which is also the reason he was friends with Jane; she was foreign, and different, and always teased by the other students, just like Max. Children can be not so nice, you know?"

I thought of Aaron and my own miserable experiences at school. Yes, I knew all too well.

"Max helped Jane, and he helped me, too." Serge paused here, searching for the right way to say what he wanted to say. "I . . . I had never been with a boy," he said. "I did not understand. I liked Max, but I never would have done that. Never would I go after a child. It was not like that. I gave him a ride home from school one day and it just happened. He knew what he was doing, more than I did. Of course I wanted to do it once we were started and I did nothing to stop him . . ."

At this point he paused again. He seemed to be staring at the glass partition between us, not seeing me at all.

"But of course we got caught," he continued. "It was one day, during the summer, when we thought Max's parents would be away. They came home and caught us together."

I remembered my grandparents then, and how they had both recoiled when I even mentioned the photo of Max.

"I was a coward," Serge said. "I ran away as soon as we were caught and left Max behind."

He paused here and his regret hung in the air. It was difficult for him to go on and he started and stopped several times.

"The odd thing about it," he said, "was the way your grandparents reacted. They didn't call the police. They didn't call the school. They didn't even call me. I guess they thought the whole thing would be too embarrassing. So instead, they beat Max."

Again Serge paused, still staring at the glass. He did not cry, but a profound sadness seemed to settle on him.

"They beat him badly," he said, "and they beat him often. It was a difficult time for all three of us. You see, Jane was around then, too, and she knew about it all. We didn't know what to do. I tried to talk to the parents, but they refused. Then I was going to turn myself in, but Max wouldn't let me. He got very angry, said he would say it was not true, said he would kill himself if I did. Jane, too, was going to report the beatings, but again, Max got very angry and made the same threats, to do himself harm, if she told. So," he said, his clear, blue eyes welling up, "we did nothing. We suffered with him.

"We always knew when the beatings had occurred because for days after, they would keep him home from school. We used to go over to his house on those nights, Jane and I, and try to talk to him at his bedroom window. Usually we couldn't get that close because the dog would bark, but when we got close enough we would flash a light at his window. Max would get up and turn on his own flashlight and send us signals. I remember he used to make the little animals, you know? with his fingers and the light on the window shade, and in that way we knew he was all right."

The tears ran slowly down Serge's tan cheeks and he made no attempt to wipe them away. I don't think he even knew they were there.

"But what about Lana?" I asked, wondering how she could possibly have sat by and done nothing. She loved Max, much more than she loved my grandparents, more than she loved me. That much I knew.

"Lana?" Serge asked. "You mean Max's sister? Oh, she was not there. She was done with school then. Done with them. Graduated. She didn't live there anymore. She had her problems with them, too, you know. Maybe worse than Max's. Your grandparents are not such good people. As soon as she was old enough, she left and took a job in the mountains. When Max did leave, he stayed with her for a while. She helped him, gave him money."

We were silent then, each holding our phones. I did not know what to say. Suddenly I saw Max differently. Another facet had been added to him and to my mother. One that I never would have imagined either of them having.

"So maybe this is all right," Serge said, giving a wave of his hand to indicate the prison. "Maybe if I stay here for a while I can do something for *him.*"

When Serge said that, I suddenly remembered the night in the cellar with Max. The night he told me he would try and dissuade Lana from sending me to camp if I promised to help him steal. "Life is like a seesaw of favors," he'd said. I saw that Serge's taking the blame for the burglaries was an odd way of bringing their relationship back into balance.

There seemed to be nothing else to say after that, so we said good-bye. Serge told me not to worry and to tell Max not to worry. I left the building in a daze and when I stepped outside it was like stepping into an oven. It was a little after two o'clock and the heat of the day was at its peak. As I walked back through Civic Center I thought of hitchhiking back home, but I felt I didn't really want to go home yet. I went a block over and started walking up Colfax. Eventually, perhaps inevitably, I found myself at the Ogden.

The movie was not scheduled to start for another twenty minutes, so I bought a ticket and went up to the balcony to wait. I sat in the back, right up against the wall by the projector, and watched as the small, matinee audience arrived and took their seats. Most people who go to movies in the middle of the day usually do so alone, so there was no conversation, just silent waiting, staring ahead at the darkened screen. Eventually the lights faded and the film began. It was, as Max had said, *Gilda.* The film was almost over before I noticed Max, seated a few rows ahead of me. He was slumped down in the seat, so all I really could see was the outline of his hand holding his cigarette, always between the third and fourth fingers. I had been so lost in my own thoughts and the film that I'd not seen him come in. I wondered if he had noticed me.

The film rolled on, slowly unraveling its dark, somewhat sinister plot until it neared the end. At that point, the two characters who "really" love each other are pushed together and the violins begin to soar in anticipation of the happy ending.

I saw Max exhale a billowing cloud of smoke and mutter something to himself. He shook his head, got up, and walked out.

I didn't get home that night until almost eight o'clock, which somehow did not surprise Lana. She gave me a wave from the sofa, where she was watching TV, but did not say anything to me, did not seem curious where I had been.

"Is Max home?" I asked.

"What?" she asked, her eyes still glued to the TV. "Max? No, no."

I knew it was useless to pump her for information so I went into the kitchen. I made myself something to eat and then went up to my room. I must have fallen asleep because when I woke up, hours later, it was dark and the house was silent. I was curious to see if Max had returned so I got up and tiptoed downstairs. The cellar door was open, so I was pretty sure he wasn't down there. I went out to the garage and flipped on the light. The Jaguar was parked next to Lana's car. I went back inside and stood at the top of the stairs to the cellar, debating whether I should go down or not. Then I heard a cough. It had come from the back deck. I went into the living room and looked at the sliding glass door. It was open, but I could see nothing outside. Then I saw it, just as I had the first day he arrived: the burning ember of his cigarette as it got brighter and then darkened. I walked silently across the living room floor and went out onto the deck. Max was standing against the railing, looking off into the empty distance. He turned when he heard me but, seeing it was me, he said nothing and turned back. I approached and stood next to him, leaning my elbows on the railing.

"Evening, Dil," he said, his voice just above a whisper. When he spoke I caught the usual smell of smoke I'd come to associate with him, but under that there was something else, something I knew all too well: alcohol. I turned and looked at him but was too shocked to say anything. I saw the glass in his hand and then, farther down along the railing, I saw the bottle.

Approaching someone who has been drinking, especially when you don't know the quantity they've consumed or the amount of time they've been consuming it, is a lot like approaching a wounded animal. It may be grateful for your help, but it's just as likely to turn and bite you. From my experience with Lana, I knew to proceed with caution.

"And how was your afternoon?" he asked. I heard the thick laziness in his speech.

"It was okay," I said. "I went to the movies."

"Oh? Were you there?" he asked.

"Yes."

There was a long silence. He continued to smoke and we both stared out at the prairie and the stars and the darkness.

"I'll do the Doris job," I said, but did not turn to look at him. "Whenever you want, I'll do it."

He did not respond, but drank the remainder of the alcohol in his glass and then set it on the railing.

"Ahh, Dil, you really don't have to do tha—"

"I know," I said. "I know." And I turned and went back into the house.

Chapter Twenty

The next morning, nothing from the day before was even mentioned. No mention of our aborted sexual encounter, no mention of Serge, and certainly no mention of the fact that I'd seen Max drinking, although I could tell by his bloodshot eyes and by the way he rubbed his forehead that he was hungover. We ate a quiet breakfast together, chitchatting over trivial items in the newspaper; and when we had finished eating and had put the dishes in the dishwasher, we set to work, once again, refining the plan to get Max's money back from Doris.

The plan was to burglarize Doris's private residence. Max had been to her condominium many times in the past (although the last time had been before he went to prison), and he knew she kept most of her yet unlaundered money in a large safe in her bedroom. He felt certain, although I was never able to ascertain why, that the money she had taken from him would be in that safe and so all we would need to do was go in and pluck it out.

The plan was more complex than that, but not much more. We were to break into her apartment (which was on the seventeenth floor of a Cherry Creek high-rise), subdue her (which is what frightened me most), and then set to work cracking the safe. That done, we would simply rappel down the building, just as we had on the Cheesman Park job, and Max would finally have enough money to get away.

The job was to be done the next day, so we had a lot to review before then. Max had broken our day down into various activities, and before we began, he handed me a small itinerary he had written up on one of the pages of the yellow legal pad. The first half of the morning we would spend working with James's stethoscope and the safe in his study, trying to decipher the combination. Later, we would do target practice in the backyard, and then, after a short break for lunch and a siesta, we would head to Eldorado canyon and practice some climbing.

We made it successfully through the first activity and were well into the second, doing our target practice out back, when the peaceful orderliness of the day was shattered by the arrival of Jane.

Max and I had plugs in our ears, so we didn't hear her screeching at us from the back deck. In fact, we didn't hear or see her at all until she had tottered across the muddy prairie in her high heels to where we stood and smacked us both on the side of our heads.

"Why the hell don't you ever answer the goddamned phone?" she yelled at Max. "You've got to go! You can't wait anymore; you've got to get out of here now!"

We removed the earplugs and looked at her, surprised.

"They'll be coming soon," she said. "You've got to go. Today!"

"What?" Max asked. "Who? The police?"

"No, not yet. It's the insurance company. They hired a private detective. He's been talking to Serge and he spent two hours yesterday talking to *me!*"

Max's face went pale and he rubbed his forehead.

"Damnit," he muttered, and then marched back toward the house, Jane and I following close behind. Inside, he paced around the living room and listened as Jane recounted her meeting with the private investigator.

"He knows it wasn't Serge," she said. "At least he knows it wasn't Serge alone, and he suspects that I know who the others are."

"What did you tell him?" Max asked.

"Not much. I was good about that. I played dumb, but it wasn't easy to keep that up for two hours. He knows that Serge was my teacher, so it's only a matter of time before he knows about you, if he doesn't already. He's even been poking around Paris, asking questions. You know everyone who works there has seen us together! You've got to go!" she cried.

"I can't," Max said, lighting a new cigarette from the butt of the one he'd just finished. "Not just yet."

"But you have to!" Jane yelled, standing up and grabbing him by the shoulders.

"Maybe you better," I added. I was suddenly very aware that the game was nearly over. The summer was at an end.

"I can't!" Max cried, waving his hands. "I don't have enough money! I—I need more money!"

"How much have you got?" Jane asked.

"Only about twenty."

"Thousand?"

"Yes."

"And that's not enough?"

"No, *chérie*, it's not. Twenty thousand probably wouldn't even get me to Paris, Texas, and as you know I need to go much farther than that. It's not like I can just go down to the travel agent and buy a ticket on the Concorde. I don't even have a passport, for Christ's sake. The old Max must be hidden away before the new one can emerge from the cocoon. That all costs money!"

He looked over at Jane, as if she might have the money he needed in one of the pockets of her purse. She let out a laugh.

"Oh, sweetie, everything I've got—and I do mean everything— is tied up in my shop. I haven't even got three hundred!"

"Can't you borrow something?" he asked, his voice cracking. She thought about this for a minute.

"I'll see what I can do," she said, "but I don't think I could get anywhere near the amount you're looking for, and I certainly couldn't get it in time. You have to go!"

"What about the egg?" Max asked, an eager, frenzied look on his face.

"Oh God!" Jane said, and turned and shook her head.

"No, no, no, now listen," he said, running over to the cellar stairs. "What if we broke it up, sold it for parts? The gold and the jewels will surely fetch something!"

And before either of us could say a word, he had disappeared into the cellar to retrieve the thing. Jane closed her eyes and shook her head again. She stubbed out her cigarette and paced around the sofa.

"I've really gotta pee," she proclaimed. "Where's the loo again?"

"There's one under the stairs," I said, and pointed her back toward the foyer. She clicked down the hall and I heard the bathroom door shut. I was nervous. Everything was happening so fast. We were going to get caught, I felt sure, and then what? My worries about what would happen to me at the end of the summer seemed almost trivial now, completely usurped by the present crisis. We had to get him away, but how? My head was spinning.

I spied Max's box of cigarettes on the coffee table. I had never smoked, but from watching Max and Jane, and even Lana, it was evidently something to do when one is nervous. Maybe it would have some calming effect, I thought, so I took one out of the box and lit it, inhaling deeply, just as I'd seen them do. Almost immediately I felt the pain in my throat and for the next several moments I doubled over, coughing violently. When I sat back up, I was surprised to see Wayne standing at the entrance to the room. He was staring straight ahead, his mouth open.

Oh boy, I thought, dropping the cigarette on the floor and quickly stamping it out. *I'll catch hell for this!*

I looked up at Wayne, and tried to appear contrite, but then I realized that he wasn't looking at me at all. I followed his gaze, back over my shoulder, and saw Max, a stunned expression on his face, holding the egg. For several moments no one moved, no one said a word. Then Wayne broke the silence.

"Hey!" he exclaimed. "That's the . . . the one that's been on the TV!" His expression darkened and he added, "But . . . what? I don't . . ."

"I can explain," Max said, but there was terror in his eyes. Again, they stood for what seemed a very long time. Neither one saying a thing.

"It's n-n-not what you think," Max sputtered, but the guilt in his voice made it all too clear that the situation was just as it appeared.

"But . . . *you* took it?" Wayne sputtered, his eyes wide with disbelief.

"No! No, no, no," Max protested. "No. We just, uh, found it. We found it."

There was another horrible silence after this. Max was struggling to think of something to say. Wayne's expression changed again, this time from one of bewildered disbelief to outrage.

"I'm calling the police!" he said, but just as he was about to turn there was a dull thud and Wayne crumpled to the floor. Behind him stood Jane, holding my clarinet in her hand like a baseball bat.

"Oh my God!" she cried and dropped the clarinet to the floor. She covered her mouth with her hands and stared, horrified, at Wayne's body. Max set the egg down and we both ran over to him. There was a big gash on the back of his head, but he was still breathing.

"I didn't . . . He's not . . . dead, is he?" Jane asked, her voice still muffled by her fingers.

"No," Max said. "But he's out."

"Oh my God," she shrieked. "I just saw him, and saw you, and saw the egg, and then he said police!"

"No," Max said, getting up and taking her firmly by the shoulders. "You did the right thing. But how did he get in?"

"I don't know," Jane said. "It's that fucking door. I must have left it open when I came in! Oh how stupid!"

"I was right here," I cried, pointing to the sofa. "I didn't even hear him come in!"

We all stared at Wayne and wondered what to do. Of course it was Max who eventually came up with a solution.

"Okay," he said, as calmly as he could, "Okay, let's get him tied up. We'll stash him in the cellar for now."

Jane and I exchanged horrified glances. Neither one of us made a move.

"If you have a better idea," Max shouted, "you have about two seconds to tell it to me! He's just knocked out, not dead. He'll wake up soon and when he does we'll really have trouble."

"We're not going to . . . kill him?" I asked.

"No," Max said. "No. I don't know. I don't know what we're going to do, but we need to get him secured so we can have time to think up what we're going to do. Now move! Go get some rope from the garage. Jane, help me get him downstairs."

We did as we were told. I headed out to the garage, but I couldn't find any rope. My hands were shaking as I opened and closed the drawers of the workbench, but my eyes weren't really seeing the contents. During the shoplifting and the burglaries, I'd been nervous. In those situations something could have gone wrong, but there was usually an easy way to fix it or at least a way to escape. This time I couldn't see any quick fixes, and the avenue of escape seemed to be narrowing with every tick of the clock. I was afraid, as I had not been afraid since that night in the van with Doris. Everything was suddenly so random and unplanned, like carrying around a bomb with a broken timer, never knowing when it would go off, but aware all the same that it *will* go off.

Finally, I found some string and the remainder of the roll of duct tape we'd used on the cook and the butler. I took these and hurried back inside.

Max and Jane were struggling to carry Wayne's thick body. Max's shirt had ridden up and I saw that he still had his pistol stuck in the waistband of his jeans. That frightened me, but I didn't say anything about it. I ran over to help lift Wayne and together the three of us carried him downstairs to the cellar. We sat him up in the only chair and secured him to it with the duct tape. He was beginning to stir.

"Go get some Rohypnol," Max ordered, "and a glass of warm water."

I nodded and bounded back up the cellar stairs and then up the main stairs to Lana's bedroom. I went to her nightstand and found the bottle, as big as a mayonnaise jar, filled with the pills. James had prescribed them for Lana to help her sleep. After he left and she realized he would not be coming back, she took one of his prescription pads and forged several of them for herself. I shook five of the pills into my hand, replaced the jar, and went back down the stairs to the kitchen. I got a mortar and pestle from the cabinet and ground the pills into powder. Then I took the pestle and a glass of water down to the cellar.

Wayne was almost completely immobilized. His hands and feet were secured to the chair with duct tape and the pretty Hermès scarf Jane had been wearing was now serving as a blindfold. I brought the pills and the water over to Max.

"How many are in here?" he asked, looking down at the powder in the pestle.

"Five."

Max looked at Wayne, trying to assess his weight. He then shook half the powder into the glass of water and looked around the cavernous room for something to stir it with.

"Where am I?"

It was Wayne. We all froze and looked over to the chair. His head was lolling from side to side and it was evident from his expression that he was in pain.

"What the . . . ?" he muttered, trying to move his hands and feet. "Why can't I move? Help! Help!"

Max stood up and took the gun from his waistband. Jane and I, clutching each other, moved back against the wine rack. Max held the barrel up under Wayne's double chin.

"Shhhhh," Max whispered.

Wayne, realizing it was a gun, began to swallow rapidly.

"Play along and you won't get hurt."

"Oh God! Dillon? Help! Help!"

"Shhhh. Shh, shh, shh," Max said, and his voice was almost soothing.

"Are you thirsty, Wayne? I'm going to give you something to drink, okay?"

Wayne gulped again and his forehead began to perspire.

"Bring me the glass," Max said, looking at me. I disentangled myself from Jane and got up. The powder was still sitting undissloved at the bottom. I took the pen from Max's French notebook and used it to stir the liquid noisily until none of the powder could be seen. Then, with a trembling hand, I gave it to Max. He instructed Wayne to open his mouth and drink, assuring him that it was not poison, but just something to help him sleep. Much of it dribbled down the front of his shirt but enough of it went into him to do the job. Once he had finished, the three of us sat silently listening to him blubber. After about twenty minutes, his head began to loll from side to side. Five minutes later he was snoring.

The silent wait had been good for all of us. Like Wayne, we were much calmer. At first the situation had, like an avalanche, caught us off guard. It was dramatic and frightening as it barreled down over us, but now the drama had stopped. We had punched out a little snow cave for ourselves and bought some time, but we still had to decide which direction to dig—before the oxygen ran out.

We went upstairs, and Max and Jane began smoking furiously. Max stood by the sliding glass door, staring out into the field behind the house. Jane paced from one end of the room to the other. I sat on the couch, absently opening and closing the egg, watching the silhouettes appear, and then disappear, and wondering if maybe the thing hadn't been cursed. No one spoke. I noticed a large bulging brown envelope on the floor near the spot where Wayne had fallen. I got up, retrieved it, and cut it open with my pocket knife. Inside there were probably twenty or so color brochures for different military academies.

So that was why he had come, I thought to myself. He'd realized Lana had never received the first batch, so he'd brought her another.

I fanned out the brochures on the table before me. They all had attractive uniformed young men on the covers, and immediately brought to mind Max's libidinous description of Bible camp. Maybe it wouldn't be that bad, I thought. Probably better than prison, which is where I felt sure all three of us were headed.

I thought about all that had happened in such a short time and I tried to make some order of it. Serge was in trouble. Max was in trouble. Jane and I were on the verge of being in trouble. Wayne was being held hostage in the basement, and soon, Lana would be home. It all seemed hopeless.

"Okay," Jane said stubbing out her cigarette. "What are we going to do?"

"Well, first we've got to get rid of the car," Max said, moving back into the room. "But I'm not quite sure how we should go about doing that in the daylight. Jane, do you remember that place everyone used to go in high school for parties?"

"Waterton Canyon?"

"Yeah. There's never anyone up there, right? I mean, it's still pretty deserted."

"What are you thinking?"

"Well, there're all those wastewater ponds from that Martin Marietta plant, remember? The ones with all the no-swimming signs. Suppose we dump the car in one of those?"

"I guess that would work," she said, "but that begs the question, what the hell are we going to do with Wayne?!"

Once again, we all fell into ponderous silence. The furious

smoking and the pacing recommenced while I sat in the middle of it all thumbing through the colorful pamphlets.

At the Waco Academy, we take pride in molding boys into men.

Discipline. Academics. Morals. Patriotism: the four pillars of life at The Jonesbourough School.

Aim for excellence! The Bosworth Preparatory School.

These places probably wouldn't be fun, I thought, but in contrast to the whirlpool of chaos and uncertainty I found myself in, they did hold an odd appeal just then: controlled, ordered environments with a decisive someone in charge who knew exactly what he was doing.

"I've got it!" Max shouted. Jane and I looked up at him expectantly.

"We need a way to keep Wayne silent about what he's seen, right?"

We nodded.

"Well, short of killing him, what is the best way to do that?" he asked, looking from one of us to the other.

"Blackmail?" Jane ventured.

"Precisely!" Max said, punching his palm.

But almost instantly the problem arose: what to use to blackmail someone who has nothing in his character that society at large would see as shameful? We all returned to the cellar and examined Wayne carefully: there was his criminal bad taste in clothing, his shamefully ugly mode of transportation, his disgraceful hairstyle— but those were just the opinions of the three of us as we stood there smoking and assessing him. We went back upstairs to discuss it. No, what we chose would have to be something that he himself would be ashamed of. Something that he would never want anyone to know about. Something really wrong. We tried to think like Wayne.

"If we could show that he'd voted for a Democrat," Jane said.

"If we could record some of his sermons and then play them backward and show that they had satanic references," I added.

"If we could get him in bed with a prostitute," said Max.

We fell silent again, all trying to think of some way to frighten Wayne into forgetting he had ever seen the egg.

"Okay, I've got it!" Max said, jumping to his feet and snapping his fingers. Jane and I looked up. I didn't like the way Max was eye-balling me, or the wicked grin spreading across his face. He looked like a cannibal sizing me up for the pot. He disappeared once again down the cellar stairs. Jane and I exchanged glances and both rolled our eyes. When Max emerged it was with a devilish grin on his face and the Polaroid camera in hand.

Chapter Twenty-one

Some would say that losing your virginity at the age of fourteen is just wrong, and many would agree that losing it with someone of the same sex makes it even worse. Now, if that same fourteen-year-old was to lose his virginity with a member of the same sex who was nearly three times his age, and was, also, the assistant pastor of the Church of the Divine Redeemer, you'd be hard-pressed to find anyone who didn't think it despicable. And that is exactly what Max was hoping for when he proposed that I pose with Wayne for a series of provocative Polaroids.

"We can't make him do that!" Jane cried, pulling me away after he'd explained his plan.

"I had thought of having *you* do it," he said to Jane, "But that didn't seem, well, seamy enough. I mean, you are, after all, a woman, and Wayne is a bachelor. If you two took pictures of yourselves, it would definitely be naughty, but it's not really blackmailable, is it?"

"Oh, God!" Jane groaned, slapping her forehead with her palm.

"I'd do it myself if I thought it would work," Max offered. "You both know that. But it's not bad enough. We're both still adults,

Wayne and I. It's not illegal the way it will be if Dil does it. Don't you see?"

I saw. The baton was being thrust toward me. I could cross my arms and refuse to accept, or I could take it and run. I looked over at Wayne's blobby body, duct-taped to the chair. He was asleep, his mouth wide open and drooling.

"If you don't want to Dil, that's fine. We'll think of something else," Max said and then added, almost under his breath, "although I don't know what."

I knew if I protested he would not make me do it (he never really made me do anything that summer), but I'd been watching Max closely throughout this latest ordeal and had noticed something in his eyes that I'd never seen there before: fear. For the first time, my hero, the one I idolized and adored in spite of everything he'd pulled over the past few days, was truly frightened. It was distressing. I hated to watch it and wanted to do whatever I could to get rid of it, to make it stop, to make him feel at ease again.

"How do we start?" I asked, solemnly stepping forward to join the ranks of Isaac, Iphigenia, and all the other sacrificial lambs.

"I don't want any part of this!" Jane said, stomping back up the cellar stairs.

It really wasn't so bad. The worst part about it was having to take off my clothes and be naked in front of Max, but he was so preoccupied trying to untape, undress, and then pose Wayne's ample body, that he didn't seem to notice me.

We decided to make it appear that Wayne was taking the pictures for his own perverse pleasure, so my role was to be largely passive. Max tried to hold Wayne up so that it looked as though he were the one using the camera, but Wayne was heavy and Max was nervous and scared, so it did not go smoothly. Max could hold Wayne, or he could hold the camera, but he could not do both, and when he tried, one or the other inevitably fell to the floor. Max's third attempt was his last. Wayne had been placed in a kneeling position, straddling me as I lay on my back. Max had his arms under Wayne's arms, and was trying to hold the camera in Wayne's hands. He had it pointed down at Wayne's flaccid penis resting on my chest and was peering through the viewfinder, about to snap the picture, when suddenly Wayne's weight began to shift and he fell to the right. Max tried to stop him, but his arms and Wayne's got tangled in the camera strap and all three—Max, Wayne, and camera—went tumbling down. The camera bounced twice on the concrete and then broke apart, pieces of it scuttling along the floor and coming to rest under the wine racks.

No one moved for a few moments. Wayne was still unconscious, my legs were trapped under Wayne's body, and Max, well, Max just lay there. Then I heard him laugh. It started out small. A tiny little chuckle at the funny absurdity of the situation, but soon the volume increased and I could feel his laughter as it shook Wayne's body beneath him. A moment later Max got up. He grabbed Wayne by the arm and rolled him over on his back, freeing my legs. I got up and wrapped myself in the blanket. Max continued laughing, pointing at Wayne and then at the pieces of the camera, all the while cackling and clutching his stomach. He leaned his back against one of the racks and lowered himself to the floor. His expression changed slightly and his laughter subtly changed to crying. Soon he was wailing like a baby, holding his head in his hands as if he thought it might break.

I was uncomfortable. I felt I was seeing something too personal, too intimate, and I took a step back into the shadows.

"Oh, God, Dil," he cried, and beat his head with his fists. "What am I gonna do? Why doesn't anything ever work out! It all goes along fine for a while, but then there's always something, some Wayne, or Meredith, or some goddamned worthless egg to come along and screw it all up! I try and try, but I'm never safe. I can never relax. I go from one mess to the next, to the next but I never fucking get on solid ground!"

He paused and stared into the darkness. Then he shook his head slowly, still holding it in his hands.

"And I'm tired, Dil. I'm so tired."

I stepped over Wayne's body and knelt down next to Max.

"You'll be okay," I said rubbing his shoulder, aware of how trite I sounded. "You *will* get out of here. You'll get to France and things will get better. You'll land on your feet," I chirped. "Just like Vautrin."

But the comparison to his fictional counterpart did not seem to make him feel any better. In fact, it had the opposite effect: he pulled away from me as if I'd pushed him, and shook his head in disgust.

"Shit!" he said, fishing in his shirt pocket for his cigarettes. "Vautrin is a fake, Dil! A fucking fake!" he cried, punching his hand into his fist.

Of course he's a fake, I thought, *he's fictional*. I stared at Max, confused, and waited for him to elaborate.

"When you took off yesterday," he said, looking at me through teary eyes, "after the, uh, after we fought . . . Well after you left, I stuck around and finished the book."

I said nothing, waiting for him to continue.

"You'll be sorry to hear," he said in a bitter tone, "that your beloved milquetoast, Lucien, gets carted off to prison and then hangs himself."

I was sorry to hear it, but life was much more interesting than fiction just then, so the fate of Lucien seemed small and unimportant. Again, I said nothing and waited for Max to continue.

"But, I'm sure you'll be less than sorry to hear that Vautrin got thrown in jail, too."

He was silent for a long time after this, so I offered a prompt.

"Did the police know it was him?" I asked. "Or was he still disguised as the priest?"

"Oh, they were pretty sure it was him," Max replied, shaking his own thoughts from his head and focusing on the story, "but they couldn't prove it. You know how well he covered up his past and made a new future. Well, the cops tell Vautrin about Lucien being dead, and at first he doesn't believe it. He's smart. He knows that they know he was in love with Lucien and he thinks it's a trap to get him to confess. Then they take him to see the body, and, well, it's pretty much all downhill after that. He loses it. He goes all soft!" Max said, his voice both angry and sad, like one betrayed. "He confesses everything and, and . . . and then he joins the police! Actually jumps the fence and becomes one of them! He sells out! It's all such bullshit!"

Max let his head fall onto his forearms. It lolled from side to side a few times but then was still. He looked exhausted, like a toy when its battery has worn down, and I wondered if he had fallen asleep. The doorbell rang. His head shot up, and there was a renewed look of terror in his eyes. A few seconds later the cellar door was opened and Jane stumbled back in.

"It's the police!" she cried. She vaulted over Wayne to where Max was seated and crouched down next to him, clinging to his arm. They looked like two hunted animals, and I suppose, in a way, that's exactly what they were.

"I'll go," I said, ditching the blanket and putting my own clothes back on. "Stay here and be quiet."

"Wait!" Max cried, pulling himself up. "Wait, what'll you tell them?"

"I don't know yet," I said, as calmly as I could. "I'll handle it. Just be quiet."

The bell rang a second time and the sound was like a shock of electrical current to Max and Jane. They stared, and shook, and did not protest as I went up the stairs and closed the door behind me. I saw the padlock on the stair, where it had remained, unused, since Max's arrival. On impulse, I picked it up and clicked it into place. I then went up the remaining steps and walked over to the front door. I opened it and saw two uniformed policemen standing on the porch. They smiled and looked past me into the house. They asked for Max.

"We'd just like to ask him some questions."

"You and everyone else!" I said, without hesitation. "You're the third ones today."

Eyebrows were raised.

"Is he here?" they asked again

"No," I said, and shook my head. "He's not."

They said nothing. The older one held my gaze for a minute, and I knew he was trying to see whether I was telling the truth. I gazed back, a smile more enigmatic than that of Jackie Kennedy on my lips.

"Do you mind if we come in and have a look?" the younger one asked. The older one frowned slightly, but said nothing.

"I don't know . . ." I replied, with the cautious tone of a children's safety film. I knew I was a little too old to go that route, but I did so anyway. "I really don't think I should," I said. "My mom's still at school and I'm not supposed to let strangers in when she's not here. She gets home about five though, if you want to come back."

They looked at each other, slightly confused and annoyed, unable to really argue against their own philosophy. The older one spoke.

"About five, you say?"

"Yes, if she doesn't get stuck in traffic. Sometimes she's a little later."

"Okay," he said, looking at his watch. "Maybe we'll pop back by about then."

They nodded good-bye and turned and walked back to where the squad car was parked in the driveway. I closed the door and then sprinted up the stairs and peered out the window on the landing. They were still sitting in the car not moving and I wondered if maybe they intended to just sit and wait until Lana came home. I tried to think of what to do if that was the case. But a moment later, I heard the engine turn over and watched as they backed into the cul-de-sac and drove away.

I gave myself a minute to relax on the stairs and took a few deep breaths. Then I went down to the main floor, got the screwdriver from the kitchen drawer, and went back down to the cellar door. When I opened the door, the whole room was dark.

"It's okay," I said. "They're gone."

I heard footsteps and then Max pulled on the light. He and Jane stood in the middle of the room staring at me expectantly. Wayne was not to be seen.

"Will they come back?" Max asked.

"Yes. At five o'clock. Probably before then. You need to go."

"We were just discussing that," Jane said, encircling Max with her arms and giving him a hug. She had been crying as well.

"Jane's going to get rid of Wayne's car," Max said, tossing her the keys to the Oldsmobile.

"I'll be back as soon as I can," she said, and ran past me up the stairs. "I'll park it at that twenty-four-hour supermarket at the bottom of the hill and then walk back up."

"What's the plan with Wayne?" I asked. "Where is he?"

Max led me over to the small crawl space beneath the basement stairs. Wayne's chair had been moved there and he'd been dressed and taped back into it.

"I need about two days, I figure," Max said. "So if you can keep him drugged and hidden for that long . . ."

"Are you sure that's enough time?" I asked.

"No, but I don't think we can keep him any longer without people poking around. If you can keep him two days, that's great. Just do the best you can. He'll probably have to pee . . ." Max laughed, "I guess you'll have to handle that somehow."

I nodded and closed the door on the sleeping Wayne.

"I'll keep him there as long as I can."

"When he does come out," Max said, "pin it all on me, understand? Everything. Jane had no idea about any of it; and as for you, I forced you to do everything, okay?"

I nodded. I felt myself starting to cry but inhaled as deeply as I could and held it.

For the next twenty minutes, Max and I tidied up the cellar. We packed up a few of his things: some clothes, his guitar, his Berlitz tapes, his notebook, his gun, and of course, the egg. He stuffed them all into the same small bag he'd arrived with and took it out to the car. Then he came back inside, and we waited for Jane to return. I sat there drumming my fingers on the table while Max paced back and forth and smoked. Jane returned about twenty minutes later, out of breath and sweating.

"All done?" I asked.

"Yes," she panted. "All done."

"You wiped off the steering wheel and door handles?"

"Gloves," she said proudly.

"The keys?"

"Dropped them in a storm drain on the way up."

She turned to Max.

"We should go," she said.

He nodded and crushed out his cigarette.

"You'll be okay with Wayne?" Jane asked me. "You know how much of the Rohypnol to give him?"

"Yes, I'll keep him as long as I can. Then I'll untie him, let him wake up, and see what he does."

Jane nodded. It was the plan we'd agreed on, but the results were unpredictable at best.

"Call me if there's any trouble," she said. "Although I don't know what good I'd be."

She gave me a kiss on the cheek and a hug.

"I'll, uh, wait out in the car," she said and then went out to the garage.

Max and I stood facing each other in the living room. The same unfinished mess of a living room into which he had arrived just three months before. I felt as though we should say something significant to each other. We'd reached the part in the movie where the characters utter eminently quotable lines, but we were both silent. Life is terribly unlike the movies sometimes and again there was nothing in my head but trite little clichés: "Take care of yourself," or "Hope to see you again real soon." "Happy Trails."

"You'd better go" is what I said, and then tapped at the face of my watch.

"Yes," he said.

He smiled and extended his hand. I took it and gave it a firm squeeze. He pulled me closer and put his arm around me.

"You're all right, Dil," he said, clapping me on the back. "You're all right."

He leaned back, smiled at me once more, and then turned and went out through the garage door. I heard the motor of the garage door opener, followed a moment later by the throaty purr of the Jaguar's engine. Again, I ran up to the window on the landing and looked out just in time to see them drive off down the hill. As if he knew I was watching, Max stuck his arm out of the driver's side window and gave a sort of salute.

The next two days were surprisingly quiet. Lana came home that evening and I did not even tell her about the police. When they arrived, she answered the door, and told them truthfully that Max was not home. The phone rang, as usual, and, as usual, we didn't answer it. We ate dinner in front of the television and spoke little.

"Max must have gone to another movie," Lana said, looking up at the clock during one of the commercial breaks.

"Probably" I replied and went back to eating my dinner.

When Lana went to bed, I snuck back down to the cellar and gave Wayne another glass of Rohypnol water. I cleaned him up as best I could and then went to bed myself. The next day I stayed home and watched over him. When Lana left, I took a chair down to the cellar and finished reading Balzac. It ended just the way Max had said. I, too, was surprised that Vautrin had joined the police, but the more I thought about it the more it made sense; he was caught, exposed, pinned against the wall. What was he supposed to do? Kill himself? That really would have been out of character. He was smart, so he made the best of it. On the surface, it appeared as if he had sold out, but it was more like a successful marketing campaign. He made his infamy and his knowledge of the criminal world into a commodity. As I closed the book, I found myself hoping that maybe Max could, wherever he ended up, do the same thing.

That night, the police came by again. This time they were looking for Wayne. He had not come home and had not shown up to work for two days. Lana jumped at the chance to enter a new drama, and this time did not hesitate to invite the police inside. Alas, she could tell them nothing, so they did not stay long and they didn't even bother questioning me. When they left, she immediately got on the kitchen phone and stayed there gossiping and speculating with the other parishioners for almost three hours. She did not even notice when I entered the kitchen, filled a glass with warm water from the tap, stirred it noisily, and then disappeared down the cellar stairs. When I returned, several minutes later, and placed the empty glass in the dishwasher, she was still talking. She had seen it all but noticed nothing.

The following day, I decided Wayne should wake up. He had not eaten anything since he arrived, and I was afraid of accidentally overdosing him. Once Lana left, I wrestled his chair into the center of the room and untaped his hands and feet. I gave him plain water to drink and then sat on the steps and waited for him to stir. By three o'clock, he still had not moved. I knew I'd better do something before Lana returned, so I brewed some very strong coffee and, when it had cooled, went back down to administer it. I was halfway down the stairs when I heard him moan. I froze. Some of the coffee sloshed out onto the stairs. More moaning. The coffee would not be necessary. I returned to the kitchen, put the cup in the sink, and then sprinted up to my room. I changed into some loose shorts and a T-shirt, threw my Walkman and a few other things in a small backpack, and then went back down the stairs and out the front door.

I had spent the entire day in the air-conditioned house, so the heat from the late afternoon sun felt wonderful on my skin. I stood basking on the porch and looked out west at the mountains. Then I turned, facing the house again, and approached the rock wall. Without any hesitation, almost without any thought to what I was doing, I began scaling the house. I had not done it since that first day when Max had arrived. It had seemed so difficult then, but now, with a summers' experience under my belt, it was easy. The handholds and footholds were large and obvious. I remembered back to that first day climbing and wondered how I could not have seen them. In about two minutes I reached the roof and pulled myself up and over the gutter.

I knew that in the next few hours things were going to get crazy down below and I didn't really want to be a part of it. At least not for a while. Wayne would wake up and he'd call the police. They'd arrive. Lana would follow, and then slowly the story would be pieced together. When that was done, probably not until much later that night, I would come down again. I would listen and determine what they knew, and then I'd ad-lib some answers and fill in the gaps in the narrative as best I could. Until then, I'd wait.

I took my Walkman out of the backpack and popped in a tape of the Carpenters' "A Song for You." I put the headphones on and lay back on the roof staring up at the afternoon clouds as they traveled across the sky, wondering what the near future held for me. There would be trouble, that much was certain. I would play the role of victim, would paint a picture of Max as an evil Rasputin, and I knew that everyone would believe it. Everyone except Lana. She knew me, and she knew Max, and she would know that the tale I told was fiction. And yet, she would probably be wise enough to keep her mouth shut. After all, trouble for me could mean trouble for her, and I knew she didn't want that. More than likely, she would go along with the tune I played. She would hear my notes and see the wisdom of jumping in and adding notes of her own. I really wasn't concerned about that. No, it was what would happen when the show was over that worried me. When the curtain went down and all the players had gone home, I wondered what Lana would do to me then. There would be more beatings, maybe even more church-going, and then there would be military school.

All summer long I had shuddered to even think of military school, but as I lay there on the roof considering it, I was no longer afraid. Oh, it might be awful; it might even be worse than junior high had been, but it would not be forever. It would be a means to an end, and to get through it, I'd just have to keep focused on the end. That much was clear. It had not been at the beginning of the summer and that was part of the reason I drank. I had thought that life with Lana and the miserable middle-school microcosm I was in was the whole world and I could not see that one day it would all be in the past, a not-so-pleasant memory, but a memory nevertheless. The summer with Max had, if nothing else, expanded my view of the world. It had given perspective to my troubles and shown me, when I stood back and took a look at them, how small and tempo-rary they really were. They might seem horrible and overwhelming at the time, but the real grace in life was to realize that they wouldn't always be that way. I knew then that no matter what hap-pened—if I stayed with Lana and returned to junior high, or if I was shipped off to military school—I would be okay. I possessed the knowledge and the strength to survive, and for that I had Max to thank.